The Last Venator

Ryan Long

Published by Ryan Long, 2025.

THE LAST VENATOR

First edition. August 29, 2025.

ISBN: 979-8999816719

Written by Ryan Long.

Table of Contents

Dedication

This book would never be written without the push and support of my loving wife.

The Last Venator

Shadows of Vengeance

Alexander slowly eased the hammer back on his rifle as he sighted in on the first shadowy figure crossing the clearing in front of the small stone cabin. He knew he could only kill one before the others broke into the cabin to feed on him. The roar of his rifle was deafening inside the cabin as it ripped through the silent night as it sent the silver infused bullet towards his hated enemy.

The vampire screamed as the bullet brought him to his knees as it ripped through his heart. Alexander followed it up with two more shots. The vamp bursted into flames leaving only its fanged skull glowing in the night. The sounds of cracking of roof timbers as crashed down behind him. Turning on his heels he empties his lever gun from the hip as he dived into another room. Two gold daggers were vibrated in the door frame. Shivering Alexander could only think how close that was. Dropping his rifle he drew his two revolvers from his belt aiming at the door way staring for any signs of movement. He was cursing himself for not turning his steam engine generator on when he arrived home from gathering supplies. Alexander guessed wrong.

The two vamps came straight through the wall. He pivoted on his heels firing both of his revolvers sending heavy .44 slugs there way.

"Damnit!" Alexander gasped as he was tackled by the last vamp with its two daggers penetrating deep into his stomach. The vamp growled.

"Seems like I get the pleasure of killing you, the last of your clan." Licking his face. "Oh boy, I see those wounds are healing pretty fast. That's a pain, just cannot take my pretties out." Tapping his blades still trapped in Alexander stomach.

Coughing "Thats okay I got a few tricks up my sleeve also." Throwing a fast uppercut, he created distance between himself and the vamp. Pulling the daggers from his stomach he tossed them underhanded distracting the vampire. Blood pooled around his feet as he drew the short sword and plasma tomahawk from his belt. The newest tech they made.

He lepted after the vamp as it regained it's bearings. Slashing and hacking at it. "Hey vamp do you know what the weirdest thing is about us Venators are?"

"Oh? Enlighten me oh great hunter?" the vamp snarled.

Alexander kept on attacking anticipating the vamps moves as like he was foreseeing the future. "We may not be as strong or immortal as you are or even as fast. Yet we have hunted and killed everything we have deemed evil even gods. Once there were many of us now only me. From my blood, my sons will bring forth the next generation to hunt the darkness. I shall not die here!"

Snarling he tried to match the vamp for speed yet failed receiving cuts all over his body. Yet the smallest mistake always decides the victor. When the vamp slipped in Alexander blood he capitalized on it. The plasma blade connected with the base of the vamps neck melting through flesh and bone separating the vamps skull from its body spraying Alexander coating him in black blood. Alexander flinched as the common room lit bright as the vamp body burst into bright flame as its skull clattered to the cold stone floor.

Stumbling towards the fireplace he willed himself to make it to his medical chest. Falling short he attempted to drag himself as he screamed through the pain the darkness closing in on him. Just touching the chest, he could hear the whirl of gears and hiss of electricity. Feeling around inside he popped three Occult pills and then stabbing in the epineedle was all he could administrate to himself before blacking out. Even in a drugged slumber his body screamed from the pain as the drugs reknitted his body together. Hours passed then there was a light so bright it hurt through his closed eyes. Opening them he was in an unfamiliar place.

It was decorated as if time had stopped before steam power was invented. Furs and blankets lined the walls. Hell looked deferent then he thought it would. Lot less hot and no brimstone. His blood ran cold as the scent of iron lingered into the room. He knew that smell, vampires.

"Oh, I see that you are finally awake." A voice so sweet it was as if honey would drip from them.

Alexander slowly propped himself up turning towards the voice. It was a girl barley out of her teens dressed in leather riding pants and a loose ruffled shirt hung from her hourglass frame. Yet all he could stare at was the rapier at the girl's hip. A royal vampire rapier. Being weak and naked all, he could replay with was a very un Venator

"Who are you?" "My name is Anna. I found you, stole your hydro steam vehicle and brought you to one of my many safe houses. We are in Slade at the moment."

"Slade? That's almost a two-day drive through the breaks. Those fuckers really did a number on me."

"Yes, but you have quit the vehicle, it was an easy trip through the breaks. However, the only things that I manage to get into your vic is what is left of your hiding place. Another band of vampires showed up, so we had to leave pretty quickly."

"But you're a vamp why would you help me?"

"I am a day walker a born vampire those monstrosities are nothing like me" she snarled. "I have been searching for you for three years Venator, the last of your line. Following the rumors, story's, tales and the fangs you sell in the wake of your hunts. I risked my life in the breaks following you for the expertise you have. You are going to kill my father for me eradicating the scum he has unleashed on this planet."

"Who the fuck is your father? There is only so many royal vamps which one is it? However, I would need an army to kill a royal it's only been done a few times in the records."

"I am the first daughter of the third wife of the dragon. Oh yes that dragon, Dracula" Alexander went cold if she was who she said she was he be able to find a way in and potentially kill him.

Revenge was at his fingertips.

The air in the room crackled with tension, each heartbeat a reminder of his vulnerability. Alexander's gaze locked onto Anna, her eyes flickering with something he couldn't quite decipher—determination, perhaps, but mixed with a hint of desperation. The weight of her lineage pressed upon him like a noose. Dracula's daughter. A potent weapon or a fatal liability.

"Do you think I can just waltz into his lair and kill him?" He spat the words, bitterness staining his tongue. The thought of facing the ancient vampire sent shards of ice through his veins. His thoughts darted to the night when he lost everything—family, home, purpose—replaced now by a burning need for vengeance that had kept him alive until now.

Anna stepped closer, her silhouette stark and defined against the soft, flickering glow of the dim light. The shadows danced around her, highlighting the intensity in her eyes. "You have no choice, Venator," she said, her voice low and urgent, resonating with an unyielding truth. "Either you end him, or he will find you. Your reputation precedes you; he would relish the hunt, savoring every moment as he tracks you down like prey in the dark."

She reached out a hand holding onto a parchment. "Maybe this will gain me a little more trust."

Anna stepped closer, her silhouette sharp against the dim light. Her hand extended, holding a parchment like a lifeline. He could see the edges were burned, the scent of singed paper wafting through the air, mingling with the metallic tang of blood still lingering in his nostrils.

"What is it?" he demanded, his voice rough and strained, each syllable an effort. The heat from his fight still pulsed in his veins but now fear clawed at him beneath that fury—fear of being cornered again, vulnerable.

"Schemes for a forthcoming assembly at the Black Spire," she whispered, her voice dripping with intrigue. "A location where my father will be utterly exposed."

He leaned forward slightly despite his wounds protesting in pain. The burning ache in his stomach was a reminder of how close he had come to death moments before. "What do you want me to do? Stab him while he's busy sipping wine and laughing with his wives or concubines as they feast on traitors' humans who enjoy the feelings of fangs in their veins?"

He pressed his tongue against a cracked tooth and let the charge of pain steady his thoughts. "You think they wouldn't notice me? I can't even piss without the Registry clocking every drop. I'm on every list. The instant I set foot in the Black Spire someone will send a runner."

Anna arched an eyebrow as if he amused her, but the effect was all sharpened edge and no warmth. "You think I don't know how the Registry works? I've sabotaged more blood vials and cracked more bracelets than you could count, Venator." She sat down across from him, boots on the table. "I can get you in. But you'll have to trust me to get you out."

Alexander scanned the room for weapons, escape routes, and, failing that, things to kill a vampire with. His own body was a disaster: bruised lungs, torn muscle, and a sickly wet pain in his gut where the daggers had ground against bone. His medical kit was gone, replaced with a flask of something that steamed faintly in the cold air. The taste on his lips was salt, iron, and whatever chemical Anna had used to keep him alive.

He snatched the parchment. The brittle sheet bore a wax seal impressed with a dragon wing. It crumbled as he unrolled it. The language was half-code, half-court formalities but the meaning was clear enough. The Black Spire. A conclave. Royals only.

He let out a short, humorless laugh. "Yeah, just walk in. Dress nice and bring a bottle."

Anna's expression didn't change, but the air about her shifted. "Listen, I can get you out. You though have to avoid capture and drive a plasma blade through the dragon's heart." She smiled "I hear that you have a friend that makes the most extraordinarily illegal weapons."

Alexander went cold "You leave Cassie the fuck out of this!"

Anna's eyes narrowed, a flicker of crimson bleeding into their dark depths. "Your weapons-maker is already involved. Every vampire hunter with decent gear knows Cassie Thornwood. My father's enforcers have been watching her workshop for months."

Alexander's throat constricted like a vise, each breath a painful reminder of his injuries. He attempted to push himself up, but his wounds howled in agony, slamming him back down onto the furs with a force that rattled his bones. The world around him spun wildly as crimson surged from his head, threatening to drag him into darkness. Cassie was his last lifeline—the only semblance of family after the brutal massacre that had shattered his world. The mere thought of her in peril sent icy tendrils of dread crawling across his skin, chilling him to the core.

"If they knew where she was, she'd be dead already," he growled through clenched teeth.

"They don't know where she is," Anna replied, folding the parchment with delicate fingers. "They only know she exists. But they're getting closer. Every Blood Registry checkpoint is scanning for traces of her handiwork. Those plasma weapons leave... distinctive signatures."

Alexander's mind raced through a whirlwind of possibilities, each one more desperate than the last, like a frantic storm brewing within him. He envisioned the steam-powered truck, a mechanical beast, hidden away in the shadows of Cassie's underground workshop, its brass fittings glinting in the dim light. He could picture the escape route winding through the treacherous northern wastes, a desolate landscape fraught with danger and uncertainty. The emergency protocols they had rehearsed countless times echoed in his mind, their familiarity providing a flicker of hope amidst the chaos. He needed to reach her, to orchestrate their evacuation with precision and haste. Thankfully, she had a dozen other workshops, each one just as well-equipped, a testament to her ingenuity and resourcefulness, ready to spring into action at a moment's notice.

"I need my gear," he said finally, voice rough. "Whatever you salvaged."

Anna pointed towards a wooden chest in the corner. "This is what little I managed to collect. Your rifle is beyond fixing, but the revolvers made it through intact. Also, I found that rather intriguing tomahawk. I took the liberty of including some new clothes and a few treats."

He forced himself to stand once more, his body trembling with a fierce determination. As he struggled to his feet, Anna raised an eyebrow, her gaze piercing. "You know you could have waited until I was gone."

Alexander shrugged, a cocky smirk playing on his lips. "A vamp like you must have seen a thousand naked humans; what's one more to you?"

Her eyes narrowed, a flash of anger igniting within them. "Maybe, just a little common courtesy would be nice?"

"Fuck off," he snapped, frustration boiling over. "I need to get Cassie out of here before we can even think about pulling this shit show together." With a grunt, he yanked on fresh clothes to replace the tattered remnants of what he'd been wearing. "How do I get in contact with you?"

Anna's lips curled into a smile that didn't reach her eyes. "There's a pub in Old Slade called The Broken Gear. Three nights from now, I'll be there at midnight. Come alone."

Alexander rummaged through the chest, inventorying what remained of his arsenal. The twin revolvers were intact, their brass chambers gleaming in the dim light. His fingers traced the etched runes along the barrels—protection sigils that had saved his life more times than he could count. The plasma tomahawk hummed faintly at his touch, its power core still charged. A small mercy.

"Three days," he muttered, strapping on his holsters. "Not enough time."

"It's all we have," Anna replied, moving toward the door. "My father grows suspicious. The Registry is being updated. New blood samples required from everyone within the month."

Alexander's jaw tightened. The Blood Registry—Dracula's perfect leash on humanity. Every citizen forced to wear those damned brass bracelets, their blood constantly monitored and tested. He'd managed to stay off the grid by harvesting blood samples from his kills, using their identities like masks, discarding them when they became dangerous.

"What about my vehicle?" he asked, checking the action on his revolvers.

"Outside. I've taken the liberty of refueling it." She paused at the threshold. "Don't be late, Venator. And don't try to run. If you disappear, I'll assume you've betrayed me. Then I'll find your precious Cassie myself."

The door closed behind her with a soft click that felt like a gunshot in the quiet room. Alexander stood alone, the weight of her threat hanging in the air like poison gas. His wounds throbbed in time with his heartbeat, a painful reminder of his mortality.

He hobbled to the window, wincing with each step as he peered through a narrow gap in the heavy, velvet curtains that seemed to absorb the very light around them. Outside, the streets of Slade sprawled beneath a thick, swirling canopy of steam and smoke, creating an atmosphere heavy with mystery. Factory chimneys loomed like dark sentinels, belching forth billowing plumes of blackened clouds that coiled and twisted into the night sky, obscuring the distant twinkle of stars. Brass-fitted airships glided gracefully between the towering spires, their navigation lights pulsating rhythmically like artificial constellations, casting a surreal glow over the industrial landscape below. The air was thick with the scent of oil and coal, a testament to the ceaseless toil of the city.

His hydro steam vehicle loomed in the shadow of the building—a colossal contraption of gleaming iron and polished brass, with massive wheels that seemed to tower over the ground and reinforced plating that glinted ominously in the dim light. Every curve and joint bore the unmistakable mark of Cassie's skilled craftsmanship, a testament to her ingenuity and precision. The mere thought of her sent a fresh wave of panic coursing through him, a turbulent mix of admiration and dread that twisted in his stomach like a coiled spring, ready to unleash its tension.

Alexander shut his eyes tightly, his mind racing as he calculated every possible distance and route. Cassie's main workshop loomed like a distant fortress, a grueling day of relentless riding through the treacherous break to reach a forgotten city that barely existed on any map. If Anna's warnings about the Registry's relentless pursuit of her signature work were even remotely true, the clock was ticking mercilessly against him. He felt the weight of the world on his shoulders, knowing it would take everything he had to return in time.

He carefully pulled out his pocket watch—a cherished family heirloom, its intricate design telling stories of generations past, and one of the few possessions he had valiantly managed to save from the harrowing night when his family was mercilessly slaughtered. The hands of the watch ticked steadily, revealing that dawn was nearly upon him. The sky began to lighten with soft hues of lavender and gold, signaling the imminent stir of the daywalkers, who would soon awaken from their shadows. They posed a significant threat to every hunter, especially to him, the last of the Venators. Meanwhile, the night-bound creatures would hastily retreat to their dark lairs, seeking refuge before the sun broke over the horizon, casting its illuminating rays upon the world.

Alexander strapped on his revolvers and placed his tomahawk in its sheath on the gun belt. His fate was sealed; he had a dragon to slay.

The Tinkerer's Haven

The workshop door let out a haunting screech, reminiscent of a dying beast, as Alexander shouldered it open with determination, causing a startled flock of mechanical birds to flutter and scatter toward the shadowy rafters above. The air inside Cassie's sanctuary enveloped him with an overwhelming sensory embrace, a volatile mix of scorching metal, the sharp bite of ozone, and the sweet, acrid tang of soldering flux—scents that had woven themselves into the fabric of his memories, oddly comforting and nostalgic over the years. Each inhalation transported him deeper into the world of creativity and invention that thrived within these walls.

"For fuck's sake, Stirling, use the bell!" Cassie's voice echoed from somewhere deep within the labyrinth of half-assembled contraptions and salvaged parts. "That's why I installed it!"

Alexander stepped carefully around a teetering pile of brass gears, each one polished to a mirror shine despite the chaos surrounding them. "The bell's wired to that crossbow mechanism again. Last time I touched it, I nearly lost an ear."

A brilliant flash of fiery red hair burst into view from behind a hulking, rusted boiler. Cassie stepped into the light, her hands smeared with dark grease as she vigorously wiped them on her already soiled overalls, the fabric a patchwork of stains and wear. Her cheeks bore smudges of soot, creating a stark contrast against her vibrant hair, yet her eyes sparkled with an intense, almost electric energy, the unmistakable enthusiasm he had grown to associate with her latest groundbreaking invention.

"That was the point," she said, a smile tugging at the corner of her mouth. "Keeps the unwanted visitors away." The smile vanished as quickly as it had appeared. "Did anyone follow you?"

Alexander checked his timepiece a habit more than necessity. "No. I took the usual precautions. Three false trails, two district crossings through the maintenance tunnels."

Cassie nodded, but her gaze flickered anxiously to the windows, their glass obscured by years of caked grime and the suffocating veil of steam condensation. Her right hand twitched toward the modified wrench strapped at her hip—a lethal tool he recognized, capable of unleashing a jolt of electricity potent enough to seize a vampire's heart in a grip of icy terror.

"Been hearing whispers on the wind," she said, her voice dropping to a conspiratorial tone as she turned abruptly, her eyes scanning the surroundings for prying ears. With an urgent wave of her hand, she beckoned him to follow closely. "The Registry's been poking around the Eastern District like a hound on a scent. Just last week, they raided two workshops—Hannon's and Glover's. Both of them were caught with modified equipment, devious contraptions designed to bypass the blood seals that keep our secrets safe."

Alexander's jaw tightened. "Alive?"

"Hannon escaped. Glover wasn't so lucky." Cassie led him deeper into the workshop, past tables laden with intricate clockwork mechanisms and steam-powered gadgets whose purposes he could only guess at. "They're getting bolder, Alexander. Not even pretending it's about regulations anymore."

Alexander's expression darkened as he spoke, "Because it's really not. They're planning a complete update and overhaul of the registry next month. But... we have even bigger issues that we really need to address."

Cassie froze mid-reach for a wrench, the tendons in her grease-blackened hand standing out like piano wires. The clatter of falling cogs from a nearby workbench made Alexander's gun hand twitch before he identified the source—a brass spider scuttling away from overturned parts.

"You look like a fool on the brink of begging for something utterly ridiculous," she shot back, her gaze fixed ahead, unwavering. Her voice had turned cold and sterile, reminiscent of the tense atmosphere that accompanied the calibration of perilous prototypes.

Alexander gently traced the raw, angry scar that marred his ribs, the jagged reminder of a close encounter with the night enforcers' daggers, hidden beneath the heavy fabric of his coat. The workshop, usually filled with the comforting hum of activity, now exuded a stifling heat that pressed in around him like a thick fog. He exhaled sharply, his heart racing as he shared the shocking news. "Dracula's daughter found me," he said, his voice barely above a whisper, laced with a mix of dread and disbelief. "She wants me to kill him at the Black Spire conclave." The words hung in the air, heavy with implication, as the shadows of the workshop seemed to deepen around him.

The wrench clanged loudly against the cold, unyielding iron plating, sending a reverberating echo through the dimly lit workshop. Cassie spun around, her eyes widening in shock, the vibrant green of her irises contrasting sharply with the white that surrounded them. "You're joking," she gasped, her voice trembling with disbelief. When he remained unfazed, not even flinching, she staggered backward, colliding with a cluttered tool cart that rattled ominously. The pungent scent of gear oil oozed into the grooves of her boot treads as she steadied herself by gripping the edge of a weathered worktable, the surface rough beneath her fingers. "That's suicide," she breathed, her heart racing, "That's... even for you..." The weight of her words hung in the air, thick with an unspoken fear.

Alex shrugged, a hollow familiarity with death etched into his demeanor. "I was born for this. My grandfather even took down the closest thing to a god before my father was born. Dracula is just a dragon."

"Dracula is a real god! Your grandfather and father failed to vanquish him. You've buried everyone you've ever cared about under that monster's shadow."

"If he bleeds, he can die," Alexander replied, his voice barely a whisper as he avoided Cassie's piercing gaze.

Her laughter sliced through the air, sharp and dissonant. Mechanical fingers—he had never dared to ask how she had lost the originals—drummed an urgent rhythm against the pressure gauge. "So, what's your brilliant plan? To swagger into the dragon's den with that charming scowl plastered on your face and last week's knife wounds still fresh?"

With a mischievous grin, he turned to Cassie, his eyes sparkling with mischief. "Scowl has thwarted a certain builder's plans more than once," he teased, his voice rich with amusement.

In a swift motion, she grabbed a nearby wench, her grip firm yet playful. "I will hurt you if you cannot take this seriously," she warned, her expression shifting to one of earnest concern. "You will die if you do this."

His face twisted with pained intensity as he replied, "And you will if I don't."

Cassie halted in her tracks, the weight of his words crashing down on her like a tidal wave. In that moment, she realized the truth: the game was over. The vampires were hot on her heels, their presence an ominous shadow looming ever closer. He wasn't merely acting out of self-preservation; his determination was fueled by a fierce desire to protect her as well.

"Need something that can breach a Spire security system. And then there are the guards to contend with, along with their nasty little pets—creatures that skitter and slink in the shadows." He observed her pupils dilate, a telltale sign that mirrored the way her mind pieced together complex equations, each thought clicking into place with precision. "We could use a modified plasma cutter, its brilliant beam slicing through barriers like butter. Distraction charges would create just the right chaos, and sun grenades—imagine the blinding light and heat they would unleash. Maybe even an automatic railgun, if you ever manage to get that ambitious idea of yours to function. Plus, I can't forget whatever ingenious contraptions you've been hiding beneath those floor panels, waiting for the right moment to reveal itself."

Cassie's throat worked soundlessly. She reached for her welding goggles, then seemed to forget why. The workshop's ever-present steam hissed louder in the sudden silence, condensing on Alexander's collar like cold sweat.

When she finally moved, it was with the jerky precision of overwound clockwork. Her boots scraped across the grated floor as she hauled up a rusted access hatch. The acidic tang of forbidden chem-powders wafted up from the darkness below.

"Bring the lift winch," she said, voice hollow as a spent shell casing. "And pray you like burning alive. This'll hurt worse than acid."

Alexander obligingly grabbed the lift winch, his heart pounding in time with the hiss of steam around them. He couldn't help but feel a twinge of trepidation as he followed Cassie into the depths of her secretive workshop, descending into a world hidden even from her closest ally. The fact that she was now letting him in spoke volumes about the gravity of their situation.

The air grew thicker and hotter as they descended, laced with the acrid tang of alchemical reagents and the ozone bite of arcane energy. Alexander's eyes watered, but he blinked away the tears, refusing to show weakness in front of her. For Cassie, who had seen more of his scars—both physical and emotional—than anyone else in this damned city, to be this on edge sent a shiver down his spine that had nothing to do with the chill emanating from the damp stone walls around them.

They reached the bottom level, and Alexander hauled on the winch, lowering a rickety-looking platform into the gloom below. He glanced at Cassie, but her expression was lost behind her welding goggles, her face a mask of grim determination. Swallowing hard, Alexander stepped onto the creaking platform and held out a hand to help her aboard.

The platform lurched as she joined him, groaning under their combined weight. Alexander silently prayed that Cassie's skills as an engineer extended to maintaining this contraption as well as she did her other creations. They sank into darkness so completely it felt like it was closing in on them, suffocating them in its inky embrace.

The descent seemed to last an eternity, but eventually, there was a clunk as the platform came to rest with a jolt that jostled their teeth. Alexander groped for a switch, praying he wouldn't electrocute himself or worse yet, blow up the entire workshop along with them.

A soft blue glow illuminated their surroundings, casting long shadows across walls lined with rows upon rows of meticulously labeled vials and canisters, the products of countless late nights hunched over her workbench.

She gazed at him, her arms outstretched, revealing a collection of ominous creations. "These are my latest and most perilous inventions," she declared, her voice tinged with a mixture of pride and excitement. "I've decided to delve fully into the realms of chemical and biohazard warfare. I've harnessed every venom I could procure, along with samples from various plagues that mysteriously arise in these small, forgotten cities. From this, I have forged weapons capable of annihilating entire cities filled with vamps."

Alexander's eyes widened as he examined the labels on the myriad canisters, his curiosity piqued. "This is astonishing. Do they work?"

"I can't say for certain; I haven't had the opportunity to test them yet," Cassie replied, a hint of uncertainty creeping into her tone. "I was hoping you would be willing to try them out on your next hunt. Why not do so when you go to confront the dragon?"

He raised an eyebrow, a mixture of intrigue and caution on his face. "And how exactly do I avoid accidentally killing myself with these?"

Cassie strolled over to a rack of meticulously designed garments, her fingers brushing the fabric with care. "With these," she explained, gesturing to the suits hanging there. "I've dubbed them Hazmat suits. They're equipped with steam gears, ventilation fans, and brass charcoal filters, all designed to keep you safe. Just toss in a thermite or a sun grenade before entering, and you can remove the suits to engage in combat with whatever remains."

"This is incredible," he exclaimed, his eyes gleaming as he examined the array of canisters laid out before him on the workbench. "I'll put them to good use, and once it's all said and done, everyone will know who helped me take him down." he paused, his expression shifting to one of urgency. "But we need you to evacuate to another workshop. I suggest you make your move through the Northern wastes at midnight in two days. That's when I'll have the whole world's attention focused on my stunt at the Black Spire." he leaned in closer, his voice dropping to a conspiratorial whisper, as he detailed the plan, his heart racing with the thrill of what was to come and the worry he might not ever see her again.

He met her gaze, willing her to understand the gravity of the situation without saying it aloud. She knew as well as he did that there might not be a second chance to end this, not without risking even more innocent lives being caught in the crossfire.

Cassie hesitated, her eyes flickering between Alexander and the myriads of inventions around them. He could see the war waging within her the desire to protect her creations versus her own survival. At last, she let out a long sigh, resignation etched into her features.

"All right," she said, her voice resolute yet laced with an undercurrent of trepidation. Her eyes, wide and shimmering with unspoken worry, searched him for a glimmer of reassurance. "I'll go. But, Alexander, you had better come back in one piece after this reckless stunt of yours."

Alexander mustered a fleeting smile, a fragile attempt to convey confidence that belied the turmoil roiling within him. "That's the plan," he replied, his tone steadier than he felt, as he carefully slipped one of the shimmering vials into the inner pocket of his coat, the cool glass pressing against his chest like a ticking clock. "Just make sure you're ready for the sirens as the attack goes down."

Alexander pressed his lips against Cassie's, the kiss heavy with the weight of impending loss, a bittersweet farewell that felt like a jagged knife twisting in his chest. The gnawing uncertainty clawed at his insides, an insatiable beast threatening to consume him. Yet, in the depths of his turmoil, he summoned the strength to push aside his own anguish, determined to be their rock amidst the chaos. With fierce resolve, he pivoted on his heels, casting one last desperate glance at the workbench, a symbol of everything that he loved about her.

Collecting the canisters in his hands, he ascended back to the surface, determination coursing through his veins as he sought out the other weapons scattered throughout the dimly lit shop. Each item he collected felt like a lifeline, essential for the perilous hunt that lay ahead—perhaps the most treacherous of his life. The weight of his responsibility pressed heavily upon him, for the fate of the one closest to him hung in the balance should he falter. This thought steeled his resolve, sharpening his focus as he envisioned the myriads of possibilities the future could hold.

Echoes of the Past

The battered stone arch of Slade's southern gate looked less like a civic entrance and more like the broken teeth of some long-dead beast. The dusk's last red was already bleeding away behind the wall as Alexander joined the shuffling queue at the checkpoint, a stagnant clot of hollow-eyed workers and faded travelers hemmed in by the snap and glare of pressurized gas-lanterns. Shadows twisted long across the yard, broken only by the harsh, regular sweep of lantern light and the steely presence of the Daywalker guard.

Alexander fixed his gaze on the battered cobbles, calculating every angle. His entire body ached from the ride, and the burden of Cassie's secret payload—four glass vials and an entire suit of untested death—hung heavy beneath the tattered coat. He kept his left hand loose near his gun belt at his hip, right cradling the forged Mechanized Steam Tech permit. Ahead, the line shuffled forward, punctuated by sharp barks and the mechanical whir of pneumatic doors.

"Next!" The Daywalker's voice was like a gunshot: abrupt, metallic, impossible to ignore. The man in front of Alexander flinched, then fumbled forward, a tremor running down the spine of his faded greatcoat. The guard took the man's papers, lifted a brass-rimmed monocle to one dead-pale eye, and scrutinized the document with a surgeon's detachment. A gloved finger slid beneath the man's chin, turning his head so that the lantern light fell full across the pale skin and the thin ring of scar tissue encircling his throat a healed feeding mark, years old, but a detail worth noting.

"District?" barked the guard.

"Fourth. Millwright."

"Show bracelet." The worker hesitated, then yanked up a sleeve, revealing the familiar brass-and-copper registry bracelet, the capsule of dried blood glinting in the lantern glare. The guard twisted it with clinical indifference, checked a number stamped into the cuff, then scrawled an annotation in his ledger. "Move." The worker stumbled on, never looking back.

Alexander stepped forward into the cone of light. The guard was younger than expected face drawn sharp as a razor strop, eyes ringed with the faint blue shadows of insufficient sleep or excessive stimulants. The Daywalker's uniform had not a single crease, the plated wool immaculate, every button and clasp gleaming as if burnished hourly. The monocle, too, caught the light: an elaborate piece, lenses arrayed like the segments of a wasp's eye, doubtless tuned to catch every minute sign of corruption or criminal intent.

"Name?" The guard's tone was neither a question nor a courtesy; it was an incantation, designed to root out lies by the blunt force of repetition.

"Stirling. First name Alexander. Out-district visitor."

"Purpose of entry?"

"Consulting on hydraulic systems for the central turbine," he recited, flipping open the permit Cassie had forged. "Summons from the Hall."

The guard took the paper, passed it through a scanner mounted in a metal frame, and waited. A shrill beep. The man's eyes narrowed. "Your permit is new," he observed. "The blood registry, though—shows you as unidentified."

Alexander affected a lazy shrug, though every nerve was coiled. "I'm due at the center for an update. My last employer lost the records in the fires up north." He let his voice go flat, just a hair away from disrespect: play the world-weary contractor. "You know how it is."

The guard's lips compressed into a slash. "I do," he said quietly. "Show your bracelet."

Alexander proffered his left wrist, the brass cuff expertly distressed, the capsule inside filled with blood that was just a touch too bright, a little too fresh. The guard's eyes flicked between the monocle and the bracelet, then back to Alexander's face, lingering on the old scar that ran like a suture line across his jaw.

"You ever get tired of being hunted?" the Daywalker asked, voice so low only Alexander could hear.

Alexander met the man's gaze head-on. "Every day." He held the stare, felt the weight of it, the implied threat and shared understanding. The registry was Dracula's leash, and every man who wore it was a slave—just some pulled harder against the collar.

A long pause. The queue fidgeted behind him, the scent of fear rippling outward.

"Your bracelet," the guard said finally, "seems to be faulty."

"Then I'll collect a new one—once I'm inside," Alexander replied, voice clipped to the bone. "I have an appointment."

The guard's hand hovered near the baton at his belt, then drifted away. "You do that." He stamped the permit with a vicious flick of the wrist, then leaned in until Alexander could smell the faint metallic tang beneath the chemical scent of his uniform. "If I see you back here without a proper registry, I'll rip that arm off myself." He said it the way some people might say see you around, a casual promise of violence.

Alexander inclined his head, accepting the threat for the mercy it was. The guard let him pass, and the next human in line shuffled forward, face already turned away.

He crossed the threshold, breath held until the gate's pneumatic locks hissed behind him. The city's nightscape bloomed ahead a maze of alleys, gaslit walkways, and the distant throb of generators pulsing through the veins of Slade. For a moment, Alexander allowed himself to stand in the arch's shadow, absorbing the shouts and hissing steam of the reeking industrial district. He had made it through, for now, but the city would not be so forgiving a second time.

He glanced down at the fake bracelet, thumbed the catch that would shatter it and scatter the blood if he was cornered. Then he shouldered deeper into the crowd, every sense tuned to the possibility of betrayal, every step taking him closer to the dragon's heart.

It was almost dawn, and the only things alive in Victor Thorn's workshop were the rats and the ghosts. Alexander found the hidden door unlatched—Victor's version of an invitation. Down the slick iron rungs of the ladder, he dropped into the subcellar, boots landing with a wet slap among the puddles of condensed steam. The heat was suffocating. Lines of copper piping choked the ceiling and walls, every joint and elbow sweating with vapor, every length running to an elaborate manifold that pulsed softly like the heart of some enormous brass leviathan.

Victor had set up shop in the heart of this mechanical underworld, surrounded by stacks of leather-bound folios and chemical-stained blueprints. The air was a blend of scorched oil, wet newsprint, and the perpetual rot of old bindings. An array of oil lamps, each hand-tuned to a different flame color, ringed the room in bloody red, sickly blue, and jaundiced yellow.

Victor hunched over a battered table, hunks of iron and unfinished clockwork bristling from the scarred surface. His beard had gone more silver than grey, and his remaining eye gleamed with the cold focus of a man who had not slept in three days. The leather patch over the other socket was stitched with a crude X, as if warning the world not to pry.

"You made good time," Victor said, not looking up from his work. "Did the city try to eat you on the way in, or was it just the usual corruption?"

Alexander let the sarcasm slide. "The checkpoint was hungry, but nothing a forged pass and a little venom couldn't handle. Might even pay him a visit if everything goes well in the next few days."

Victor's right hand flexed, the knuckles cracked and thickened by years of recoil and wrenching. "Sit." He jerked his chin toward a chair on the far side of the table, its seat worn to the bone. "Let's get it over with."

Alexander sat, careful to keep his movements deliberate. He scanned the tabletop: three unfinished pistols, an open tin of oiled brass casings, and a single glass of black liquor that smelled like it had been strained through a corpse. In the middle, scattered like the debris field of a small disaster, were blueprints: some Cassie's, some Victor's, all annotated with overlapping rivers of red ink.

He slid the nearest sheaf aside, revealing a battered ledger beneath. "You ever going to tell me how Dracula went from exile to king in a decade? Or are we still playing it close?"

Victor's jaw clenched. He wiped his hands on an oily rag and, with a grunt, levered himself upright. From a cavity in the wall, disguised as a cracked tile, he drew a heavy volume, its cover the color of dried blood and its spine bristling with faded index tabs. Dust plummeted as he dropped it onto the table between them.

"Here's what's left," Victor said, voice stripped of humor. "The complete record of the venator line. Or at least, the pages not burned."

Alexander leaned in, hands braced on the ledger's corners. The first dozen leaves were missing, torn away with surgical precision. He flipped through entries in a tight, old-world script: battle rosters, lists of the fallen, receipts for holy water and ammonium nitrate. Some pages were annotated with what looked like rust but smelled unmistakably of blood.

"After your father's death, the registry was purged," Victor said, seating himself with a hiss of pain. "The city lords made a pact: hunt down the survivors or be hunted in turn. The venators went underground, scattered. Dracula picked us off like vermin."

"He did it with help," Alexander said. He didn't ask so much he knew. "Which house was first?"

"The Marcelli. Always hungry for power, and their bastard son owed the Dragon a favor."

Alexander flipped to the bookmarked section: The Fall. He traced the margin with a gloved finger, the print nearly blurred to oblivion by years of handling and, in one corner, a smudge of dried crimson that made the words hard to read.

Victor's voice dropped to a grave whisper. "He brokered alliances with the elder houses. Gave them immunity, status, and the promise of new prey once the registry was complete. The humans who cooperated were elevated; the ones who resisted were... well, you've seen the Ten Spears."

Alexander nodded. He had seen the Spears, all right. The wasteland of charred timber and bone that used to be the venators' last redoubt, his family's legacy reduced to black glass and grave markers.

Victor poured two shots of the corpse liquor, slid one across the table. "He didn't just kill us," Victor said, "He erased us. Every record, every line. The only reason you're still breathing is that you're more valuable as a myth than a corpse. And even that's running thin."

Alexander lifted the glass, let the scent scald his sinuses, and set it back down untouched. "Show me the moment. Where the houses turned."

Victor's hand trembled as he peeled back three pages. There, beneath a jagged watermark, was a ledger entry in a different hand—Victor's own, dated twenty years past. It detailed the betrayal: a midnight council, the opening of the gates to the registry enforcers, the slaughter of the venator apprentices in their sleep.

"I warned them," Victor said. "But your father—he believed in loyalty, even after it was a joke. He trusted Marcelli, trusted the council. The Dragon paid them in children and cities."

Alexander scanned the page, every word a knife. "So, what's left to kill him with, then? If the council is gone, the houses are loyal, and the humans are too busy eating each other to care?"

Victor's smile was a rictus. "You ever hear of the Decembrists?"

"No."

"They were the last resistance. Didn't fight with guns or knives. Fought with secrets. Bombed the Dragon's supply lines, sabotaged his blood farms, poisoned the wells. Made him bleed, even if they bled more."

Alexander's pulse quickened. "Did they win?"

Victor shrugged. "Does it matter? They hurt him. Made him mortal for a day, two at most. If you want to kill the Dragon, you need to make him feel that again."

Alexander closed the ledger with a soft thud. "And the weapon? Cassie thinks she's made something that can do it."

Victor's face softened, for just a second, at Cassie's name. "Maybe. But you'll need a way in. And you'll need to not die long enough to use it."

A grim amusement flickered in Alexander's eyes. "That's the easy part."

Victor snorted. "Then I hope you've kept up with your reading. There's a dossier in the back. Detailed maps, updated registry lists, even a few of the old guard still walking."

Alexander slid the ledger into his bag, careful not to crush the vials. "Why help me?"

Victor's gaze went distant, focused on a memory that Alexander could almost see reflected in the glass of the oil lamp. "Because you're the last. And if you die, so does every name in that book."

They sat in silence, the only sound the slow drip of condensation and the far-off, echoing clang of pipes above.

When Alexander rose to leave, Victor's voice stopped him at the ladder. "You kill the Dragon, you let me know before you die. I'd like to see it with my own eyes."

Alexander nodded. Then he was gone, up the rungs and into the predawn gloom, the heavy ledger in his pack and the truth heavier in his gut.

He remembers what it was like before. Before his world was turned upside down.

Years before the city ever burned, the woods behind Victor Thorn's estate were a cathedral of dusk and silence. The clearing was ringed by sentinel oaks, their gnarled limbs knotted with decades of old training scars—cuts from sabers, axes, even the occasional explosive charge. The air stank of sap and scorched powder, but at this hour it was the rot of leaf mold that dominated, a ripe, earthy fug that Alexander had come to associate with the worst kind of instruction.

He was twelve, maybe a wiry thirteen, and his shirt was already soaked through with sweat as he circled the row of wooden dummies. Each post was with old gouges, dark lines where the lacquer had never fully covered up blood or resin. He kept his sword low, just as Victor had drilled into him a thousand times and watched the instructor's silhouette hover at the edge of the ring, arms folded, and one leg cocked in perpetual impatience.

"Again," Victor said, and the word cracked across the clearing like a musket shot.

Alexander grits his teeth, feinted left, then swept the practice blade at the nearest dummy's midsection. The wood clacked hollow, sending a splinter of bark flying, but it wasn't clean—he'd overextended, and he knew it.

Victor's cane lashed out, catching Alexander's shin with a jolt of pain that brought him back upright.

"You're not cutting lumber. You're cutting flesh," Victor snapped. "Efficiency, not bravado. Every inch you overreach is an inch you lose to your enemy."

Alexander scowled but reset his stance. "Wouldn't matter against a real vamp. They'd just heal it."

Victor snorted. "They heal slower with half their spine on the ground. Again."

He did as told, the rhythm of attack, retreat, and reset all but automatic now. Victor watched with a predator's patience, never correcting twice for the same flaw, always finding some new detail to clarify with him.

"You waste motion," Victor said. "You telegraph your anger." Another blow, this time to the upper arm, and Alexander staggered, more from humiliation than pain.

"I'm trying," he hissed.

"Try harder. Because when the time comes, you'll be the only one left to try at all."

The forest deepened around them, blue light slipping from the air, and for a moment even the insects seemed to go silent.

Alexander finished the last drill, lungs burning, and let the sword drop to his side. "Did you hate your instructor this much?"

Victor's smile was a ghost. "He's dead, so he must have done something wrong." He limped forward, snatched the blade from Alexander's hand, and inspected the notched edge. "Next time, focus on the kill. You get one shot. After that, it's all running."

The sound came then: the distant crack of branches, the slow-building drum of hoofbeats on soft earth. Victor went still, cocked his head, and listened with an intensity that made Alexander's skin crawl.

"Inside. Now." Victor tossed the practice blade to the ground, eyes scanning the shadowed timberline. "Go."

Alexander didn't hesitate. He sprinted for the back door, heart thudding. He made it halfway up the slope before he looked back.

Victor stood unmoved, hands at his sides, watching the darkness gather at the edge of the woods. The light had gone red, the last rays of sun warped by the smoke of distant burning. Among the trees, Alexander saw the first glint of torchlight, then the silhouettes of men—too many, moving with military precision, faces masked and weapons ready.

The front of the house erupted in shouts, the sound of glass shattering, then a terrible, layered silence. Alexander ducked behind the root cellar, breath ragged. The torches drew closer. He could hear Victor shouting, the voice no longer instructor-cold but brimming with panic.

"Alexander! In now!

Victor met him at the side door, shoved him inside with a force that sent him skidding across the stone floor. "Upstairs. Third room. Don't come out unless you hear my voice."

"But—"

Victor's palm cracked across his cheek. "No arguments. Not tonight."

Alexander staggered up the stairs, the shouts below rising to a fever pitch. He ducked into the third room, as ordered, and closed the door behind him.

It was his father's old study, lined with thick books and the heavy stink of stale pipe smoke. He knelt beneath the window, peered through the warped glass.

Outside, men poured across the yard, their weapons out. Victor held the porch, cane in one hand and a heavy, ancient revolver in the other. He fired twice, the flashes bright even against the torchlight, and two men fell.

Then the Daywalkers hit, moving so fast the eye could barely follow. Alexander saw Victor go down under a tide of black coats, then the vampires themselves—taller, heavier, faces painted with ritual scars—tear into the line of attackers, heedless of friend or foe.

He ducked as something crashed through the window, a hail of splinters raining down on his back. He crawled to the desk, found the revolver hidden in the bottom drawer, and clutched it to his chest.

The house was burning now, the heat and smoke seeping into every crevice. Alexander curled into a ball, pressed his forehead to the cold floor, and waited for the end.

Through the roar and the screams, he heard Victor's voice, battered but unmistakable: "Remember every lesson!"

The memory snapped off like a switch.

He dressed in silence, checked his weapons with the slow, deliberate ritual Victor had drilled into him, and stepped into the night. There was no safety in the world anymore, only motion, and the thin hope that this time, when the monsters came, he'd be ready.

Carrying a carefully wrapped bundle of food, he navigated the familiar corridors, his footsteps echoing softly against the aged wooden floorboards. The scent of freshly prepared meals wafted around him, mingling with the musty aroma of old books and leather that filled Victor's old study. As he approached the door, a sense of nostalgia washed over him, the memories of countless hours spent in this room flooding his mind. He paused for a moment, his heart quickening, knowing he still needed the wise counsel that lingered in the corners of this space. What he was about to undertake weighed heavily on his thoughts, and he yearned for the guidance that Victor had always provided.

The twilight bled through Victor Thorn's study, painting the crumbling plaster and steam-pitted steel with a wash of orange and sickly gray. The torches in the wall sconces were new—high-efficiency, paraffin-fed, their flames sharp as razors and just as hungry. The air in here was always a little too warm, the smell of scorched paper and old parchment thick enough to settle on the tongue.

Victor waited behind his desk, the battered slab of iron banded with steel rivets and so scarred it looked like it had survived a dozen wars. Scrolls and ledgers fanned across its surface, many still open to whatever disaster Victor had been consulting before Alexander's arrival. There was no chair on Alexander's side, so he stood, posture rigid, hands locked behind his back. The show of discipline wasn't lost on Victor; he smirked, just barely.

"Thought you'd be dead by now," Victor said, voice sandpaper rough.

Alexander shrugged, let the silence between them stretch. "Didn't want to be followed."

"Then why lead them straight to my door?" Victor's one good eye flicked to the shadowy corners, where the old tripwires and flame-traps hid. "You sure you weren't tailed?"

"If I was, you'd be the first to know."

Victor's gaze sharpened, as if daring Alexander to say otherwise. He folded his hands atop the desk, the gnarled fingers interlaced and nodded at a file resting dead center on the blotter. Thats all I could find regarding the building of the Black Spire. Trusting Anna might be placing your head on a silver platter."

Alexander shrugged "She did save my life and seems very hell bent on killing the dragon."

Victor grunted. "She rescued you, but her loyalty ends at her own advantage. She's not family, Alexander."

Alexander set the building plans down, then closed the main letter, snapping the file shut with a hollow click. "Doesn't matter," he said. "If she thinks I'll play by her script, she's more naïve than I thought she be."

Victor shook his head. "No one's naïve anymore. Not since the Dragon burned the last of us out. What do they really have to fear. One Venator left hiding like a rat killing from the shadows?"

They stood in silence, both men eyeing the folder as if it might explode. Alexander felt the old bitterness rise—every memory of betrayal, every name crossed out in the ledger. He forced it back down. There was a job to finish, and not even the ghosts would save him from it.

Victor's eyes drifted to the ancient revolver mounted on the wall behind the desk. "You know what you're walking into?"

"I know I don't have a choice."

"Then at least go in with your eyes open." Victor's voice was almost gentle, or as close as it could get. "Don't mistake Anna's kindness for a weapon. She'll turn it against you the second she's in danger."

Alexander's lips curled in a humorless smile. "I'm counting on it."

Victor pushed a final item across the desk—a tin of matches, each head lacquered a dull gray. "You ever get close enough, these'll burn right through a Daywalker's coat. Just mind the blast radius." He paused, the lines in his face deepening. "And don't bring them back here if you get caught."

Alexander pocketed the matches, then straightened, eyes fixed on Victor. "You know what happens if I fail."

Victor nodded. "It won't be quick." His hand traveling to his face before he realized being caught in an old memory.

Alexander turned to go, his shadow stretching long across the flagstones. At the door, he hesitated, then glanced back. "Thanks for the warning."

Victor's voice followed him out, low and unyielding: "Don't die for nothing, Alexander."

He left the old man in the study, the echoes of torchlight flickering along the books and steel. The city outside was already bracing for nightfall, every window shuttered, every lamp lit. He drew his coat tight, felt the hard weight of glass vials and weapons against his ribs, and let the darkness carry him toward whatever waited at the Spire.

If Anna had already planned her betrayal, that was fine. He'd learned from the best. And in the end, monsters or not, it would come down to who made the first cut.

Unlikely Allies

The Broken Gear squatted like a wounded beast at the end of a narrow lane in Old Slade, its weathered facade peeling away to reveal the rotted bones beneath. Alexander pressed his shoulder against the crumbling brick of the adjacent building, watching the tavern's entrance for twenty silent minutes before even considering approaching it. Three patrons had entered, two had left. The mathematics of survival were never complicated—they were just absolute.

His fingers brushed the grip of his revolver, thumb tracing the worn checkering that had become smoother with each kill. The weight was reassuring against his hip, a constant companion that had never betrayed him. Unlike people.

From his vantage point, he cataloged every detail that might save his life later: the second-story windows with their moth-eaten curtains, the rusted fire escape that looked ready to collapse under a child's weight, the unmarked door beside the main entrance that likely led to a stockroom or cellar. The worn cobblestones in front of the tavern told their own story—scuff marks from hurried exits, dark stains that rain had failed to wash away.

A drunk staggered out, humming a tuneless melody as he pissed against the wall, then wobbled away into the gathering darkness. Alexander counted to one hundred before pushing off from his hiding place.

The Broken Gear's sign hung from a single chain its painted cogs and gears faded to ghostly outlines. The sound of clinking glasses and muted conversation leaked through cracks in the warped doorframe. Beneath it all, the low hum of steam pipes pumping heat into the building provided a constant baseline to the evening's uncertain symphony.

The iron handle was cold against his palm as he pushed the door open, bracing himself against the wave of stale air that rushed to meet him—a potent mixture of spilled beer, unwashed bodies, and the greasy smoke of tallow candles. Every instinct screamed for him to turn back, to trust no one, to find another way. But revenge made for strange bedfellows, and if Anna's information about her father was true...

He stepped inside, allowing his eyes to adjust to the dim interior. The tavern's layout unfurled before him: bar along the right wall, a dozen mismatched tables scattered across a floor sticky with spilled drinks, a narrow staircase at the back leading to rooms he'd rather not imagine. A single exit that wasn't the front door—a kitchen passage, half-hidden behind a ragged curtain.

Alexander moved with deliberate casualness toward a table near the bar, positioning himself with his back to the wall and clear lines of sight to both exits. The chair creaked under his weight as he settled into it, coat arranged to allow quick access to his weapons.

The bartender—a barrel-chested man with arms like tree trunks and scars suggesting he'd survived at least one vampire attack—glanced his way without expression. No recognition, which was good. No curiosity either, which was better.

The patrons were a typical Old Slade mix: factory workers drowning the day's monotony, a pair of merchants concluding some transaction in hushed tones, a trio of Registry officials still in their brass-buttoned uniforms—Daywalkers, Alexander noted, the telltale pallor of their skin visible even in the tavern's forgiving light. They paid him no attention, absorbed in their cups of synthetic blood and conversations.

A waitress approached, her movements careful and measured. She wore her dark hair pulled back severely, exposing a neck marked with the thin white lines of feeding scars—old ones, healed over many times. Her eyes flicked across his face without lingering, trained never to stare.

"What'll it be?" she asked, voice neutral, neither friendly nor cold.

"Draft cider," Alexander replied, matching her tone. "And whatever passes for food."

Her lips twitched in what might have been amusement. "Duck jerky's the least likely to turn your stomach inside out."

He nodded, and she moved away, disappearing behind the bar. Alexander's gaze swept the room again, cataloging faces, postures, and weapons. The Registry officials were the only obvious threat, but they seemed more interested in their drinks than surveillance. Still, he kept them in his peripheral vision.

The waitress returned with a dented pewter mug of amber cider and a plate of dark meat sliced thin and glistening with oil. As she set the plate down, her fingers moved with practiced efficiency, slipping something between the slices. The movement was so subtle that anyone not looking for it would have missed it entirely.

"Bread costs extra," she said, loud enough for nearby tables to hear, then moved on to her next customer.

Alexander took a sip of the cider—sour but not unpleasant—and casually rearranged the jerky on his plate. A corner of parchment peeked out from beneath the bottom slice. He glanced around, confirming no one was watching, then extracted it with nimble fingers and slipped it into his palm.

Under the table, he unfolded the note, the paper soft and worn as if it had passed through many hands. The message was written in a tight, elegant script that betrayed an education far beyond what a tavern waitress should possess:

"Follow the arrow. Come alone. Speak to no one."

Below the text was a crude drawing of a rat, its tail forming a directional pointer. Alexander refolded the note and tucked it into his inner pocket. He took another sip of cider, considering his options. This could be a trap—probably was a trap. Anna had resources he couldn't begin to guess at, and enemies he couldn't name. Trusting her was a calculated risk, one that could end with his blood adding another stain to Old Slade's cobblestones.

But he was hunting the Dragon. And to reach such prey, sometimes you had to wade into the swamp.

He chewed a piece of the jerky—tough and oversalted, but better than he'd expected—and washed it down with the last of his cider. The Registry officials were paying their tab, preparing to leave. Better to wait until they were gone.

Five minutes later, they filed out, and Alexander stood, leaving a few coins on the table. The waitress caught his eye from across the room and gave an imperceptible nod toward the back door. He acknowledged nothing, simply adjusted his coat and moved toward the exit.

The night air hit him like a slap, carrying the metallic tang of factory smoke and the underlying sweetness of decay that permeated Old Slade. He circled around to the alley behind the tavern, hand never straying far from his revolver.

Whatever waited in the darkness ahead, he was ready. Or as ready as a man could be when walking knowingly into a trap. After all, sometimes the only way to kill a predator was to let it think you were prey.

The alley behind The Broken Gear was a throat of shadows, narrow and choked with the refuse of a hundred desperate meals. Alexander moved with practiced silence, each step placed deliberately to avoid the broken glass and splintered wood that might announce his presence. His breath came shallow through his nose, tasting the rancid air without allowing it to fill his lungs. Old Slade's back passages were never empty—rats and worse things claimed these territories after dark—but tonight the silence pressed against his ears like cotton wool.

His eyes adjusted to the darkness, picking out shapes among the discarded crates and moldering sacks. Twenty paces in, something caught his attention—an arrangement too deliberate to be chance. Three rats lay dead on the filthy cobblestones, their bodies positioned tip-to-tail in a perfect arrow shape. Their fur was still sleek, deaths recent enough that the city's scavengers hadn't yet found them. The precision of their placement sent a chill up his spine that had nothing to do with the night air.

Alexander crouched, careful not to touch the grotesque marker. No blood pooled beneath the small corpses—killed elsewhere, then arranged here. A message meant only for someone who knew to look for it. He followed the direction of the arrow with his eyes, tracking its path to a rusted sewer grate set into the stone a dozen paces ahead.

The shadows seemed to thicken as he approached the grate. A crude capital "D" had been scrawled across the oxidized metal in what appeared to be dried blood, its edges flaking away like rust. Dracula. Dragon. Death. The letter could stand for any of them—or all three.

Alexander glanced over his shoulder, confirming he was alone, then slipped his fingers through the grate's bars. The metal was cold and rough against his skin as he lifted. It came away with surprising ease, suggesting recent and frequent use. The hole beneath gaped like an open wound, exhaling the musty breath of Old Slade's bowels.

He lowered himself into the darkness, boots finding purchase on slick iron rungs embedded in the tunnel wall. The smell hit him immediately, sewage and stagnant water, overlaid with the chemical tang of industrial waste that the factories pumped through the city's underbelly. He descended carefully, counting each rung until his feet touched solid ground fifteen steps down.

The tunnel stretched before him, a single vaulted passage barely tall enough for him to stand upright. What little light filtered through the open grate above quickly surrendered to the underground gloom. Alexander reached for the small steam-powered torch at his belt, then hesitated. Light would make him a target in this confined space.

As his eyes adjusted, he noticed a faint blue-green glow emanating from patches along the curved walls and ceiling. Phosphorescent fungi, feeding on the damp and dark, cast just enough illumination to navigate by. Their light pulsed gently, almost like breathing, dripping luminescence onto the slick stone path.

Alexander moved forward, keeping his back to one wall, hand resting on his revolver. The tunnel's acoustics amplified every sound, the soft splash of his footsteps, the distant drip of water, the occasional scuttle of something small and quick retreating from his approach. Each noise echoed, making it impossible to determine if he was truly alone.

The air grew thicker as he progressed, heavy with moisture that was collected on his skin and clothes. His lungs protested each breath, the tainted oxygen burning slightly as it filled his chest. Time became difficult to track in the unchanging passage, but he estimated he'd traveled nearly half a mile when the tunnel began to slope upward.

Water ran in thin rivulets down the center of the path now, flowing against his direction of travel. The streams caught the fungi's glow, creating snaking lines of blue-green light that twisted around his boots. Alexander's jaw tightened as he pushed forward, disgusting warring with determination. Anna had chosen this route deliberately testing his resolve, perhaps, or ensuring that only the truly desperate would follow her breadcrumb trail.

A rhythmic tapping reached his ears, too regular to be natural. Alexander froze, pressing himself against the curved wall, listening intently. Three taps, followed by two, then three again. Not an SOS, but close enough to be meaningful. It grew louder as he advanced, leading him toward a patch of darkness that resolved into another grate overhead.

Three more dead rats hung by their tails from the metal bars, suspended by fine copper wire that glinted in the fungi's glow. Their bodies twisted slowly in the stale air currents, forming a macabre mobile that pointed upward. The message was clear: this was the exit.

Alexander reached up, testing the grate with gentle pressure. It shifted slightly but didn't lift. He braced himself, set his shoulders against the damp stone, and pushed upward with both hands. The metal protested with a low groan, then gave way, scraping across stone as he shifted it aside.

Cool night air rushed into the tunnel, sweet compared to the fetid atmosphere below. Alexander hauled himself up and out, emerging onto a narrow cobblestone lane lined with crumbling flats. The buildings hunched shoulder to shoulder, their facades pockmarked with age and neglect. Windows stared like blind eyes, most boarded up or broken, curtains hanging in tatters where they remained at all.

He replaced the grate and oriented himself, identifying this as the northeastern quarter of Old Slade—a warren of abandoned factories and tenements left to rot after the Registry deemed it too costly to maintain. No functioning gas lamps illuminated these streets; the only light came from a waning moon partially obscured by smoke from distant factory stacks.

Alexander moved along the wall, counting doorways until he reached the seventh building. Its windows were intact but clouded with grime, preventing any view of the interior. As he approached, something caught the meager moonlight—a small brass statue placed deliberately on a windowsill, visible through a crack in the otherwise filthy glass. A dragon, its wings spread in flight, jaws open in silent challenge.

The door before him was weathered but solid, reinforced with bands of iron that hadn't succumbed to the rust that claimed most metal in Old Slade. No knob or handle marred its surface—just a smooth expanse of wood worn by countless hands. Alexander raised his fist to knock, then hesitated, ears straining for any sound from within.

Before his knuckles could touch the wood, the door swung inward on silent hinges. Anna stood framed in the narrow opening, her silhouette sharp against the warm light spilling from behind her. Her eyes met his with unwavering intensity, neither welcoming nor hostile—simply watchful, calculating.

"You're late," she said, her voice low and controlled. She stepped aside, a silent invitation that promised nothing but further complication.

The safehouse was a study in controlled paranoia. Alexander stepped across the threshold; cataloging exits and potential weapons before the door closed behind him. Three windows, all reinforced with iron latticework. A staircase leading to the second floor. A heavy oak table dominating the center of the room, its surface covered with maps and diagrams illuminated by a quartet of oil lamps with polished reflectors. The light cast Anna's features in sharp relief as she secured the door with three separate locks—mechanical, not magical. She believed in steel, not superstition.

"You smell like the sewers," she said, wrinkling her nose as she moved past him toward the table. Her movements were precise, economical, the grace of a predator conserving energy.

"Your invitation lacked certain amenities," Alexander replied, remaining near the door. His back itched, exposed in this unfamiliar space. "The rats were a nice touch."

Anna's lips curled into the ghost of a smile. "I needed to ensure you weren't followed. The Registry has eyes everywhere, but they rarely look down." She gestured to a basin of steaming water in the corner. "Clean your hands, at least. The maps are delicate."

Alexander approached the basin cautiously, noting the strange copper implements arranged beside its surgical tools, perhaps, or instruments of torture. He washed quickly, the hot water turning gray against his skin. The soap smelled of lye and something sharper, medicinal.

"Why the elaborate game?" he asked, drying his hands on a cloth that hung nearby. "You could have simply told me where to meet."

Anna's gaze was cool, assessing. "Trust is earned, Venator. I needed to see if you could follow instructions without drawing attention." She pulled out a chair at the table. "Sit. We have much to discuss."

He joined her at the table, positioning himself so that he could watch both her and the door. The maps spread before him were hand-drawn on aged parchment, the lines precise and detailed. Architectural plans of some massive structure—a fortress or palace, its dimensions dwarfing any building he'd seen in Slade.

"Before we begin," Anna said, leaning forward, elbows on the table, "I want to be clear about my intentions. I am not helping you for the sake of humanity or some noble cause. I want my father dead for my own reasons."

Alexander met her gaze. "I assumed as much. Family quarrels among vampires tend to end in bloodshed."

"It's more than a quarrel." Her voice hardened, eyes flashing with something that might have been pain. "He's an abomination. The pure bloodlines—the Daywalkers, born vampires like me—we lived in balance with humans for centuries. We fed, yes, but we didn't slaughter indiscriminately. We didn't create armies of turned vampires to police the streets and terrorize the populace."

Alexander's jaw tightened. "You expect me to believe you care about human lives?"

"I care about order," she replied. "The Blood Registry, the walls around the cities, the constant surveillance—these are perversions of our natural relationship with humanity. My father has created a system that will eventually collapse, and when it does, humans will hunt us to extinction."

Her words were practiced, rehearsed, but beneath them Alexander sensed genuine conviction. He didn't trust it—couldn't afford to—but it was useful information. Anna had a stake in this beyond mere power or revenge. She believed herself to be protecting her species' future.

"And what happens after he's dead?" Alexander asked, voice low and even. "You take his place?"

Anna's fingers traced the outline of the fortress on the map. "I have no interest in ruling. I want to dismantle the Registry, dissolve the enforcer corps, return to the old ways." She looked up, meeting his eyes directly. "But that's a discussion for after the Dragon is dead."

"No this is a discussion for now." Alexander growled

"I want it no different from before my father took his rein." Anna answered coldly.

Alexander nodded slowly. He didn't believe her, not entirely, but her immediate goals aligned with his. That was enough for now. "Show me what we're facing."

Anna spread her hands across the blueprints, anchoring them flat against the table. "The Black Spire," she said. "My father's stronghold is at the center of the city. A hexagonal main tower surrounded by four guard turrets connected by skybridges." Her finger traced the structure's outline. "The outer walls are fifteen feet thick, reinforced with steel and warded against both physical and arcane attacks."

Alexander studied the diagrams, committing each detail to memory. The central tower rose twenty stories above the surrounding city; its apex crowned with a glass observatory. The four smaller turrets were positioned at the compass points, each housing a contingent of elite guards—Daywalkers like Anna, judging by the notation.

"These eastern vents," he said, pointing to a series of narrow openings along the tower's eastern face. "They look like potential entry points."

Anna shook her head. "They're heavily warded—anyone attempting entry would be incinerated instantly. I've seen it happen." Her finger moved to the western spire. "Our target is here—a maintenance hatch on the roof of the western turret. The wards are weaker there due to the need for regular access."

Alexander frowned. "The guards?"

"Patrols every fifteen minutes along the skybridges, but the rooftop itself is only checked at the change of shifts—midnight and noon." She pulled another diagram from beneath the others patrol schedule, meticulously annotated with times and numbers. "The midnight shift is smaller, just four guards instead of six. The darkness makes them overconfident."

The plan was taking shape in Alexander's mind. "We'd still need to approach unseen," he said. "The Spire is visible from every point in the city."

Anna's smile was cold and satisfied. "That's why we're not approaching from the ground." She revealed another document, the schematic for an airship, smaller than the commercial vessels that drifted between city districts. "I've know where to acquire a Scout-class patrol ship. We'll approach from above, using the factory smoke for cover, then rappel down to the western turret.

Alexander's pulse quickened despite himself. The plan was audacious, borderline suicidal, but it might work. If they timed it perfectly, if the guards maintained their routine, if Anna's information was accurate... a lot of ifs, but fewer than he'd expected.

"And once we're inside?" he asked.

"My father's quarters are three levels below the observatory. He holds court there each night, surrounded by his favorites. During the Black Spire conclave, security will be focused on the main entrance and the grand hall. The upper levels will be relatively unguarded."

Alexander traced the path with his finger, mentally calculating distances and timing. "We'd have minutes at most before they realized something was wrong."

"Minutes is all we need," Anna replied. She reached beneath the table and produced a small wooden box, its surface carved with intricate patterns. She opened it to reveal a vial of viscous black liquid nestled in velvet. "This is extracted from the heart of an Elder—one of the original vampires. It will weaken my father long enough for your weapons to finish the job."

Alexander's eyes narrowed. "An Elder's heart? Those are mythical."

"So was Dracula, once." Anna closed the box with a decisive snap. "Believe what you will, but this is our only advantage."

He sat back, weighing all he'd heard against the burning need for vengeance that had driven him since the night his family died. The plan was desperate, the alliance treacherous, but the opportunity...

"When?" he asked finally.

"Two nights from now. The conclave begins at midnight—we make our move at eleven-thirty, when the guards are preparing to change shifts and the guests are still arriving at the main entrance."

Alexander nodded, decision made. "I'll need to prepare a weapon harness of some kind."

"Bring only what's necessary," Anna warned. "We'll be descending on ropes—every ounce matters."

They spent the next hour refining details—drop points, extraction routes, and contingencies for discovery. The tension between them never dissipated, but it transformed into something productive—the wary respect of two predators with a common prey.

As dawn approached, Alexander gathered his notes and committed the final details to memory. "If this fails," he said, standing, "and you betray me—"

"You'll kill me," Anna finished for him, her expression unreadable. "And if you betray me, I'll ensure you suffer far longer than my father would allow." She extended her hand across the table, pale fingers steady in the lamplight. "Until then, we are allies."

Alexander took her hand. Her skin was cool but not cold, her grip firm. Not quite human, but not the corpse-chill of a turned vampire either. Born of darkness but not consumed by it. He wondered, briefly, what that meant for her soul if such things existed anymore.

"Allies," he agreed, releasing her hand. "For now."

The word hung between them, fragile as glass and just as likely to shatter when pressure was applied. But it was enough to build on—a foundation for the vengeance they both craved, for reasons neither fully trusted the other to understand.

The Crimson Trail

The dawn above Old Slade was the color of a two-week bruise, sickly purple at the rim and jaundiced with sulfur nearer the city wall. They'd chosen the south gate because the Daywalkers rotated here at shift-change, half-drunk and clumsy, barely bothering to check papers. Anna and Alexander cleared the checkpoint with three words between them and the subtle pressure of her cold fingers against his arm, which somehow convinced the guards not to make eye contact for the duration of their passage.

They followed the wall's shadow for half a mile, boots echoing over the empty concourse, until the surface underfoot changed from the even shudder of flagstone to a more treacherous debris field—fractured asphalt, humped and gored with exposed rebar, every step its own equation in balance and intent. Beyond the wall, the city's outskirt slumped into a wasteland called the "breaks": collapsed industrial parks, razed tanneries, and those neighborhoods judged too rebellious or too sick for the Registry to bother saving.

Alexander had always hated this part of the world, the place where civilization ended not with a whimper but with the mechanical shriek of a city's last exhale. He walked ahead, letting the brittle wind whip the edges of his coat, pretending that Anna's predatory calm behind him was just a trick of acoustics, a product of the broken windows and hollowed cement.

They made the rendezvous point in twenty minutes. The outpost was a hunk of stone, possibly a remnant of a pre-Registry tollhouse, now split wide by centuries of freeze-thaw and occupation. Anna ducked inside first, scanning the mossy interior with her odd, refocused stare. She said nothing but Alexander could tell by her measured breathing and the way she flexed her left hand, as if preparing for a slap, that she'd checked for traps. There were none.

"Give it a moment," he said, settling against a slab of wall. "I don't start the vehicle cold. Makes a noise you wouldn't believe."

Anna let her eyes linger on him, mouth a straight line. "There are ears everywhere," she said.

"You ever driven one?" he asked.

"No," she said. "I can't stand machines. They always lie."

He barked a humorless laugh, surprised by how close her words mapped to his own distrust. "All right. Stay behind me. And keep your hands off the brasswork unless you want a thumb melted."

They threaded through a slot in the back wall and into a sunken alley, its surface scabbed with fifty years of street battles. The thing lay waiting under a tarpaulin, the pattern of acid burns and bullet holes giving it the appearance of a sleeping animal. Alexander peeled the tarp away, fingers numb from cold and nerves and revealed his other inheritance: a hydro-steam car, scavenged from at least three separate eras of the city's life. The body was low and squat, plated with strips of pounded iron and bristling with anti-personnel mesh. The front end had a cowcatcher welded in place, its tips honed to a dull blue. The rear chassis was half-lifted, armored like a gunboat, the tires overbuilt to run on mud or snow or worse. Cassie outdone herself he couldn't help but think.

He double-checked the perimeter—nobody, not even rats in the drains—and reached for the access panel. Anna watched with her arms crossed, one boot resting on a loose cobble. She didn't look bored, just terminally unimpressed.

He unlatched the hatch, exposing a shallow cockpit lined with faded leather. From beneath the seat, he withdrew a battered oilcan and dribbled a line of lubricants along the piston rods. The tank was half full of water; he topped it with a waterskin sewn to the inside of his coat. Then came the fuel—a double shot of ethanol poured into a side compartment, then a primer pellet for the ignition. The boiler's hiss filled the alley, sharp and urgent, accompanied by the familiar rattle of the pressure gauge. He counted to thirty, then slapped the starter.

The engine answered with a raw, gurgling roar that rattled his teeth. The smell of hot iron and old sweat filled the cockpit. For a moment, Alexander grinned—he couldn't help it. It always started. Not every time, not even most times, but enough to make a man feel like the world might not win after all.

He slid behind the controls, motioned Anna to the jump seat. She settled in with an economy of movement, showing no reaction as the engine's vibration set the brasswork trembling against her thigh.

"What's the route?" she asked.

"We take the old canal bed south to the grain mill. If they're watching the main highways, we cut through the blast zone at Miser's Field and double back on the access roads. No one follows us unless they know the car's sound, and even then, they'll lose us in the fog."

Anna nodded. "The mill. You sure that's where he's keeping the shipments?"

"Not sure of anything," Alexander said, twisting the throttle. "But the registry's been bleeding slaves from every block between here and the waterworks. My guess is he's stockpiling something big, and he needs it moved out before the conclave. The mill's the only spot left with the right infrastructure. Plus, if we can destroy whatever he is preparing for the enclave should make him angry enough to send his enforcers on a wild goose chase as allowing us to have more leeway as we slip in."

Anna's mouth quirked. "You're not as dumb as you look."

"Neither are you," Alexander shot back, and gunned the accelerator.

The car spat a plume of scalding steam and jerked forward, tires grinding over broken glass and the bones of smaller machines left to rot by less hopeful men. The blast shield rattled, but the welds held. Within a quarter mile, they'd left the city's last lamps behind and entered the bone field: acre after acre of failed outbuildings, each a collapsed tent of rust and soot. Feral birds—engineered to eat corpses and keep the city's perimeter clean—took flight as they passed, filling the dawn with a scratchy, metallic chatter.

Alexander kept his eyes on the terrain. The canal bed was a scar through the landscape, its sides slicked with years of chemical runoff and layered with bricks slick as wet soap. He knew better than to trust the surface; sinkholes, the size of carriages opened at random, sometimes filled with water, sometimes with things worse than water. He steered wide, always keeping an escape vector open.

After a moment, the car cleared the last of the bone field and shot up onto a stretch of old turnpike, the surface here intact enough to allow for speed. He floored the accelerator, feeling the engine's heat bloom against his boots. Ahead, the silhouette of the grain mill rose above the flatland, its silo ringed by the faintest suggestion of guards—human, probably, but not definitely.

He throttled down a hundred yards short of the perimeter. Anna hopped out before the car stopped rolling, her movements silent as she thought. She knelt behind a crumbling embankment and surveyed the approach with a focus that made Alexander uneasy.

"Three on the north wall," she said, "one in the yard. No dogs." She paused, head cocked. "And a watcher in the silo window. That's where they'll keep the registers."

Alexander took out his new railgun that Cassie had gifted him she was the definition of someone with a taste for overkill—and checked the load. Seeing the small rod of silver in the chamber, he then checked the magazine. He kept his eyes on Anna, but she gave no sign of nervousness, just the cold arithmetic of a killer lining up a plan.

"Want the lead?" he asked.

Anna flashed a smile—just a line of teeth, no more—and disappeared into the low fog. Alexander gave her thirty seconds, then moved out, keeping to the shallow ditches and the shifting angles of the mill's outer yard. In the east, the sun had risen to the point where even the smoke-stained sky could not entirely conceal it. Shadows grew sharp and deep, the air thick with the smell of mold and cut wheat.

He reached the north wall, pressed himself flat against the rough-hewn timber, and counted the guards: three, as Anna had said, all looking in the wrong direction. He could hear them talking, voices muffled by the masks they wore to keep out the spores that sometimes drifted in from the slaughterhouse next door.

Anna was already on the wall, her body nearly invisible against the faded boards. She dropped behind the nearest guard, slid a wire around his throat, and pulled him backward into the mud. The other two saw the body drop, but Anna was already among them, her movements, a blur of elbows and knees and something sharp Alexander could not see. Both men were down in a matter of seconds.

He sprinted for the door, boots pounding the hard ground. Anna met him there, a smear of blood across one cheek.

"Easy," she whispered. "Inside's worse."

They pushed through the door, straight into a corridor reeking of ammonia and the sweeter tang of fermenting grain. The floor was slick and the walls pulsated with the drone of machinery. Down the hall, Alexander could see the outline of more guards, all clustered around a bank of punchcard readers and a battered abacus the size of a coffin. At the far end, perched on a chair with his legs propped up on a crate of what might have been cured meat, was a man Alexander recognized from a dozen wanted posters in a dozen cities: Marcelli, the Registry's golden boy, a man who'd signed the death warrants for half of Alexander's family.

Anna saw the recognition on his face. She nodded once, then faded left into a blind spot created by a buckled support beam.

Alexander didn't bother with subtlety. He flicked the safety off of the railgun. The sound echoed off the metal and leveled it at the cluster of men.

"Hands up," he said, voice dead even. "Now, or your boss picks you out of the walls for a month."

The men hesitated, then raised their hands in slow, fearful synchrony. Marcelli remained unmoved, his eyes never leaving Alexander's face.

"Well, well," Marcelli said. "If it isn't the last Venator. I'd say I was surprised, but I've been betting the pool on you for years."

Alexander kept the gun trained on the group. "Empty your pockets. Slowly."

Marcelli smiled. "What's your angle, Stirling? You can't shoot your way out of this. Even if you get to me, the fail safes in this building will cook you alive before you get three steps."

Alexander stepped forward, just enough to put himself in line with the others. He never took his eyes off Marcelli.

"Fail safes," he said. "You mean the cyanide sprayers in the ceiling, or the self-sealing doors? Because I disabled both on my way in."

That was a lie, but a convincing one. Marcelli blinked, uncertain for the first time.

"You're bluffing," he said.

"Try me," Alexander said.

Marcelli looked to his men. They looked to each other, then back to Alexander. He saw it in their eyes: a split, a fracture in the chain of command. It was always like this with the Registry's top men. They could kill in cold blood but the moment they thought someone might kill them back, the calculation changed.

"You don't have to die here," Alexander said, softening his tone just enough. "Step away from him. Drop your weapons, and you walk out."

The first man did so, then the next. Within seconds, all three were backpedaling down the hallway, leaving Marcelli alone on his makeshift throne.

Anna reappeared behind Marcelli, silent as air. She slid a thin, glittering knife across his throat, not enough to kill, but enough to make him yelp and clutch the wound.

"You'll need to talk, Marcelli," she said, her voice a low purr in his ear. "The Dragon's plans. Where's the shipment, and what's in it for the conclave?"

Marcelli gasped, blood seeping between his fingers. "Vault," he managed. "Below the mill. Access code is in the ledger." He gestured weakly to the abacus.

Anna glanced at Alexander, who nodded. She slammed Marcelli's head into the crate, hard enough to leave him twitching, then went for the ledger.

Alexander followed, railgun at the ready, every step through the grain-slick corridor, a reminder that trust was still currency and he had none left to spend.

They reached the vault in under a minute, bypassing two more security doors and a tripwire that Anna found and disarmed with one clawed nail. Inside, the air was colder kept that way for whatever was stacked in the racks. Glass vials, sealed boxes, a crate of human teeth that rattled when Alexander shook it.

He turned to Anna, who had already found the manifest. "It's here," she said, voice shaking for the first time. "They're moving it tonight. Everything."

Alexander felt a sour twist in his gut. "Can we stop it?"

Anna ran a finger down the page, her brow furrowed. "Not by ourselves. But we can bleed them. Hard."

Alexander nodded. "Let's do it."

Together, they emptied the shelves of anything useful—blood vials, old world toxins, a packet of sun grenades someone had hidden among the shipment—and set the rest to explode. As they sprinted out, Anna flung a match over her shoulder, igniting the trailing fuse Alexander had left.

The blast was muffled by the thick walls, but the fire that followed was visible from a mile away. In the predawn light, the mill burned like a signal flare, a message to anyone watching that the world's end wasn't coming quietly.

Alexander and Anna watched from the safety of the hydro car, lungs aching with exertion, eyes locked on the rising plume.

"Round one," she said, and for once, there was a trace of pride in her voice.

Alexander smiled, his teeth stained with soot. "Round one."

They drove until the city was a rumor behind them, the world ahead nothing but open road and the long, red memory of what they'd left burning.

The road wound south and east in a ragged spiral, clinging to the edges of long-dead rivers and the humped backs of once-cultivated hills. By the time they reached the high plateau, the sun had risen high enough to bleach the world to a single merciless glare, every shadow cast with razor precision. Anna navigated by dead reckoning, eyes fixed on the horizon where the scorched plains met the fractured teeth of the southern range. Alexander steered by paranoia, never letting the car run too far in a straight line, never trusting the silence of the wilderness to last more than a mile.

They crested the last switchback, engine laboring, and the landscape opened up—a wide shelf of stone and brittle dirt, dotted with the corpses of fire-shrubs and skeletal trees. At the far end, the gutted remains of an observatory loomed, its dome sheared off and the black glass of its lens pointed like a weapon at the cloudless sky. Even from this distance, Alexander saw the signs of recent passage: gouged earth, a trail of animal droppings that glistened with chemical rot. He killed the engine a hundred yards out and let the car coast on momentum.

Anna was out of the seat before the wheels stopped turning. She walked the perimeter in a slow, measured spiral, hands open and empty. Alexander thumbed the scattergun's action and followed, keeping his distance—he had no interest in what she might do if startled from behind.

The air here was thin, tainted with the burnt plastic scent of the city's waste fires. A wind scoured the plateau, picking up grit and the bitter dust of old bones. Alexander kept his eyes on the ruins ahead, but it was Anna who noticed the change in the air: a tremor, almost below hearing, that set the hairs on his neck prickling.

He didn't have to wait long. The attack came all at once, from two sides, shrieking, impossibly loud rattle that overrode every other sense. Six shapes emerged from behind the observatory's shell, two loping in a high-stepping gait, the others flying low to the ground. They were snarlskulks, though Alexander had never seen so many at once, or this close to the city. Eight feet tall, all blade-edged bone and oil-slick muscle, their wings more for steering than flight. Faces that split vertically, jaws packed with teeth the color of old ivory. They moved with the hunger of things that had never eaten enough in their lives.

Anna didn't wait for orders. Her eyes went red, not just the pupils but the whites as well, and she launched herself at the nearest skulks. Her first strike was almost beautiful a hard, clean arc that took the lead beast's head off above the jawline, sending it cartwheeling across the dirt. She caught the spray of acidic saliva on her forearm, wincing but not retreating. The next beast fanned its wings, dropping low, and Anna leapt over its charge, her boots landing square on its spine with a wet crack. She rode it to the ground and ripped its neck open with her teeth.

Alexander went for the railgun, squeezing the trigger and sending a rod of steel into the next two skulks. The first staggered, lost a chunk of its chest, but kept moving, undeterred by the pain or the fist-sized hole that now steamed and fizzed with leaking acid. The fourth creature flanked him, wings beating the dust into a swirling curtain. He fired point-blank, the blast tearing off a wing and a good portion of its left side.

Anna was in the thick of it now, moving too fast to follow, her form a blur of pale flesh and blackened leather. She grabbed one beast by the upper jaw and tore its face apart, using the lower mandible as a weapon to club the next attacker. Acid hissed against her coat and skin, leaving angry red streaks that healed almost as quickly as they formed. She shrieked, a sound so inhuman that Alexander felt it rattle through his bones.

He pivoted, caught the next skulks with the last two rods in the magazine. One dropped, convulsing and snapping at its own entrails. The other caught Anna's leg, claws digging through her calf with a sound like tearing silk. She spun, drove her fist through its skull, and let it fall.

For a moment, there was silence—just the wind, the smell of cooked meat, and Anna's heavy breathing. Alexander watched as she knelt beside one of the corpses, tore a strip of flesh from its neck, and smeared the blood over her wounds. The red faded from her eyes; her skin sealed, scars disappearing beneath a fresh coat of pallor.

He reloaded, hands trembling only a little. "Didn't know you could do that," he said.

Anna glanced up, teeth still bared. "I don't like to," she said. "But it works."

"Better than the needles and pills I got," Alexander conceded, stepping over the mess of bodies. The ground sizzled where the snarlskulks' blood hit stone, carving shallow trenches that smoked and spat. He checked the perimeter, found no more movement, then motioned for Anna to follow. "Come on. Not safe here."

They made it halfway back to the car before the next wave hit.

This time, it wasn't monsters. It was men.

Three of them, all in makeshift armor: boiled leather patched with sheet metal, faces hidden by strips of cloth and the hollowed-out jaws of small animals. They came in low, using the snarlskulk corpses as cover, and opened up with crossbows. The bolts were dipped in something sticky and bright—incendiary gel. Alexander saw the first bolt catch Anna's coat, felt the heat as it burst into flame. She didn't flinch, just shrugged the burning sleeve off and kept moving.

He fired a snapshot at the lead men, but the men were already spreading out, trying to flank. Anna darted right, using the windbreak of a ruined kiosk to gain ground, then vaulted onto the lead bandit before he could recock his weapon. She bit into his neck, spat out the flesh, then used his limp body as a shield against the next barrage of bolts.

The second bandit, seeing his friend fall, panicked and ran for the car. Alexander intercepted him with a single shot to the chest. The impact sent the man spinning, blood fountaining from the ragged exit wound.

The third was smarter. He waited for Anna to close, then dropped his crossbow and drew a machete—a mean-looking thing, welded from a car leaf spring and honed to a mirror shine. He swung at Anna's head, but she ducked, caught his wrist, and twisted until the bone snapped. The machete clattered to the ground. Anna picked it up, appraised its weight, and buried it in the man's stomach. He tried to scream, but she put a hand over his mouth and held him there until the kicking stopped.

She looked at Alexander, expression unreadable. "Someone hired them," she said, voice flat. "They knew where we'd be."

Alexander nodded. "The city doesn't forget its debts. We move fast, or we'll have company."

They dumped the bodies off the road, wiped what blood they could from the car, and left the rest for the scavengers. Anna took the machete, cleaned it on her shirt, and tucked it into her belt.

The drive from the plateau was tense, neither of them speaking, both staring at the horizon as if expecting it to collapse inward at any moment.

When they finally stopped, it was at a ridge overlooking a long, low building set into the side of a dry riverbed. The manor. The last waypoint before the Spire.

Alexander killed the engine, leaned back in his seat, and let the silence settle.

"You all right?" he asked, eyes on the blood drying on Anna's face.

She touched her cheek, then wiped it clean with a slow, deliberate motion. "Better than most," she said.

Alexander smiled, despite himself. "You're a real piece of work."

Anna smiled back, a thing of cold geometry and sharp angles. "We're not so different," she said.

He laughed, bitter and true. "No. We're not."

They watched the manor for a while, letting the wind carry away the last of the plateau's violence. When night finally fell, it did so suddenly and without warning, draping the world in black and gold and the promise of one more fight before the end.

They waited until the last light had gone out behind the hills before moving in. The manor, up close, was less a house than a tumor: a brick-and-timber mass swollen with annexes and sheds, all festooned with rusted pipes and shrouded in the stink of dead animals. The yard was a killing floor—pitted with runnels where blood had soaked the earth, every patch of grass dead and brittle underfoot.

Alexander led the way, machete drawn, boots sucking at the sodden ground. Anna kept to the shadows, her presence a cold certainty behind him, senses tuned to any hint of movement. The main door hung from one hinge, the wood gnawed away by termites or worse. Inside, the air was even thicker with rot. Somewhere, far below, machinery thumped and wheezed like the heart of a giant beast.

They crossed the foyer, past heaps of moldy burlap sacks and a tangle of old chain. The floor was sticky with something unnamable; every step left a slow, reluctant print. In the parlor, a body slumped over a card table, most of its face melted away by some caustic agent, the hand clutching a half-finished letter. Anna paused to read, her lips curling in distaste.

"Inventory report," she said. "Two barrels of grain, one of blood. Delivery schedule... every three days. The city's been feeding this place."

Alexander felt his stomach lurch. "It's a livestock operation," he said. "But the stock is people."

Anna nodded, face grim. "And whatever's left goes to the Spire."

They found the hatch under a pile of straw in the kitchen—rectangular, set into the stone, with an inset handle worn smooth by decades of use. Anna lifted it effortlessly, revealing a short flight of iron stairs slick with condensation.

"After you," she said, voice hollow.

The basement was colder by twenty degrees, the stone sweating in the dark. A single bulb, powered by an ancient dynamo, swung above the space and cast mad, spinning shadows across the walls. Tables lined the perimeter, each loaded with a different atrocity: glass jars of pickled eyes, hearts suspended in a clear jelly that pulsed gently as if remembering old rhythms. One table held nothing but hands, all tagged and numbered, some tiny and still childlike.

But the centerpiece was what lay against the far wall—a man, or the ruin of one, strapped to a gurney with leather bands. His limbs had been replaced, joint by joint, with lengths of copper pipe and clockwork gears. Tubing snaked from his chest into a pump that gurgled at every breath. His head had been shaven; the scalp tattooed with lines of script and formula. His eyes, when they opened, were bright blue and lucid.

He tried to speak, but the only sound was a whistle of air through a cracked larynx.

Anna knelt beside the gurney. "Can you hear me?" she asked, softly.

The man nodded, once.

Alexander scanned the room for weapons, traps, anything that might turn this into an ambush. But it was clear: the only threat here was time, and what it might let the city do next.

Anna touched the man's forehead, then made a small, clean cut on his wrist and let a few drops of her blood fall into his mouth. The effect was immediate—the blue in his eyes brightened, and the tremor in his body eased.

She straightened, eyes burning with fury. "They're testing new blends," she said. "Trying to perfect the next generation. Faster, smarter. Immune to the old weapons."

Alexander felt the familiar chill of failure. "Then we just need better weapons" he said, but he didn't believe it. He'd seen what happened when you underestimated the Dragon's patience.

They found the journals in a box near the pump. The leather was slick with blood, but the title was clear enough: "Project Chimera." Anna read aloud as Alexander flicked through the pages, each one packed with spidery diagrams and lists of reagents.

"'Hybridization of subject matter achieved at last. Early attempts resulted in catastrophic tissue rejection, but the addition of regenerative agent'—" She paused, glancing at Alexander. "It's my blood. They're using it as a template."

Alexander stared at the diagram on the next page. It was a monster—ten limbs, half of them jointed backward, a head sheathed in metal, the mouth replaced by a respirator mask. There were notes in the margin: "Field test pending. See log 8." Below that, a smear of dried red.

Anna flipped to the last entry. "'Dragon to inspect progress in person. All records to be sealed prior to his arrival.'" She closed the book, jaw set.

"We burn it," Alexander said.

Anna didn't argue. They doused the tables in ethanol from a nearby jug, set the papers on the gurney, and lit the whole pile with a single match. The blue flames licked at the jars, which exploded one by one in a sequence of sharp pops, the air filling with the smell of sweet, chemical death.

As they climbed the stairs, Anna turned to look back. The man on the gurney watched her with eyes that did not blink, even as the fire consumed the rest of him. She mouthed something—maybe an apology, maybe a promise—then closed the hatch and sealed it with the length of chain.

Outside, the sky was black and the wind bitter. They could see the glow of the manor burning from a mile away, a beacon to anyone who cared to look.

Alexander packed the journals into his coat, hands shaking. "You think it'll make a difference?" he asked, not really expecting an answer.

Anna's face was unreadable. "It has to," she said.

They got back in the car, neither speaking for a long time. The road ahead was empty, the future less so.

In the rearview, the last light from the burning manor faded, but Alexander knew better than to hope. The city was still out there, still hungry, and now it knew he was coming.

They drove in silence, past the ruins and the bone fields and the empty places where people once believed in something. The world was smaller every day, but their enemy was not.

As the night deepened, Anna watched the horizon, eyes shining with a light Alexander could not name. Maybe it was hope. Maybe just the reflection of another fire waiting to be lit.

He pressed the accelerator and didn't look back. They had a Airship to steal.

The Ghost Rider Gambit

The road ahead spiraled into a razor-toothed maw of fractured earth and skeletal remains of pre-Registry structures, their twisted metal frames reaching skyward like the fingers of those long buried beneath. Alexander gripped the controls of the hydro-steam car tighter, the vibrations through the chassis telling him they couldn't push much further without risking a breakdown. The Ash Chasm waited beyond—a thousand-foot drop into a wasteland of toxic fog and scavenger beasts that had evolved to thrive on flesh and metal alike. No one crossed it without a guide who knew the hidden paths. No one sane, at least.

"We stop here, this is it" Alexander said, easing the steaming vehicle into the shadow of a half-collapsed water tower. "We're walking from this point."

Anna's eyes narrowed as she surveyed the hellscape ahead. "I don't see a path."

"That's the point," he replied, killing the engine. The sudden silence felt oppressive, broken only by the tick-tick-tick of cooling metal and the distant shriek of something hunting in the fog below. "The only way across is with someone who knows the unmarked bridges. Someone who's crossed it enough times to map the stable ground."

"I assume you have someone in mind?" Her voice remained cool, but Alexander caught the flicker of concern that crossed her face as she stared into the Ash Chasm's depths.

"A smuggler. Goes by Niko." Alexander checked his weapons before exiting the car. "We've done business. I've never had to kill him, which is as close to trust as it gets out here."

They set out on foot, following a barely visible trail that snaked between piles of rusted machinery and heaps of ash that shifted in the wind. The silence between them was a living thing, hungry with unspoken questions and the knowledge that each step brought them closer to the Dragon's lair.

After twenty minutes of careful navigation through terrain that seemed designed to slice open boots and catch unwary ankles, they crested a small rise. Below, nestled in the hollow between two defensive berms, sat a trapper's cabin—or what passed for one in the breaks. The structure was cobbled together from salvaged materials: corrugated steel, bulletproof glass panels likely scavenged from military vehicles, and thick wooden beams blackened with age and smoke. A thin plume rose from a crooked chimney, the only sign of habitation.

"He's there," Alexander said, noting the distinctive arrangement of trip wires around the perimeter—Niko's signature. "And he's not expecting company."

Anna touched his arm, a rare gesture that sent an involuntary chill across his skin. "How dangerous is he?"

Alexander considered the question, weighing years of scattered interactions and half-truths. "Dangerous enough to survive out here alone. Smart enough to know when cooperation pays better than betrayal." He paused. "Usually."

They approached the cabin carefully, Alexander stepping deliberately over the nearly invisible wire strung across the path. He rapped on the door with the butt of his revolver—three short taps, pause, two more. The universal code of the breaks: I'm not here to kill you, but I'm armed.

Silence followed, stretching long enough that Alexander began to wonder if they'd made the journey for nothing. Then came the metallic scrape of multiple locks disengaging, and the door swung inward to reveal a wiry man whose weather-beaten face split into a grin that never reached his calculating eyes.

"If it isn't Alexander fucking Stirling," Nikolai Petrov sneered, his accent a jagged blade that could slice through the tension thick in the air. "The last time I laid eyes on you, you were sprinting from Registry enforcers, half your coat ablaze. I assumed they'd already displayed your head on a pike."

Alexander's face remained a mask of cold indifference, refusing to yield to the taunt. "Still trying to scrape together coins from foolish treasure hunters?"

"Still clinging to the delusion that your crusade carries any weight?" Niko's gaze flickered to Anna, his interest sharpening like a knife's edge. "And who might this be? She certainly doesn't fit your usual entourage."

"Someone who'll end your life if you dare stare any longer." Anna shot back, her voice a silky whisper wrapped in razor wire.

Niko's laughter erupted, a sound both genuine and laced with malice. "I like her." He stepped back, arms wide in mock hospitality. "Come in, come in. The walls have ears, and the Registry lavishes gold for the juiciest of tales."

The interior of the cabin was a study in organized chaos. Maps covered one wall, each overlaid with annotations in a cipher only Niko could read. Weapons of various origins hung within easy reach—Registry issue intermixed with black market modifications and the occasional piece Alexander recognized from Cassie's workshop. A pot bubbled on a small stove, filling the space with the smell of something almost, but not quite, like food.

"Drink?" Niko offered, already pouring amber liquid into chipped glasses. "Local moonshine. Only slightly poisonous."

Alexander took the glass but didn't drink. "We need to cross the Ash Chasm. Tonight."

Niko's eyebrows rose. "Ambitious." He swirled his drink, studying the liquid as if it held secrets. "The patrols have doubled since whatever you two did at the mill. Seems someone important is very, very angry."

Alexander and Anna exchanged a glance. News traveled fast in the breaks, but not this fast. Not unless someone was feeding information.

"How do you know about the mill?" Alexander asked, hand drifting to his revolver.

Niko smiled thinly. "Please. I make it my business to know which way the wind blows. Especially when it smells like opportunity." He drained his glass. "So, the Chasm. That'll cost you. Not just money."

"Name your price," Anna said.

"Information first. Then we talk payment." Niko leaned forward, suddenly serious. "Word is you're going after the Dragon himself. That true?"

Alexander maintained a neutral expression. "Would that change your price?"

"It changes everything," Niko replied. "Including whether I help you at all. I've built a nice life avoiding suicide missions."

Anna stepped forward, her patience visibly thinning. "We're wasting time." slowly drawing a small blade from beneath her wrist.

Niko held up a placating hand. "Relax, lady. Just making sure I know what I'm getting into." He turned back to Alexander. "Three hundred in gold, plus whatever you're carrying from the old man's stash."

Alexander stiffened. "What old man?"

"Don't play dumb. I saw you leaving Victor's place." Niko's grin widened. "Those journal pages in your coat? Worth more than your life to the right buyer."

The silence that followed was thick enough to choke on. Alexander weighed his options. Niko knew too much already. The question was whether he'd sell that knowledge, and to whom.

"Two hundred," Alexander countered. "And you don't get to look at what's in my coat."

Niko seemed to consider this, though Alexander knew he'd already calculated exactly what he would accept. "Two-fifty, and you tell me where you're headed after the Chasm. Just in case I need to avoid that area for a while."

"Done," Alexander said, too quickly. Anna shot him a warning glance, which he ignored.

Niko clapped his hands together. "Excellent! Now, about those patrols. The Registry has checkpoints every three miles along the normal routes. But there's a maintenance line—old railway tunnel, partially collapsed—that cuts under the worst of it. Not comfortable, and definitely not safe, but it'll get you across."

He unrolled a map, pointing to a nearly invisible line that snaked through the shattered landscape. "Sensor blind spots here, here, and here. We'll need to move fast between them. And there's something else you should know."

Alexander leaned in despite himself trying to be unexcited.

"They've deployed new scouts," Niko said, voice dropping. "Not human, not vampire. Something... else. They don't follow patrol patterns. They hunt."

"Chimeras," Anna whispered, the word barely audible.

Niko's eyes widened fractionally. "You know about those?"

"We've seen the research," Alexander said grimly. "How many?"

"At least two in this sector. Nasty pieces of work." Niko rolled the map up with practiced efficiency. "We leave in an hour. I need to gather supplies."

As Niko busied himself with preparations, Anna pulls Alexander aside.

"I don't trust him," she murmured.

"You shouldn't," Alexander replied. "But we need him."

"He knows too much."

"That's why he's still alive." Alexander watched Niko check his weapons with the methodical precision of someone who'd survived on their reliability. "He's the best guide in the breaks, and he knows it. His loyalty is to his own skin."

"And if someone offers him more for ours?"

Alexander's hand rested on the butt of his revolver. "Then he'll learn why the Venators were feared for more than just killing vampires."

Niko glanced up, as if sensing their conversation. His smile was easy, charming, and utterly devoid of warmth. "Ready for a pleasant stroll through hell, friends?"

Alexander nodded, the weight of the journals heavy against his chest. The path to the Dragon narrowed with each step, choices dwindling like bridges over the Ash Chasm. But as long as there was a path, he would walk it. Even if it meant trusting someone who'd sell him to the Registry for the right price.

The maintenance tunnel yawned before them like the throat of some industrial leviathan, its rusted tracks disappearing into darkness that swallowed the feeble light of Niko's oil lamp. The stench of ancient oil and chemical residue hung thick in the air, burning Alexander's nostrils as they descended into the gloom. Above them, the last rays of sunlight vanished behind the jagged ridgeline of the Ash Chasm, plunging the world into the hungry dark where monsters—both mechanical and flesh—ruled unchallenged by humans or vamps.

"Stay between the rails," Niko warned, his voice oddly flattened by the tunnel's acoustics. "The ground beside them is unstable. One wrong step and you'll fall through to the old sewers. Trust me, you don't want to know what lives down there now."

Alexander kept his revolver drawn, thumb resting on the hammer. The darkness pressed against them from all sides, broken only by the swinging circle of Niko's lamp and the occasional phosphorescent fungus clinging to the tunnel walls. The air grew thicker as they descended, charged with the metallic tang of old machinery and something else—a coppery scent that reminded Alexander of freshly spilled blood.

"How much further?" Anna asked, her footsteps unnaturally silent on the rusted tracks.

"Another mile," Niko replied, pausing to consult a brass compass whose needle wavered erratically. "We're under the Registry's western sensor net now. Good news is they can't detect us down here. Bad news is that means they've got other ways of keeping people out."

"Like what?" Alexander kept his eyes on the darkness behind them, where shadows seemed to shift and writhe with a life of their own.

The answer came in the form of a low, mechanical groan that shuddered through the tunnel walls. Dust and fragments of concrete rained down from the ceiling as the vibration intensified. Niko froze, the lamp swinging wildly in his hand, casting monstrous shadows that danced across the walls.

"Like that," he whispered, dousing the lamp with a quick twist. "Don't move. Don't breathe."

The darkness became absolute. Alexander felt Anna's shoulder press against his, her body tense but steady. The groaning grew louder, accompanied now by a rhythmic thudding that shook the ground beneath their feet. Whatever approached was massive, its tread heavy enough to dislodge debris from the tunnel ceiling that pattered down like deadly rain.

A glow appeared ahead—sickly green light that pulsed in time with the thunderous footsteps. It illuminated the tunnel in stroboscopic flashes, revealing glimpses of the horror that hunted them.

The Sentinel loomed ominously, its towering form stretching nearly to the ceiling, a grotesque amalgamation of salvaged machinery and what unmistakably resembled human remains, twisted and melded into its very structure. Six enormous limbs, a blend of metal and sinew, propelled it forward with an unsettling grace, each limb ending in a menacing pneumatic claw that crushed the ground beneath it with a thunderous thud with every deliberate step. Where one would expect a head, a chaotic cluster of brass and glass observation devices spun and swiveled independently, their lenses glinting menacingly as they scanned the environment in every conceivable direction. Steam hissed and erupted from vents along its torso, producing a sound akin to a chorus of enraged serpents, each puff of vapor swirling and dissipating into the air, adding to the oppressive atmosphere surrounding this mechanical monstrosity.

"Registry's newest toy," Niko breathed, his lips so close to Alexander's ear that he felt rather than heard the words. "Part machine, part chimera. It doesn't see like we do—it senses body heat and movement. Standstill, and we might not end up as spare parts."

Alexander's pulse hammered in his throat as the monstrosity lumbered closer. Through the strobing light, he saw what decorated the thing's chassis: human skulls, dozens of them, wired into the framework like grotesque ornaments. Fresh ones, some still bearing scraps of flesh.

The Sentinel paused twenty yards ahead, its observation cluster rotating with a sound like grinding teeth. A plume of steam erupted from its core, momentarily obscuring it from view. When the vapor cleared, Alexander saw that one of the "eyes" was pointed directly at them.

"Run," Niko hissed, shoving Alexander backward. "Now!"

They bolted down the tunnel, abandoning stealth for speed. Behind them, the Sentinel let out a mechanized shriek that sent splinters of pain through Alexander's skull. The ground shook as it gave chase, its limbs clattering against the rails with a sound like artillery fire.

"Side passage!" Niko shouted, suddenly veering left. "Twenty feet ahead!"

Alexander saw it—a narrow maintenance shaft barely wide enough for a man to squeeze through. He pushed Anna ahead of him, covering their retreat with a snap shot from his revolver. The bullet struck one of the Sentinel's observation devices, shattering it in a spray of glass and fluid. The creature roared, a sound so inhuman it seemed to come from the depths of hell itself.

Niko reached the passage first, diving through with a serpentine grace that belied his wiry frame. Anna followed, vanishing into the darkness. Alexander fired twice more, aiming for the joints where flesh met metal, then scrambled after them.

The passage was claustrophobic, the walls pressing in from all sides. They ran blind, guided only by Niko's urgent commands—"Left here!" "Duck now!" "Jump!"—as they navigated a labyrinth that seemed to exist in defiance of logical architecture.

Behind them, the Sentinel's rage shook the very foundations of the tunnel. It couldn't follow through the narrow passage, but Alexander heard the screech of tearing metal as it attempted to dig its way through.

"Almost there," Niko panted. "One more—"

His words cut off as the floor suddenly gave way beneath them. Alexander felt himself falling, a moment of weightless terror before he slammed into a sloping surface that sent him sliding uncontrollably into deeper darkness. Niko's cursing and Anna's controlled breathing told him they'd fallen too.

They landed in a heap on what felt like a bed of something soft yet crunchy—bones, Alexander realized with a surge of nausea. Niko fumbled with his lamp, finally coaxing it to life. The weak flame revealed a chamber that might once have been a maintenance depot, now transformed into a charnel house. Skeletons lined the walls, arranged in poses of supplication around a central platform.

"Fuck," Niko breathed. "Sentinel's feeding ground."

Alexander scrambled to his feet, helping Anna up. "Which way out?"

Niko hesitated, eyes darting between three identical doorways. "I... I'm not sure. This shouldn't be here."

"You said you knew these tunnels," Anna hissed, fangs glinting in the lamplight.

"I do! But this..." Niko gestured helplessly. "This is new."

A terrible realization dawned on Alexander. "You've never actually crossed this way before, have you?"

Niko's silence was answer enough.

Above them, the Sentinel's digging grew louder. Dust and fragments of concrete showered down from the ceiling.

"That door," Niko said suddenly, pointing to the rightmost exit. "The airflow—it's stronger there. Has to lead outside."

Alexander weighed their options, which were rapidly dwindling to none. "Lead on."

They sprinted for the door, even as the ceiling began to collapse behind them. The passage beyond was tight and winding, forcing them to move single-file through near-darkness. The air grew fresher, tinged with the scent of ash and open sky.

After what felt like hours but was likely minutes, they emerged onto a narrow ledge halfway up the Chasm wall. Below them, toxic fog swirled like a living entity. Above, the first stars pierced the darkening sky.

"There," Niko said, pointing across a precarious natural bridge to a structure built into the opposite cliff face. "The Manor."

The building seemed to grow organically from the rock, its architecture a blend of ancient stone and modern reinforcement. High windows gleamed with a faint amber light, and a tower rose from its eastern edge—a docking spire for airships. Tethered to it was their target: a Scout-class vessel, its brass hull gleaming in the last light of day.

"You actually did it," Alexander muttered, unable to keep the surprise from his voice.

Niko grinned, the expression never reaching his eyes. "Don't sound so shocked. I got us here, didn't I?"

"After nearly getting us killed," Anna observed coldly.

"Details," Niko waved dismissively. "The point is there's your airship. Now, about the rest of my payment..."

Alexander studied the Manor through narrowed eyes. "Not until we're aboard that ship."

"Fine." Niko shrugged. "But you should know—the Manor belongs to Lord Carmilla. Not someone you want to meet without an invitation."

"You're just telling us this now?" Alexander's hand tightened on his revolver.

"Would you have come if I'd mentioned it earlier?" Niko smiled thinly. "Besides, he's away for the conclave. Only a skeleton crew remains—a few Daywalkers, maybe some human servants. Nothing we can't handle if we're careful."

Alexander exchanged a glance with Anna, seeing his own suspicion mirrored in her eyes. Niko's convenient omissions were stacking up faster than the Registry's body count. But the airship was right there, their passage to the Spire and the Dragon beyond.

"We wait for full twilight," he decided. "Then we move."

As the sun sank lower, casting the Chasm in deep shadow, Alexander watched Niko carefully. The smuggler's eyes kept darting to the journal pages visible in Alexander's coat pocket, his fingers twitching slightly as if already counting the coin they'd bring from the right buyer.

Alexander made a mental note to watch his back once they reached the Manor. The path to revenge was treacherous enough without a knife between the shoulder blades from their guide.

The last light faded, plunging the world into a darkness broken only by the faint glow from the Manor windows. It was time to steal an airship.

Whispers In the Machine

T he natural bridge stretched before them like a skeletal finger pointing toward Lord Carmilla's Manor, its ancient stone worn smooth by centuries of wind and the careful tread of those who valued their lives. Alexander studied the narrow passage, calculating the odds of collapse against the weight of three bodies moving in tandem. The toxic fog below churned hungrily, as if sensing potential prey, while the Manor's amber windows watched their approach with the indifferent malice of a predator who knew its territory was inviolable. The brass hull of the Scout airship gleamed tantalizingly in the darkness, tethered to the eastern tower like an obedient beast awaiting its master's return.

"Single file," Alexander whispered, his breath visible in the chilly night air. "Anna leads, Niko follows so that I can watch you."

Niko's face twitched with barely concealed annoyance, but he nodded. "Trust issues, Venator? I'm hurt."

"Save it," Alexander replied, testing the first step onto the bridge. The stone held firm beneath his boot. "The only reason you're still breathing is because we need a pilot."

They crossed in silence each footfall measured against the groaning protests of the ancient span. Halfway across, a gust of wind sent a tremor through the structure, forcing them to crouch low against the surface. Alexander's fingers brushed the cold stone, feeling the vibrations that whispered of imminent collapse.

When they finally reached the Manor's outer wall, Alexander pressed his back against the weathered stone, scanning for entry points. The wall rose twenty feet above them, its surface slick with moisture and dotted with iron spikes designed to discourage exactly this sort of approach.

"There," Anna murmured, pointing to a recessed section ten yards to their right. "Servant's entrance. All vampire lords maintain their tradition demands a separate path for those who bring blood."

Alexander raised an eyebrow. "Convenient."

"Practical," she corrected. "My father's court has similar arrangements. The lesser nobles copy his designs out of fear and flattery."

They edged along the wall, Alexander keeping one hand on his revolver. The entrance Anna had identified was barred by an iron gate, its hinges thick with rust. Beyond it, a narrow passageway disappeared into darkness.

Niko produced a set of lock picks from inside his coat. "Allow me," he said, kneeling before the gate. His fingers worked with practiced precision, manipulating the ancient mechanism until something clicked deep within the lock. The gate swung inward with a reluctant groan.

"Wait," Anna hissed, grabbing Alexander's arm as he moved to enter. She knelt, examining the flagstones just beyond the threshold. "Pressure plates. Standard issue in vampire strongholds."

"Traps?" Alexander asked.

"Worse. Alarms. Step on the wrong stone and every Daywalker in the Manor will converge on this spot." She ran her fingers along the wall beside the entrance, finding an almost invisible seam. With a precise twist of her wrist, she pressed a hidden panel, and the floor beyond the gate shifted subtly, revealing a narrow safe path through the pressure plates.

"How did you know?" Niko asked, eyes narrowed with suspicion.

"Vampire politics 101," Anna replied, stepping confidently onto the revealed path. "Know your enemies defenses better than they do."

Alexander followed her lead, careful to place his boots exactly where she had stepped. The passageway opened into a low-ceilinged chamber lined with pipes that hissed with escaping steam. The air was thick with heat and the smell of oil and metal, making Alexander's lungs burn with each breath.

"Maintenance tunnel for the Manor's heating system," Niko observed, running a hand along one of the copper pipes. "These will lead us to the main building."

They had barely taken ten steps when a metallic clicking echoed through the chamber. Alexander froze, hand flying to his weapon. From the shadows ahead emerged a creature that defied natural classification a mechanical hound whose body was a latticework of brass gears and iron plates, its head a grotesque approximation of canine features. Glass eyes glowed with an unnatural blue light, focusing on the intruders with predatory intensity.

"Guardian," Anna whispered. "Don't move."

The clockwork hound advanced, each step a symphony of grinding metal and hissing steam. It lowered its head, sensors scanning their heat signatures, jaws opening to reveal rows of serrated steel teeth.

"It just Id us as threats," Alexander muttered. "Any suggestions?"

Anna reached into her coat and withdrew a small vial of dark liquid. "Vampire blood," she explained, uncorking the container. "These guardians are programmed to recognize the scent of their masters. This should confuse it long enough for us to pass."

She flicked her wrist, sending droplets of blood arcing through the air to land on the floor before the mechanical beast. The hound paused, its head tilting as it processed the conflicting information. After a moment of apparent confusion, it turned and retreated back into the darkness, metal claws clicking against the stone floor.

"Nice trick," Niko said, sounding genuinely impressed.

"Not a trick. Knowledge." Anna wiped her hands on a handkerchief. "These security systems are primitive compared to my father's."

They continued through the maintenance tunnel, eventually emerging into what appeared to be the Manor's cavernous kitchen space dominated by iron stoves and preparation tables stained dark with substances Alexander preferred not to identify. Copper pots hung from the ceiling, swaying slightly in the artificial breeze created by a massive ventilation system that churned the air with slow, methodical purpose.

"Servant quarters are through there," Anna whispered, pointing to a door at the far end of the kitchen. "Then the main hall, and finally the eastern tower where the airship is docked."

As they moved toward the door, Alexander noticed the floor had changed—no longer stone, but metal plates arranged in a precise grid pattern. He grabbed Niko's arm just as the smuggler was about to step onto the grid.

"Wait," he warned. "Look at the seams."

The metal plates were separated by hairline cracks that gleamed with an oily residue. Alexander picked up a wooden spoon from a nearby counter and tossed it onto the nearest plate. Instantly, the floor came to life—plates dropping away to reveal spike-filled pits, others rising to form crushing walls, and from the ceiling descended a series of curved blades that sliced through the air with mathematical precision.

"Shit," Niko breathed. "How do we get past that?"

Anna studied the mechanical trap room, her eyes tracking the patterns of movement as the floor reset itself. "It's a sequence," she said after a moment. "Vampire lords are creatures of habit and vanity. The sequence will be something meaningful to the owner."

She closed her eyes, recalling some distant memories. "Seven, three, nine, one. The year his house gained nobility. Follow me exactly, and step only where I step."

With deadly precision, Anna navigated the trap room, stepping on specific plates in the exact sequence she had determined. Alexander followed, counting under his breath, conscious of the lethal machinery waiting to activate at the slightest misstep. Niko came last, his usual confidence replaced by uncharacteristic caution.

They reached the far door unscathed. Beyond it lay a corridor lined with portraits of pale-faced nobles whose eyes seemed to follow their progress. The air here was colder, carrying the unmistakable scent of vampiric presence—like old copper and winter frost.

"The tower access is ahead," Anna whispered, leading them toward a spiral staircase at the corridor's end. "But it will be guarded."

As if summoned by her words, a pair of Daywalkers appeared at the top of the stairs—tall, aristocratic figures in tailored uniforms bearing Carmilla's crest. Their hands rested on ornate daggers at their belts, eyes scanning the corridor with predatory focus.

Alexander felt the familiar ice of battle slide through his veins. The airship was within reach now, separated from them only by these final obstacles. He exchanged a glance with Anna, who nodded almost imperceptibly.

It was time for the last phase of their infiltration—and the most dangerous.

Alexander locked eyes with Anna, a silent conversation passing between them in the space of a heartbeat. His hand tightened around the grip of his revolver, the checkered surface warm against his palm, while she shifted her weight to the balls of her feet—a predator preparing to strike. The Daywalkers at the top of the spiral staircase hadn't noticed them yet, their aristocratic profiles outlined against the ambient glow of steam lamps that lined the tower walls. Alexander counted his breaths, slowing his heart rate deliberately, preparing for the violence that would bridge the gap between him and the airship that represented their only hope of reaching the Dragon.

"Wait here," Anna whispered to Niko, the command leaving no room for argument. She glided forward, her movements liquid and silent as she ascended the first few steps.

One of the Daywalkers stiffened suddenly, his nostrils flaring as he caught Anna's scent on the air. His head turned, eyes widening in recognition—not of Anna specifically, but of what she was. "Noble blood," he hissed to his companion. "We have an intruder."

Both guards drew their daggers in perfect synchrony, the blades gleaming with a faint blue phosphorescence that spoke of alchemical enhancements. Alexander knew those weapons could slice through bone and metal with equal ease.

Niko swallowed hard as he watched Anna's almost dance-like movements—graceful yet brutal at the same time. She moved like a tiger stalking its prey, each step measured and deadly. The Daywalkers never stood a chance against her since she incorporated more elements from their kind into her fighting style.

But the sounds...oh, the sounds that filled the narrow corridor! The crunch of bone as she twisted one guard's wrist until it snapped sent shivers down Niko's spine; the wet tearing noise as she slammed his companion's head against the stone wall made him want to vomit. He'd seen violence before, but never on this scale or with such precision.

As they neared the top of the spiral staircase, Niko could smell it now: coppery blood mixed with something metallic and acidic—the tang of spilled gut and ruptured organs. He forced himself to move faster, eager to escape this place before he lost what little breakfast, he'd eaten that morning.

They reached a landing halfway up where remnants of another battle littered the floor: shattered bones poking out from underfoot; chunks of flesh and clothing splattered against walls stained dark with age; an arm here, a leg there...Each step was louder than usual now; not just from their own footfalls but also from the sound of pulsing blood pumping out from gruesome injuries left by Anna's swift assault on her foes.

"Clean," Alexander muttered, already moving up the stairs past the fallen guards. He stepped over the bodies with practiced indifference, checking the corridor beyond additional threats. Empty.

"You could have left one alive for questioning," Niko observed, joining them at the top of the stairs. He nudged one of the bodies with his boot, grimacing at the spreading pool of blood.

"No time," Alexander replied. "And dead vampires tell no tales to their masters."

The corridor branched in two directions at the top of the stairs. To the left, a passageway led deeper into the Manor's eastern wing. To the right, a shorter hallway ended at a heavy oak door reinforced with bands of blackened iron.

"That way," Anna said, pointing to the door. "Carmilla's private study. If there's information about the airship's security, it will be there."

The study door was locked but yielded easily to Niko's picks. Beyond lay a chamber that seemed transported from another century, walls lined with leather-bound books, a massive desk carved from a single piece of dark wood, high windows that offered a commanding view of the toxic fog swirling below the Manor's perch. Oil lamps cast a warm glow over the room, highlighting the gleam of brass instruments arranged on shelves and the dull sheen of maps pinned to the walls.

But it was what lay spread across the desk that captured Alexander's attention. Architectural drawings, rendered with exquisite precision on yellowed parchment, depicting a structure of such complexity that his eyes struggled to make sense of it. Brass gears and iron cogs featured prominently in the design, alongside what appeared to be thousands of glass tubes arranged in concentric circles.

Anna moved to his side, her breath catching as she examined the plans. "The Blood Registry calculation engine," she whispered, her voice tight with recognition. "My father's magnum opus."

Alexander leaned closer, trying to decipher the notations that crowded the margins of the drawings. "What exactly am I looking at?"

"The future," Anna replied, her finger tracing a section of the design that resembled a massive clockwork heart. "A machine that can process every drop of blood in the Registry, analyze it for patterns, predict behavior, identify dissidents before they even act."

"Thought crime detection?" Niko asked, peering over their shoulders.

"Worse," Anna said. "Complete control. The current Registry requires vampires to feed directly from humans to monitor them effectively. This engine would eliminate that requirement. It would process the blood mechanically, cataloging every human's potential usefulness, resistance tendencies, even their compatibility as food sources."

Alexander's mind raced through the implications, each one more horrifying than the last. The Registry was already a leash around humanity's collective neck, but this would transform it into something far more invasive. A system that could predict rebellion before it formed, that could identify and eliminate threats with mechanical efficiency.

"The vampires could expand their control indefinitely," he realized aloud. "No more limits on how many humans they could monitor."

Anna nodded grimly. "My father's been working on this for decades. These must be recent refinements the calculation matrices are far more sophisticated than anything I've seen before."

Alexander studied the plans with new urgency, seeing beyond the technical specifications to the human cost they represented. Each gear and valve in the design was a link in a chain that would bind what remained of human freedom. His vendetta against Dracula had always been personal revenge for his family, for the venator line. But this was different. This was extinction by another name.

"We need to take these," he decided, carefully rolling up the plans. "Cassie and Victor need to see them. Maybe they can find a weakness, something we can exploit."

"Assuming we survive long enough to deliver them," Niko said dryly. He had moved to a cabinet against the far wall and was rifling through its contents. "Ah, here we go." He withdrew a smaller scroll, unfurling it to reveal schematics of the Scout airship tethered to the Manor's eastern tower.

"Maintenance schedules, security protocols, even the ignition sequence," Niko said, his eyes gleaming with professional appreciation. "Carmilla runs a tight operation."

Alexander tucked the calculation engine plans inside his coat, securing them alongside the journals. The weight of the documents felt heavier than their physical mass, laden with the knowledge of what they represented. His mission had evolved beyond mere assassination it was now about preventing a future where humans existed solely as resources to be cataloged and consumed.

"There's more," Anna said, her voice drawing him back to the desk. She had uncovered additional papers beneath the main plans—correspondences between Carmilla and other vampire lords, all discussing preparations for the Black Spire conclave. "The gathering isn't just a social event. It's the unveiling of the calculation engine prototype. My father's presenting it to the noble houses as the final solution to the human question."

Alexander felt cold certainty settle in his gut. "Then we're not just killing a tyrant. We're stopping the end of humanity as we know it."

"Poetic," Niko commented, rolling up the airship schematics. "But we should move. Those guards won't be missed forever, and I'd prefer to be airborne before their replacements arrive."

Alexander nodded, but his mind was already racing ahead, recalculating odds and consequences. The Dragon's death had always been his endgame, the culmination of years of hunting and loss. Now it was merely a necessary first step in a larger war—one that might not end with Dracula's heart on a stake.

"The eastern corridor leads directly to the airship dock," Niko said, heading for the door. "According to these plans, there should be minimal security Carmilla's overconfident about his outer defenses."

As they slipped back into the corridor, Alexander cast one last glance at the study. The room's quiet opulence seemed suddenly obscene a testament to vampire nobility built on centuries of human suffering. The calculation engine would only perfect what the Registry had begun, transforming that suffering into a science.

For the first time since his family's murder, Alexander felt something beyond the cold burn of vengeance. Something that tasted like purpose.

The eastern corridor stretched before them like the throat of some mechanical beast; its walls lined with copper pipes that pulsed with steam and pressure. Alexander moved with calculated steps, the weight of the stolen plans heavy inside his coat, their revelations heavier still in his mind. Each turn brought them closer to the airship dock, the Manor's defensive measures notably scarcer in this section a testament to Lord Carmilla's overconfidence or perhaps his resource limitations. The distant hum of engines grew steadily louder, a mechanical heartbeat that promised escape if they could just reach it without triggering the Manor's remaining alarms.

"Hold," Anna whispered, raising a hand as they approached a final bend in the corridor. She pressed herself against the wall, peering cautiously around the corner. "Docking platform ahead. Two guards at the gangplank, one mechanic working on the port-side engine housing."

Alexander joined her, taking in the scene with a hunter's practiced eye. The airship dock was a cavernous space carved directly into the eastern face of the cliff, its ceiling lost in shadows above. Wind howled through the massive opening that faced the Ash Chasm, bringing with it tendrils of toxic fog that swirled around the boots of the guards. The Scout airship itself was smaller than Alexander had expected, its brass hull gleaming with fresh polish, the gondola slung beneath reinforced with steel plating that suggested combat capability.

"Minimal security," he muttered. "Just as the plans indicated."

Niko shifted impatiently behind them. "So, what's the plan? Shoot our way in?"

Alexander shook his head. "Too much noise. We need to be in the air before the Manor realizes what's happening." He studied the platform's layout, noting the positions of the guards and the mechanic's absorption in his work. "Anna, can you handle the guards? Quietly?"

She nodded, lips curling into a smile that didn't reach her eyes. "Leave them to me."

"Niko, you get to the control cabin and prep for launch. I'll deal with the mechanic." Alexander checked his revolver, then tucked it back into its holster. This called for subtler methods.

Anna moved first, stepping out onto the platform with the confident stride of someone who belonged there. The guards straightened immediately, hands moving to their weapons, but the sight of her—aristocratic features, the unmistakable bearing of noble blood—gave them pause.

"State your business," the taller guard demanded, though his tone already carried the deference ingrained in those who served vampire nobility.

Anna approached with languid grace, her voice pitched to carry just far enough. "Lord Carmilla requested an inspection of the vessel before departure. There have been... concerns about Registry saboteurs."

The guards exchanged uncertain glances, clearly unaware of any such order but unwilling to challenge someone of apparent rank. That moment of hesitation was all Anna needed. She closed the distance in a blur of motion, her hands striking with surgical precision at the guards' throats. They collapsed without a sound, unconscious before they hit the platform's metal grating.

Alexander was already moving toward the mechanic, who remained oblivious to the silent takedown, his head and shoulders buried deep in the engine housing. The smell of oil and heated metal grew stronger as Alexander approached, using the constant hiss of steam valves to mask his footsteps.

"Hand me the pressure wrench, would you?" the mechanic called out, assuming Alexander was one of the guards. "This coupling's shot to hell."

Alexander picked up the requested tool from a nearby tray and tapped the mechanic's leg with it. As the man backed out of the housing to take the wrench, Alexander brought the handle down hard on the back of his skull. The mechanic slumped forward, a small trickle of blood disappearing into his already oil-stained collar.

"Clear," Alexander called softly.

Niko darted from the corridor and made straight for the airship's gangplank, nimble as a rat navigating familiar territory. "Get aboard," he called back. "We need to be away before someone comes looking for our new friends."

Alexander and Anna dragged the dead bodies onto the airship, stowing them in a storage compartment near the gondola's stern. The interior of the vessel was cramped but efficient, every inch of space utilized with typical vampire precision. Brass instruments lined the walls, their needles and dials monitoring a dozen different systems. The air was thick with the scent of engine oil and the peculiar tang of the alchemical fuel that powered the craft's main propulsion system.

Niko was already in the control cabin, his fingers dancing across levers and valves with practiced ease. "Registry maintains a fleet of these for patrol duty," he explained, not looking up from his work. "Stole one back in '38 during the border uprising. Basic design hasn't changed much."

Alexander strapped himself into one of the navigation chairs, studying the array of controls with growing concern. "How long until we're airborne?"

"Minutes," Niko replied, spinning a pressure valve to full open. The engines responded with a throaty roar that vibrated through the entire gondola. "Just need to build up enough steam for the initial lift."

Anna secured the hatch, then joined them in the cabin. "Someone will have heard that," she warned, eyeing the platform beyond the gondola's windows. "We need to move now."

As if confirming her words, an alarm began to wail somewhere deep within the Manor, its distant howl carried to them on the swirling winds. Lights flashed along the dock's perimeter, bathing the platform in alternating red and amber.

"Almost there," Niko muttered, his face beaded with sweat as he manipulated the engine controls. The airship shuddered, lifting slightly against its moorings. "Release the tether on my mark."

The door at the far end of the platform burst open, disgorging a squad of guards with drawn weapons. Alexander drew his revolver, preparing to provide covering fire if necessary.

"Now!" Niko shouted.

Anna yanked the emergency release lever. The tethers fell away with a sound like snapping bones, and the airship lurched upward, nearly throwing them from their seats. Niko shoved the propulsion throttle forward, and the craft shot toward the platform's edge, engines screaming in protest at the sudden demand for power.

Gunshots rang out behind them, bullets pinging harmlessly off the gondola's armored hull. Then they were past the edge, dropping momentarily before the lifting tanks fully engaged, sending them soaring into the open air above the Ash Chasm.

Alexander watched the Manor recede, its windows blazing with alarmed activity. They had done it stolen an airship from under a vampire lord's nose, escaped with plans that could change the course of the war between humans and the undead. But the real test still lay ahead.

"Set course for the eastern wastelands," he instructed Niko. "We need to stay below the Registry's sensor grid until we're ready to make our approach to the Spire."

Niko nodded, adjusting their heading with small, precise movements of the control yoke. "We've got about sixteen hours of fuel at cruising speed. Enough to get us positioned for the attack, with a bit to spare for evasive maneuvers if needed."

The airship climbed steadily through layers of industrial haze, eventually breaking into clearer air where the first stars were visible through gaps in the perpetual smoke cover. Alexander felt a moment of vertigo as he gazed down at the world below—a patchwork of darkness broken only by the occasional glow of settlements or the sullen red of factory districts.

"We've done it," Anna said quietly, coming to stand beside him at the viewport. "The first piece is in place."

Alexander nodded, hand unconsciously moving to touch the plans concealed within his coat. "But taking down the Dragon is just the beginning now. The calculation engine, the Registry—the whole system needs to be dismantled."

"One monster at a time, Venator," she replied, her eyes reflecting the distant stars. "First we kill my father. Then we can worry about saving the world."

Alexander turned his gaze toward the horizon, where the faintest suggestion of the Black Spire could be made out against the night sky a darker shadow among shadows, waiting for them like the inevitable conclusion to a story written in blood and betrayal.

"Two days," he said, more to himself than his companions. "Two days until we face the Dragon."

The airship sailed on through the night, its brass hull gleaming like a promise, carrying them toward destiny or doom with equal indifference. Below, the toxic fog of the Ash Chasm swirled and eddied, hungry for those who fell. Above, the stars watched with cold, eternal patience—witnesses to the small rebellion taking shape within the gondola, a desperate plan born of vengeance and newfound purpose.

Alexander Stirling, the last Venator, allowed himself a moment of grim satisfaction. They had taken the first step. The rest would be written in the Dragon's blood, or their own.

The Midnight Market

Twilight bled into the night as Alexander crouched behind a rusted hopper car, the cold metal pressing against his spine. The abandoned rail yard stretched before him like a graveyard of industrial ghosts, each derelict car and twisted track a monument to Slade's decaying infrastructure. Beside him, Anna's pale face caught the last dying rays of sun, her features sharp as a blade in the fading light. Niko worked silently at the airship's hull, draping heavy tarpaulins over its brass fittings to muffle the telltale gleam that would attract Registry eyes from the wall looming just half a mile east.

"Final approach to the Spire will be cleaner if we have ward-breaking tech," Alexander whispered, his breath forming small clouds in the cooling air. "The black market's our only option at this point. It's a different sort of place, never really know what you can find."

Anna nodded, her eyes never leaving the silhouette of Slade's eastern gate. "My father's defenses are layered—magical and mechanical. We'll need both countermeasures if we want to reach him."

The stolen Scout airship now resembled nothing more remarkable than another piece of abandoned machinery, its silver hull obscured, and its engine dampened by the thick coverings. Alexander had insisted on hiding it here rather than risking the more obvious airship docks; Registry enforcers would be combing every official landing site by now.

"Done," Niko announced, wiping grease from his fingers onto an already stained handkerchief. "She'll wait for us. Assuming no one stumbles on her in the next twelve hours."

"Let's move," Alexander said, checking his revolvers one final time before sliding them back into their holster. The weight of the stolen plans felt heavier against his chest with each passing hour—knowledge that could shift the balance of this eternal war, if they lived long enough to use it.

They slipped between the rail cars, boots crunching softly on gravel and dead weeds, until they reached a maintenance gate set into the yard's eastern fence. The bars were corroded, peeling with decades of rust and neglect. Niko produced his lock picks, but Anna simply gripped two bars and wrenched, the metal giving way with a low groan that spoke more of her inhuman strength than any verbal reminder could have.

Beyond the fence lay the entrance to the abandoned mine shaft, its wooden support beams sagging beneath the weight of years and disuse. A faded sign, half-rotted and barely legible, warned trespassers of collapse. Alexander ducked beneath it without hesitation. The acrid tang of damp earth and leaking oil assaulted his nostrils as they descended, the darkness swallowing them whole until Niko struck a match, lighting a small lantern he produced from his coat.

"These tunnels run under most of Old Slade," he explained, voice barely above a whisper. "The Registry sealed the official entrances decades ago, but they've never managed to close all the access points. Too many people with reasons to stay off the streets."

They followed corroded rails deeper into the earth, the path sloping gently downward. The walls wept moisture, creating slick patches that threatened treacherous footing. Anna moved ahead, her crimson-brown eyes adapting to the darkness far better than her human companions. Her boots made no sound as she navigated the treacherous ground, while Niko's quiet footsteps echoed softly in the confined space.

Flickering gas lamps appeared along the tunnel walls at irregular intervals, casting sickly yellow pools of light that revealed graffiti some of them was mundane territorial markings, others elaborate symbols Alexander recognized as ward-signs against Registry tracking.

"Close now," Niko murmured after they had walked for what felt like an hour. "Mouth shut, eyes open. This isn't a place for outsiders."

They rounded a final bend, and Alexander saw a massive iron hatch set into the stone wall, marked with a wolf sigil painted in what appeared to be dried blood. Two figures stood guard, their faces obscured by cloth masks, their hands resting on modified steam pistols. One stepped forward as they approached, the barrel of his weapon rising slightly.

"Business?" The guard's voice was muffled by his mask, but the threat was clear enough.

Niko stepped ahead. "Looking to trade. I vouch for these two."

The guard stared at them for a long moment, eyes cold above his mask. Then he nodded once and stepped back, turning a massive wheel that caused the hatch to swing open with a groan of protesting metal.

The sound that escaped was a tangible force, a cacophony of noise that enveloped the senses, a wall of voices haggling in a symphony of a dozen languages, each tone rising and falling like waves crashing against a shore. The sharp hiss of steam valves punctuated the air, mingling with the rhythmic clank of machinery grinding away relentlessly. Beneath it all lingered the low, haunting moan of human misery, echoing like a distant lament. Then came the smell, an assault on the olfactory senses: the acrid scent of sweat and blood mingled with harsh chemicals, the metallic tang of scorched metal and the sickening odor of burned flesh. All of it coalesced into an unmistakable miasma, bound together by the pervasive, suffocating reek of fear that hung heavily in the air.

Alexander stepped through the hatch into a vaulted brick chamber pulsing with lantern light and billowing steam. The ceiling arched twenty feet overhead, ancient masonry reinforced with modern steel beams. Stalls lined both sides of a central corridor that stretched into darkness, each one a microcosm of forbidden commerce.

In the nearest booth, a withered woman with mechanical arms stitched to her shoulders sorted through a pile of severed bat wings, each one tagged with a location and date of harvest. Beside her, venom vials whispered within cracked glass containers, their contents shifting with hypnotic patterns.

Further down, Alexander's gaze fell upon grim cages, some imprisoning creatures he could scarcely recognize, while others held human souls in torment. The laborers within trembled violently, their hollow eyes reflecting a void of despair, the telltale registry bracelets conspicuously missing from their wrists. They were liberated from one monstrous system yet shackled to the merciless hands of those who had bought their freedom at a ghastly price.

His jaw clenched tight enough to ache. This was the underbelly of the Registry's perfect order, the black market that serviced those with coin and connections enough to skirt the Dragon's laws, while still profiting from the misery they created.

Overhead, a massive chandelier crafted from gryphon claws cast a sickly light across the proceedings, each talon holding a flickering oil lamp that sent shadows dancing across the brick walls. From darkened side passages came the rattle of chains and occasional cries quickly silenced.

"Don't stare," Niko cautioned, his voice low. "And don't touch anything unless you mean to buy it."

They paused five paces in, allowing their senses to adjust to the overwhelming stimuli. A distant steam hammer roared somewhere deeper in the complex, its rhythmic pounding vibrating through the floor beneath their feet. Torchlight danced on Anna's pale skin, giving her an otherworldly glow that drew sidelong glances from nearby traders.

Racks of forbidden gear lined one wall—weapons, tools, and devices all stamped with official Blood Registry seals, stolen or salvaged from government stores. Alexander recognized gear that would fetch a venator's yearly salary on the open market, now being bartered for by haggard traders whose hushed voices barely carried over the ambient noise.

The metallic scent of spilled monster blood permeated everything, the floor beneath their boots sticky with substances Alexander preferred not to identify. Coins clinked as transactions completed, goods and currency exchanging hands with furtive movements.

"The ward-breaker dealer is deeper in," Niko said, gesturing toward the far end of the main corridor. "Nasty piece of work, but he's the only one who might have what we need."

Alexander nodded, taking a deep breath of the fetid air. This hidden market held both their salvation and grave danger, one wrong move, one hint of their true purpose, and they would never leave these tunnels alive. Yet without the tools they sought, the Spire would remain impregnable, the Dragon untouchable.

"Lead on," he said, hand never straying far from his revolver as they pressed deeper into the undercity's forbidden heart.

The stall squatted at the dead end of a narrow passage, isolated from the market's main thoroughfare by strategic design rather than chance. Red velvet drapes, tattered and stained with substances Alexander preferred not to identify, hung from rusted pipes overhead, creating a makeshift tent lit by a single sodium lamp that cast everything in sickly yellow. Behind a scarred wooden counter stood Torben Krav, a mountain of a man whose burn-scarred cheek pulled his mouth into a permanent sneer. His left arm ended not in a hand but in a sharpened brass hook that gleamed wickedly in the lamp's unsteady light as he placed a small, cloth-wrapped bundle on the counter with exaggerated care.

"The venator lives," Krav's voice rasped like steel on stone, his coal-black eyes never blinking as they fixed on Alexander. "Thought the Registry had mounted your head years ago."

Alexander kept his expression neutral, though his fingers itched to reach for his revolver. "News of my death has always been premature."

Krav's laughter sounded like bones breaking. "Clearly." His gaze shifted to Anna, recognition dawning in those pitch-dark eyes. "Interesting company you keep these days."

Two guards stood silently behind Krav, their features half-hidden in shadow. The larger one tapped a jagged obsidian dagger against his steel-plated gauntlet in a rhythmic pattern that set Alexander's teeth on edge. The smaller was motionless as a statue, but no less dangerous for his stillness.

Krav unwrapped the bundle with agonizing slowness, revealing an amulet no larger than a pocket watch. It was crafted from tarnished silver and what appeared to be human bone, inscribed with glyphs that seemed to shift and writhe under direct observation. At its center sat a chip of ivory, etched with symbols Alexander recognized from the oldest venator texts warding signs, inverted and corrupted.

"The last of its kind," Krav said, his hook tracing the central glyph with surprising delicacy. "Crafted from the thigh bone of a hedge witch who specialized in boundary magic. Quite difficult to acquire the materials these days."

Anna stepped forward, her face, a mask of aristocratic disdain that didn't quite hide the hunger in her eyes. "You said it bypasses every ward in a stronghold?"

Krav's crooked grin widened, revealing teeth filed to points. "Every one of them. Thermal detection, blood-recognition gates, even the soul-sensing portals at the inner sanctum." His hook lingered on the ivory chip. "The wearer becomes a ghost to magical security—present but undetectable. Like walking through morning mist."

"And mechanical security?" Alexander asked, calculating odds and angles, marking the positions of both guards in his peripheral vision.

"That's your problem," Krav replied with a shrug that made his massive shoulders roll like tectonic plates. "I sell magic countermeasures, not skeleton keys."

Niko leaned against a support beam, affecting casual disinterest while his hand hovered near his holstered revolver. "Price?"

"For this?" Krav caressed the amulet with his remaining hand. "Sixty sovereigns or a favor owed." His eyes gleamed. "Though I'd prefer the favor, especially from such... unique clientele."

Alexander's boots scuffed the dusty floor as he shifted his weight, buying seconds to think. Sixty sovereigns was a fortune—more than they could afford to part with before the Spire assault. And a favor owed to someone like Krav was tantamount to signing away your soul on an open contract.

"Thirty," Alexander countered, "and information on Registry patrol schedules for the eastern perimeter."

Krav's face hardened. "You insult me, venator. This isn't a haggler's market stall." He nodded almost imperceptibly, and the larger guard stepped forward, knuckles cracking like gunshots in the confined space. "Full price. Now. Or leave empty-handed."

The lamp's glow cast long shadows across Anna's sharp features as she moved with fluid grace to stand at Alexander's side. Her pulse visibly tightened at her throat—not from fear, Alexander realized, but from carefully controlled rage.

"Perhaps a demonstration first," she suggested, her voice honeyed poison. "I've heard counterfeit charms are becoming common, even in... establishments of your reputation."

Krav's scarred face twisted in fury. "You dare question my merchandise?" His hook slammed into the wooden counter, embedding itself deep in the aged oak. "I don't deal in fakes, blood-drinker."

"And yet you seek payment without proof," Anna replied, unmoved by his display. "Curious business practice."

The tension in the stall thickened to something almost tangible. The smaller guard's hand drifted to a bulge beneath his coat, a pistol, Alexander guessed, probably loaded with silver. Niko's fingers now rested openly on his revolver's grip, his casual pose abandoned for combat readiness.

"Payment. Now." Krav's voice dropped to a dangerous growl. "Or my men will extract it from your flesh, piece by piece."

For a moment, no one moved. Then Anna reached into her cloak with deliberate slowness and withdrew a small velvet pouch. She tossed it onto the counter with a heavy clink of metal striking wood.

"Registry regalia," she announced. "Worth triple your asking price to the right collector."

Krav's eyes narrowed with suspicion, but greed won out. He reached for the pouch, only to freeze as Anna's other hand emerged from her cloak holding a slender vial filled with luminescent crimson liquid.

"Insurance," she explained, lips curving in a smile that didn't reach her eyes. "In case your merchandise fails to meet expectations."

Alexander recognized the vial instantly alchemical fire, unstable and devastating in enclosed spaces. The kind of weapon that didn't discriminate between friend and foe once unleashed.

Krav recognized it too. "Put that away," he hissed, genuine fear flickering across his face. "One wrong move and you'll burn this entire section to ash."

"Precisely." Anna's smile widened. "So perhaps we understand each other better now."

With lightning speed, she snatched the amulet from the counter, simultaneously flinging the vial to the floor at Krav's feet. The glass shattered with a delicate tinkle that belied its deadly contents. Crimson liquid splashed across wood and boot leather, instantly igniting in a hissing arc of unnatural flame that climbed up the counter and licked at Krav's sleeve.

The merchant recoiled with a howl, yanking his hook free from the counter as his guards scrambled back from the spreading fire. Smoke billowed upward, acrid and thick with chemical stench, filling the small space with impenetrable darkness.

Alexander felt Anna's hand close around his wrist, pulling him toward the exit. Niko was already ahead of them, clearing a path through the sudden press of curious onlookers drawn by the commotion. Behind them, Krav's curses turned to threats, then to promises of retribution that faded as they plunged deeper into the twisting passages of the underground market.

"Was that necessary?" Alexander asked when they finally stopped running, three corridors and two levels away from Krav's burning stall.

Anna opened her palm, revealing the ward-walking charm nestled against her pale skin. "Yes," she replied simply. "The regalia were counterfeit he would have discovered that within the hour. And we need this." Her finger traced the central glyph, which pulsed faintly in response to her touch. "Without it, we'd never reach my father's inner chambers."

Niko glanced nervously over his shoulder. "We should keep moving. Krav has connections throughout the undercity. Once he recovers, he'll have every mercenary and cutthroat in Slade looking for us."

Alexander nodded, aware that they had just made a powerful enemy—one more name on a list that grew longer by the day. But the amulet was worth the risk. It represented the difference between a suicide mission and a fighting chance against the Dragon.

As they moved toward the market's eastern exit, the clamor of bartering voices drowning out the distant sound of Krav's still-burning stall, Alexander watched Anna slip the charm into an inner pocket of her coat. Her expression remained unreadable, but he caught the slight tremor in her hand it was not fear, but anticipation.

They were one step closer to the Spire, one step closer to the Dragon. And with each step, the weight of their purpose grew heavier, crushing any hope of retreat beneath its inexorable mass.

Betrayal's Kiss

Anna slipped through the iron-barred exit of the Midnight Market, the rusted hinges protesting with a low groan that scraped against her sensitive ears. The service alley beyond lay narrow and slick with industrial runoff, hemmed in by brick walls that seemed to lean inward like the sides of a coffin. She paused, nostrils flaring at the complex mixture of scents—hot metal, rotting food, human sweat, and beneath it all, the unmistakable cold-copper smell of vampire. Not just any vampire. Her body tensed, muscles coiling like springs as the sound of armored boots scraped against the cobblestones ahead, punctuated by a voice she knew all too well.

"Search every exit," Lucian Grigorescu commanded, his aristocratic accent bouncing off the oil-streaked bricks. "The Countess has grown predictable in her desperation. She leaves a scent even a half-blind hound could follow."

Anna pressed herself against a recessed doorway, one hand closing around the ward-walking charm still warm in her pocket. Through the steam rising from a nearby grate, she counted silhouettes—six, no, eight armored thralls, their serrated sabers gleaming dully in the sickly lamplight. And at their center, tall and imperious, stood Lucian himself.

The lamplight caught his pale, veined face as he turned, highlighting the sharp angles of his aristocratic features. His steel-gray eyes scanned the alley with predatory focus, lips curled in what might have been amusement or disgust. The black greatcoat he wore hung perfectly tailored despite the filth of their surroundings, its brass buttons and mechanical augmentations glinting with each measured step.

"I can smell your noble blood, Anna," he called, voice pitched just loud enough to carry down the confined space. "Always so distinctive. Your father's lineage, but... tainted with something else. Rebellion, perhaps? Or is it merely fear?"

Anna felt her fangs elongate in response to the threat, pressing against her lower lip as her body prepared instinctively for combat. Her fingernails hardened and extended into claws, the transformation sending waves of heat through her limbs. The ward-charm pulsed against her palm, almost as if sensing the proximity of another vampire noble.

"You're a long way from the Spire, Lucian," she called back, stepping deliberately into the open. No point in hiding now. "Did my father send his favorite lapdog to fetch me, or are you hunting strays on your own time?"

Lucian's smile widened, revealing teeth too perfect to be natural. "The Dragon grows impatient for your return. The conclave approaches, and your absence has been... noted." He gestured casually, and his thralls fanned out, blocking both ends of the alley. "Come willingly, and I'll ensure your punishment is merely educational."

Anna snarled, her elongated fangs fully visible now. "I've had enough of my father's education."

She surged forward like a bolt of lightning, the world dissolving into a kaleidoscope of chaos as she closed in on the nearest thrall. Her claws ripped through his steel-reinforced vest with the ease of tearing paper, the brutal impact sending him crashing backward into a heap of hissing, steaming crates. Before the second thrall could even lift his saber, she was upon him, one hand clamping viciously around his throat while the other wrenched the weapon from his grip, a primal growl escaping her lips.

Blood erupted from her latest victim, splattering across the cobblestones as she spun, the stolen blade slicing through the air to carve a gash across another attacker's chest. Behind her, she heard the ominous click-whir of Lucian's mechanical gauntlet springing to life, the air thick with the electric tang of ozone and volatile alchemical energy crackling around her.

A flicker of movement caught her attention—two thralls closing in from behind, their every step choreographed with the deadly precision of relentless training. She dropped low, using her momentum to roll beneath their guard, then sprang to her feet in one fluid motion, her claws driving upward through the first thrall's jaw with a sickening crunch. Without missing a beat, she pivoted and slammed the second thrall into the wall with bone-shattering force, the bricks around him cracking under the impact.

The echo of a pistol shot reached her ears a fraction of a second before pain bloomed in her left thigh as a silver bullet seared a hole, the wound burning with unnatural intensity as the metal reacted with her flesh. She staggered, regaining her balance in time to see three more thralls advancing, their weapons raised.

Anna bared her teeth in a feral grin. "Silver? How predictable. Weapons for a bunch of Bitches."

She launched herself at the wall, using it as a springboard to land behind the thrall formation. Before they could turn, she had seized one by the shoulders, using his body as a shield against the next volley of shots. The impact of bullets drove them both backward, but she maintained her grip, feeling the thrall's body jerk with each hit.

Metal-groaned and anguished shrieks filled the air as she tore through their ranks, her movements a blur of calculated violence. Blood hers and theirs slicked the cobblestones, making footing treacherous. A second silver bullet grazed her shoulder, leaving a smoking furrow in her flesh that sent waves of nausea through her system.

Through the chaos, she caught glimpses of Lucian not fighting directly, but observing, analyzing her technique with the cold detachment of a chess master studying an opponent's moves. His calculated restraint infuriated her more than any attack could have.

She closed on him, ducking beneath a mechanical arm that shot out to intercept her. Her claws raked across his chest, tearing through expensive fabric to the flesh beneath exposing his lungs and heart. Black blood older and thicker than humans spattered his pristine coat.

Lucian hissed, more in annoyance than pain, and struck with his gauntleted hand. The blow caught Anna across the jaw, sending her sprawling backward into a puddle of foul water. Her vision swam, ears ringing from the impact.

"Impressive," Lucian conceded, pressing a handkerchief to the gash across his chest. "Your time among humans hasn't dulled your edge. But this pointless rebellion cannot last, Anna. The calculation engine will be unveiled at the conclave, with or without your attendance."

Anna spat blood onto the cobblestones, forcing herself to stand despite the silver burning in her veins. "Then why hunt me at all? Afraid I might spoil the Dragon's grand moment?"

Something flickered across Lucian's face uncertainty, perhaps, or a more complex calculation. He glanced at his remaining thralls, most now sprawled broken across the alley.

"Your father values family appearances," he said finally. "Even wayward daughters have their uses in politics."

He raised his gauntlet, not in attack but in a gesture of reluctant retreat. The mechanical fingers flexed once, then closed into a fist. "We will meet again at the Spire, Countess. By choice or by force."

With that, he backed away, maintaining eye contact until he reached the mouth of the alley. His remaining thralls gathered their wounded and followed, disappearing into the labyrinth of Old Slade's underground.

Anna remained standing until the echo of their retreat faded, then allowed herself to slump against the wall, breath coming in ragged gasps. Black ichor dripped from half a dozen cuts across her body, each silver wound burning like a brand pressed into her flesh. She probed the bullet hole in her thigh with trembling fingers, wincing as they made contact with the metal still lodged in the muscle.

The flickering lamplight cast her shadow long and distorted against the bricks as she gritted her teeth and dug the silver round from her leg. It came free with a wet sound, smoking slightly as she flicked it away. Her heightened healing would take care of the wound eventually, but silver poisoning would slow the process considerably.

She had to find Alexander and Niko and reach the airship before Lucian returned with reinforcements. The Dragon's calculation engine, the conclave, the fate of humans under vampire rule all of it now balanced on a knife's edge, with her father waiting at the center of the web.

Anna limped toward the deeper shadows, leaving bloody footprints that slowly faded to nothing as her body began the painful process of healing around the silver's taint.

Alexander's back slammed against the cracked concrete wall of the mine-shaft junction, the impact sending shock waves of pain through his already battered body. Sweat and blood mingled as they trickled down his face, stinging his eyes as he blinked frantically to clear his vision. The junction stretched before him like a spider's web of narrow tunnels and fractured support beams, each path potentially leading to safety or death with equal probability. His lungs burned with each breath, the air thick with industrial dust and the metallic tang of ruptured steam pipes. Through the haze, the unmistakable sound of coordinated footsteps echoed from the eastern tunnel Registry troops, and they were closing fast.

He wiped his sleeve across his face, smearing blood and grime but clearing his vision enough to assess his surroundings. The junction was a natural cavity in the rock, reinforced with ancient timber supports that groaned under the weight of the mountain above. Scalding steam vents punctuated the rough floor, releasing pressurized jets that hissed and spat with unpredictable rhythm. The air wavered with heat distortion, casting the emergency lamps glow into fractured, dancing patterns across the rough-hewn walls.

Alexander pressed his palm against his side, feeling the warm wetness of blood seeping through his shirt. Not fatal but slowing him down exactly what he couldn't afford with Registry forces converging on his position. He'd lost Anna and Niko in the chaos following their theft from Krav, the market's alarm systems splitting them in three different directions as they fled. Now he was alone, cornered, with the stolen documents from Carmilla's manor still tucked inside his coat a prize worth dying for, or killing for.

The footsteps grew louder, more distinct. Not the chaotic patter of market security but the measured tread of trained soldiers. Through the steam-choked tunnel mouth, he counted the silhouettes—six, no, eight armored troopers pouring into the confined space, their faces obscured by breathing apparatus, their chests protected by registry-issue plate designed specifically to withstand conventional weapons.

"Target confirmed," called the lead trooper, his voice muffled but clear enough through his mask. "Last Venator, armed and wounded. Lethal force authorized."

Alexander's mind raced through options that dwindled with each passing second. The tunnel behind him had collapsed in his desperate flight, while the western passage would only lead deeper into the mountain's labyrinth, away from the rendezvous point. Direct confrontation was suicide their armor would turn his bullets, and in his current state, hand to hand combat against multiple opponents was out of the question.

His fingers brushed against the cylindrical shape nestled in his coat's inner pocket. The blood-boiling vapor grenade—last of three he'd acquired from Cassie before this mission began. A desperate measure, designed for use against vampires in confined spaces, but equally effective against humans unwise enough to be caught in its mist. The caveat was simple: its effects didn't discriminate between friend and foe. Deploying it here meant subjecting himself to the same toxic cloud that would engulf his attackers.

No choice. The troopers were spreading out in standard formation, creating overlapping fields of fire that would cut him down the moment he moved. Alexander subtly shifted his weight, gauging distances and angles, calculating the optimal trajectory in the split second before commitment.

With practiced efficiency, he yanked the grenade from his coat, the motion flowing seamlessly as he hooked his thumb under the pin. The safety mechanism released with a metallic click that seemed to echo in the cavernous space. The lead trooper's head snapped up, recognition dawning too late.

"Grenade!" he shouted, but Alexander had already hurled the device directly into the center of their formation. It arced through the steam-filled air, trailing a thin ribbon of crimson vapor even before impact.

The moment the grenade left his hand something slammed into Alexander's side with the force of a runaway train. One of the troopers had fired not a bullet, but a compressed air projectile designed to incapacitate rather than kill. The impact lifted him off his feet, sending him hurtling backward into a tangle of exposed pipes and jagged rock. His ribs cracked with an audible snap that was drowned out by his own involuntary cry of pain.

The grenade detonated with a sound more like a wet slap than an explosion, releasing its payload in a rapidly expanding cloud of crimson mist. Unlike conventional explosives, the blood-boiler's effect was almost silent but the screams that followed were not. The mist enveloped the troopers before they could retreat, clinging to exposed skin and seeping through the breathing apparatus of those too slow to seal their masks.

Alexander watched through pain-blurred vision as the first effects took hold. The vapor reacted with human blood on contact, rapidly increasing its temperature beyond what flesh could withstand. Troopers clawed at their armor, desperate to escape the burning sensation spreading through their veins. Some fell immediately, their nervous systems overloaded by the sudden pain. Others staggered in circles, firing blindly into the mist, their shots ricocheting off the stone walls and metal pipes.

A stray bullet shattered one of the steam pipes above Alexander's head, releasing a fresh jet of scalding vapor that rained down on his already battered form. He rolled aside, coat shredding against the jagged rock as he sought shelter behind a fallen support beam. The movement sent fresh waves of agony through his broken ribs, each breath becoming a deliberate act of will against the body's instinct to remain still.

The crimson mist continued to spread, filling the junction with its deadly haze. Alexander pulled a rag from his pocket, pressing it over his mouth and nose in a futile attempt to filter the air. Too late, he could already feel the first tendrils of the vapor working their way into his lungs, bringing with them the distinctive copper taste of blood and chemicals.

Metal pipes clattered and hissed around him as the troopers' blind fire struck the junction's infrastructure. Water lines burst, mixing with the chemical cloud to create a toxic slurry that pooled on the uneven floor. Emergency lamps flickered and died as their power sources were severed, plunging sections of the cavern into near darkness broken only by the eerie red glow of the blood-boiling mist.

Through the chaos, Alexander crawled toward a narrow crevice in the western wall not an official tunnel, but a natural fault in the rock that might provide escape from the rapidly deteriorating chamber. His lungs burned with each shallow breath, the chemical residue of his own weapon scorching his throat and nasal passages. The stolen documents pressed against his chest inside his coat, their edges jabbing into the fresh bruises with each movement.

The sounds of struggle behind him gradually faded, replaced by the wet, ragged breathing of the dying and the persistent hiss of damaged infrastructure. Alexander dragged himself the final few feet, collapsing in the space between two flickering emergency lamps that had somehow survived the destruction. His hunting coat, once Victor's pride and the mark of a Venator, hung in tatters around his shoulders, shredded beyond recognition by the jagged rock.

He lay there, chest heaving with the effort of drawing breath through damaged lungs, each inhalation bringing fresh pain from his broken ribs. The chemical fallout from the grenade had left a film on his skin that burned like acid, slowly eating through layers of tissue. His vision swam, darkness encroaching at the edges as his body fought against the combined effects of injury and toxin exposure.

Through the fog of pain, one thought remained clear: the documents. He had to ensure the plans for the calculation engine reached safety. His fingers groped weakly at his coat, confirming that the inner pocket remained intact despite the garment's outward destruction.

Empty.

Alexander's heart seized with a new kind of pain. The pocket had been torn open, its precious contents now missing. In the chaos of the fight, the blast, the desperate scramble for safety, the documents that detailed the Registry's most devastating weapon had vanished. If they'd fallen into the toxic slurry behind him, they might already be destroyed. But if someone had taken them...

The implications crashed through his fading consciousness like a physical blow. He tried to rise, to return to the junction and search, but his body refused to respond. The lamps flickered overhead, their rhythm matching the slowing beat of his heart as darkness crept further into his vision.

Alexander's last thought before unconsciousness claimed him was of Anna, and whether she'd fared any better in her own escape from the market's depths.

Niko darted from the fractured junction, his boots barely touching the ground as he fled through the labyrinth of underground passages. The stolen journal pages crackled against his chest, tucked hastily inside his shirt when Alexander had been thrown by the Registry trooper's impact weapon. He hadn't planned the theft—opportunism was simply his nature, a survival instinct honed through decades of navigating Slade's deadliest corners. When Alexander went down and chaos erupted, Niko's fingers had moved of their own accord, slipping into the torn coat and extracting what might be the most valuable documents in the city. His betrayal wasn't personal; it was just business; he told himself as his heart hammered against the papers with each frantic stride.

The tunnels twisted ahead of him, a maze he had memorized over years of smuggling contraband beneath Registry noses. Each intersection represented a choice—toward safety or into the waiting arms of enemies whose faces he couldn't yet determine. The crimson mist from Alexander's grenade had barely touched him; he'd been moving backward at the first sign of the weapon, an instinctive reaction born from surviving a hundred similar situations.

His lungs burned with exertion, each ragged breath drowned by the omnipresent hiss of steam escaping from ruptured pipes. The infrastructure beneath Old Slade was decaying like everything else in this godforsaken city, held together by rust, prayer, and the stubborn refusal of engineers to acknowledge defeat. Moisture beaded on the rough-hewn walls, collecting in rivulets that traced paths through decades of industrial grime.

Niko paused at a Y-shaped split in the tunnel, pressing his back against the damp stone as he listened for pursuers. Nothing but the distant groan of settling earth and the persistent drip of water from somewhere above. Only then did he pull the crumpled papers free from his shirt, examining his prize in the weak light of a distant emergency lamp.

The documents were a mess, creased and spotted with what might have been Alexander's blood, their edges singed from proximity to the detonated grenade. But the contents remained legible: schematics, formulae, and detailed notes about something called the "calculation engine." Niko's eyes widened as he scanned the first page, comprehension dawning. This wasn't just valuable information; it was potentially world changing.

"Shit," he whispered, fingers trembling slightly as he turned to the second page. The Registry's plan to mechanize blood monitoring, to track and categorize humans with unprecedented precision—this was the kind of intelligence that could start a revolution. Or end one before it began.

Footsteps echoed from the direction he'd come, accompanied by the rhythmic thud of Registry-issue boots. Decision time. Niko quickly folded the papers and tucked them inside his vest, securing them in the hidden pocket he'd specially reinforced for contraband. The weight of the documents seemed to burn against his chest, heavier than their physical mass should allow.

He veered left at the fork, ducking into a dank side shaft that most would overlook. The ceiling here dropped low enough to force him into a crouch, his shoulders brushing against slick walls as he navigated by touch more than sight. The air grew thicker, laden with the musty scent of fungal growth and the metallic tang of mineral deposits leaching through the rock. Timber supports, half-collapsed and groaning under the mountain's weight, framed his path like the ribs of some petrified beast.

Water seeped through his boots as he splashed through shallow puddles of indeterminate origin, each step producing a sound that seemed magnified in the confined space. The darkness pressed in from all sides, broken only by the occasional phosphorescent patch of cave fungi that cast everything in a sickly blue-green glow. In these brief illuminated moments, Niko caught glimpses of his surroundings, discarded tools from mining operations long abandoned, bones of small animals that had wandered in and found no exit, the rusted remnants of rail tracks that once carried ore carts to the surface.

He counted his steps automatically, an old smuggler's habit. Fifty paces from the fork to the first major support beam. Another thirty to the natural stone arch that marked the transition from the excavated tunnel to natural cavern. Twenty more to the narrow squeeze that most Registry enforcers, encumbered by armor and weapons, couldn't navigate. Niko slipped through this bottleneck with practiced ease, his lean frame designed by genetics and honed by necessity for such escapes.

Beyond the squeeze, the tunnel widened again, transitioning from natural cave back to human construction. This section had been a service corridor once, connecting different parts of the mine before structural failure had rendered it officially unusable. Unofficially, it remained one of the most reliable smuggling routes in Old Slade for those who knew its secrets and respected its dangers.

The ceiling had partially collapsed, forcing Niko to navigate a treacherous path between fallen beams and chunks of concrete. His hands found familiar handholds in the debris, muscle memory guiding him through obstacles he'd traversed dozens of times before. Each movement was calculated to minimize noise, his boots finding solid purchase on islands of stable flooring amid the ruin.

He emerged into a relatively intact section where a single sputtering gaslight cast wild, dancing shadows across walls stained with decades of soot and moisture. The flame within the glass housing flickered erratically, starved for oxygen in the stale underground air, threatening to plunge the corridor into complete darkness with each wavering pulse. Rust-colored water dripped from exposed pipes overhead, collecting in brackish puddles that reflected the unsteady light in distorted patterns.

Niko paused here, chest heaving as he pressed himself against the wall and listened. The distant sounds of pursuit had faded, replaced by the ambient creaks and groans of the underworld's perpetual decay. He forced his breathing to slow, fighting against the adrenaline that demanded flight. Panic was a luxury he couldn't afford not when clear thinking was the only currency that might keep him alive.

His fingers brushed the documents in his vest, confirming their presence for the hundredth time since the theft. The calculation engine plans represented more than just information; they were leverage, power, a key to doors that had remained locked to someone of his station. The question now was which lock to try first—the Registry would pay handsomely for their return, but so would the resistance movements scattered throughout the city's shadows. Even vampire noble houses opposed to the Dragon might offer a king's ransom for insight into their ruler's latest scheme.

He peered into the choking gloom beyond the gaslight's feeble reach, mentally mapping the remaining route to the surface. Three more junctions, a vertical shaft with rusted ladder rungs, then a maintenance hatch that would deposit him in the basement of a abandoned apothecary two districts away from the market. From there, he could disappear into Old Slade's winding streets, anonymous among the thousands of desperate souls who scraped out existence beneath the Registry's boot.

The documents weighed heavier with each passing moment. Niko had never considered himself a man of conscience—survival had always taken precedence over morality in the breaks. But Alexander had hired him in good faith, had trusted him despite ample evidence suggesting such trust was misplaced. And Anna... Niko suppressed a shudder. The vampire countess would not view his betrayal as a simple business transaction. She would hunt him with the single-minded focus of her kind, and her vengeance would be neither quick nor merciful.

"Just business," he whispered again to the empty corridor, the words hollow even to his own ears. "Nothing personal."

He pushed away from the wall, decision made. The surface first, then a message to his contact in the smugglers' guild. The documents would fetch their highest price if multiple parties believed they had an exclusive opportunity to bid. It was a dangerous game, but then, life in Slade had never been anything else.

Niko took one last look behind him, gauging how fast his pursuers might be closing in. The corridor remained empty, the gaslight's struggle the only movement visible in the subterranean stillness. He turned away, slipping deeper into the choking gloom with the practiced stealth of a man whose life had been built on escaping consequences just barely ahead of their arrival.

The Healer's Price

Consciousness returned to Alexander in cruel increments. First came the taste. Copper and chemicals coating his tongue like a toxic film. Then the smell of damp stone, rusted metal, and the faint lingering trace of his own blood-boiling grenade. Pain followed, a symphony of broken ribs and chemical burns that transformed each shallow breath into an exercise in agony. He opened his eyes to perfect darkness, his body wedged into a space barely wider than his shoulders, cool metal pressing against his cheek. Not the crevice he'd collapsed in an air duct. Somehow, he'd dragged himself here before consciousness had abandoned him entirely.

He tested each limb cautiously, cataloging injuries with the detached precision Victor had drilled into him since childhood. Three ribs cracked, possibly four. Left shoulder dislocated but crudely reset the work of his own hands before memory failed. Chemical burns across his exposed skin, their edges crusted and weeping. Internal damage from the vapor he'd inhaled, evident in the wet rattle accompanying each breath. Survivable. Barely.

The documents. Memory slammed into him with physical force. His hand flew to his coat's inner pocket, fingers finding only torn fabric and dried blood. Gone. The calculation engine plans, the registry's ultimate weapon against humanity, lost in the chaos or...

"Niko," he whispered, the name tasting like betrayal on his tongue.

Priorities crystallized with cold clarity: escape, find Anna, recover the documents. In that order, because the dead saved no one.

Alexander braced his palms against the duct's sides and pushed himself forward, inch by excruciating inch. The metal protested beneath his weight, decades of rust and moisture having compromised its structural integrity. Each movement sent fresh waves of agony through his chest, broken ribs grinding against each other with nauseating precision. He bit his lip until blood flowed, using the sharp new pain to focus his mind away from the deeper damage.

Faint light appeared ahead, a grated opening where the ventilation system connected to a larger chamber. Alexander paused, listening intently for any sign of Registry troops. Only the distant drip of water and the settling groan of abandoned mine works reached his ears. He pressed his face against the grate, vision swimming as he tried to make sense of the shadows beyond.

An abandoned storage room, its contents long since salvaged or destroyed. Emergency lights flickered weakly overhead, their batteries nearly exhausted after hours or days of continuous operation. No movement, no sound of breathing beyond his own labored gasps.

He braced himself against the sides of the duct and kicked at the grate with both feet. The rusted metal gave way on the third attempt, crashing to the floor with a sound that echoed through the chamber like a gunshot. Alexander froze, counting heartbeats as he waited for the inevitable response. Nothing. He eased himself through the opening, dropping to the floor with as much control as his battered body could manage.

His legs buckled instantly, sending him sprawling across the cold concrete. For a moment, darkness threatened to reclaim him, black spots dancing across his vision as pain threatened to overwhelm consciousness. Alexander fought it back through sheer force of will, dragging himself to his knees, then to his feet using a nearby shelving unit for support.

The doorway stood open, leading to a corridor dimly lit by the same emergency system. Alexander staggered forward, one hand pressed against his ribs, the other trailing along the wall for support. Each step was a negotiation between determination and physical limitation, his body screaming protests that his mind refused to acknowledge.

Twenty paces down the corridor, he heard a faint scrabbling, the sound of someone or something fighting against immobility. Alexander tensed, reaching for his revolver only to find an empty holster. Defenseless, wounded, but still moving. Still hunting.

He followed the sound to a junction where the corridor branched into three separate tunnels. The ceiling had partially collapsed here, massive support beams and chunks of concrete creating a chaotic barrier. The noise grew louder as he approached someone trapped beneath the debris, still alive enough to struggle.

"Hello?" he called, voice rasping through his damaged throat.

The movement stilled, then intensified. Not words, but a desperate increase in effort. Alexander climbed over the smaller pieces of rubble, ignoring the fresh blood seeping through his shirt as the exertion reopened wounds. He peered into the gap between two fallen beams and saw pale fingers scrabbling against stone, smeared with blood so dark it appeared black in the dim light.

"Hold on," he grunted, bracing himself against the larger beam. The wood was rotted through in places, its structural integrity compromised by years of moisture and neglect. Alexander positioned himself at its midpoint and pushed upward with legs and back, a scream tearing from his throat as broken ribs shifted beneath the strain.

The beam moved inch by agonizing inch, revealing more of the trapped figure beneath. A woman's arm, pale as marble but streaked with blood and dirt. The limb was ravaged, muscle and tendon laid bare to bone in places, the pattern of damage distinctive—silver bullet wounds, interspersed with deep lacerations that could only come from Registry sabers.

"Anna," Alexander gasped, recognition flooding through him.

He redoubled his efforts, adrenaline temporarily masking the worst of his pain as he levered the beam high enough to create a gap. Anna's fingers grasped weakly at the opening, their usual strength absent. Alexander kicked smaller debris aside and reached into the space, his hands closing around her wrist with care to avoid the worst of her wounds.

He pulled steadily, guiding her broken form through the narrow gap until she lay fully revealed in the emergency lights' sickly glow. The sight stole what little breath remained in his lungs.

Anna's normally immaculate appearance was destroyed beyond recognition. Her right arm hung uselessly, shredded from shoulder to wrist, white bone gleaming through ribbons of torn flesh. Silver bullet wounds peppered her torso, each one smoking faintly as her body fought against the toxic metal. A deep puncture wound beneath her ribs leaked thick, black blood that pulsed with each shallow breath. Her face was a mask of dirt and dried blood, features barely recognizable beneath the grime.

"Lucian," she whispered, the name barely audible. "Registry... knows..."

Alexander knelt beside her, hands hovering uselessly over her broken form. Vampire healing was powerful, but silver poisoning would slow the process to near-human levels. And the blood loss... even creatures like Anna had limits.

"Save your strength," he murmured, tearing strips from his already ruined shirt to bind the worst of her wounds. "We need to move before they come back."

Anna's eyes flickered open at the sound of his voice, heterochromatic irises focusing with visible effort. Recognition dawned slowly, her cracked lips parting in what might have been relief or despair.

"Alexander," she breathed, the word carrying a weight he couldn't decipher. Then her eyes rolled back, consciousness fleeing as her body surrendered to the combined assault of silver, blood loss, and trauma.

Alexander gathered her limp form into his arms, his own injuries screaming in protest. She weighed less than she should, as though the encounter had burned away substance along with strength. He cradled her against his chest, feeling the faint flutter of her heart against his broken ribs, a rhythm too slow and unsteady for comfort.

"Hold on," he whispered into her matted hair. "Just hold on."

He turned toward the exit tunnel, mind already mapping the shortest route to the one person in Slade who might save her—and by extension, their mission. The calculation engine plans could wait. Without Anna's knowledge of the Spire's defenses, they were useless anyway. One impossible task at a time. First, survival. Then vengeance.

Alexander took the first step of many, each one a fresh testament to his refusal to surrender to either pain or failure. The darkness ahead promised only more suffering, but somewhere beyond it lay a chance, however slim a chance of salvation.

The sewers beneath Old Slade ran like festering veins through the city's diseased heart, carrying waste both physical and metaphorical away from Registry-approved districts. Alexander descended through a maintenance shaft, each rung of the corroded ladder threatening to give way beneath the combined weight of his and Anna's bodies. The stench hit him like a physical force human excrement, industrial runoff, and the distinctive sweet-rot smell of bodies decomposing in forgotten corners. He adjusted Anna's limp form across his shoulders, her blood seeping through his tattered shirt and mingling with his own. Down here, far below Registry sensors and patrol routes, they were just two more pieces of human wreckage being flushed away by a system that had deemed them disposable.

His boots splashed into ankle-deep filth at the bottom of the shaft. The main channel stretched before him, its curved ceiling barely visible in the wan light filtering through periodic grates far overhead. Alexander had mapped these passages years ago, during his early days hunting registry enforcers. The memory of those simpler missions, straightforward assassination rather than world-altering sabotage he was attempting now, twisted his mouth into a grim smile that reopened his split lip.

"Just a few miles," he whispered to Anna's unconscious form, though whether to reassure her or himself remained unclear.

He shifted her weight into a fireman's carry that kept her head above the sewage while distributing her mass more evenly across his damaged frame. Each step sent daggers of pain through his broken ribs, the bones grinding against each other with nauseating precision. Alexander focused on his breathing shallow sips of the fetid air, carefully timed between footfalls to minimize agony.

The tunnel curved and branched, its geography familiar yet treacherous. Alexander tracked his route by counting junction markers, faded numerals stenciled onto the brick walls decades or centuries ago. Three lefts, a right at the major intersection beneath what had once been the financial district, then straight for half a mile where the ceiling lowered to force him into a stooped position that sent fresh waves of torture through his spine.

Anna stirred against him, a faint moan escaping her lips as the movement jostled her silver-poisoned wounds. Her skin burned with unnatural heat where it pressed against his neck, her body fighting the toxic metal with every resource at its disposal. Without treatment, even her vampire constitution would eventually succumb. Alexander increased his pace despite the protests of his own failing body.

The sound reached him before the sight, a rhythmic splashing that echoed off the curved walls, approaching from a side tunnel ahead. Alexander froze, straining his ears to identify the source. Too regular for rats, too heavy for the feral cats that sometimes hunted them. Human. Or something that had once been human.

He pressed himself against the wall, easing Anna down into the shallow alcove formed by a maintenance access point. The footsteps grew louder, accompanied now by the distinctive metallic click of Registry-issue reinforced boots. A patrol, down here where they rarely ventured. The market raid had them searching every corner of the undercity.

Alexander reached for a weapon that wasn't there, his empty holster, a stark reminder of his vulnerability. If discovered, he could neither fight effectively nor flee while carrying Anna. They would both die in this filth, their mission unfinished, the Dragon's plans unopposed.

The patrol passed the junction just ahead, the beam of their electric torches sweeping across the opposite wall. Three enforcers, moving with the mechanical precision of those who feared punishment for inadequate thoroughness. Their voices echoed in the enclosed space.

"Nothing down here but rats and shit."

"Orders are orders. Check every tunnel, every alcove."

"The sooner we finish, the sooner we can return to breathable air."

Alexander pressed deeper into the alcove, one hand covering Anna's mouth in case consciousness returned at this most inopportune moment and the other on his revolver. The torch beams swung toward their hiding place, light creeping along the curved ceiling. He held his breath, time stretching like hot metal pulled to breaking.

The beams moved on. The footsteps receded. Alexander released the breath he'd been holding, the exhale carrying a small prayer of thanks to deities he no longer believed in.

The journey resumed with increased urgency. Alexander calculated the patrol's route, adjusting his own to avoid potential intersections. This added precious minutes to their travel time, but confrontation would add hours or eternity. He chose the lesser cost.

They emerged from the sewers through a collapsed drainage culvert that opened into the basement of a bombed-out tenement building. The Gray Zone—a district claimed by neither the Registry nor the rebel factions that occasionally contested its authority. Here, neutrality was maintained through strategic weakness rather than strength; the area simply wasn't worth the resources required to control it.

Alexander navigated through the skeletal remains of what had once been homes. Collapsed staircases forced detours through holes in walls, each transition requiring him to shift Anna's deadweight in ways that threatened his precarious balance. Twice he stumbled, falling to one knee and biting through his already damaged lip to prevent a cry of pain that might attract unwanted attention.

In his arms, Anna stirred again. Her eyes flickered open, unfocused and glazed with fever. "Alexander," she whispered, her voice a broken shadow of its usual imperious tone. "The plans..."

"Shh," he soothed, continuing his careful progress through the urban ruin. "Save your strength."

Her hand clutched weakly at his shirt. "My father... knows we're coming..." Her eyes rolled back as consciousness fled once more, but the warning had been delivered. Somehow, the Dragon had learned of their planned assault on the Spire. The already suicidal mission had just become even more impossible.

Mariana Florescu's clinic occupied what had once been a luxury hotel, its marble facade now pockmarked with artillery scars from conflicts long concluded. Steel shutters covered the windows, and the entrance was reinforced with salvaged armor plating. No sign announced its purpose; those who needed Mariana's services already knew where to find her. Those who didn't were better kept ignorant of her existence.

Alexander approached the service entrance at the building's rear, a heavy iron door monitored by a brass camera apparatus that swiveled to track his movement. He stood in its field of vision, Anna's broken form clearly visible in his arms.

"I need Mariana," he called, voice cracking with exhaustion and thirst. "It's Alexander Stirling. I have payment."

The camera whirred, lens extending to examine them more closely. A moment later, the door unlocked with the heavy thunk of retreating bolts. Alexander shouldered it open, stepping into a narrow corridor lit by oil lamps that cast dancing shadows on walls lined with anatomical diagrams, some human, some distinctly not.

A young assistant in a bloodstained apron appeared from a side room, eyes widening at the sight of them. Without a word, he motioned for Alexander to follow, leading them deeper into the converted hotel. The sounds of medical equipment hissing steam valves, clicking mechanical timers, the wet suction of pumps moving fluids grew louder as they approached the central treatment area.

Mariana Florescu stood beside an operating table; her hands submerged in a basin of glowing blue liquid. She looked up as they entered, her serene face betraying no surprise at their condition. Her chestnut hair was pulled back in a severe bun, streaked with premature silver that caught the lamplight. Her eyes, a shade of green too vivid to be entirely natural assessed them with clinical detachment.

"The Last Venator," she said, her voice carrying the faint accent of lands far beyond Slade's walls. "And Dracula's rebellious daughter. What interesting company you keep these days, Alexander."

"She's dying," Alexander replied, cutting through pleasantries with the directness of desperation. "Silver poisoning, blood loss, multiple traumatic injuries."

Mariana dried her hands on a towel, approaching them with measured steps. Her fingers, marked with faint alchemical burns, gently probed Anna's wounds. "Yes, she is. The silver has penetrated deeply, and her healing abilities are suppressed. Without intervention, she has hours at most."

"Can you save her?"

A smile crossed Mariana's lips—not cruel, but not entirely kind either. "I can. My methods could have her healed within a day, perhaps less. But my services require compensation, Alexander. You know this."

Alexander shifted Anna's weight, his muscles trembling with fatigue. "Name your price. I have gold, weapons—"

"Information," Mariana interrupted, her eyes never leaving Anna's damaged face. "About your mission. The real purpose behind this suicide run against the Dragon. What you hope to accomplish by storming the Black Spire during the conclave."

Alexander's jaw tightened. The mission's details were their only advantage the element of surprise already compromised according to Anna's fevered warning. To reveal more could doom them entirely. But without Anna's knowledge of the Spire's defenses, the mission was already failed.

"Treatment first," he countered. "Information after I see results."

Mariana considered this, head tilted slightly like a predator assessing prey. Finally, she nodded. "Agreed. But understand me clearly, Alexander: if your information proves... unsatisfying, there are ways to reverse healing. Even vampire healing."

She gestured to her assistants, who rushed forward with a stretcher. "Bring her to the main theater. Prepare the silver extraction apparatus and three units of mixed blood. We begin immediately."

As they took Anna from his arms, Alexander felt a curious emptiness—as though something essential had been removed along with her weight. He watched them carry her away, her pale face peaceful in unconsciousness, unaware that her salvation might come at the cost of their mission's secrecy.

"Rest and drink" Mariana told him, gesturing to a side room equipped with a simple cot. "You're no use to anyone in your current state. We'll discuss payment when you can speak without swaying on your feet."

Alexander nodded, the room already spinning around him as adrenaline ebbed and the full impact of his injuries reclaimed his awareness. The cot beckoned, promising temporary escape from pain and decision. Tomorrow would bring choices with consequences that stretched far beyond his own survival but tomorrow was not yet here, and his body had reached its limit.

Alexander awoke to the muted hiss of steam valves and the rhythmic clicking of mechanical timers. Pain still radiated from his ribs and chemical burns, but the sharp edge had dulled to a manageable throb. Mariana's assistants had treated him while he slept, bandages wrapped his torso with professional precision, and the raw patches of skin where the blood-boiling vapor had burned deepest now glistened with a medicinal salve that smelled of copper and crushed herbs. He lay still for a moment, cataloging improvements and lingering damage with a venator's practiced detachment. Not fully healed, but functional. Capable of continuing the mission, assuming Anna had survived Mariana's treatments, and the Dragon hadn't already dismantled their plans entirely.

The room swam briefly as he sat up, blood rushing from his head. Late afternoon light filtered through narrow slits in the steel shutters, casting prison-bar shadows across the simple cot and bare floor. His clothing had been removed, replaced with loose cotton trousers and nothing else. His weapons, what few, remained after the mine incident, were nowhere to be seen.

Alexander pulled himself upright, testing each muscle group methodically. His body responded with the grudging cooperation of machinery kept running beyond its intended lifespan. Good enough. It would have to be.

He found his boots beside the cot, cleaned of sewer filth and partially repaired. His coat or what remained of it hung from a hook near the door, the tears roughly stitched, and bloodstains mostly removed. No sign of his other possessions. Typical of Mariana to keep potential leverage close at hand.

The corridor outside his room bustled with quiet efficiency, the assistants in blood-spattered aprons moved between treatment rooms carrying instruments and medications, their faces bearing the flat effect of those who had seen too much suffering to register it consciously anymore. One nodded to Alexander, gesturing toward a set of double doors at the corridor's end without breaking stride.

The main treatment theater lay beyond those doors, a cavernous space that had once been the hotel's grand ballroom. Now it housed a bewildering array of medical equipment, some conventional, others clearly of Mariana's own design. Brass and copper pipes snaked along the walls, connecting pressurized tanks to distribution systems that fed a dozen different workstations. Glass containers of varying sizes held fluids in colors nature never intended, bubbling and circulating through elaborate filtration arrays.

At the room's center stood what could only be described as a mechanical sarcophagus a human-sized brass chamber connected to pulsing tubes and monitoring devices, its transparent viewing panel revealing the occupant within. Anna lay suspended in luminescent blue fluid, her eyes closed, her shredded arm now held together by an intricate framework of thin metal rods and alchemical sutures. The silver bullet wounds across her torso had been opened wider, surrounded by brass extraction cups that drew darkened fluid away from the injuries. Her skin, normally pale, had taken on the alabaster sheen of porcelain, making her appear more statue than living creature.

"Impressive, isn't it?" Mariana's voice came from behind him, startling Alexander despite his trained reflexes. She moved to stand beside him, her eyes fixed on the healing chamber. "Vampire physiology responds remarkably well to the right combination of alchemical stimulants and mechanical assistance. The silver is being drawn out molecule by molecule. Another few hours and she'll be stronger than before the injuries occurred."

Alexander studied the unconscious vampire's face, searching for signs of discomfort or awareness. "And the cost for this miracle?"

"Remains as stated." Mariana's tone carried the finality of a contract already signed. "Information, Alexander. The truth about what you and the Dragon's daughter plan to accomplish at the Black Spire conclave."

Alexander's gaze never left Anna's suspended form. How much could he reveal without endangering what remained of their mission? The calculation engine plans were gone, presumed stolen by Niko, but their objective remained unchanged kill the Dragon before he could implement his new system of control. Without those plans, however, they lacked crucial intelligence on the device's weaknesses, making their task even more impossible than before.

"I need to know she'll recover completely," he countered, buying time to consider his options. "No hidden complications from your treatment."

Mariana's lips curved in a smile that contained neither warmth nor malice just merely professional satisfaction. "See for yourself. Her belongings are there." She nodded toward a side table where Anna's effects had been laid out with forensic precision.

Alexander approached the table cautiously, aware of Mariana watching his every move. Anna's clothing had been cut away during treatment, but her other possessions remained intact: the ward-walking charm stolen from Krav, a silver-bladed dagger with glyphs etched along its length, and most interestingly, a small leather journal bound with what appeared to be human skin.

He hesitated, then opened the journal, justifying the invasion of privacy as necessary intelligence gathering. The pages contained diagrams and notes in Anna's elegant hand—most concerning the Black Spire's defenses, information they had already discussed. But the final pages held something new: detailed plans for the aftermath of Dracula's death, a power structure with Anna at its center, controlling a coalition of younger vampire nobles committed to a different relationship with humanity. Not freedom, precisely, but a more sustainable form of coexistence. Humans would still be managed, still provide blood, but without the brutal efficiency of the calculation engine. A negotiated peace rather than total subjugation.

Alexander closed the journal, his mind racing. Anna had never mentioned these plans during their preparations. She had presented their mission as simple vengeance of hers against a father who had used and controlled her, his against the creature who had ordered his family's execution. This was something else entirely: revolution disguised as assassination.

"She's waking," Mariana observed, moving to the control panel beside the healing chamber. Valves hissed as she adjusted pressures and chemical flows, the blue fluid beginning to drain from around Anna's body.

Anna's eyes opened slowly, focusing first on Alexander, then darting to Mariana with a flash of calculation that belied her weakened state. The viewing panel slid open as the last of the fluid drained away, leaving her suspended in the framework of medical apparatus.

"How long?" she asked, voice raspy from disuse.

"Eighteen hours," Mariana replied, checking monitors with clinical efficiency. "The silver poisoning was extensive. You would have died without intervention."

Anna's gaze returned to Alexander, a question in her heterochromatic eyes. "The plans?"

"Gone," he confirmed. "Niko took them during the confusion."

Something flashed across Anna's face not surprise, but a cold anger quickly masked. "Then we proceed without them. The calculation engine must still be destroyed, whatever the cost."

"Is that all you intend?" Alexander asked, watching her reaction carefully. "Just destruction?"

Anna held his gaze, understanding the implication instantly. "You read my journal."

"I needed to know what I'm fighting for. What I'm potentially dying for."

She was silent for a moment, the only sound the mechanical whir of apparatus as Mariana's assistants began disconnecting her from the healing chamber. Finally, she spoke, her voice low but steady.

"My father's reign must end. What follows... must be different. The cycle can't continue."

Before Alexander could respond, Mariana interjected, her tone conversational despite the tension hanging between her patients. "So, the Last Venator and the Dragon's daughter plan to assassinate Dracula during the conclave, destroy his calculation engine, and install a new regime with modified human-vampire relations." She shook her head, a small smile playing at her lips. "Ambitious. Nearly impossible. And exactly as Victor and Cassandra described when they contacted me three days ago."

Alexander's head snapped toward her, muscles tensing despite his injuries. "What?"

"Did you think you were operating in a vacuum, Alexander?" Mariana raised an eyebrow. "Victor has been planning ways to kill the dragon since the betrayal. Cassandra's been manufacturing specialized weapons and equipment for months knowing that you would one day attempt the impossible. They needed to ensure you would have medical support when the inevitable occurred." She gestured to their injuries. "As it has."

Anna struggled to sit upright, her newly healed arm still stiff but functional. "Then why demand information as payment? Why the pretense?"

"Because I needed to confirm your commitment," Mariana replied simply. "Plans change. Alliances shift. I needed to hear from you directly that the mission remains, despite setbacks." Her gaze sharpened. "The Registry controls medicine, blood distribution, life itself. The calculation engine would make that control absolute, eliminate what little autonomy remains for healers like myself. I have practical reasons for wanting it destroyed."

She moved to a cabinet on the far wall, unlocking it with a key she wore around her neck. From within, she withdrew a wooden case inscribed with alchemical symbols. "These are healing potions—my finest work. Accelerated tissue regeneration, pain suppression, toxin neutralization. They will keep you functional regardless of what you encounter at the Spire."

Alexander accepted the case, feeling the weight of dozens of glass vials within. "Your neutrality is well-known, Mariana. This is an unusual position for you to take."

"Neutrality is a luxury purchased through careful balance," she replied, her eyes momentarily shifting color in the chamber's artificial light. "When one side threatens to eliminate all others, balance becomes impossible. Self-preservation requires... adaptation."

Anna slid from the healing chamber, testing her repaired limbs with cautious movements. Her naked form bore the marks of Mariana's work, thin silver scars where bullets had been extracted, the faint outline of mechanical sutures where her arm had been reconstructed. She dressed quickly in the clean clothes provided, her movements growing more fluid with each passing minute as her vampire physiology incorporated the treatments.

"We've lost time," she said, buckling the silver dagger at her waist. "The conclave begins tomorrow night. Without the airship—"

"Your transportation concerns are addressed," Mariana interrupted. "Another of Victor's arrangements. A cargo dirigible will be waiting at the eastern loading docks at midnight. Registry inspection seals are already forged."

Alexander studied Mariana's face, searching for signs of deception or hidden agenda. He found only the composed mask of a survivor who had calculated odds and chosen sides accordingly. Not an ally, precisely, but aligned with their interests for the moment. In Old Slade, that was often the closest thing to friendship one could hope for.

"We'll need weapons," he said, thinking of his empty holsters and the challenges that awaited at the Spire.

Mariana smiled a genuine expression this time, touched with something almost like affection. "Already arranged, Alexander. Victor may be paranoid, but his contingency planning is unmatched. Everything you need will be aboard the dirigible."

She handed him a small brass key. "The eastern service exit will take you through the underground markets without Registry interference. My people have cleared the path." Her expression grew serious. "What you attempt may fail. The Dragon has survived centuries of assassination attempts. But if you succeed..."

"If we succeed, what follows will be different," Anna finished, retrieving her journal and the ward-walking charm. "For everyone."

Alexander pocketed the healing potions, mind already plotting their route to the loading docks. The mission parameters had shifted, their resources diminished, but the objective remained unchanged. Kill the Dragon. Destroy the calculation engine. Prevent the final subjugation of humanity. And now, apparently, usher in Anna's new vision for vampire-human relations, a detail she had conveniently omitted during their planning.

Trust remained a luxury he couldn't afford, even with his supposed ally. But common purpose would have to suffice. For now.

"Dawn approaches," Mariana observed, glancing toward the shuttered windows. "Rest here until nightfall. Conserve your strength for what comes next."

As she left them alone in the treatment chamber, Alexander turned to Anna, questions burning in his throat. But she spoke first, her eyes holding his with uncharacteristic directness.

"When this is done, we will talk of what follows," she said. "But first, we must survive the Spire. First, my father must die."

On that point, at least, they remained in perfect accord. Alexander nodded, sealing their pact anew. Tomorrow night, they would either change the world or die in an attempt. Neither outcome permitted half measures or divided focus.

The Dragon awaited, and with him, the future of two species balanced on the edge of a blade.

Sin's Of A Father

Night had fallen over Old Slade, the darkness a welcome shroud as Alexander and Anna slipped from Mariana's clinic through the eastern service exit. The brass key turned smoothly in the lock, mechanisms clicking with precision as the door swung open to reveal a narrow passage lit by sputtering gas lamps that cast long shadows across the damp brick walls. Alexander's ribs still ached beneath the fresh bandages, but Mariana's healing potions dulled the worst of the pain to a manageable throb. Beside him, Anna moved with renewed strength, her reconstructed arm fluid and graceful once more, though the faint silver scars that mapped her recent wounds still gleamed in the lamplight when she turned just so.

"Two hours until midnight," Alexander murmured, checking the brass chronometer Victor had given him years ago. The device had survived the sewers, the mine collapse, and countless other brushes with destruction. Like its owner, it refused to die easily.

They descended through a series of maintenance tunnels that connected Mariana's domain to the underground markets. Here, the passages were deliberately confusing, built to frustrate Registry patrols and provide multiple escape routes for those who lived in the shadows of vampire rule. Steam hissed from corroded pipes overhead, mixing with the perpetual fog of human breath and machinery to create a thick haze that clung to skin and clothing like a second skin.

Anna moved with practiced ease through the labyrinth, her aristocratic bearing incongruous in these grimy surroundings. She paused at a junction, head tilted as she listened for sounds beyond human hearing.

"Registry checkpoint ahead," she whispered. "We'll need to take the low road."

The "low road" proved to be a crawlspace beneath the main tunnel, so narrow that Alexander's shoulders scraped the rough stone on either side as he inched forward on his elbows. The space smelled of mold and human waste, the floor slick with substances he preferred not to identify. Anna followed behind him, her breathing unnaturally controlled, without the labored quality that marked his own.

When they emerged on the far side of the checkpoint, she helped him to his feet with a strength that belied her slender frame. For a moment, she didn't release his hand, her fingers cool against his skin.

"I never thanked you," she said, eyes fixed on some middle distance. "For carrying me from the mine. For taking me to Mariana when you could have left me to die."

Alexander shrugged, uncomfortable with the gratitude. "The mission needs you. Your knowledge of the Spire—"

"Is that all?" Her tone was light, but something vulnerable flickered across her face, there and gone so quickly he might have imagined it.

He didn't answer, unsure what response she sought. After a moment, Anna continued walking, leading them deeper into the undercity's twisted heart. They passed through abandoned storerooms filled with rotting crates, ancient machinery workshops where rusted tools still waited for hands that had turned into dust centuries ago and collapsed living quarters where personal effects lay scattered as if their owners might return at any moment.

"I was nine when my father first beat me to the edge of death," Anna said suddenly, her voice so soft Alexander almost missed the words. She didn't turn to look at him, her steps never faltering as she navigated the treacherous footing. "I had shown kindness to a human servant, a child younger than myself who had spilled wine on the dining room floor. I intervened when the overseer moved to whip her."

Alexander remained silent, sensing that interruption might close this unexpected window into Anna's past.

"My father watched the entire incident, then summoned me to his private chambers afterward. He explained that kindness was weakness, that humans were cattle, and that my behavior reflected poorly on our bloodline." Her voice remained steady, but her fingers brushed unconsciously against her throat, tracing scars visible only in memory. "The beating lasted hours. He was methodical, breaking bones in a specific sequence to maximize pain while ensuring I remained conscious. When my regenerative abilities began to heal the damage, he would start again, targeting fresh areas."

They ducked through a partially collapsed doorway into what had once been a wine cellar, its empty racks stretching into darkness. Anna's pale skin seemed to glow in the weak light of Alexander's lantern, her eyes distant with remembrance.

"That was merely the first lesson," she continued. "There were hundreds more over the last 50 years. Lessons in obedience, in cruelty, in the proper hierarchy of things." Her lips twisted in a smile that contained no humor. "When physical pain proved insufficient, he found other methods."

Alexander's throat tightened, the implications clear enough. "You don't need to—"

"But I do," she interrupted, turning to face him fully. "You need to understand what we face. My father isn't merely a tyrant; he's a creature who has perfected control through centuries of practice. He loaned me to other nobles when it served his political purposes—my body, my blood, my dignity all commodities to be traded for advantage."

Her words hung in the dank air between them, heavy with centuries of pain and rage. Alexander had hunted vampires his entire adult life, had witnessed their cruelty firsthand when they slaughtered his family, but the cold calculation of Dracula's abuse struck him differently. This wasn't the mindless bloodlust he'd encountered in lesser vampires; this was something more insidious, a power wielded with precision to break and reshape another being.

They resumed walking, the silence now charged with unspoken horrors. Anna led them through a maintenance shaft that angled steadily upward, bringing them closer to the surface and the docks beyond.

"The worst part," she said after several minutes, "isn't the pain or the humiliation. It's fighting what he tried to make me become." She paused, fingers trailing along the rough stone wall. "Vampirism brings certain... hungers. The need for blood is only the most basic. There's a desire for dominance, for power over others, a predatory instinct that whispers constantly in the back of the mind."

Alexander had seen those instincts unleashed in combat; he had witnessed Anna's transformation from controlled aristocrat to something feral and lethal in moments of danger. The memory of her tearing through Registry troopers in the alley flashed through his mind, the inhuman grace of her movements, the savage efficiency of her attacks.

"My father embraced these aspects of our nature, refined them into a philosophy of rule," she continued. "He taught me that giving in to these impulses was our birthright, our evolutionary advantage over the 'lesser species.' For decades, I believed him. I..." Her voice faltered for the first time. "I did things to humans that I cannot speak of without disgust. Things that pleased him, that earned his rare approval."

They reached a ladder that led upward to a street-level grate. Alexander tested the rungs, finding them solid despite their apparent age. Anna remained at the bottom, looking up at him with eyes that held centuries of complicated pain.

"Then what changed?" he asked, the question slipping out before he could consider its wisdom.

"I met a human who didn't fear me," she replied simply. "A woman in my father's household who looked at me not as predator or prey, but as a person capable of choice. She showed me kindness without expectation, spoke to me as an equal. My father discovered our friendship and had her executed while I watched just another lesson in the proper order of things."

Anna ascended the ladder with fluid grace, brushing past Alexander to lift the grate. Night air, thick with industrial smoke and the briny scent of the river docks, poured down through the opening.

"That was the moment I began planning his destruction," she whispered, her face illuminated from below by Alexander's lantern, throwing her features into sharp relief. "Not for vengeance, though God knows I crave it, but because he represents a system that must end if either of our species is to have any future worth claiming."

She climbed through the opening, then reached down to help Alexander navigate the final rungs with his injured ribs. They emerged in an alley between abandoned warehouses, the eastern dockyard visible at the street's end a forest of loading cranes and mooring towers silhouetted against the night sky. And there, exactly as Mariana had promised, a cargo dirigible waited, its brass hull gleaming dully in the glow of the dock's few functioning lamps.

Anna's hand lingered on Alexander's arm, her touch light but insistent. "Now you know what we face," she said. "Not just a monster, but the architect of monstrosities that not even nightmares can create."

Alexander met her gaze, seeing for the first time the weight she carried decades of abuse transformed into purpose, into a vision of something different for both their kinds. Whether that vision would prove better than what came before remained to be seen. But in this moment, with the final confrontation just hours away, the truth of her pain was enough to cement their alliance anew.

The cargo dirigible loomed before them; its elongated hull suspended beneath a massive gas envelope reinforced with a latticework of brass supports that gleamed dully in the dock's sparse lighting. Unlike the sleek Scout airship they'd stolen from Carmilla's manor, this vessel was built for utility rather than speed – a converted freight hauler with its registry markings crudely painted over and replaced with commercial identifiers. Alexander eyed the craft with professional assessment, noting the reinforced gondola and the tell-tale bulges along the hull that suggested hidden weapon ports. Victor's preparations were thorough, as always.

A lone dockhand waited beside the mooring line, his face obscured by a heavy hood. He nodded once at their approach, then gestured toward the boarding ramp without speaking. The man's silence spoke volumes he was another one of Victor's agents, paid well enough to see nothing and remember less.

"We have one hour before the midnight patrol makes its rounds," Anna murmured as they ascended the ramp. "They'll check registrations, even for authorized vessels."

The dirigible's interior surprised Alexander with its spaciousness. The main cargo hold had been converted into an operations center, with maps of the Black Spire and surrounding districts pinned to portable bulletin boards. Weapons crates lined one wall, their lids already unlatched to reveal an arsenal that would make even the most hardened Registry officer blanch. Alexander ran his fingers over a custom-built revolver he recognized immediately – one of Cassie's special designs, with chambers that could accommodate multiple ammunition types.

"Six silver-core rounds with tungsten jackets," he noted, checking the accompanying ammunition box. "Armor-piercing incendiaries. Blood-boiler capsules." He glanced at Anna, who was examining a slender rifle with similar appreciation. "Victor and Cassie wasn't taking any chances."

"Or perhaps he simply believes in our mission more than we realized," she replied, her tone thoughtful as she lifted a sealed packet labeled with her name. Inside was a set of lightweight armor designed specifically for her frame – reinforced leather with strategic metal plating over vital areas, all treated with alchemical compounds to resist both conventional weapons and more esoteric attacks.

Alexander found a similar package with his own gear, along with medical supplies that complemented Mariana's potions. As he sorted through the equipment, arranging it in order of priority for the coming assault, his mind kept returning to Anna's journal and the vision she'd concealed from him until now.

"In your journal," he said finally, setting down a box of ammunition to face her directly, "you outlined plans for after your father's death. A coalition of younger nobles, with you at its center."

Anna stilled, her hands pausing in their examination of a set of throwing knives. She didn't appear surprised by his knowledge – she'd acknowledged at Mariana's clinic that he'd read her private thoughts – but something guarded entered her expression, nonetheless.

"Yes," she said simply. "The Dragon's death will create a power vacuum. Nature abhors such things. Without a plan to fill it, the resulting chaos would likely make conditions worse for humans, not better."

"You never mentioned these plans during our preparations."

She set the knives down with deliberate care. "Would you have trusted me if I had? A vampire seeking to rule over other vampires, and by extension, over humans?"

Alexander didn't answer immediately. The truth was complicated. He'd partnered with Anna for her knowledge of the Spire and her personal vendetta against Dracula, which aligned with his own mission of vengeance. The idea that she sought not just the Dragon's death but also his throne albeit with different methods raised questions he'd conveniently avoided until now.

"Tell me about this coalition," he said instead. "These younger nobles who would follow you."

Anna moved to the operations table, adjusting one of the Spire maps to reveal a secondary chart beneath a hierarchy of vampire noble houses, with notes on their politics and loyalties. "There are those among the younger generation who see the unsustainability of my father's methods," she explained. "The Registry's brutality, the calculation engine's purpose – these aren't just moral failings but practical ones. A system that treats humans as nothing more than cattle."

Alexander leaned against the cold wall of the chamber, watching Anna test her newly healed arm. The limb moved with the fluid grace of expensive clockwork, each motion precisely calibrated as she flexed her fingers and rotated her wrist. Silver scars traced patterns across her pale skin where bullets had torn through flesh and where Mariana's instruments had extracted them. He studied her with the detached focus of a hunter assessing both ally and potential threat, the weight of her journal's revelations settling like lead in his gut. A new regime. Modified human-vampire relations. Anna at its center. Not freedom for humanity, but a different kind of cage one she considered more humane.

"When would you have told me about the plans for how things would be governed? Alexander asked

Anna's movements paused, her eyes finding his with that unnerving directness that reminded him she was not human, despite her appearance. "Eventually. When the time was right."

"When would that have been? After I'd helped you kill your father? After we'd destroyed the calculation engine?" Alexander pushed away from the wall, anger flaring sudden and hot. "Or perhaps after you'd installed yourself as the new Dragon?"

"Not the Dragon." Her voice remained steady, but he caught the slight tightening around her eyes. "Something different."

"Different how? Your journal speaks of humans still providing blood, still being 'managed.' How is that not just exchanging one tyrant for another?"

Anna sighed, rolling down the sleeve of her borrowed shirt to cover the silver scars. "You think in absolutes, Alexander. Freedom or slavery. Good or evil. The world has never been so simple."

"Explain it to me, then." He moved closer, close enough to see the slight mismatch in her heterochromatic eyes—one brown with hints of crimson, the other a blue so dark it bordered on black. "Make me understand how your vision differs from your father's reign. Because I never had freedom. My life has been constant misery trying to survive and destroy those who snuffed out my family."

She met his gaze without flinching. "My father sees humans as cattle—resources to be drained efficiently until they're useless, then discarded. The calculation engine would perfect that system, reducing humans to numbers in a ledger, their worth measured only in blood quality and obedience metrics."

"And you?"

"I see potential for balance. Vampires need blood to survive—that's biological necessity, not cruelty. But the taking doesn't need to be exploitative. It can be an exchange. Protection, medical care, technology all provided to human communities in return for voluntary donations."

Alexander's laugh was sharp and humorless. "Voluntary. Under a vampire regime. Those words don't belong together."

"They can." Anna's voice hardened. "They must. The alternative is extinction—either yours or ours. If yours goes extinct then so does mine. My father's system is unsustainable. It breeds resistance, wastes resources on control mechanisms, and ultimately fails. The calculation engine is his attempt to forestall the inevitable collapse, but it will only accelerate it."

Alexander turned away, pacing the small confines of the chamber. The glass vials in Mariana's case clinked softly with each step, reminding him of the immediate mission ahead. The Dragon. The Spire. The calculation engine. Those targets remained clear, regardless of what might follow.

"You've lived among humans," Anna continued, softer now. "You've seen how they adapt, how they build communities even under Registry control. Imagine those communities protected rather than exploited. Imagine blood donation as taxation—regulated, limited, with benefits in return."

"I've seen Registry 'taxation,'" Alexander replied, the memory of his family's execution flashing unbidden across his mind. "I've seen what happens to those who resist."

"I'm not my father." The words came out clipped, precise, edged with centuries of resentment. "I've been his prisoner as much as any human. Do you think I enjoyed watching him drain children to prove points about Registry authority? Do you think I approve of the venator extermination, the mass executions to instill fear?"

Alexander turned back to her, studying the genuine anger that tightened her features. "You participated. You fed."

"I survived." Her gaze didn't waver. "I survived so that one day I could end it. But ending it means replacing it with something sustainable, not just tearing it down and watching the world burn."

Silence fell between them, heavy with unspoken history and divergent visions of the future. Alexander found himself mentally tracing the scars visible on Anna's neck—old wounds that her vampire healing had never fully erased. He'd always assumed they were battle marks, but now he wondered if they were punishments from the Dragon himself.

"The younger nobles," he said finally. "Your journal mentioned a coalition."

Anna nodded. "Many have grown disillusioned with my father's methods. They see the waste, the inefficiency of ruling through terror. Some even have human... companions they value beyond mere feeding." A flicker of something crossed her face—pain, or perhaps memory. "Sustainability serves vampire interests too. A stable human population with decent living conditions provides better blood, less resistance, fewer security requirements."

"How utilitarian of you." Alexander's tone remained skeptical, but some of the edge had left it. "And the Blood Registry?"

"Modified. Voluntary registration in exchange for benefit medical care, education, housing. No more forced feeding, no more segregation into feeding districts."

Alexander snorted. "And those who choose not to register?"

"Free to live beyond vampire territories. The breaks would remain neutral ground—dangerous, but uncontrolled."

He considered this, turning the vision over in his mind like a strange artifact discovered in the ruins. Not freedom as he'd imagined during his years of hunting—not the complete destruction of vampire rule and the liberation of humanity. But perhaps... perhaps something that could reduce suffering, that could give humans space to breathe, to live with some dignity. The calculation engine would offer none of that; it would only perfect their subjugation.

"Why keep this from me?" he asked finally.

Anna's expression softened marginally. "Because your hatred for vampires is foundational to who you are, Alexander. It drives you. I needed that drive focused on my father, not distracted by debates about what comes after."

He absorbed this, recognizing the manipulation but also the pragmatism behind it. "And now?"

"Now we're hours away from attempting the impossible. My father dies tonight, or we do. The calculation engine burns, or the last hope for a different future dies with it." She stepped closer, close enough that he could smell the faint copper tang that hung around all vampires. "Our reasons for wanting him dead may differ, but the necessity remains absolute."

Alexander nodded slowly. His vengeance and her revolution required the same first step. Whether her vision was truly better than the current system was a question for tomorrow assuming they lived to see it.

"The dirigible leaves in less than an hour," he said, his decision made. "We should prepare."

Anna held his gaze a moment longer, then turned toward her remaining belongings. "Yes. We should."

The matter wasn't settled, not truly. Alexander still harbored deep reservations about any future with vampires in positions of power. But for now, the path forward remained clear: reach the Spire, kill the Dragon, destroy the calculation engine. Beyond that... beyond that lay questions too complex for this moment of preparation for war.

He retrieved his coat, feeling its weight lighter without the stolen plans, heavier with the knowledge of what truly hung in the balance tonight. Not just vengeance, not just Anna's revolution, but the shape of the world to come.

Alexander needed air decided to walk outside of the airship to get some. They were only a few minutes from releasing the tethers and attempting the impossible.

"Don't shoot. Please."

Niko emerged from the shadows of a derelict loading dock, his hands raised shoulder-high in the universal gesture of surrender. He looked worse than Alexander had ever seen him clothes torn and stained with what might have been blood, his face sporting a fresh bruise that had swollen his left eye nearly shut. The smuggler's usual cocky demeanor had vanished, replaced by something Alexander barely recognized: genuine fear.

"Give me one reason I shouldn't put a bullet between your eyes," Alexander growled, revolver aimed steadily at Niko's forehead.

"Because I brought these back." Niko slowly lowered one hand to his jacket movements telegraphed with exaggerated care. He withdrew a bundle of papers, their edges charred and stained but unmistakable the calculation engine plans stolen during the mine collapse.

Alexander's finger tightened on the trigger. "Throwing away the price on your betrayal won't save you."

"I deserve that," Niko said, his voice lacking its usual sardonic edge. "I deserve worse. But hear me out before you pull that trigger."

Anna stepped out, her posture relaxed in a way that Alexander knew meant she was ready to strike with lethal force if necessary. "Make it quick," she said. "We have an appointment to keep."

Niko swallowed visibly. "I sold you out. Both of you. Took the plans thinking I'd auction them to the highest bidder—Registry, resistance, whoever paid best." He gestured to his battered face. "Turns out your information had too many interested parties. Got jumped by Registry enforcers and resistance fighters within an hour of each other. Barely escaped with my life."

"And you expect sympathy?" Alexander's aim didn't waver.

"No. I expect nothing." Niko's voice cracked slightly. "But I got a look at those plans, really looked at them while hiding in the sewers. I've seen some vile things in the breaks, but this—this is extinction dressed up as progress. This would be the end of everything, even for rats like me who survive in the cracks."

Alexander exchanged a glance with Anna, whose expression remained unreadable. "So, your conscience finally found you. How convenient."

"Not conscience. Self-preservation." Niko took a tentative step forward, stopping immediately when Alexander tensed. "There's no profit in the world the Dragon's building. No angles to play, no margins to exploit. Just perfect control." He held the papers out farther. "I could have disappeared with these. Could have run to the wastelands beyond Registry reach. Instead, I tracked you through three districts using contacts who'd spotted you heading for Mariana's clinic."

"Why?" Anna asked, her voice cool and measured.

"Because I want to help finish what we started. Because I'm a selfish bastard who wants to keep living in a world with enough chaos to make a living." A hint of Niko's old smirk surfaced, though it looked more like a grimace on his battered face. "And because I'd rather die helping take down the Dragon than live knowing I could have made a difference and ran instead."

Alexander's finger eased slightly on the trigger, though his aim remained true. The calculation engine plans were the missing piece they needed the detailed schematics of the device's core architecture, potential weaknesses, fail-safes. With them, their assault on the Spire gained precious percentage points of possibility.

"You're asking us to trust you again," Alexander said, the words tasting bitter. "After you stole from us once already."

"I'm not asking for trust. I'm offering service." Niko slowly lowered the plans to the ground and stepped back. "Use me, watch me, put a bullet in my head at the first sign of betrayal. But let me help undo what I nearly ruined."

Anna moved forward with vampire speed, snatching the plans from the ground before retreating to Alexander's side. She examined them briefly, then nodded.

"They're genuine. Undamaged in any meaningful way."

Alexander considered their options. Killing Niko would be satisfying just simple justice for betrayal. But another pair of hands, especially hands connected to the extensive network of contacts the smuggler maintained throughout Slade, could prove valuable in the chaos to come.

"We could use a distraction," Anna said, seeming to follow his thoughts. "The Spire will be heavily guarded during the conclave. Drawing forces away from the around the building to the main entrance would improve our chances significantly."

Niko nodded eagerly. "I know people. People who hate the Registry, who'd welcome any chance to bloody its nose. I could organize something maybe a riot, an attack on a collection center, something big enough to pull guards from the Spire."

Alexander finally lowered his weapon, though he kept it ready in his hand. "And why would these people follow you into Registry gunfire?"

"Because I'll pay them. Every coin I have left." Niko's expression hardened into something like resolve. "And because I'll be leading them myself."

The silence that followed was broken only by the distant sound of steam venting from industrial pipes. Alexander studied Niko's face, searching for signs of the deception he'd come to expect from the smuggler. Instead, he found a desperate sincerity that seemed foreign to the man's usual calculating demeanor.

"The southern approach to the Spire," Anna said finally. "The Registry maintains fewer guards there because of the defensive landscape. A significant disturbance, something that threatens to spread to the privileged districts would be enough to draw forces from all sectors, including the Spire itself."

Niko nodded. "I can make that happen. When?"

"Could you get it done and started in an hour? That would be just before we dropped in." Alexander said, the decision made. "We'll be entering from the north while your distraction pulls attention south."

"Casualties will be high," Anna warned, her tone matter of fact. "The Registry won't hesitate to use lethal force against rioters."

"I'll make that clear to everyone who joins. They won't be the only ones to cause casualties." Niko's hand drifted to a pouch at his belt. "And I'll make sure the payment reflects the risk."

Alexander stepped closer, close enough that Niko had to tilt his head back slightly to maintain eye contact. "If this is another betrayal another setup, I will find you and flay you. No matter how this ends tonight, no matter where you run. I will hunt you until one of us is dead."

"I believe you," Niko said quietly. "I've earned that and worse."

Alexander stepped back. "Then go. You have your mission. Make it count."

Niko nodded once, then turned and melted back into the shadows with the practiced ease of someone who had spent a lifetime navigating the margins of society. His footsteps faded quickly, leaving Alexander and Anna alone in the dank canal path.

"Can we trust him?" Alexander asked, already knowing the answer.

"Of course not," Anna replied, carefully securing the plans inside her coat. "But his fear is genuine it was strong enough that I could smell the pheromones, and fear is a more reliable motivator than loyalty ever was."

They resumed their journey toward the eastern docks, each step bringing them closer to the final confrontation. Alexander found himself wondering how many others like Niko were out there in the city. People who had glimpsed the calculation engine's true purpose and recoiled from the perfect order it promised. People who preferred the messy, dangerous freedom of the breaks to the sterile security of absolute control.

Perhaps that preference was the last, most human thing left in this broken world. And perhaps it would be enough to give their desperate mission the edge it needed to succeed.

The dirigible awaited its engine finally warmed up. The Dragon's hour approached. And somewhere in Old Slade, a traitor turned ally was gathering forces for one final act of redemption or betrayal.

The Iron Harvest

The dirigible cut through the night like a knife through dark water, its brass hull dulled to a matte finish by Cassie's specialized coating. Alexander peered through the small viewing port, watching as the towers of the Registry's sensor grid passed below them, their crimson warning lights dim and unaware of the intruders slipping through their blind spots. His broken ribs ached with each small turbulence, the pain a constant reminder of how close they'd come to failure already. The calculation engine plans sat heavy in Anna's coat pocket, their weight more psychological than physical, the final piece needed for their desperate gambit against the Dragon.

"Three minutes to descent point," the pilot called from the control cabin, his voice barely audible over the muffled thrumming of the engines. Victor had found them a veteran of the underground resistance, a man whose face had been partially replaced with brass fittings after a Registry raid left him half-dead. His mechanical eye whirred as it adjusted to the darkness, focusing on instruments that glowed with faint alchemical light.

Alexander turned from the viewport to where Anna stood checking her equipment. Her movements were precise, economical, betraying none of the tension that must surely grip her as they approached her father's domain. She secured the last of Cassie's stealth devices to her belt—small brass spheres that emitted a field designed to confuse both mechanical sensors and vampire senses.

"These will only work for twenty minutes once activated," Alexander reminded her, running through his own gear with methodical thoroughness. "After that, we're visible to anything with eyes or sensing equipment."

Anna didn't look up from her preparations. "Twenty minutes is sufficient to cross the outer perimeter and reach the ward boundary. Beyond that, this charm is our only protection."

Alexander checked Cassie's other gifts: phosphorous grenades that could temporarily blind even vampire vision; miniature steam-powered grappling hooks capable of piercing stone; and most precious of all, the specialized ammunition for his custom revolvers. Each bullet contained a complex alchemical core designed specifically to disrupt vampire physiology on contact. He loaded both weapons with practiced efficiency, despite the pain that flared through his bandaged ribs with each movement.

"There," Anna said suddenly, moving to his side at the viewport. She pointed toward the horizon where a dark shape rose against the night sky, blotting out stars like a hole torn in reality itself. "The Black Spire."

Alexander felt something cold slip down his spine as he took in the massive structure. Even at this distance, its scale was overwhelming, the central tower reaching up from a sprawling complex of buildings and walls like a skeletal finger pointing accusingly at the heavens. Sickly green lights pulsed at irregular intervals along its length, the glow casting the surrounding architecture in an unhealthy pallor.

"My childhood home," Anna added, her voice flat with carefully controlled emotion. "Though 'prison' would be more accurate."

The dirigible began its descent, engines throttling back to a whisper as they approached the drop zone. Alexander secured his coat, checking that Mariana's healing potions were safely stowed in inside pockets. The vials clinked softly against each other, their contents glowing faintly through the thick glass.

"Ready," he said, moving toward the cargo hatch where their descent equipment waited.

The pilot guided them into the shadow of a massive rock formation. One of many that dotted the blasted wasteland surrounding the Spire's domain. The dirigible hovered fifteen feet above the roof, its bulk concealed from casual observation by both the natural feature and Cassie's stealth coating.

"Deploying in five," the pilot announced. "Registry patrol schedule gives you eighteen minutes before the next aerial sweep."

Alexander gripped the descent line, securing its mechanical harness around his chest. The pain from his ribs intensified as the straps tightened, but he pushed the sensation away, focusing instead on the mission parameters. Anna finished activating the stealth devices, their brass casings now emitting a barely perceptible hum that made Alexander's skin prickle.

"After you," she said, gesturing to the open hatch.

He dropped first, the descent line playing out with a soft mechanical whir as counterweights controlled his fall. The roof rushed up to meet him. He released the harness at the last moment, rolling to absorb the impact despite his injuries. His ribs protesting angerly.

Anna followed moments later, her landing silent and graceful as a falling leaf. Above them, the dirigible's engines spooled up, carrying the craft back to a higher altitude where it would circle until their extraction signal or until it became clear no extraction would be needed.

"This way," Anna whispered, leading him across the broken roof toward the first ward that simmered in the moonlight.

They moved in silence, picking their way through a rooftop that seemed designed to inflict injury. Jagged rock formations erupted from the roof at irregular intervals. The air carried a metallic tang that coated Alexander's tongue with each breath, accompanied by an almost subliminal vibration that set his teeth on edge.

At the second roof edge, Anna knelt, producing the ward-walking charm they'd stolen from Krav's black market stall. In the pale moonlight, the amulet's components—tarnished silver and human bone—took on a sickly sheen, the central ivory chip seeming to absorb rather than reflect the available light.

"My father's defenses are layered," she explained, voice barely above a whisper. "Physical, mechanical, magical. This outer ward detects intention as much as physical presence. Anyone approaching with hostile thoughts toward the Dragon is detected instantly." She traced the central glyph with one pale finger. "The charm creates a bubble in the ward-fabric, space where intentions become... illegible to the detection system."

Alexander studied the barrier before them. To normal sight, it appeared as nothing more than a slight heat distortion in the air, but his venator training had equipped him to perceive the magical structures that most humans missed. To his enhanced vision, the ward revealed itself as a vast, shimmering curtain stretching in both directions until it vanished over the horizon. Runes and sigils pulsed within its substance, each one a different shade of sickly green, matching the lights that crawled up the distant Spire.

"How long will the effect last?" he asked, watching as Anna pressed the charm between her palms.

"Long enough to pass through. After that, we'll be within the perimeter, where different protections apply." She glanced up at him, her heterochromatic eyes reflecting the ward's unhealthy glow. "The sensation will be... unpleasant for you. For me, less so."

Before he could ask for clarification, Anna began to whisper words in a language that slithered unpleasantly against Alexander's eardrums. The charm between her palms began to glow, first with a dull red light that gradually shifted through the spectrum until it pulsed with the same sickly green as the ward itself.

With a final word that seemed to echo despite its softness, Anna thrust the charm forward toward the shimmering barrier. The effect was immediate and dramatic as a circular opening appeared in the ward, its edges rippling like disturbed water. Beyond the opening, the landscape appeared unchanged, but Alexander knew they were looking at the first step into the Dragon's domain.

"Now," Anna commanded, stepping through the portal without hesitation.

Alexander followed, and pain crashed through him like a physical blow. Every nerve in his body seemed to ignite simultaneously, while the air in his lungs crystallized into shards of ice. He staggered forward, feeling as though he were pushing through molasses that had been heated to just below boiling. His vision fragmented, each eye suddenly operating independently, showing him overlapping versions of reality that refused to align properly.

The crossing took perhaps three seconds of objective time, but to Alexander it stretched into a nightmarish eternity. When he finally stumbled through to the other side, he dropped to one knee, fighting the urge to vomit as his senses slowly realigned.

Anna stood watching him, her expression a mixture of sympathy and impatience. She had passed through the portal with no visible discomfort, her movements as fluid and controlled as ever.

"Vampire wards," she explained simply. "Designed to incapacitate humans while allowing my kind to pass freely. The charm protected you from detection but couldn't completely shield you from the physical effects."

Alexander forced himself upright, swallowing back the copper taste of blood where he'd bitten his cheek during the crossing. Behind them, the portal sealed itself with a sound like a sigh, leaving no trace of their passage.

"We're inside the interior perimeter now," Anna said, her gaze turning toward the peak of the Spire that loomed ever larger before them. "The first line of defense is breached."

Alexander checked his weapons and equipment, ensuring nothing had been damaged during the crossing. "And the next?"

Anna's lips curved in something too grim to be called a smile. "The next is where the real nightmares begin."

The rooftop garden of horrors stretched before them, a twisted mockery of nature that made Alexander's skin crawl. What had once been ordinary vegetation now writhed with unnatural life, trees fused with copper pipes and brass fittings that pulsed like veins, carrying some unknown fluid through their twisted trunks. Flowers bloomed with petals of thin-hammered metal, their centers spinning gears that clicked and whirred as they tracked movement. The ground beneath their feet was a patchwork of soil and metal plates, warm to the touch and occasionally shifting with mechanical purpose. Anna moved through this abomination with the wary familiarity of one revisiting a childhood nightmare.

"The Dragon's Garden," she whispered, gesturing toward a particularly monstrous growth that resembled a weeping willow, its branches tipped with hypodermic needles that dripped a phosphorescent green fluid. "My father's earliest experiments in melding the organic with the mechanical. These were the... successful ones."

Alexander ducked beneath a low-hanging vine threaded with copper wire, careful not to brush against its surface. Every instinct honed through years of venator training screamed danger at him. He studied the patterns of movement around them, noting how certain plants reacted to their proximity while others remained dormant.

"Pressure plates," he murmured, pointing to a section of ground ahead where metal discs were barely visible beneath a layer of loamy soil. "And those flowers—they're sensory arrays, aren't they?"

Anna nodded. "Motion detectors, heat sensors, even chemical analyzers that can identify individual scents. Follow exactly in my footsteps. The safe path changes weekly, but some constants remain from my time here."

Alexander matched her movements with precision, placing his boots in the exact indentations left by Anna's smaller feet. He retrieved a small device from his coat pocket it was one of Cassie's inventions, a brass compass-like object whose needle pointed not north but toward active mechanical systems. It vibrated in his palm as he swept it before them, indicating hidden mechanisms buried beneath the surface.

"Three paces ahead," he warned. "Something large. Probably a capture system."

Anna paused, studying the seemingly innocent patch of ground. "The patterns have changed. In my day, the trap was two paces to the right."

Alexander swept the detector in a slow arc, building a mental map of the threats surrounding them. With practiced efficiency, he retrieved a small vial from his belt another of Cassie alchemy concoctions, this one designed to temporarily disrupt mechanical systems. He thumbed off the cap and flicked three drops onto the suspect area.

The reaction was immediate and alarming. The ground heaved upward, soil falling away to reveal a massive brass contraption resembling a mechanical spider, its legs twitching spasmodically as the potion corroded its activation mechanisms. Alexander and Anna froze, waiting for alarms or secondary systems to trigger, but the device merely shuddered once more before collapsing back into its pit, disabled.

"Crude but effective," Anna commented, skirting the now-revealed trap. "My father values function over elegance in his defensive systems."

They continued through the garden, Alexander relying on his venator training to spot the telltale signs of mechanical traps and magical wards. Twice more they were forced to disable security systems. Once a network of trip wires connected to steam-powered alarm bells, and later a pressure-sensitive pathway that would have released caustic chemicals from the surrounding vegetation.

The distant howl froze them both in place—a sound no natural creature could produce, part mechanical screech and part organic rage. It echoed across the garden, setting the metal flowers trembling on their stems.

"Hounds," Anna said, her voice tight. "We need to move faster."

They increased their pace, abandoning caution for speed where possible. As they rounded a particularly dense thicket of metal-infused brambles, Alexander caught his first glimpse of the "hounds" Anna had mentioned. The creatures paced along a perimeter path fifty yards away, their movements a jerky parody of canine motion. Even at this distance, he could make out the horror of their construction the once living dogs whose bodies had been split open and reinforced with steel ribcages, their organs partially replaced with steam-driven mechanical components. Glass cylinders protruded from their backs, filled with bubbling red fluid that circulated through tubes connected to what remained of their natural cardiovascular systems.

"Exposure to the pain drives them mad," Anna explained, noting Alexander's horrified fascination. "The rage makes them more effective hunters. They can track a normal human's heartbeat from half a mile away. Good thing your barley changes like ours."

One of the creatures paused in its patrol, raising a head that was more metal than flesh. Sensor arrays where its eyes should have been swiveled independently, scanning the garden. Rotary saw blades extended from its jaws, spinning up with a high-pitched whine that set Alexander's teeth on edge.

"It's caught something," he whispered. "Not us, or it would be charging already."

The hound's attention fixed on a point beyond their position. With another howl that summoned its pack mates, it bounded off in pursuit of whatever unfortunate creature had drawn its interest. Alexander released the breath he'd been holding, tension momentarily easing from his shoulders.

"There," Anna said, pointing toward what appeared to be a solid rock formation abutting the garden's edge. "Behind that outcropping is a maintenance entrance. The servants used it to tend the garden without disturbing my father's contemplation."

They crossed the remaining distance in tense silence, every sense alert for returning hounds or other patrols. The rock formation proved to be partly artificial, a cleverly designed facade covering a narrow doorway set into the Spire's outer wall. Anna pressed her palm against a seemingly unremarkable section, and a mechanism clicked softly within. The door swung inward on well-oiled hinges, revealing a dark passage beyond.

"The staff passages run throughout the lower levels," she explained as they slipped inside. "Servants are meant to be unseen, their labor invisible to noble eyes."

The passage closed behind them, plunging them into darkness broken only by the faint glow of emergency lamps set at irregular intervals along the ceiling. The air here was thick with the stench of hot metal, industrial lubricants, and beneath it all, the unmistakable copper tang of blood. Not fresh, but a persistent undertone as if the very walls had absorbed decades of spillage.

Alexander's boots rang softly against metal grating as they descended into the Spire's lower levels. Pipes of various diameters ran alongside the walls and ceiling, carrying steam, chemicals, and other substances he would prefer not to identify. The ambient temperature rose steadily, sweat beginning to bead on his forehead as they penetrated deeper into the complex.

"The calculation engine would be housed in the central tower," Anna whispered. "But first we need to understand what defenses surround it. These maintenance tunnels should lead us to an observation point overlooking the main laboratory."

The narrow passage eventually opened onto a metal catwalk suspended above a vast chamber that throbbed with mechanical activity. Alexander crouched beside Anna, peering through a ventilation grate that offered a clear view of the horrors below.

The laboratory stretched at least a hundred yards in each direction, its floor crowded with operating tables, each illuminated by harsh electric lights suspended from articulated brass arms. Upon these tables lay human subjects in various stages of transformation—some still recognizably human despite the metal ports implanted along their spines, others so heavily modified that only their agonized expressions revealed their original nature.

White-coated scientists moved between the tables, their faces obscured by elaborate respiratory apparatus. They worked with the detached efficiency of butchers, cutting flesh and installing mechanical components with identical precision. Steam hissed from pneumatic tools that drove metal spikes into bone, while articulated brass hands performed microsurgery with inhuman steadiness.

In the chamber's center stood a massive vat of bubbling red liquid—human blood, Alexander realized with sickening clarity, mixed with chemicals that gave it an unnatural luminescence. Tubes ran from this central reservoir to each operating table, pumping the mixture into the subjects' bodies through cruel metal needles.

"The living core of the Blood Registry," Anna breathed, her face rigid with controlled horror. "Human blood, alchemically enhanced to serve as both fuel and control mechanism for the hybridization process. They cannot take them and install them in the Blood Registry tower"

A team of scientists clustered around one particular table, their excitement evident in their animated gestures. As they stepped back, Alexander saw their creation rise. A human male whose entire chest cavity had been replaced with a transparent chamber containing brass gears and pulsing tubes. The subject's eyes were gone, replaced with telescopic lenses that whirred as they focused. When he opened his mouth to scream, the sound that emerged was the same mechanical-organic howl they'd heard from the hounds in the garden.

"Success," one scientist announced, his voice distorted by his breathing apparatus. "Subject 274 shows complete integration of the control mechanism. Neural override is functioning at ninety-three percent efficiency. Prepare him for the Dragon's inspection."

Anna's fingers dug into Alexander's arm with bruising force. Her face had gone even paler than usual, her heterochromatic eyes wide with a mixture of horror and rage. "This is worse than I imagined," she whispered. "The calculation engine isn't just a monitoring system—it's the brain that will control an army of these... abominations."

Alexander watched as more "successful" subjects were activated, their movements jerky but coordinated as they were led to a holding area at the chamber's far end. Each bore the same vacant expression, all individual will be subsumed by the mechanical components grafted to their flesh.

"The Black Spire conclave," he realized aloud. "Your father isn't just unveiling the calculation engine to the noble houses—"

"He's demonstrating its control capabilities," Anna finished, her voice hardening with renewed determination. "Creating an army that will ensure no one can challenge his rule—not humans, not even other vampires." Her jaw clenched, the muscles working beneath her pale skin. "He must be stopped. Tonight. Whatever the cost."

The shriek of steam whistles shattered the relative quiet, the alarm system activating with sudden brutality that made Alexander wince. Red emergency lights began to pulse throughout the laboratory below, casting the nightmarish scene in alternating shadows and bloody illumination. The scientists immediately abandoned their work, securing instruments and activating protective measures around their most valuable subjects. Anna's hand closed around Alexander's forearm, her grip like iron as she pulled him away from the observation grate.

"That's not for us," she whispered, pressing her ear to the wall as if listening to the building itself. "Different pattern—it's an arrival alert. High-ranking nobles for the conclave, earlier than scheduled." Her eyes met his, decision crystallizing. "We need to split up. Now."

Alexander shook his head. "Not part of the plan. We stay together until—"

"The plan is already compromised." Anna's voice cut through his objection with cold efficiency. "If nobles are arriving early, security protocols will change. Every inch of this place will be swept for intruders." She pressed something into his hands, small brass key with unusual teeth. "This will access the maintenance shaft behind the main calculation chamber. The new engine core will be there, still being calibrated for tonight's demonstration."

"And you?" Alexander pocketed the key, already calculating alternate routes through the complex based on the partial schematics they'd studied.

"I'll head to my father's inner sanctum. I'm expected for the conclave. My absence would be noted immediately." Her expression hardened. "I can move freely as the Dragon's daughter, gather intelligence about the exact timing of the demonstration. When the moment comes, I'll ensure his attention is divided."

Alexander recognized the logic even as he despised it. Separated, they were more vulnerable, but their chances of successful sabotage improved. He checked his weapons, ensuring each was primed and accessible.

"If I'm compromised, don't wait," he told her. "Destroy the engine, then the Dragon. That's the priority."

Anna's hand brushed his cheek in a gesture so unexpected it momentarily stole his breath. "Twenty years I've planned this, Alexander. Don't make me do it alone." She stepped back, already transforming before his eyes—her posture straightening into aristocratic rigidity, her expression smoothing into the cold mask of vampire nobility. "South passage leads to the calculation chamber. Stay in the maintenance tunnels as long as possible."

Before he could respond, she slipped through a small access door, vanishing into the complex's arterial network of service corridors. Alexander allowed himself three seconds to recalculate, adjust, then set off in the opposite direction. The maintenance tunnels grew narrower as he progressed, the pipes overhead more numerous and complex. He had to crouch in places, his injured ribs protesting each awkward movement with sharp stabs of pain.

The calculation chamber, according to Anna's intelligence, occupied the Spire's heart—a massive circular room spanning multiple levels, housing the mechanical brain that would soon control the Blood Registry's next evolution. Alexander moved carefully, using Cassie's detection device to avoid triggering security systems embedded in the walls and floor. Twice he froze as patrols passed on the other side of thin metal barricades, their heavy footsteps and mechanical breathing marking them as the same hybrid monstrosities they'd observed in the laboratory.

He found the access point Anna had described. An unassuming maintenance hatch set into a wall otherwise crowded with pipes and junction boxes. The brass key slid into the lock with satisfying precision, tumblers clicking softly as he turned it. Beyond lay a narrow crawlspace that angled sharply downward, barely wide enough for his shoulders. Alexander secured his equipment, ensuring nothing would catch or make noise, then eased himself into the confined space.

The shaft descended for what felt like hours but was likely only minutes, the walls gradually transitioning from metal to stone as he penetrated deeper into the Spire's original structure. Eventually, the passage terminated in another hatch, this one warmer to the touch than the surrounding stone.

Alexander pressed his ear against it, listening for movement beyond. Hearing nothing, he eased it open just enough to peek through.

The calculation chamber exceeded even Anna's descriptions in its terrible grandeur. A vast, cathedral-like space stretched before him, dominated by concentric circles of brass and copper machinery that rose from floor to ceiling in an intricate lattice. Glass tubes thicker than his arm carried glowing red fluid—human blood, he realized with a chill throughout the structure, pulsing in rhythmic patterns that mimicked a massive heartbeat. At the chamber's center stood what could only be the engine core: a perfect sphere of transparent crystal, within which floated a human brain suspended in luminescent fluid, its surface crawling with fine metal filaments that connected it to the surrounding machinery.

Alexander eased the hatch open further, scanning for guards or technicians. The chamber appeared deserted—the scientists likely pulled away to prepare for the arriving nobles. He slipped through the opening, crouching behind a bank of machinery that hummed with contained power. From his coat, he retrieved Cassie's sabotage package. Collection of alchemical compounds designed to disrupt the specific alloys used in Registry technology.

He had just begun to move toward the core when the sound reached him. The distinctive click of mechanical limbs against stone, approaching from multiple directions. Alexander froze, calculations racing through his mind. The maintenance shaft behind him offered retreat but would trap him if discovered. The chamber's main entrances were likely already

The mechanical limbs clicked against stone with unnatural rhythm, the sound bouncing off the chamber's vaulted ceiling to create a disorienting echo. Alexander pressed himself against the humming machinery, mind racing through dwindling options. The maintenance shaft offered retreat but would become a trap if discovered. The chamber's main entrances were already sealed. He was cornered in the Dragon's heart, surrounded by the pulsing glow of human blood flowing through glass arteries. His hand closed around Cassie's sabotage package, a crystallizing decision - if capture was inevitable, he would at least destroy the core before they took him.

He slipped three vials from the package and armed them with quick, practiced movements. The first contained a corrosive compound that would eat through the engine's brass conduits; the second, an alchemical catalyst designed to coagulate the blood-fuel; the third, a simple but effective incendiary that would ignite whatever remained. Twenty seconds after activation, they would transform the calculation engine from technological marvel to molten ruin.

The clicking grew louder, now accompanied by the hiss of steam-regulated breathing. Alexander risked a glance around the machinery bank. What he saw froze his blood mid-flow.

Six guards approached from different angles, but these were no ordinary sentries. Each had been transformed through the same grotesque process they'd witnessed in the laboratory. Human forms surgically violated and reconstructed with mechanical precision. Their legs terminated in articulated brass feet that clicked against stone with metronome regularity. Chest cavities had been opened and replaced with transparent chambers housing modified hearts that pumped a sickly luminescent mixture through visible tubes. Eyes were gone, replaced with telescopic lenses that whirred as they focused, scanning the chamber in mechanical sweeps. Most horrifying were their arms, ending not in hands but in modular weapons - retractable blades, miniature harpoon launchers, even small-caliber firearms integrated directly into the bone and muscle.

Alexander's mind categorized them automatically: enhanced vampire guards, Registry elite, likely nobles who had volunteered for "improvement." The modifications explained their methodical movement patterns - they were partially controlled by the calculation engine itself, their remaining free will be subservient to programmed imperatives.

No time for subtlety. Alexander activated all three sabotage vials simultaneously and hurled them toward the crystal sphere housing the suspended brain. In the same fluid motion, he drew both revolvers, muscle memory overriding the pain in his injured ribs.

"Contact!" The lead guard's voice emerged as a mechanized approximation of speech, vibrating through a metal diaphragm implanted in its throat. "Venator detected!"

Alexander fired in rapid succession, his first shots deliberately targeting the glass tubes carrying blood to the guards' mechanical hearts. Two found their marks with perfect precision, shattering the tubes and sending the glowing mixture spraying across the chamber floor. The affected guards staggered, their movements becoming erratic as their control systems struggled to compensate for the sudden pressure loss.

"Get to the sabotage devices!" another guard commanded, its optical lenses expanding as it spotted the vials tumbling through the air toward the core.

Alexander took advantage of the momentary distraction, diving sideways as he switched ammunition types. The specialized rounds Cassie had provided slid into place with a satisfying click. His next shots carried alchemical charges designed specifically to disrupt the electrical systems powering the guards' mechanical components.

The first guard he hit jerked violently as the charge dispersed through its modified nervous system, metal limbs spasming in uncoordinated frenzy before it collapsed. But the others were closing fast, adapting to his tactics with the cold efficiency of machines learning from observation.

A harpoon whistled past his ear, embedding itself in the machinery behind him with enough force to shower him with sparks and fragments of metal. Alexander rolled beneath a bank of equipment, using the limited cover to reload as sweat trickled into his eyes. His broken ribs screamed protest with each movement, the partially healed fractures threatening to separate anew.

One of his sabotage vials reached its target, shattering against the crystal housing. The corrosive compound immediately began eating through the support structure, releasing a cloud of acrid vapor that temporarily obscured the core. The guards moved through the cloud without hesitation, their respiratory systems modified to filter such contaminants.

Alexander emerged from cover on the opposite side, firing both revolvers in a thunderous cascade that dropped another guard. Four remained, and they had adjusted their formation to minimize vulnerable angles. One launched itself into the air, mechanical legs propelling it in an inhuman leap that would bring it down directly on Alexander's position.

He rolled again, but not fast enough. Metal claws raked across his shoulder, tearing through coat and flesh with equal ease. Pain lanced down his arm, nearly causing him to drop his right-hand revolver. Alexander countered by pressing the barrel of his left revolver directly against the guard's chest chamber and pulling the trigger.

The alchemical round shattered the glass, its contents igniting on contact with the blood mixture. The guard's torso erupted in a blue-white flame that crawled through tubes and mechanical components with unnatural hunger. It staggered backward, its optical sensors going dark as control systems failed catastrophically.

But the momentary victory cost him crucial positioning. The remaining three guards converged from different angles, cutting off retreat paths with tactical precision. One fired a compressed air weapon similar to what had broken Alexander's ribs in the mine. He twisted sideways, avoiding a direct hit but catching enough of the impact to send him sprawling across the chamber floor.

"Target damaged but operational," one guard reported, its voice devoid of satisfaction or rage. "Proceeding with capture protocols."

Alexander's second sabotage vial had fallen short, rolling beneath machinery without reaching the core. The third was intercepted mid-air by a guard, its metal hand closing around the vial with delicate precision that belied its monstrous appearance.

Still, the corrosive compound continued its work on the core housing, eating through support struts with quiet efficiency. Alarms began to sound throughout the chamber, urgent and shrill. Alexander managed to regain his footing, backing toward the maintenance shaft, both revolvers tracking separate targets.

"Surrender unnecessary," the lead guard announced. "Neural compliance will be achieved regardless of cooperation."

Alexander's response came in the form of his last two alchemical rounds; both fired at the chamber's lighting system. The bullets shattered the main electrical junction, plunging the vast space into momentary darkness broken only by the pulsing glow of blood-filled tubes and the guards' mechanical eyes.

He used the confusion to make a desperate break for the maintenance shaft, but a guard had anticipated this move. Metal arms closed around him from behind, pinning his right arm with inhuman strength. Alexander drove his elbow backward, connecting with something that yielded slightly before hardening flesh transitioning to mechanical reinforcement.

The guard didn't flinch. Its grip tightened until Alexander's revolver clattered to the floor. Another guard approached from the front, optical lenses adjusting to the low light with mechanical whirs. A third circled to retrieve the fallen sabotage vial.

Alexander struggled with the determination of a man who had survived impossible odds before, but the guard's strength was beyond human limitation. Metal fingers dug into his flesh with precise pressure, finding nerve clusters that sent waves of paralyzing pain through his limbs.

"The Last Venator," the guard before him observed, its voice carrying the faintest trace of what might have been satisfactory. "The Dragon will be pleased."

Alexander's vision began to fade at the edges, the pain from his injuries combining with the guard's nerve manipulation to push him toward unconsciousness. The last thing he saw was the calculation engine's core, its crystal housing now compromised, fluid leaking around the suspended brain as emergency containment systems activated with hisses of steam and mechanical groans.

Not destroyed, but damaged. It was something, at least.

Darkness claimed him.

Consciousness returned in sluggish increments, each one accompanied by a fresh wave of pain. Alexander's eyes opened to red-tinged darkness, his vision swimming as he tried to focus on his surroundings. His mouth tasted of copper and chemicals, his tongue thick and unwieldy. Every muscle in his body ached with the distinctive aftereffects of electrical stunning which seemed to be the Registry's preferred method of ensuring compliant prisoners.

He lay on a metal floor that vibrated subtly with the pulse of massive machinery somewhere below. Slowly, carefully, he pushed himself upright, taking inventory of injuries with clinical detachment. Ribs still broken, now with fresh fractures joining the partially healed ones. Deep lacerations across his right shoulder where the guard's claws had torn through flesh. Numerous contusions and electrical burns across his body. Painful, but survivable. Nothing immediately fatal.

His surroundings gradually resolved into coherence his cell was approximately eight feet square, three walls of solid metal, the fourth comprised of interlocking brass bars that pulsed with faint electrical current. Beyond the bars stretched a circular chamber containing other cells arranged like spokes on a wheel, all facing a central guard station currently unoccupied. The air carried the distinctive scent of ozone and steam, punctuated by the occasional hiss of pressure valves releasing excess energy.

Alexander ran his hands across his body, cataloging what had been taken. Both revolvers, obviously. The visible sabotage equipment. His coat with its many pockets of specialized tools. His boots had been replaced with flimsy slippers that would provide no protection or leverage in a fight.

But not everything.

They had missed the thin metal strips sewn into the seams of his trousers. Lockpicks disguised as reinforcement stitching. The hollow tooth at the back of his mouth still contained Mariana's most potent healing compound, designed to be activated by crushing it between molars in moments of dire emergency. And most importantly, they'd overlooked Cassie's masterpiece. A mechanical scarab secreted beneath the skin at the base of his skull, its metal legs anchored to his cervical vertebrae, waiting for the specific sequence of pressure points that would activate it.

Alexander allowed himself the ghost of a smile. Not helpless. Not yet.

A low moan drew his attention to the neighboring cells. The chamber housed at least a dozen prisoners, their forms dimly visible through the electrified bars. To his left languished a human male, middle-aged, his once-muscular frame now withered by captivity. Fresh surgical scars traced patterns across his exposed chest and arms - preparation marks for the conversion process Alexander had witnessed in the laboratory.

To his right, more surprising, sat a vampire - female, young by their standards, perhaps only decades rather than centuries old. Her aristocratic features were marred by silver burns that left weeping wounds across her face and hands. Unlike the human prisoner, she remained alert, her eyes tracking Alexander's movements with calculating intensity.

"The famous Last Venator," she observed, her voice barely above a whisper. "They said you were a myth. A story the humans told themselves for comfort."

Alexander studied her without responding immediately, noting the distinctive emblem tattooed on her forearm - a lesser noble house, one of many that served the Dragon while harboring quiet resentments. He had killed her kind before, many times. Now they shared the same fate.

"The famous part is exaggerated," he finally replied, matching her whisper. "The last part, unfortunately accurate."

From cells further around the circular chamber came other sounds - weeping, muttered prayers, the occasional scream quickly muffled. A community of the damned, awaiting whatever horrors the Dragon's scientists had planned for them.

"Why is a vampire in the Dragon's prison?" Alexander asked, keeping his voice low.

The vampire's lips twisted in a bitter smile that reopened one of her silver burns. "The same reason as anyone else. I displeased him. My house questioned the wisdom of the calculation engine, suggested more... traditional methods of control should be maintained."

"And for that, you're here?"

"The Dragon tolerates no dissent, not even from his own kind." Her eyes flicked toward the central guard station. "Especially not with the conclave approaching. Those who aren't absolutely loyal become either examples or experiments." She nodded toward the surgical scars on the human prisoner. "Some become both."

Alexander leaned back against the cell wall, mind already calculating angles, timings, weaknesses in the security systems. The guard station would be manned soon. Feeding schedules, interrogation rotations, shift changes all potential opportunities if he could just determine the patterns.

"How long until the conclave begins?" he asked.

The vampire studied him with renewed interest. "You really are hunting him, aren't you?" She glanced toward a steam clock visible on the chamber's far wall. "Four hours. When the clock strikes midnight, the Dragon will unveil his masterpiece to the noble houses. Those who applaud will be rewarded. Those who hesitate..." She gestured to her cell.

Four hours. Alexander closed his eyes, focusing on his breathing to manage the pain. Four hours for Anna to navigate the treacherous politics of her father's court. Four hours for him to find a way out of this cell and back into the fight.

The calculation engine had been damaged but not destroyed. The Dragon still lived. The mission continued, even from behind electrified bars.

Alexander opened his eyes, gaze fixing on the empty guard station. Patience had never been his preferred strategy, but sometimes, the hunter had no choice but to wait for the right moment to strike.

Anna glided into the grand court with measured steps, her face a perfect mask of aristocratic indifference. The journey through the Spire's upper levels had given her time to shed Alexander's influence. The human warmth that had begun to seep into her demeanor during their shared mission. She had buried those feelings beneath centuries of practiced cruelty, assuming once more the mantle of the Dragon's daughter. Her return would already arouse suspicion; any softness would be fatal and not just to her, but to Alexander, whose absence from the calculation chamber would surely have been discovered by now.

The Dragon's court occupied the highest level of the Black Spire, a circular chamber whose domed ceiling depicted the conquests of vampire-kind in gruesome mosaic. Massive windows of leaded glass lined the walls, their panes treated with alchemical compounds that filtered sunlight to safe levels during day hours. Now, under night's protection, they stood open to the cold air, framing views of the blasted wasteland that surrounded the Spire like a moat of desolation.

Vampire nobles filled the space, arranged in precise hierarchies that Anna read as easily as text. Those closest to the Dragon's elevated throne represented the oldest bloodlines, their pale flesh almost translucent with age, their eyes holding centuries of calculated malice. The younger nobles lingered at the periphery, hungry for advancement, watching their elders with predatory patience. All wore the markers of their stations. Jewelry crafted from human bones, garments dyed with blood-based pigments, mechanical enhancements that merged with flesh in displays of Registry technology.

At the chamber's center, seated upon a throne of brass and bone, waited her father. Dracula—the Dragon—looked much as he had when she'd fled his court two years prior. His form remained that of a man in his prime, tall and broad-shouldered, with features that human artists had once used as models for their depictions of angels. Only his eyes betrayed his true nature—crimson irises surrounded by black so deep they seemed to absorb light rather than reflect it. He wore a simple black suit tailored to his powerful frame, the only ornamentation a single ring on his left hand, its stone containing a droplet of blood suspended in perpetual motion.

His gaze found her immediately, pinning her with the weight of centuries. "My wayward daughter returns," he announced, his voice carrying effortlessly across the suddenly silent chamber. "How fortuitous that you should arrive on this historic evening."

Anna approached the throne and sank into a deep curtsy, her eyes downcast in the perfect performance of submission. "Father. I could not bear to remain away when whispers of your latest triumph reached me."

He studied her for a long moment, his expression unreadable to all but her, who had spent decades learning to interpret the smallest shifts in his demeanor. She saw calculation there, and suspicion, but also something like satisfaction. The pride of a predator whose prey has returned to the trap of its own accord.

"Rise," he commanded finally. "Tell us of your travels. We have heard such... interesting reports of your activities."

Anna stood, keeping her posture perfect, her hands folded before her to hide their slight trembling. "Mere observation, Father. I wished to understand the human condition better, to learn how they function outside our direct influence. Such knowledge can only strengthen our control systems."

A murmur rippled through the assembled nobles. Some approving, others skeptical. From the corner of her eye, Anna noticed Lucian Grigorescu, the nobleman who had attacked her in Old Slade. His partially healed wounds from their encounter were visible beneath his high collar, and his eyes burned with barely concealed hatred.

"Indeed?" The Dragon leaned forward slightly, the movement causing several nearby nobles to flinch. "And what conclusions did you reach about our... livestock?"

The word choice was a deliberate test. Anna felt the weight of the court's attention, measuring her response. She allowed a cold smile to touch her lips, an expression she had learned from her father centuries ago.

"That they remain predictable in their desperation," she replied. "They build their little resistance movements, their pathetic attempts at sabotage, never understanding that each act of rebellion has been anticipated, even encouraged. They mistake the space we allow them for freedom."

The Dragon's lips curved in what might have been approval. "You always were an apt pupil, when you chose to apply yourself." He gestured to an empty place at his right hand. "Join us. Tonight's demonstration will benefit from your perspective."

Anna ascended the dais with measured steps, taking the indicated position beside her father's throne. The closeness revolted her, memories of centuries of abuse threatening to crack her carefully maintained facade. She focused instead on scanning the chamber, noting which noble houses were represented and which were conspicuously absent. The missing ones would be those already eliminated for questioning the calculation engine like the young vampire in Alexander's neighboring cell.

"The final calibrations proceed as scheduled, my lord," a white-coated scientist reported, approaching the throne with a reverent bow. "Despite the recent... incident in the central chamber, the core functions remain intact. Full operational capacity will be achieved within the hour."

Anna's pulse quickened, though she kept her expression neutral. Incident. Alexander had managed to damage the engine before his capture. Not enough to halt the demonstration, but perhaps enough to create exploitable weaknesses.

"And the saboteur?" the Dragon inquired, his tone casual as though asking about the weather.

"Secured in the holding cells beneath the eastern tower," the scientist replied. "Initial scans confirm he is the Last Venator, as suspected. His genetic profile matches our records from the purge."

"How fascinating." The Dragon's gaze slid to Anna, watching for any reaction. "The Last Venator, in my Spire, on the very night of the calculation engine's unveiling. Such remarkable timing."

Anna met his eyes without flinching, centuries of practice allowing her to maintain her composure despite the terror gripping her heart. "The desperate last gasp of a dying breed," she observed. "Perhaps he should be included in the demonstration. Show our guests what happens to those who oppose progress."

Her father studied her face, searching for cracks in her performance. Whatever he sought, he apparently didn't find it. He turned back to the scientist. "Prepare the venator for integration. I want his conversion to be the culmination of tonight's events. A symbolic end to human resistance."

"Integration" – the euphemism chilled Anna's blood. She had witnessed the process during her years in her father's court. The subject's consciousness remained intact while their body was systematically violated, mechanical components replacing organic systems until only enough humanity remained to experience the horror of what they had become. Alexander would be transformed into one of the hybrids they had observed in the laboratory, his will be subsumed by the calculation engine's control.

"A fitting end," she agreed, hating herself for the words.

The Dragon rose from his throne, silencing the murmurs that had broken out among the assembled nobles. "The hour approaches," he announced. "Let us adjourn to the demonstration chamber. Tonight marks the beginning of perfect order—the final evolution of the Blood Registry System."

He offered Anna his arm in a gesture of false courtesy that none present would dare refuse. As she placed her hand upon it, his fingers closed over hers with crushing strength, hidden from the observers by the drape of his sleeve.

"We shall speak privately of your absence after the demonstration, daughter," he whispered, his lips barely moving. "I find myself curious about certain coincidences."

"I look forward to it, Father," she replied, matching his tone.

The court processed from the chamber in strict order of precedence, descending through the Spire's levels toward the demonstration chamber where the calculation engine awaited. As they walked, Anna listened carefully to the conversations flowing around her, gathering fragments of crucial intelligence.

"...neural compliance at ninety-eight percent efficiency..."

"...full implementation within six months across all Registry territories..."

"...expanded harvesting protocols to meet the increased blood requirements..."

The pieces assembled into a nightmarish whole. The calculation engine wasn't merely a monitoring system or even a control mechanism for an army of hybrids. It was the foundation for a fundamental transformation of human society. From penned livestock to integrated components in a vast machine. Humans would not simply be tagged and tracked; they would be systematically converted, their bodies and minds merged with Registry technology until free will became a distant memory.

They passed through the Spire's medical level, where Anna glimpsed rows of human subjects in various stages of preparation. Some still looked fully human, their vacant expressions suggesting chemical sedation. Others had already begun the conversion process, surgical scars and mechanical ports mapping the progress of their transformation. All wore identical expressions of resigned horror, aware enough to understand their fate but powerless to resist it.

Her father's grip remained painfully tight as they descended further, entering a level Anna had never been permitted to access during her previous time in the Spire. The architecture here was older, predating the Registry's formation, its stone walls carved with symbols that made her eyes hurt if she looked at them directly.

"The original foundations," the Dragon explained, noting her interest. "Built upon technologies far older than our kind. The calculation engine merely refines what was always here, waiting to be rediscovered."

The demonstration chamber opened before them, a vast circular space dominated by what appeared to be a miniature version of the calculation engine's core. The same crystal sphere containing a suspended brain, the same network of tubes carrying luminescent blood, but scaled down to showcase the principles without revealing all the technical details to the assembled nobles.

As the court filed into their assigned positions, Anna carefully memorized every aspect of the chamber's layout. The number of guards and their positions. The locations of access panels and maintenance hatches. The rhythm of the steam vents that regulated the chamber's temperature and pressure.

Four levels below, Alexander waited in his cell, likely planning his own desperate countermoves. Three hours remained until midnight, when the demonstration would reach its climax with the full activation of the calculation engine—and Alexander's scheduled "integration."

Anna took her place at her father's side, the perfect image of the loyal daughter returned to the fold. Beneath that mask, her mind raced through calculations and contingencies, weighing risks against necessities. The Dragon's suspicions were already aroused; any move she made would need to be perfectly timed and executed.

As the scientists began their preliminary explanations to the assembled nobility, Anna fingered the small vial concealed within her sleeve. A poison synthesized from her own blood, designed to target the specific vulnerabilities in her father's ancient physiology. One chance, requiring perfect proximity and timing.

The Dragon placed his hand on her shoulder, the gesture appearing paternal to observers while his fingers dug into her flesh with warning pressure. "Welcome home, daughter," he murmured. "I've prepared a special celebration for your return."

Anna smiled up at him, centuries of hatred concealed behind a daughter's adoring gaze. "I wouldn't miss it for the world, Father."

Alexander counted the seconds between guard rotations, his mind constructing a mental map of the prison's rhythms. Thirty-seven minutes between the heavy footfalls of the enhanced sentries. Twelve minutes for the steam pressure to build in the pipes running beneath the cell floor before the release valve hissed. Eight minutes from the distant screams of "processing" to the return of guards with empty stretchers. Each detail a potential advantage, each pattern a possible escape route. The venator texts had taught him that even the most perfect cage contained flaws. Though only if one could observe long enough to find them.

The pain in his ribs had settled into a dull throb, familiar enough to ignore. Alexander shifted position, moving to the front of his cell where he could better observe the circular chamber. The guard station remained empty except during shift changes and prisoner transfers, but he'd identified at least three mechanical monitoring devices scanning the cells at irregular intervals. One resembled a brass spider, scuttling along the ceiling pipes with a clicking of tiny gears. Another was built into the floor itself, a pressure plate disguised as ordinary metal grating. The third was more sophisticated, some kind of alchemical sensor that detected rapid movement or elevated heart rates, triggering a soft whine when prisoners became agitated.

"They'll come for you first," the vampire noblewoman in the adjacent cell observed, her voice barely audible. "New arrivals always get priority processing, especially ones as... valuable as the Last Venator."

Alexander turned slightly toward her, careful to keep his movements casual, his lips barely moving as he replied. "You know my reputation. Do you have a name, or should I just call you 'vamp?'"

A faint smile crossed her silver-burned face. "Eliza. House Corvinus. A minor bloodline, though we predate the Registry by several centuries." The smile faded. "Or we did, until my father questioned the Dragon's wisdom. Now I am the last."

"The Dragon doesn't tolerate dissent within his own kind," Alexander noted. It wasn't a question.

"The calculation engine threatens traditional vampire authority," Eliza explained, her eyes constantly scanning for monitoring devices. "Some houses preferred the old ways—direct control through fear and blood bonds. The engine makes noble bloodlines unnecessary. Why maintain an aristocracy when machines can monitor and control humans more efficiently?"

The human prisoner on Alexander's other side shifted closer to the bars separating their cells. His movements were stiff, surgical incisions across his chest and arms still raw and weeping. "It's worse than that," he whispered. "I was in the engineering corps. Worked on the engine's hydraulic systems before I made the mistake of asking questions."

Alexander studied him with renewed interest. "What kind of questions?"

"About the integration protocols. Why we needed to merge human neural tissue with the mechanical components." The man's hands shook as he spoke, fingers tracing the incision marks on his arms. "They're not just monitoring us. They're... absorbing us. Turning us into components."

"I'm Mills," the man added. "Chief Engineer. Second tier." His eyes held the haunted look of someone who had glimpsed horrors beyond their comprehension. "The engine needs human minds to function. Not just the brain at its center, but thousands of... contributors."

Alexander processed this information against what they'd already discovered about the calculation engine. "The hybrid guards," he said. "They're connected to the engine somehow."

Mills nodded. "Neural compliance. The mechanical implants link their consciousness to the central brain. They see what it sees, know what it knows. Perfect soldiers who can never rebel because they're no longer fully individuals."

"And the Registry plans to expand this process to the general population," Alexander concluded, pieces falling into place.

"Not all at once," Eliza interjected. "First the troublemakers. Then key professionals' engineers, physicians, teachers. Anyone who might organize resistance. Eventually, everyone except a small breeding population to maintain the blood supply."

A new voice joined their whispered conversation—an elderly woman in a cell across the chamber. "I was a record keeper in the western district," she said, her voice cracking with age. "Saw the classification protocols. They've already tagged everyone in the Registry. Color-coded for processing priority."

Alexander's mind raced through implications. The calculation engine wasn't merely a monitoring system or even a control mechanism—it was a hive mind in development, with the Dragon at its center. Humans wouldn't just be cattle; they'd be cells in a vast organism directed by vampire consciousness.

"When?" he asked.

"Full implementation begins after tonight's demonstration," Mills replied. "They're bringing noble representatives from every district to witness the engine's capabilities. After that, processing centers activate across all Registry territories."

The distant clank of metal doors interrupted their conversation. Alexander tensed, recognizing the sound pattern that preceded prisoner transfers. Heavy footsteps approached—multiple guards, moving with mechanical precision.

"Someone's getting processed," Eliza whispered, shrinking back from her cell bars.

Three enhanced guards appeared at the chamber entrance; their movements synchronized with disturbing precision. Between them walked a white-coated scientist, checking notations on a brass clipboard. They stopped at the central guard station, the scientist running his finger down a list of names.

"Subject 387," he announced. "Final preparation phase."

The guards moved to a cell containing a young woman who couldn't have been more than twenty. She screamed as they deactivated the electrical current in the bars, her terror giving way to eerie calm as one guard pressed a device against her neck that hissed with the release of sedative compounds.

Alexander watched with calculated focus, noting every detail of the security protocol. The scientist used a mechanical key card to disable the electrical current. The guards' movements followed predictable patterns optimized for efficiency rather than adaptability. Most importantly, he observed a three-second delay between the electrical system's deactivation and the bars' retraction into the floor—a tiny window, but potentially enough.

As they carried the sedated woman away, Alexander turned back to his fellow prisoners. "The demonstration tonight, what form will it take?"

Mills swallowed hard. "They'll activate the full network. All existing hybrids will demonstrate synchronized responses to central commands. Then they'll conduct a live integration—show how quickly a human can be converted and brought under control."

"The final demonstration subject hadn't been selected when I was brought in," Eliza added. "But rumor suggested someone significant. A symbol of resistance whose conversion would break human morale."

Alexander didn't need to ask who that would be. The Dragon's announcement in Anna's presence had confirmed his fate—integration as the culmination of the night's events. The clock on the chamber wall showed barely two hours remaining until midnight.

"I don't plan to be here for that demonstration," he said quietly.

Eliza's eyes narrowed. "The cells are escape-proof. The electrical current in the bars would stop your heart before you broke through, and even if you somehow managed it, the enhanced guards would have you before you reached the door."

"I've heard that before," Alexander replied. "From people who are now dead."

With subtle movements, he began working one of the metal strips from his trouser seam, his body angled to block the monitoring devices' view. The improvised lockpick was Cassie's design, flexible enough to manipulate tumblers but strong enough to serve as a weapon if necessary.

"You'd need to disable the electrical system first," Mills observed, catching on to Alexander's intentions. "And for that, you'd need access to the control panel in the guard station."

Alexander's fingers continued their careful work, freeing the metal strip without drawing attention. "Or an alternative power source strong enough to create a temporary surge. Overload the system."

Eliza's expression changed, understanding dawning. "The steam pipes beneath the cells. They're part of the Spire's main power distribution network. Rupture one at the right moment..."

"And the electrical systems would temporarily reset," Alexander finished. "Creating a window of opportunity."

Mills leaned closer. "I could help. I know the Spire's engineering systems better than most who designed them. There's a junction box behind that wall panel." He nodded toward a section of the guard station that appeared slightly discolored compared to surrounding areas. "It controls this entire cell block."

Alexander assessed the man's condition—weakened from captivity and preliminary processing, but still functional. His knowledge could prove invaluable, assuming he could move when the moment came.

"I can create a distraction," Eliza offered unexpectedly. "My kind can withstand more electrical current than humans. Not indefinitely, but long enough to draw attention."

Alexander studied her, surprise momentarily breaking through his carefully maintained composure. "Why would you help a venator? I've killed your kind before. Many times."

Eliza's hand unconsciously touched the silver burns on her face. "Because the Dragon destroyed my house. Because his vision of the future leaves no place for vampire nobility or human independence. Only his perfect, mechanical order. Because sometimes survival requires unlikely alliances."

A sentiment Alexander understood all too well. His current mission with Anna represented exactly such an alliance.

"We'll need to coordinate precisely," he said. "The next guard rotation comes in approximately twenty minutes. After they leave, we'll have thirty-seven minutes until the following patrol."

As the others nodded their agreement, Alexander's fingers located a loose section of flooring near the steam pipe junction—a maintenance access point, likely used for pressure adjustments. The metal was thin enough that his improvised tools might pry it open, giving him access to the steam system beneath.

He worked silently, methodically, using his body to shield his actions from the mechanical monitors. Years of venator training had prepared him for this. Patience and precision under pressure, turning captivity into opportunity.

The clock on the chamber wall continued its inexorable countdown toward midnight. Less than two hours remained until the demonstration that would transform human society forever. Less than two hours for Alexander to escape, find Anna, and destroy the calculation engine.

His fingers touched the mechanical scarab embedded at the base of his skull, Cassie's masterpiece of engineering, designed for precisely this kind of desperate situation. The device contained enough explosive compound to breach the cell floor but using it would be his final option. The resulting damage to his cervical vertebrae would likely paralyze him if it didn't kill him outright.

A faint vibration traveled through the cell floor with regular pulses that Alexander recognized as machinery being activated elsewhere in the Spire. The demonstration preparations were accelerating.

"They're bringing the engine to full power," Mills whispered, feeling the same vibrations. "Once it reaches operational capacity, the enhanced guards will be at peak efficiency. Our window is closing."

Alexander's lockpick finally caught the edge of the floor panel, creating a tiny gap he could exploit. "Then we move at the next guard rotation," he decided. "Be ready."

As if in response to his declaration, the distant doors clanked open once more. But the footsteps that followed weren't the mechanical precision of enhanced guards. These were heavier, more deliberate—the tread of someone whose authority required no hurry.

The vampire prisoners tensed visibly, shrinking back from their cell bars. Even Eliza's composure cracked, fear flashing across her aristocratic features.

"The Dragon," she breathed. "He never comes to the cells himself."

Alexander continued working at the floor panel, movements now microscopic to avoid detection. Whatever was coming, it changed nothing. The plan remained the same, he had to escape, find Anna, destroy the engine.

The footsteps grew louder, accompanied now by the distinctive click of mechanical limbs. The Dragon was not coming alone.

Alexander slid the lockpick back into his trouser seam, assuming a posture of defeated exhaustion. Whatever game the Dragon was playing, Alexander would use it to his advantage. Every interaction was information. Every confrontation, an opportunity.

The Last Venator waited, counting heartbeats, ready to face the architect of humanity's enslavement. One way or another, their long-delayed confrontation was about to begin.

Gears of Deception

The Dragon's footsteps echoed through the cell block like measured drumbeats, each impact reverberating through the metal floor beneath Alexander's feet. He remained motionless, feigning exhaustion while his fingers stayed wrapped around the concealed lockpick in his trouser seam. The approaching figure emerged from the steam-clouded corridor he was tall, aristocratic, radiating power that seemed to dim the emergency lights through some impossible physics. Behind him walked Anna, her face, a perfect mask of daughterly obedience that only Alexander could recognize as meticulously crafted deception. Since if it wasn't he was truly dead.

Eliza hissed softly from her adjacent cell, pressing herself against the far wall as if trying to melt into the metal. Even Mills went utterly still, his breath held in terrified suspension. The other prisoners followed suit, a wave of silence rolling through the circular chamber as Dracula approached the guard station.

"The Last Venator," the Dragon said, his voice carrying the weight of centuries. He didn't raise it above conversational volume, yet it filled the chamber completely. "A disappointing specimen, considering your reputation."

Alexander met his gaze without flinching, counting the seconds between steam valve releases beneath the floor. Thirty-seven, thirty-six, thirty-five...

"Nothing to say?" Dracula smiled, revealing teeth that were perfectly, unnaturally white. "Perhaps you're conserving your strength for tonight's demonstration. Wise, though ultimately futile."

The Dragon circled the guard station, running one pale finger along the control panel. Behind him, Anna's eyes flickered to Alexander for the briefest momenta warning or perhaps encouragement. Her right hand drifted toward her pocket, where Alexander knew she carried the poison intended for her father.

"I studied your family's techniques, you know," Dracula continued, moving closer to Alexander's cell. "The Stirlings had such... innovative methods. It's a shame they proved inadequate when my enforcers came calling."

Rage flared hot in Alexander's chest, but he channeled it into focus. Twenty-six, twenty-five, twenty-four...

"Perhaps you'll be interested to know that I preserved your younger sister's body. Such a promising subject with her neural tissue showed remarkable compatibility with the early calculation engine prototypes."

Alexander's hand tightened around the lockpick, knuckles whitening. His mind filled with mechanical calculations, not the memory of his sister's smile. Not now. Not when timing meant everything.

"Father," Anna interrupted smoothly, moving to his side with practiced deference. "The demonstration begins in less than an hour. Shouldn't the subject be prepared?"

Dracula smiled indulgently at his daughter. "Always so efficient, my dear. Yes, the scientists should begin the preliminary work." He turned slightly. "Summon the medical team. I want to witness the first incisions personally."

As a guard moved to obey, Alexander caught Mills' eye across the narrow gap between their cells. The engineer nodded imperceptibly, his fingers already working at the loose panel near his own steam pipe junction. Fifteen, fourteen, thirteen...

Anna positioned herself carefully, angling her body to block the Dragon's view of Alexander's hands. "The nobles are gathering in the demonstration chamber, Father. I've heard whispers of dissent among the lesser houses. Your presence might be required to ensure loyalty."

While Dracula contemplated this, Alexander slid the lockpick free and eased it toward the cell's control mechanism. Cassie's design was brilliant in its simplicity—the metal strip's unique alloy could disrupt electrical currents without conducting them back to the user. Seven, six, five...

"Perhaps you're right," Dracula conceded. "The calculation engine represents such fundamental change requires some hands may need to be held through the transition." His gaze returned to Alexander. "Don't worry, Venator. I'll return for your integration ceremony."

Three, two, one...

The steam valve released with a hiss, and Alexander jammed the lockpick into the cell's control panel. Simultaneously, Mills slammed his weight against the loosened floor panel, exposing the steam junction beneath. The timing had to be perfect if not the electrical disruption from Alexander's lockpick creating a momentary failure in the system would fail. Just as Mills redirected superheated steam into the conduit that fed the cell block's power distribution.

Alexander withdrew a tiny brass scarab from where he'd concealed it in his mouth another one of Cassie's marvels, this one containing corrosive compounds that would eat through metal on contact. He spit it toward the exposed steam junction just as the lights flickered from his electrical sabotage.

The reaction was instantaneous and catastrophic. Metal corroded in a spreading wave, weakening the pressurized pipes from within. A thunderous crack split the air as steam erupted through the cell block, shattering pipes and sending shrapnel flying in all directions. Emergency systems triggered, klaxons wailing as backup power stuttered and failed.

"Now!" Alexander shouted, slamming his shoulder against the cell bars as the electrical current died. The three-second delay before mechanical retraction gave him just enough time to brace his feet against the opposite wall and heave with all his strength, ignoring the stabbing pain from his broken ribs.

The bars groaned, then gave way with a shriek of protesting metal. Alexander tumbled forward onto the main floor just as chaos erupted throughout the chamber. Eliza was already moving, her vampire strength allowing her to wrench her own damaged cell door open. Mills followed seconds later, ducking beneath a geyser of escaping steam.

Dracula roared a sound more felt than heard, vibrating through Alexander's bones with physical force. Through the blinding clouds of steam, Alexander saw the Dragon's silhouette elongate, shoulders broadening as his true form began to emerge. Anna backed away, her hand slipping inside her pocket.

Alexander rolled beneath a guard's wild swing, coming up behind the confused sentry. He struck precisely at the junction between mechanical components and flesh, where Anna had once explained the control systems were most vulnerable. The guard staggered, neural connection temporarily disrupted, and Alexander stripped him of a wicked-looking blade with a serrated edge that seemed to make his mouth water for blood.

All around him, the cell block dissolved into bedlam. Prisoners who'd managed to escape their cells fought desperately against disoriented guards. Emergency lights pulsed crimson through clouds of steam, casting everything in bloody illumination that made movement a stuttering, nightmarish ballet. The floor vibrated beneath Alexander's feet as distant machinery responded to the security breach, lockdown protocols engaging throughout the Spire.

"This way!" Mills shouted over the din, gesturing toward a maintenance access near the chamber's edge. "Service corridor leads to the upper levels!"

Alexander fought his way toward the engineer, blade flashing as he parried attacks from two partially mechanical guards. Their movements were sluggish, erratic and not up to par with the guards he faced before. The calculation engine's control compromised by power fluctuations. He exploited the weakness ruthlessly, striking at exposed hydraulic lines and severing connections to their mechanical limbs.

Eliza appeared at his side; her face twisted in a savage grin despite the pain from silver burns. She moved with vampire speed, tearing mechanical components from a guard's chest with her bare hands. "Never thought I'd fight alongside a venator," she gasped, ripping out a fistful of wires that sent the guard collapsing in a heap.

"Survival makes strange allies," Alexander replied, driving his blade through another guard's control module.

They reached the maintenance access, where Mills was already working on the lock with a piece of scavenged metal. Other prisoners gathered behind them. Those strong enough to fight or desperate enough to seize this unexpected chance at freedom.

Alexander looked back through the chaos, searching for Anna. He spotted her near the stairwell, ostensibly struggling to pull her father away from danger. Her eyes met his across the churning mass of bodies and steam, her expression unreadable at this distance. But her left hand, hidden from Dracula's view, made a sharp gesture toward the upper levels—Go!

The maintenance door groaned open under Mills' efforts, revealing a narrow passage beyond. Alexander ushered the escapees through, counting each one, organizing them with terse commands that cut through their panic. "Mills, lead them toward the eastern corridors. Eliza, watch our backs."

The thunder of approaching reinforcements echoed from the stairwell. More enhanced guards, these moving with coordinated precision that suggested direct control from the calculation engine itself. Alexander slammed his weight against a fallen storage cabinet, pushing it into a position to barricade the corridor after their escape.

As the last prisoner slipped through, Alexander paused, his eyes finding Anna once more. She stood at her father's side, steadying him as he recovered from the initial shock of the attack. But her fingers, splayed against the Dragon's back, formed a deliberate pattern that Alexander recognized from their planning sessions: twenty minutes. The demonstration chamber. She would meet him there.

Alexander nodded once, then disappeared into the maintenance shaft, pulling the heavy door closed behind him. The Last Venator was free, and the hunt resumed. And this time, he was the predator once again and not prey.

Crimson warning lights pulsed through the fortress corridors, painting Alexander's world in alternating waves of blood-red illumination and pitch darkness. His breath came in controlled, measured pulls despite the fire in his broken ribs as he ducked beneath a hissing steam pipe that had partially detached from the ceiling. The escape had triggered emergency protocols throughout the Spire. Pressure doors slamming shut in distant corridors, mechanical sentries deploying from wall recesses, and the ever-present wail of alarms that vibrated the very stones beneath his feet. He pressed on, counting intersections and memorizing landmarks as Mills had instructed before they'd separated to increase survival chances.

"Three levels up, follow the brass conduits," the engineer had whispered before leading the other escapees toward the eastern service tunnels. "The demonstration chamber connects to the main library through maintenance shafts that's probably your best chance to reach it undetected."

Alexander flattened himself against a wall as heavy footsteps approached, the distinctive hydraulic hiss of enhanced guards echoing from around the corner. Their movements were more coordinated now. The calculation engine regaining control after the initial disruption. He slipped into an alcove just as they passed, their optical sensors sweeping methodically across the corridor.

The fortress architecture itself worked against intruders. Corridors twisted at irregular angles, designed to disorient. Ceiling heights changed abruptly, forcing awkward movements that slowed progress. Brass pipes carrying steam and alchemical compounds crisscrossed overhead like mechanical veins, their contents occasionally venting through safety releases that filled sections with vision-obscuring vapor.

Alexander followed the largest conduit, reasoning it would lead to critical infrastructure. His stolen blade remained clutched in his right hand, its edge already notched from encounters with two solitary guards who'd had the misfortune to cross his path. Their bodies lay hidden in maintenance closets, neural control modules carefully disabled to prevent the calculation engine from pinpointing his location through their implants.

A distant explosion shook the corridor, sending dust raining from ancient stone ceilings. Eliza's work, perhaps—the vampire noblewoman had promised to create diversions to pull security away from the central tower. Or maybe Mills had found his way to an engineering control room and was wreaking targeted havoc on the Spire's systems.

Alexander reached a junction where five corridors met beneath a domed ceiling. A massive gear mechanism rotated slowly overhead, driving chains that disappeared into wall apertures. The central passage was wider, its floor polished stone rather than utilitarian metal grating. Nobility used that corridor which was meant to led toward important chambers.

He started forward, then froze as a door slammed somewhere ahead, followed by running footsteps. Alexander pressed himself into a shadowed recess, calculating angles and preparing for combat. But the figure that emerged through the steam wasn't a guard.

Anna sprinted from a side passage, her aristocratic composure abandoned for raw speed. Her normally immaculate appearance was disheveled—hair wild, clothing torn at one shoulder where something had caught the fabric. She glanced behind her eyes wide with urgency rather than fear.

Alexander lunged from his hiding place, clamping one hand over her mouth to prevent a startled cry as he dragged her sideways into the nearest doorway. She reacted instantly, her vampire strength nearly breaking his grip before recognition dawned in her heterochromatic eyes.

They tumbled together through a heavy oak door marked "Bibliotheca" in tarnished brass letters. Alexander kicked it shut behind them just as shouts erupted in the corridor came a patrol of guards responding to movement sensors.

"Eight enhanced sentries," Anna whispered, pulling away from his grasp. "My father sent them after me when I slipped away claiming to organize his personal guard. He suspects something."

The library stretched before them in shadowed grandeur—a vast chamber with vaulted ceilings supported by stone arches that disappeared into darkness overhead. Towering bookshelves dominated the space; their ancient wood warped from years of exposure to the Spire's ever-present steam and moisture. Leather-bound tomes lay scattered across cracked marble tiles where they'd fallen from rotting shelves. A single iron-reinforced window cut into the far wall offered a narrow glimpse of the night sky beyond was black and starless under heavy cloud cover.

Alexander dragged a heavy reading table toward the door, its legs screaming against the marble floor. Anna immediately understood, helping him position it as a barricade before kicking a fallen bookcase into place beside it. It wouldn't hold enhanced guards for long, but they needed only minutes.

"The calculation engine?" Alexander demanded, his voice low as he scanned the chamber for alternate exits.

Anna moved to a large map tacked to the wall—a detailed schematic of the Blood Registry tower. "Damaged but operational. My father accelerated the demonstration timeline after your escape. The noble houses are gathering now."

Alexander examined the map, committing key details to memory. "How many access points to the central chamber?"

"Three." Anna traced them with a gloved finger. "Main entrance, heavily guarded. Service tunnel from the eastern tower, less security but longer approach. And..." She hesitated, then pressed a section of the map that appeared unremarkable. "My father's private entrance, directly from his quarters. Security is minimal because only he's supposed to know of its existence."

Alexander's eyes narrowed. "And you know the access codes."

"I've been planning this for twenty years, Alexander." There was something wounded in her tone, a flash of the centuries of abuse she'd endured. "Every detail, every contingency."

Outside, boots thundered past their hiding place. The barricade wouldn't confuse pursuers for long.

"The tower itself is the vulnerability," Anna continued, fingers moving to the Registry structure's foundation. "The calculation engine draws power from steam generators at the base. Disrupt those, and the entire system fails temporarily including the neural controls on the enhanced guards."

Alexander nodded, mind already calculating explosive placements. "I can access the generators through maintenance shafts. Plant charges at structural weak points."

"And I can return to my father's side," Anna added. "Create confusion among his forces, delay the demonstration until you're in position." She met his eyes directly. "He trusts me less with each passing minute. If I disappear completely, he'll lock down everything."

Alexander studied her face, searching for deception despite their shared ordeal. The question that had haunted him since their partnership began resurfaced: how much could he trust the Dragon's daughter?

As if reading his thoughts, Anna stepped closer. "I could have let him capture you in the cell block. Could have exposed your escape plan before it began." Her voice dropped lower. "We both want him dead, Alexander. My reasons may differ from yours, but the goal remains the same."

Metal screeched against stone in the corridor outside—enhanced guards testing the door. The barricade shifted slightly, wood groaning under pressure.

"We have minutes at most," Alexander said, already moving toward a servant's passage Anna had indicated on the map. "If your plan is to take his place, what then?"

Anna's expression hardened. "First we survive. First, we kill him. Then we can debate the future."

She reached inside her torn clothing, withdrawing a small leather pouch that clinked with metallic contents. "Explosive charges. Small but potent. Cassie's design, acquired through contacts before I returned to the Spire."

Alexander accepted them, recognizing the craftsmanship. "Fifteen minutes?" he asked, indicating when they should reconvene.

"At the registry base. I'll ensure the noble witnesses are evacuated we do not need innocent casualties." Anna's hand caught his wrist as he turned to leave, her grip strong but not threatening. "Alexander. Whatever happens... my father must die tonight. If I fall, you must finish it."

Their eyes held for a moment longer than necessary, an unspoken current passing between them. Not trust, not quite—but something adjacent to it. Shared purpose forged in blood and desperate circumstance.

The barricaded door shuddered under renewed assault. Wood splintered as enhanced strength was applied methodically to the weakest points.

Truth And Consequences

The barricaded door exploded inward with a sound like breaking bones, shards of wood and metal flying across the library's marble floor. Alexander grabbed Anna's wrist, pulling her deeper into the shadowed stacks as enhanced guards poured through the shattered entrance. Their mechanical limbs clicked against stone with the precision of clockwork predators, optical sensors sweeping methodically through the dust-filled air. Alexander's broken ribs screamed in protest as he ran, but survival meant pushing past the pain that threatened to double him over with each labored breath.

"West wing," Anna whispered, tugging him toward a narrow passage between towering oak shelves. "There's a service exit through the reading gallery."

They slipped between aisles of ancient tomes, leather-bound volumes coated with decades of dust that rose in choking clouds as they brushed past. Alexander's boots slid on the marble floor, leaving betraying streaks in the grime. Distant shouts echoed through the vaulted space as the guards organized their search, the metallic rasp of weapons being drawn sending ice through Alexander's veins.

He spotted an abandoned weapons rack near a reading alcove the remnants of the library's guardians from centuries past. Among the ceremonial halberds and tarnished swords lay a repeater crossbow, its brass fittings dull with age but its mechanism sound. Alexander snatched it up, checking the tension with practiced hands.

"Still functional," he muttered, sliding a handful of bolts from a nearby quiver into his belt.

Anna's eyes never stopped scanning their surroundings, her vampiric senses detecting threats beyond human perception. The torches along the walls sputtered in drafts from broken windows, casting writhing shadows that mimicked the movements of pursuers. She pressed closer to Alexander, her voice barely audible even to his trained ears.

"The wards begin at the gallery threshold. I can bypass them with the charm, but we'll have seconds before the system resets."

Alexander nodded, wincing as his ribs shifted beneath bandages now damp with sweat and blood. The crossbow felt heavy in his hands, its weight reassuring despite its antiquity. They moved swiftly through the stacks, passing reading tables where open books lay forgotten, pages turning in ghostly breezes like the restless thoughts of long-dead scholars.

The flickering torchlight cast Anna's features in stark relief, her pale skin seeming to absorb the wavering glow rather than reflect it. Her fingers worked at the silver charm—the ward-walker they'd stolen from Krav's black market stall—preparing it for activation. Alexander noted the tension in her shoulders, the tight control in her movements that belied the fear she would never verbally acknowledge.

"Almost there," she breathed as they approached an arched doorway at the end of a long aisle. Beyond it lay the reading gallery, its high windows offering glimpses of night sky and distant citadels of the Blood Registry's domain.

They stepped through the archway together, Alexander scanning for threats while Anna focused on the ward barrier she alone could see with vampiric sight. The gallery stretched before them, circular in design with radiating aisles like spokes from a central hub. Broken glass crunched beneath their feet, the floor littered with shards from damaged display cases. Alexander's tactical mind registered multiple exits, calculating escape routes even as his finger rested lightly on the crossbow's trigger.

Then his blood turned to ice.

At the far end of the gallery, silhouetted against a massive stained-glass window depicting the Dragon's rise to power, stood a figure Alexander recognized immediately. Lucian Grigorescu's aristocratic frame cut a perfect line against the colored glass his posture relaxed with the confidence of a predator who knows its prey is cornered.

"I must commend your persistence," Lucian called, his voice carrying effortlessly across space. "Breaking into the Spire, infiltrating the Dragon's own sanctum..." He stepped forward into a pool of torchlight, revealing a face marked with the same cold calculation Alexander had seen in Anna's father. "And you, daughter of the Dragon. Your betrayal is particularly... disappointing."

Alexander raised the crossbow in one fluid motion, muscle memory overriding the pain in his ribs. The weapon's sights aligned perfectly with Lucian's chest, where a heart would beat if the creature possessed one. Anna slid behind him, not in fear but in tactical positioning, her silver blade appearing in her hand as if conjured from shadow.

"You should have stayed hidden, Lucian," Anna hissed, her voice low and controlled despite the danger surrounding them. "Father will be displeased when he learns you've interfered with his plans for the venator."

Lucian's lips curved in amusement, teeth gleaming unnaturally white in the torchlight. "Oh, I think not. The Dragon sent me personally to retrieve you both." He snapped his fingers, the sound sharp and final as a guillotine's fall.

From alcoves on either side of the gallery emerged two armored vampire thralls, their movements fluid and predatory in contrast to the mechanical guards. These were old-school enforcers, creatures who had earned their position through centuries of loyal service rather than technological enhancement. They wore the distinctive black armor of the Dragon's personal guard, emblazoned with crimson sigils that seemed to pulse with their own heartbeat.

Alexander released a bolt without hesitation, the crossbow's mechanism singing as it launched the projectile toward Lucian's smirking face. But the nobleman moved with inhuman speed, shifting just enough that the bolt thunked harmlessly into the marble statue behind him.

"Predictable," Lucian sighed, brushing an imaginary speck of dust from his immaculate sleeve. "The Last Venator. Such a disappointment in person."

The thralls circled wider, cutting off potential escape routes with practiced efficiency. Alexander shifted his stance, placing himself at an angle that protected Anna while maintaining sight lines to all three vampires. His mind calculated odds, finding them increasingly unfavorable with each passing second.

"The calculation engine has already been damaged," Anna said, her voice carrying the aristocratic authority she'd been raised to wield. "Father's demonstration will fail. You're backing the wrong side of history, Lucian."

Lucian's amusement vanished, replaced by something colder and more ancient. His eyes flashed crimson in the torchlight as he raised his hand and whispered a command in a language Alexander didn't recognize but instinctively feared.

The response was immediate and overwhelming. Panels hidden in the gallery's ornate walls slid open with oiled precision, revealing passage after passage filled with guards. Some were enhanced, with mechanical limbs and glowing sensor arrays. Others were pure vampires, their movements silent and deadly as they flowed into the gallery like water finding its level.

Alexander's finger tightened on the trigger as the ring of steel and malice closed around them. The air itself seemed to thicken with the scent of oil, blood, and ancient magic, the unholy trinity of the Dragon's power.

They were trapped, surrounded on all sides, with Lucian's triumphant smile promising horrors beyond even the calculation engine's integration protocols. Alexander met Anna's eyes briefly, seeing in them not defeat but cold determination. Whatever happened next, they would face it as they had faced everything since their unlikely alliance began—together, against impossible odds.

Alexander didn't wait for Lucian's order to attack. He lunged forward with explosive force, ignoring the white-hot pain that lanced through his ribs as he swung the heavy crossbow in a vicious arc. The brass-reinforced stock of the weapon connected with a guard's helmet, the impact sending vibrations up Alexander's arms and ringing through the library like a broken bell. The guard staggered back, the visor dented, momentarily disoriented as fluid leaked from ruptured hydraulic lines in his neck.

"The east window!" Anna shouted, already in motion.

She moved with the fluid grace unique to vampire nobility, her form blurring as she launched herself at the nearest thrall. Her fingers extended into lethal claws. A partial transformation that Alexander had witnessed only twice before. She raked them across the vampire's face, tearing through flesh with a sound like fabric ripping. The creature howled, blood spattering across leather-bound books as it stumbled sideways into a shelved alcove. Ancient scrolls cascaded to the marble floor, their brittle parchment crumbling under armored boots.

Alexander pivoted, barely avoiding a thrust from a mechanized pike. The weapon's electrified tip crackled past his ear, close enough that he felt the hairs on his neck rise from its charge. He countered with a swift kick to the guard's knee joint, the weakest point in the Registry's enhanced armor. Metal buckled with a satisfying crunch, sending the guard sprawling.

Three more converged on his position, their movements jerky but coordinated, like puppets controlled by a distant master. The calculation engine was directing them remotely, compensating for individual weaknesses with collective tactics. Alexander recognized the pattern from previous encounters, they attempted to herd him into a corner, limiting his mobility until he could be subdued.

He wouldn't give them the chance.

The library's west wing opened before them, its high ceiling disappearing into shadow above elaborate chandeliers that swung precariously from their mounts. Massive stained-glass windows lined the outer wall, their colored panes depicting the Dragon's conquest of human territories centuries ago. Below them, at least fifty feet down, lay the dark waters of the canal that surrounded the Spire's base. A moat designed less to keep attackers out than to trap those inside.

Alexander's world narrowed to the immediate threats surrounding him: the hiss of steam vents from mechanized limbs, the metallic tang of oil and blood in the air, the pounding of his heart that seemed to echo off the vaulted ceiling. He loaded the crossbow one-handed while retreating, backing toward Anna who had dispatched another guard with ruthless efficiency.

"We're outnumbered twenty to one," he said, voice tight with controlled urgency.

"Then they should have brought more," Anna replied, a hint of her father's arrogance showing through her usual reserve.

The soldiers—half-human, half-machine—fanned out across the gallery in standard Registry containment formation. Their faces betrayed their nature: some still mostly human, with fear making their eyes wild despite the mechanical precision of their movements; others more machine than man, optical sensors whirring where eyes should be. All moved with the singular purpose of capture rather than kill, they wanted Alexander alive for the demonstration, and Anna for her father's personal attention.

From across the gallery, Lucian directed the assault with casual gestures, his aristocratic features arranged in an expression of mild interest, as though watching children at play rather than a desperate battle. He made no move to engage directly, confident in his overwhelming numerical advantage.

A lanky guard with more human features than most stumbled forward, fumbling nervously with something clipped to his belt. Alexander recognized the distinctive brass casings of Registry stun grenades, non-lethal but devastating in enclosed spaces. The guard's hands shook as he tried to activate the primer mechanism, his eyes darting between Alexander and his commander.

"Down!" Alexander shouted, diving toward Anna as the guard's trembling fingers slipped.

Two grenades activated in rapid succession, their primer pins falling to the marble floor with a sound like distant bells. The guard looked down in horror at the devices now pulsing with alchemical energy in his hands.

The first explosion ripped through the gallery with concussive force, the blast wave shattering display cases and sending fragments of glass and wood flying in all directions. The second detonated a split second later, multiplying the chaos. Stained-glass windows that had survived centuries cracked, then exploded outward in a shower of colored shards. The blast lifted Alexander and Anna off their feet, throwing them against the far wall with bone-jarring force.

Alexander felt something crack in his already damaged ribcage, fresh pain blooming across his torso like spilled ink. His ears rang with a high-pitched whine that blocked all other sounds, disorienting him as the room seemed to tilt and spin. Through watering eyes, he saw Lucian staggering back, his perfect composure finally broken as blood streamed from cuts across his face where glass shards had embedded themselves.

Alexander groped blindly for Anna, his hand finding her sleeve amidst the debris. She pulled him upright with vampiric strength, her mouth moving in words he couldn't hear through the ringing in his ears. But her intent was clear as she pointed toward the largest window, now nothing but a gaping frame with jagged glass teeth lining its edge.

They stumbled forward together, leaning on each other as the floor seemed to shift beneath their feet. Guards lay scattered across the gallery, some motionless, others struggling to rise through the haze of dust and smoke that filled the air. Lucian's shape loomed through the chaos, his eyes burning crimson with rage as he shouted orders that were swallowed by the aftermath of the explosions.

Alexander felt hot splinters embed in his arm as a secondary explosion—perhaps from ruptured steam pipes—sent another shockwave through the gallery. The force hurled him and Anna the final distance toward the broken window, their bodies crashing through the remaining glass. He felt shards slice through his coat, cutting into the flesh beneath like dozens of tiny knives.

Then they were through, suspended in open air above the dark waters of the canal. Alexander's stomach lurched as gravity reclaimed them, the momentary weightlessness giving way to the sickening acceleration of free fall. Anna's hand remained locked around his wrist, her hair whipping upward as they plummeted together.

Time stretched like heated metal, allowing Alexander to register absurd details: the moon breaking through clouds above the Spire; Lucian's face appearing at the shattered window, contorted with fury; the reflection of fires now spreading through the library dancing on the water's surface far below.

The night air rushed past them, cold and damp against Alexander's face, tearing the breath from his lungs in a single, terrifying instant before darkness and water rose to meet them.

Alexander broke the surface with a desperate gasp, canal water flooding from his mouth as he heaved for air. The impact had driven what little breath remained in his lungs, replacing it with brackish water that tasted of industrial runoff and centuries of decay. He thrashed for a moment, disoriented by the fall and the cold that immediately seeped through his torn clothing to chill his core. Above him, the shattered library window glowed orange with spreading flames, smoke billowing into the night sky like a signal flare announcing their escape.

A splash beside him announced Anna's emergence. She surfaced more gracefully, water cascading from her black hair in rivulets as she immediately scanned their surroundings with predatory focus. Her pale skin seemed almost luminous against the dark water, every movement efficient despite the sodden weight of her clothing. Alexander noticed she kept one arm raised clear of the water, clutching something protectively against her chest.

"The schematics," she explained, following his gaze. She carefully unfolded her hand to reveal several waterlogged journal pages, their ink beginning to run but the crucial diagrams of the Blood Registry still visible. "I grabbed them before we jumped. Without these, we have no chance of targeting the structural weaknesses."

Alexander nodded, too breathless to speak as pain radiated from his ribs in waves that threatened to pull him back under. The fall had aggravated his injuries, each movement sending fresh daggers of agony through his torso. He tasted copper in the back of his throat—internal bleeding, most likely, though Mariana's potions still coursing through his system would slow the damage.

Both fighters gasped for breath, treading water as they took stock of their situation. Alexander's crossbow was gone, lost in the explosion or the fall. His coat hung in tatters, the careful arsenal of tools and weapons he'd collected now scattered across the library floor or sinking to the canal's murky bottom. Anna's clothing was similarly damaged, tears revealing pale flesh crisscrossed with rapidly healing cuts from the window glass.

The slate-gray sky stretched above them like tarnished metal, clouds obscuring stars and moon alike. The Spire loomed behind them, its towering bulk silhouetted against the night, countless windows gleaming with electric light. From their position in the water, it seemed to stretch impossibly high, its upper levels disappearing into low-hanging clouds.

Alexander spat a mouthful of canal water onto the surface, grimacing at the taste of soot and chemicals that coated his tongue. "We need to move," he managed, voice rough. "They'll have guards at every canal access point within minutes."

His gaze swept the silent waterfront, tactician's mind cataloging details despite the pain that threatened to cloud his thoughts. Fog curled over the canal's surface, providing some cover but limiting visibility to mere yards.

Distant lanterns flickered along the embankment, marking the positions of Registry checkpoints. From the Grand Docks several hundred yards downriver came the faint rumble of patrol boats, their steam engines chugging to life as alarms spread throughout the compound.

"He knows," Anna said suddenly, her voice a whisper that trembled with anger and regret. Her knuckles whitened as she clutched the precious schematics more tightly to her chest. "Lucian's presence in the library wasn't coincidence. He was waiting for us."

Alexander's jaw clenched against the cold as he processed the implications. "Your father suspected your return wasn't genuine."

"Not suspected. Knew." Anna's heterochromatic eyes reflected the distant fires still raging in the library. "He tested me, and I failed. Now he'll accelerate the demonstration timeline, perhaps begin it immediately."

Alexander kicked toward the far edge of the canal, every stroke sending fresh pain through his damaged body. Anna kept pace beside him, her vampire physiology already repairing the worst of her injuries. The water around them was filthy with industrial waste and the accumulated refuse of centuries, but it had saved their lives—the fifty-foot drop would have shattered human bones on solid ground.

"This is our only chance to destroy the registry," Anna continued, determination hardening her voice. "If my father completes the demonstration and brings the calculation engine fully online, resistance becomes impossible. The neural compliance protocols will spread beyond the enhanced guards to the general population."

Alexander nodded grimly, the cold water numbing his extremities but doing nothing to dull his resolve. They had come too far, sacrificed too much to abandon the mission now. The damage to the calculation engine core had been significant but not fatal—they needed to finish what they'd started, regardless of the escalated risk.

They reached the canal's edge, a moss-slicked stone embankment littered with broken machinery and discarded metal parts. Alexander dragged himself up with trembling arms, collapsing onto the wet stones as water streamed from his clothing. Every breath sent spikes of pain through his chest, but he forced himself to his knees, then to his feet, swaying slightly as his body protested the movement.

Anna emerged beside him, water sluicing from her form as she carefully tucked the registry schematics inside her torn blouse. Despite their bedraggled appearance, her eyes burned with the same cold fire that had driven her to betray her father and join forces with the Last Venator. The unlikeliest of alliances, forged in shared hatred and desperate necessity.

"We still have Cassie's explosives," Alexander said, patting his waterlogged trousers where he'd secured the small devices in waterproof pouches. "And we know the approach route through the maintenance tunnels."

"They'll have doubled the guards," Anna countered, wringing water from her hair with quick, efficient motions. "And my father will have moved the nobles to the secure level for an expedited demonstration."

Alexander straightened to his full height, ignoring the protests of his battered body. In the distance, searchlights swept across the Spire's lower levels, illuminating the decorative gargoyles and steam vents that adorned its façade. Registry patrol boats had begun moving up the canal, their searchlights cutting through the fog in widening arcs.

"Then we adapt," he said simply. "We find another way in."

Anna studied his face, seeing the determination that had carried him through years of hunting, surviving, and planning his revenge against the creature who had ordered his family's execution. The same determination that now drove him to prevent the final subjugation of humanity, regardless of the cost to himself.

She nodded once, a gesture that contained both agreement and respect. "The western maintenance shaft. It's older, less monitored. Designed for waste disposal rather than access, but it connects to the lower levels where the power distribution systems are housed."

Together they moved away from the canal edge, slipping into the shadows between dilapidated warehouses that lined the waterfront. Steam rose from their soaked clothing as their body heat began to dry the worst of the dampness. They left wet footprints on the cobblestones, but the spreading fog would conceal these traces before patrol guards could follow them.

The Dragon awaited in his Spire, surrounded by vampire nobility and protected by an army of enhanced guards. The calculation engine hummed with power, preparing to extend its control beyond the walls of the Registry and into the minds of every human within its reach. All that stood against this terrible future were two figures moving through the fog: a vampire daughter turned against her kind, and the Last Venator, united in their determination to strike at Dracula's heart and shatter the machinery of absolute control.

Tinkerer's Gambit

Alexander followed Nikolai "Niko" Petrov across the shattered outskirts of Slade, his boots crunching on glass and broken cobblestones with each careful step. His broken ribs protested with each movement, the damp clothes from their canal escape still clinging uncomfortably to his skin. The smuggler moved with surprising agility for someone who'd been beaten nearly senseless the day before, slipping between collapsed walls and burned-out storefronts with the practiced ease of a man who'd spent his life navigating society's margins. Behind them, fires raged where Niko's distraction had drawn Dracula's forces away from the Spire.

"Keep low," Niko hissed over his shoulder, his swollen eye a purple testament to the price of his earlier betrayal. "Registry patrols are everywhere since your escape."

Alexander tightened his grip on the rifle butt, a battered piece salvaged from a dead guard during their frantic rush through the back alleys of Old Slade. The weapon felt inadequate against what awaited them, but it was better than facing Dracula's forces unarmed. His finger brushed against the trigger guard, the cold metal a small comfort in a world gone mad.

Ahead, flames licked at wooden barricades where terrified townsfolk lobbed stones and bottles at Dracula's armored jackboots. The Registry soldiers advanced with mechanical precision, their movements unnervingly synchronized as steam hissed from regulation joints in their armor. Behind them prowled clockwork hounds, their glass eyes glowing red in the darkness as they sniffed for prey with mechanical snouts.

Alexander felt a flicker of grim satisfaction at the chaos Niko had sown. "Your distraction seems effective," he muttered, ducking behind a scorched carriage as a patrol thundered past.

"Had to call in every favor I was owed," Niko replied, his usual sardonic tone subdued by the gravity of their situation. "Half the underground thinks

I've lost my mind, attacking the Registry directly. The other half joined because they've seen what happens to those who get 'processed' by the calculation engine."

They paused at an intersection where the street gave way to a tangled maze of twisted metal and broken stone. Niko scrambled over a pile of scorched crates, his movements nimble despite his injuries. He waved Alexander forward, pointing toward a narrow gap between two half-collapsed buildings.

"Through there. She's waiting."

Alexander ducked beneath torn canvas walls that once marked the boundary of a thriving market, now reduced to charred timber and scattered merchandise. The alley beyond stank of burned cloth and spent alchemical charges, the distinctive copper tang of blood underlying it all. His venator senses cataloged the smells automatically, calculating how recently the violence had swept through this area.

In the shadows of a recessed doorway, Anna waited. Her pale skin seemed to glow in the dim light, her heterochromatic eyes scanning the sky for Registry airships or worse, the winged thralls that sometimes, accompanied major Registry operations. Her clothing was different from when they'd separated at the canals, she'd found something dry, practical, with multiple belts and pouches that spoke of preparation rather than fashion.

"You made it," she said, relief briefly softening her aristocratic features. "I thought perhaps..."

"It'll take more than a fall and some water to finish me," Alexander replied, the joke falling flat as fresh pain lanced through his ribs. He pressed a hand against his side, feeling the dampness that might be water or blood. "Your father's men?"

"Everywhere," Anna confirmed, her voice tight. "He's mobilized everything. Enhanced guards, Registry enforcers, even the noble houses' private security. The calculation engine demonstration was a success."

Alexander checked his timepiece, barely an hour remained. "Then we're out of time for subtlety."

A commotion drew their attention to the main road. Steam-spewing cloaked figures—Registry technicians with experimental weapons—directed a pack of mechanical wolves toward the barricades. Their metal paws sparked against cobblestones as they bounded forward, jaws designed to crush bone snapping at the air in anticipation.

"They're heading for the breach in the eastern quarter," Niko observed. "My people opened a false path to the Spire from that direction. Should keep them occupied for twenty minutes, maybe thirty."

As the patrol thundered past their hiding spot, Alexander caught Anna's eye. She nodded once, understanding passing between them without words. They had survived the impossible, escaped the Spire itself. Whatever came next, they would face it together.

"Now," Niko hissed, shoving Alexander toward a rusted door set into the foundation of what had once been a Registry substation. The hinges protested as he forced it open, revealing stone steps descending into darkness.

The supply bunker below was illuminated only by a single oil lamp, its weak light revealing stacks of pitted rifles leaning against crumbling walls. Wooden crates lined one side of the room, their contents partially visible through broken slats—grenades stamped with Cassie Fairweather's distinctive emblem, her technical brilliance repurposed for destruction. Barrels filled with incendiary vials stood in neat rows, their contents glowing faintly through green glass.

"Your resistance friends have been busy," Alexander observed, inspecting a rifle more closely. The weapon showed signs of heavy use, but its mechanism was clean, well-maintained.

"Not the resistance," Niko corrected, securing the door behind them. "At least, not just them. These are from Cassie's private stockpile. She's been preparing for this day longer than any of us realized."

Anna moved through the bunker with silent efficiency, examining each weapon with the critical eye of someone who had spent centuries learning the art of war. She slung a rifle over her shoulder, the movement graceful despite the weapon's awkward bulk. Her pale fingers tested a grenade's pin, measuring its resistance with practiced precision.

"These will do," she said finally. "Not enough to storm the Registry Spire directly, but enough to create the opening we need."

Alexander checked the barrel of his chosen rifle, finding it straight and true. The wooden stock was worn smoothly from use, fitting against his shoulder like an old friend. He loaded it with mechanical precision, each motion practiced until it required no thought.

Distant howls echoed from above. Dracula's enforcers, hunting through the streets for any sign of the escaped prisoners. The mechanical baying gradually receded, drawn away by the chaos of the riot Niko had orchestrated.

Only when the sounds faded entirely did Alexander allow his shoulders to drop, the tension he'd been carrying since their desperate plunge from the Spire's window momentarily easing. He slumped against a wall, suddenly aware of how close to collapse his body had come.

"You look terrible," Niko observed, offering a flask of something that smelled like industrial solvent. "Drink. It won't heal you, but it'll make you care less about the pain."

Alexander accepted the flask, taking a careful sip that burned all the way down. "We still need to reach the Registry engine," he said, passing the flask to Anna. "And your father will have tripled the guards since our escape."

Anna took a measured drink before returning the flask. "We won't use the same approach. The explosion in the library damaged more than just books. It compromised part of the outer ward system. There's a vulnerability we can exploit if we're quick."

"And I've arranged one final distraction," Niko added, a ghost of his old confidence returning. "Something even the Dragon won't be able to ignore."

Alexander pushed himself upright, ignoring the protest from his broken body. They had weapons now, a plan, and the desperate courage of those with nothing left to lose. The calculation engine awaited, and with it, the fate of both their species.

"Then let's finish this," he said, checking his timepiece again. Fifty-two minutes until midnight. Until Dracula unleashed his perfect vision of control upon the world. "Once and for all."

Alexander crept through Slade's canal district, keeping his body low against slick cobblestones still wet from evening mist. The moonless sky offered perfect cover but also concealed the movements of Dracula's patrols. He clutched his stolen rifle tight against his chest, every sense heightened by the venator training that had kept him alive for years in this hellish world. Distant clangs of metal against stone marked the methodical search pattern of steam-patrols, their mechanical breathing audible even from streets away. Behind him, Niko moved with uncharacteristic silence, fear having finally taught the smuggler caution, while Anna's steps fell soundless beside him, her vampire nature allowing her to glide like a shadow across the uneven ground.

"Junction ahead," Niko whispered, his breath forming small clouds in the chill air. "Registry checkpoint usually staffed with four guards and at least one enhanced."

Alexander nodded, the movement sending fresh waves of pain through his damaged ribs. The binding he'd applied in the supply bunker was already soaked through with a mixture of canal water and blood. Every breath felt like glass shards in his lungs, but he pushed the pain aside with practiced discipline. The mission mattered more than his comfort or survival.

"Can we bypass it?" he asked, studying the darkened intersection where three canals met beneath an ornate bridge of wrought iron and tarnished brass.

"No time," Anna replied, her heterochromatic eyes reflecting what little light filtered through the cloud cover. "Forty-three minutes until midnight. We take the direct path."

Alexander assessed their options with a tactician's precision. The checkpoint stood between them and the most direct route to the Blood Registry tower, whose upper spires were just visible over the rooftops, green lights pulsing along its length like a diseased heartbeat. To go around would cost precious minutes they couldn't spare.

"I'll draw them off," Niko offered, already reaching for a smoke grenade from his belt. "Give you a thirty-second window, maybe less."

Before Alexander could respond, Anna's head snapped up, her body tensing in alarm. "Too late," she hissed. "They've found us."

The sound reached Alexander's human ears a moment later, the distinctive snarling of vampiric enforcers, their boots thundering on marble blocks as they bounded across rooftops with inhuman speed. Unlike the shambling enhanced guards or the methodical steam-patrols, these were pure predators, trained to hunt and kill without the encumbrance of mechanical augmentation.

"Run," Alexander commanded, abandoning stealth for speed as he sprinted toward the checkpoint. Behind them, the enforcers howled, the sound echoing off stone buildings and across the still water of the canals.

They raced through narrow alleys, past boarded-up shops and abandoned homes whose owners had fled or been "processed" by the Registry. Alexander's legs burned with exhaustion, his lungs struggling for air as his broken ribs limited each breath. Anna could have outpaced them easily, her vampire strength undiminished by their ordeal, but she matched her pace to Alexander's, unwilling to leave her human ally behind.

"There!" Niko gasped, pointing to a collapsed structure ahead. The building had once been a Registry transport depot, its roof caved in from some past attack or structural failure. Among the rubble lay several hover carts, their brass hulls dented but largely intact.

Alexander vaulted over a low wall and into the wreckage, his eyes immediately assessing each vehicle for viability. Most were beyond repair, their levitation coils shattered, or power cores depleted. But one, half-buried beneath fallen beams, still showed the faint blue glow of a functioning power system.

"Help me," he grunted, heaving a splintered beam aside to access the cart's controls. Anna joined him, her strength making quick work of obstacles that would have stymied human efforts.

The cart was smaller than standard Registry models, designed for maintenance rather than transport. Its exposed power conduits sparked dangerously, the insulation burned away to reveal glowing copper beneath. The control lever was bent but functional, its brass handle worn smooth from use.

Niko scrambled in behind them, his face pale with exertion and fear. "They're right behind me," he panted, fumbling with his remaining grenades. "I count six, maybe more."

Alexander yanked the cart's lever, praying to gods he'd stopped believing in years ago. The vehicle shuddered, ancient machinery protesting as power surged through damaged circuits. For a heart-stopping moment, nothing happened. Then the hover cart lurched upward, clearing the ground by inches as its levitation coils screamed in protest.

"Hold on," Alexander warned, slamming the throttle forward. The cart shot through the collapsed depot's open side, showering them with sparks as exposed power conduits scraped against broken beams.

They burst into the open street just as the first enforcers rounded the corner, their crimson eyes widening in surprise at the unexpected sight. One leaped forward with supernatural speed, clawed hands extended to catch the cart's rear edge.

Niko was faster. He lobbed a grenade with perfect accuracy, the device detonating in a blinding flash that sent the enforcers reeling backward, temporarily blinded. The cart accelerated, leaving their howls of rage behind as it skimmed low over the cobblestones.

"Head for the eastern approach," Anna directed, her voice raised over the cart's whining engines. "The Registry checkpoint there will be undermanned with all patrols searching the city for us."

Alexander steered through narrow streets, the cart's controls fighting him as damaged systems struggled to maintain stability. Ahead loomed the wrought-iron gates that marked the outer perimeter of the Blood Registry complex. Beyond them rose the tower itself, a monument to vampire dominion over humanity that had stood for centuries. Tonight, if they succeeded, it would fall.

The cart skidded beneath the steel archway, guards shouting in alarm as they flashed past too quickly for even enhanced reflexes to respond. Alexander's heart hammered against his damaged ribs, adrenaline briefly masking the pain as they penetrated the outer defenses with surprising ease.

"Stop here," Anna commanded as they approached a darkened courtyard some distance from the tower's main entrance. "We go on foot from here."

Alexander killed the power, the cart settling to the ground with a metallic groan that seemed too loud in the sudden silence. They'd made it inside the perimeter, but the real challenge still awaited them. Reaching the calculation engine at the tower's heart before Dracula could activate it fully.

He was about to step from the cart when movement ahead caught his attention. A figure stepped into the pool of lantern light, tall and broad-shouldered, with a leather patch covering his left eye socket. The patch stood dark against a face mapped with scars earned in decades of battle against the Registry's forces.

"Victor," Alexander breathed, recognizing the venator master who had trained him after his family's slaughter.

Victor Thorn's remaining eye narrowed as he assessed his former pupil's condition with professional detachment. "You look like hell, boy," he growled, his voice like gravel underfoot.

Behind him stepped a smaller figure, a woman whose vibrant red hair was pulled back in a practical knot, soot streaking her face and hands. Cassie Fairweather clutched a reinforced chest in her arms, its brass surface etched with protective sigils and mechanical locks.

"You're late," she said, though relief softened the accusation. "We thought you'd been captured again."

Alexander stepped from the cart, his legs almost buckling as exhaustion and pain reasserted themselves. "How did you find us?" he asked, eyes darting to the shadows around them, searching for threats or traps.

"Niko's message reached us," Victor replied, nodding to the smuggler who hung back, uncomfortable under the venator master's scrutiny. "Though I'd have words with him later about loyalty and the price of betrayal."

Cassie stepped forward, setting the chest on the ground between them. Her fingers, stained with oil and soot from her workshop, worked the complex locks with practiced efficiency. "No time for that now," she insisted. "We have minutes, not hours."

The chest opened with a soft hiss of equalizing pressure, revealing its precious contents—rolled parchments covered in intricate diagrams and technical specifications, along with a dozen or more pulse-disruptor charges nestled in protective casings.

"These schematics map every ward anchor and kill-switch inside the tower," Victor explained, his voice dropping to ensure it wouldn't carry beyond their small group. "Dracula rewires them at dawn for full implementation. Tonight's demonstration is just the preview of what's to come."

Alexander knelt beside the chest, his fingers tracing the detailed floor plans of the Registry's inner sanctum. The calculation engine's location was clearly marked, along with power conduits, security checkpoints, and most critically, structural weaknesses that could be exploited.

"How did you get these?" he asked, unable to keep the awe from his voice. Such intelligence would have taken years to compile, countless lives sacrificed to gather each fragment.

"Does it matter?" Victor countered. "Use them. Finish what your father started before the Registry purged the venators."

Alexander clenched his fists at the sight, each detail confirming that their final assault now depended on the intelligence they carried. With these schematics, they had a fighting chance—without them, they would have been blindly stumbling through the Registry's defenses until capture or death found them.

"Thirty-six minutes," Anna announced, checking a timepiece pulled from her pocket. "We need to move now."

Victor's eye lingered on the vampire noblewoman, decades of ingrained hatred battling with the pragmatic necessity of their alliance. "You're really doing this?" he asked her. "Betraying your father, your kind?"

Anna met his gaze without flinching. "My father betrayed what vampires could be long before I betrayed him. The calculation engine will enslave humans and vampires alike—just in different ways."

Alexander gathered the schematics and charges, distributing them among the group with tactical precision. "We'll approach through the maintenance tunnels here," he decided, pointing to a service entrance marked on the plans. "Four charges at these junction points should create enough structural damage to disable the power grid without destroying the entire tower."

"And Dracula?" Victor asked the question hanging heavy in the air between them.

Alexander's face hardened, years of grief and rage condensing into cold certainty. "He's mine."

The last venator checked his weapons one final time, the rifle slung across his back alongside Cassie's specialized explosives. Thirty-four minutes remained until midnight. Thirty-four minutes to prevent humanity's final subjugation under the Dragon's claw.

"Let's move," he ordered, and the unlikely alliance of venator, vampire, inventor, and smuggler melted into the shadows, advancing toward their date with history.

Assault On the Iron Tower

Alexander crept forward through the rubble-strewn outskirts of Slade, his broken ribs screaming protest with each careful step. The moonless sky hung like a shroud above them, perfect cover for their approach but also perfect concealment for Dracula's patrols. Behind him, Anna moved with preternatural silence, her pale skin the only betrayal of her presence in the shadows, while Cassie and Victor followed with the practiced stealth of those long accustomed to evading Registry detection.

The Blood Registry tower loomed before them, its silhouette carved against the night like a knife wound in darkness. Green lights pulsed along with its height in irregular patterns, signaling the calculation engine's increasing power. Alexander checked his timepiece: twenty-nine minutes until midnight. Twenty-nine minutes until Dracula's vision for humanity's enslavement would become irreversible.

"Niko's distraction should draw the bulk of the patrols to the western quadrant," Victor murmured, his voice barely audible over the distant hiss of steam vents. The venator master's remaining eye constantly scanned their surroundings, decades of battle instincts never at rest.

Alexander nodded, not wasting breath on unnecessary words. Each inhale sent daggers through his torso, the bindings around his broken ribs now stiff with dried blood. He focused instead on the approach vector, identifying the maintenance entrance marked on the stolen schematics. A rusted service door partially concealed behind waste processing units.

They skirted the fractured remains of what had once been Registry worker housing, now nothing but hollow shells after the last uprising. The stench of burned insulation and chemical residue hung in the air, marking where flame throwers had purged resistance fighters from their hiding places months ago.

"Wait," Cassie whispered sharply, dropping to one knee beside a massive steam vent. Her fingers, blackened with grease and soot, worked at a brass device hanging from her belt. "Thermal scan pulse incoming. They'll see us if we don't—"

She didn't finish, instead twisting the central dial on her device with practiced precision. A faint blue shimmer washed over the group as the stealth field generator activated. Alexander felt the hair on his arms rise as the field took effect, bending heat signatures away from Registry sensors.

"How long?" he asked, eyes fixed on the tower's upper levels where scanning equipment rotated on mechanical arms.

"Three minutes, maybe less," Cassie replied, already repacking the generator. "Batteries can't handle more without—"

The words died in her throat as metal scraped against stone behind them. Alexander turned, rifle already rising to his shoulder, to see them—half-human, half-machine abominations shambling into view around the corner of a collapsed warehouse.

Five hybrids, their movements jerky yet purposeful, optical arrays glowing sickly yellow in the darkness. Their torsos had been surgically opened and reinforced with brass plating, internal organs visible through transparent panels filled with bubbling fluids. What had once been arms now terminated in articulated claws or crude weapons fused directly to bone and sinew. They sniffed the air like hunting dogs, their partly human faces contorted in expressions of permanent agony.

Alexander's tactical assessment was instant and cold. The stealth field concealed them from thermal scans but not visual detection. The hybrids had spotted them, heads swiveling in unison with mechanical precision as commands from the calculation engine directed their movements.

"No choice," Anna hissed, her heterochromatic eyes flashing with predatory focus. "Take them quickly, before they can alert others."

Victor moved first, decades of venator training condensed into a blur of lethal efficiency. He launched forward from a half-crouch, twin silver-bladed stakes appearing in his hands as if conjured from air itself. The stakes found their marks with surgical precision, driving through reinforced thoracic cavities where hybrids' control modules were housed.

Alexander was only half a step behind, his wrist-mounted ether bolt launcher discharging with a soft thump. The projectile struck the third hybrid squarely in its exposed chest cavity, the alchemical charge disrupting the electrical impulses that kept its human and mechanical components functioning in horrible harmony. The creature convulsed, tubes and wires rupturing in a spray of fluids and sparks before it collapsed.

Anna's movement was too fast for human eyes to track properly—a pale streak resolving into brutal efficiency as she closed with the remaining hybrids. Her hands found vulnerable connection points between flesh and machine, twisting with inhuman strength. The sound of vertebrae snapping echoed like brittle twigs breaking, her expression unchanged throughout the slaughter.

The fifth hybrid, larger than its companions and sporting what appeared to be experimental armor plating, raised an arm-mounted sonic weapon. Cassie reacted immediately, thumbing the activation switch on her disruptor. The device emitted no sound audible to human ears, but the effect on the hybrid was immediate and catastrophic. Its enhanced auditory systems, designed to detect the faintest human heartbeat at a hundred paces, overloaded instantly. The creature staggered, internal fluids leaking from rupturing containment vessels as its mechanical components vibrated at resonant frequencies they were never designed to withstand.

"The gate," Alexander hissed, gesturing toward the maintenance entrance now just thirty yards ahead. He seized Cassie's arm, pulling her forward as the hybrid thrashed in its death throes, metal components tearing through its own flesh in a desperate attempt to silence the unbearable frequencies assaulting its systems.

They reached the reinforced gate, its surface etched with Registry wards and mechanical locks designed to resist both physical and magical intrusion. Victor produced tools from inside his coat with practiced efficiency, working at the complex mechanism while Alexander and Anna stood guard, weapons ready.

"Almost," Victor grunted, sweat beading on his scarred face despite the night's chill.

The lock yielded with a grudging click, metal pins retracting into housing. Alexander pressed his shoulder against the gate, muscles straining as the hinges protested with a sound like distant screaming. The gap widened inch by agonizing inch, just enough for them to slip through one at a time.

"Cassie, you first," Alexander ordered, maintaining pressure on the reluctant gate.

She nodded, squeezing through the narrow opening, her tool belt catching momentarily before she yanked it free. Anna followed, her slender form passing through with vampiric grace. Victor gestured for Alexander to go next, but he shook his head stubbornly.

"After you," he insisted, the venator code ingrained too deeply to abandon even now.

Victor's mouth tightened, but he didn't waste time arguing. He turned sideways to slip through the gap, his broad shoulders barely clearing the opening. As he passed, a shadow detached itself from the darkness behind them—the fifth hybrid, somehow still functioning despite catastrophic damage to its systems. Its barbed tail whipped forward with terrible speed, the serrated edge slicing through the air toward Alexander's unprotected back.

"Down!" Victor shouted, shoving Alexander aside with desperate force.

The tail missed Alexander by inches, instead lashing across Victor's back as he interposed himself between his former student and certain death. Leather and flesh parted beneath the razored edge, blood spraying in a dark arc visible even in the dim light. Victor grunted, more in anger than pain, as he stumbled forward through the gate.

Alexander didn't hesitate. He fired his ether bolt directly into the hybrid's face, the alchemical charge detonating with a wet thump that splattered organic and mechanical components across the wall behind it. Shoving the gate closed behind him, he spun to where Victor had collapsed against the courtyard's inner wall, clutching his left shoulder.

"How bad?" Alexander demanded, already assessing the wound with clinical detachment. The gash ran diagonally across Victor's back from shoulder to mid-spine, deep enough to expose muscle but having missed vital structures by millimeters.

"Had worse shaving," Victor growled, though the tightness around his eye betrayed the pain he refused to acknowledge. "Just bind it. We don't have time for more."

Anna appeared at Alexander's side, pressing a cloth torn from her own clothing against the wound. "The courtyard is clear for now," she reported, "but we have minutes at most before patrols discover the bodies."

Alexander nodded, helping Victor to his feet once the makeshift bandage was secured. Blood already soaked through the cloth, but the venator master stood firm, refusing to be slowed by mere injury. Together they moved deeper into the shadow of the tower, toward the calculation engine that represented humanity's doom and their last chance for victory.

"Twenty-six minutes," Cassie whispered, checking her timepiece as they approached the tower's service entrance. Alexander felt time's pressure weighing on him like a physical force as they slipped inside, the first barrier breached but the real challenges still ahead.

The entry hall yawned before them like the gullet of some mechanical beast; its high ceiling lost in shadow and steam. Rotating cog-doors intersected the chamber at irregular intervals, their brass teeth grinding against stone floors with sounds like distant screams. Alexander's eyes traced the network of steam-flecked corridors branching from the central hub, each one bristling with warded vents and pressure-sensitive floor plates designed to trigger lethal countermeasures. The air itself felt hostile, thick with the metallic tang of blood-infused steam that powered Dracula's unholy machinery.

"Surveillance grid," Cassie whispered, pointing toward brass observation spheres suspended from the ceiling on articulated arms. Their glass lenses rotated in mechanical precision, sweeping the hall in overlapping patterns. "They'll spot us in ten seconds unless I—"

She didn't finish, instead darting toward a bank of brass conduits running along the eastern wall. Alexander and Anna flanked Victor, supporting him as blood continued to seep through his makeshift bandage. The venator master's face had gone ashen, but his remaining eye burned with fierce determination.

"Keep pressure on it," Alexander murmured to Anna as they followed Cassie's path, staying in the blind spots between surveillance spheres. The vampire noble nodded, her pale fingers pressing against Victor's wound with calculated force.

Cassie knelt beside the conduit junction, her tools appearing in her hands with practiced speed. She pried open an access panel, revealing a nest of copper wiring and glass tubes filled with bubbling red liquid, human blood, alchemically treated to power the Registry's systems. Alexander recognized the configuration from the schematics they'd studied: the central control nexus for the entry hall's defenses.

"Cover me," Cassie muttered, her fingers already tracing connections with confident precision. "Need forty seconds."

Alexander scanned their surroundings, counting threats with venator instinct. The cog-doors continued their relentless rotation, each pass revealing glimpses of corridors beyond. Steam vented from pressure release valves at irregular intervals, the controlled bursts concealing subtle shifts in the hall's architecture as defensive measures realigned themselves.

"Movement," Anna hissed, her vampire senses detecting threats before human eyes could perceive them. "Eastern corridor. Blood-sworn guards."

Alexander positioned himself between the threat and Cassie, rifle raised in readiness. Behind him, the inventor's tools clicked against metal as she bypassed security measures and rewired control mechanisms. Victor struggled to stand straighter, refusing to be dead weight despite his injury.

"Almost..." Cassie's voice was tight with concentration. "Just need to reroute the pressure through the secondary—"

The hall's lighting flickered as her bypass took effect. The grinding of cog-doors stuttered, then halted entirely. Surveillance spheres drooped on their mounts, lenses going dark as power was diverted from security systems to emergency protocols. From somewhere deep within the tower's structure came the sound of massive pistons powering down, followed by the metallic groaning of pressure valves locking into safety positions.

"Done," Cassie announced, securing her tools with quick efficiency. "We have maybe three minutes before the backup systems engage."

Anna stepped forward, her heterochromatic eyes scanning the now-static cog-doors. "This way," she commanded, her voice carrying the authority of centuries. "Through the northern passage. The wardstones are weaker there. Deliberately so, to allow my father easier passage."

They followed her lead, moving swiftly through the temporary stillness of the entry hall. The northern passage narrowed quickly, its walls lined with black obsidian that seemed to absorb light rather than reflect it. Flame gratings punctuated the corridor at irregular intervals, blue-tinged fire dancing behind ornate metalwork. With each grating they passed, Alexander felt the distinctive prickling sensation of magical wards washing over his skin.

"Blood wards," Anna explained, her voice dropping to an antiquated cadence that betrayed her true age. "Designed to admit only those of noble lineage or their sanctioned servants." She produced the black-market charm from within her clothing, its surface now glowing with an unhealthy purple light. "Stand close. The effect extends mere inches beyond my person."

Alexander pressed closer to her side, feeling Victor and Cassie do the same. The charm's light pulsed in time with Anna's heartbeat as she traced complex patterns in the air before each ward they encountered. The magical barriers shimmered visibly at her approach, then reluctantly parted like curtains drawn aside by invisible hands.

"Your father's magic recognizes you still," Alexander observed, noting how the wards seemed almost to hesitate before yielding.

"Not recognition," Anna corrected, her lips tightening. "Confusion. It senses my blood but cannot reconcile it with my intent. The charm exploits that uncertainty."

They had navigated past the seventh warded grating when the attack came. Figures in gossamer coats materialized from alcoves cunningly designed to conceal their presence—loyalist vampires, their eyes burning crimson with fanatical devotion to their Dragon lord. Unlike the mechanically enhanced guards outside, these were pure vampire nobility, their movements fluid and lethal as they closed from multiple directions.

"Traitor-daughter," hissed the lead vampire, his aristocratic features twisted with hatred as he focused on Anna. "The Dragon will wear your skin as a trophy for this betrayal."

Alexander didn't waste breath on response. His rifle came up in one fluid motion, specialized incendiary rounds punching through the first vampire's chest. The creature shrieked as alchemical fire ignited its internal organs, spreading through undead tissue with unnatural hunger. A second shot caught another in the face, the round detonating on impact and reducing its head to charred fragments.

Anna moved like liquid shadow, her vampire speed making her nearly invisible to human perception. She materialized behind a third loyalist, driving a silver blade through the base of its skull with brutal precision. The creature collapsed, its nervous system severed from the brain that controlled it.

Victor, despite his injury, proved why he had survived decades as a venator. His movements were slower than usual but no less lethal, each strike targeting vulnerable points with economical precision. His remaining silver stake found a vampire's heart, the creature's dying scream cut short as its body crumbled to ash.

Cassie held her own with technology rather than combat skill. Her sonic disruptor emitted focused pulses that disoriented vampire senses, creating openings that Alexander and Anna exploited with ruthless efficiency. Within moments, the corridor was littered with dissolving corpses, the stone floor slick with fluids that steamed in the cold air.

"We need to move," Alexander urged, reloading his rifle with practiced speed. "That was just the advance guard."

Anna nodded, already turning toward the end of the corridor where a spiraling stairwell twisted upward into darkness. "The calculation engine's central chamber lies five levels up," she said. "These stairs are the most direct route."

The stairwell was carved from solid obsidian, each step worn slightly concave by centuries of use. No railings protected against the dizzying drop at its center, the spiral continuing upward far beyond what Alexander's human eyes could perceive in the gloom. They ascended as swiftly as Victor's condition allowed, the venator master's breathing becoming increasingly labored with each level they climbed.

They had reached the fourth level when Anna suddenly froze, her body tensing like a hunting cat's. "Elite sentinels," she whispered, pointing upward to where the stairwell opened onto a wide landing. "Steam-armored. At least eight."

Alexander peered upward, his venator-trained eyes picking out details that would be invisible to ordinary humans. The sentinels stood in perfect formation, their armor unlike anything he'd seen before. Steam vented from joints in the metal plating, the brass surfaces etched with runic protections against both physical and magical attacks. Each sentinel carried an electrified halberd, the weapons humming with lethal potential.

"They're blocking the only approach to the inner sanctum," Anna continued, her voice tight with controlled urgency. "We cannot go around."

Victor straightened, his face gray with pain but his eye clear. "I'll handle them," he announced, his gravelly voice allowing no argument.

"Victor—" Alexander began, but the venator master cut him off with a sharp gesture.

"I'm bleeding out, boy. We both know it." Victor reached into his coat, producing a brass sphere that pulsed with barely contained energy. Cassie's prototype pulse grenade, far more powerful than standard Registry explosives. "Better to go out taking some of the Dragon's pets with me."

Alexander recognized the truth in Victor's words, even as he rejected it emotionally. The older venator had perhaps minutes left, the wound in his back having severed more than was immediately apparent. Victor saw the realization in his former student's eyes and nodded once, a warrior's acknowledgment.

"Get to the engine," Victor commanded. "Finish what we started."

Before Alexander could respond, Victor lurched forward, ascending the remaining stairs with sudden speed born of desperate purpose. The sentinels reacted instantly, their halberds leveling in perfect unison as they detected the intruder. Victor didn't slow, instead activating the pulse grenade with a twist of its upper hemisphere. The device began to emit a high-pitched whine that rose rapidly in pitch and intensity.

"Down!" Cassie shouted, dragging Alexander and Anna backward as Victor hurled the grenade into the midst of the sentinel formation.

The explosion transcended sound, becoming a physical force that slammed into Alexander's chest like a battering ram. The stairwell's obsidian walls shattered under the blast wave, chunks of stone flying outward as the entire section of tower seemed to fold in upon itself. Steam pipes ruptured, their contents escaping in scalding jets that filled the air with blinding vapor. Through the chaos, Alexander glimpsed Victor's silhouette, standing firm as the blast engulfed him and the sentinels alike.

Then the floor beneath them gave way, dropping them into swirling dust and debris. Alexander felt Anna's hand close around his wrist with vampire strength, pulling him toward a jagged opening that had appeared in the inner wall. Cassie was already scrambling through the gap, her smaller frame allowing her to navigate the twisted metal and shattered stone.

"Move!" Anna shouted above the continuing rumble of collapsing architecture. "The support won't hold!"

Alexander followed her through the breach, ignoring the glass-sharp edges that tore at his clothing and skin. They tumbled together into a corridor beyond, Cassie slamming a massive blast door shut behind them just as the stairwell collapsed completely. The sound of Victor's sacrifice was suddenly muffled, reduced to distant vibrations felt through the floor rather than heard.

Alexander leaned against the wall, breathing in ragged gasps as his broken ribs protested the rough treatment. Anna stood perfectly still, her eyes closed as she processed the loss of their ally. Cassie busied herself checking her remaining equipment, her hands moving with mechanical precision that belied the emotion tight around her eyes.

"Victor knew the odds," Alexander said finally, straightening despite the pain. "He chose his end."

Anna's eyes opened, revealing a hardness that reminded Alexander whose daughter she truly was. "Then let's ensure it wasn't wasted," she replied. "The calculation engine lies just ahead."

They moved forward into the heart of Dracula's domain, one ally fewer but their resolve undiminished.

The calculation engine chamber stretched before them in terrible grandeur, a vaulted cathedral to human subjugation. Colossal brass and copper machines lined the circular walls, their pistons driving with the rhythm of mechanical heartbeats as they processed millions of blood samples collected from Registry citizens. Glass tubes thick as Alexander's arm carried glowing crimson fluid throughout the apparatus, pulsing with unnatural life as they fed data into computation engines that whirred and clicked with relentless purpose. The chamber's center held a raised platform ringed by control stations, each attended by white-coated technicians who fled in panic as the intruders burst through the damaged entrance.

Alexander's his Venator senses immediately cataloged the obscenity before him. Each piston stroke, each mechanical click represented a human life reduced to data—blood samples extracted by force, processed, categorized, and stored within the Registry's vast archives. The machine didn't simply monitor humans; it quantified them, reducing individual lives to variables in Dracula's equation of perfect control. The massive chamber processed ten thousand samples per minute, rendering humanity's diversity into uniform data points for vampire consumption.

"There," Anna whispered, pointing toward a crystal sphere suspended above the central platform. Inside floated what appeared to be a human brain, its surface crawling with fine metal filaments that connected it to the surrounding machinery. "The neural core. It coordinates all Registry functions across the territories."

Cassie pulled a compact brass device from her tool belt, its surface covered with dials and tiny pressure gauges. "I need access to the primary distribution nodes," she said, eyes already assessing possible approaches. "If I can overload the hydraulic systems, the entire network crashes."

Alexander nodded, his attention shifting to the far entrance where movement caught his eye. "Company," he warned, rifle already rising to his shoulder.

They emerged from arched doorways with choreographed precision. Six figures in brass-trimmed velvet tailcoats, their aristocratic features marked by the unnatural pallor of vampire nobility. Unlike the common soldiers they'd encountered before, these were Dracula's lieutenants, ancient creatures who had served the Dragon for centuries. They carried halberds of archaic design, the weapons' edges glinting with silvery enchantments designed to wound even vampire flesh.

"The traitor-daughter and her pet venator," announced the foremost lieutenant, his voice carrying the refined accent of long-dead European courts. "How disappointing that you've come so far only to fail in sight of your goal."

Alexander didn't waste breath on response. He fired three rapid shots, the specialized rounds arcing toward the lieutenant's chest. The vampire moved with blinding speed, his halberd twirling to intercept the projectiles with uncanny precision. Sparks flew as rounds detonated against enchanted metal, the explosion insufficient to breach the lieutenant's defense.

"Anna, left flank," Alexander commanded, already moving right to split the lieutenants' attention. "Cassie, go!"

The inventor needed no further urging. She darted between massive engine pylons, her small form vanishing among the forest of pipes and conduits that fed the calculation engine's insatiable appetite. Two lieutenants' broke formation to pursue her, their movements fluid as mercury as they leaped over control stations with inhuman grace.

Alexander met the first lieutenant's charge with grim determination, parrying the halberd's thrust with his rifle barrel before countering with a silver-edged combat knife that materialized in his left hand. The blade scored across the vampire's cheek, drawing a thin line of blackish blood that hissed on contact with air. The creature snarled, aristocratic pretense dropping away to reveal the predator beneath.

Across the chamber, Anna fought with the cold precision of one born to vampire nobility. Her movements matched her opponents in speed and grace, centuries of enforced training evident in every strike and parry. She had produced twin blades from hidden sheaths, the weapons flashing in the gaslight as she drove one lieutenant back while fending off another's attacks.

"You would betray your own kind for them?" one lieutenant demanded, genuine incomprehension in his ancient eyes as he circled Anna. "For livestock?"

"I betray nothing but tyranny," Anna replied, her voice carrying despite the chamber's mechanical cacophony. "The Registry perverts what we could be."

The lieutenant's response was a lightning-fast thrust that would have impaled a human opponent. Anna twisted aside, the halberd's edge slicing through her sleeve but missing flesh by millimeters. Her counterstrike took the vampire's hand at the wrist, the severed appendage dissolving into ash before it hit the floor.

Alexander found himself driven back by two lieutenants working in perfect coordination, their halberds creating a web of lethal steel that threatened to ensnare him with each exchange. His ribs screamed protest with every movement, the earlier bindings now soaked through with fresh blood. He ducked beneath a horizontal sweep that would have decapitated him, using the movement to close distance and drive his knife up beneath one lieutenant's ribcage.

The blade struck true, silver edge burning through undead flesh to find the heart beneath. The vampire's eyes widened in shock—a venator should never have penetrated his defense—before his body collapsed inward, crumbling to fine ash that scattered across polished floor tiles. Alexander had no time to celebrate the small victory as the second lieutenant redoubled his attack, rage replacing the cold calculation in his ancient eyes.

Through the battle's chaos, Alexander caught glimpses of Cassie's progress. The inventor moved with surprising agility between engine components, her tools flashing as she severed critical connections and inserted her sabotage devices at key junctions. Wherever she passed, mechanical rhythms faltered, pressure gauges spiked into red zones, and warning lights began to pulse along control panels.

A lieutenant cornered her against a massive gear housing, his halberd raised for a killing stroke. Cassie didn't flinch. Instead, she jammed a specialized tool into the nearest pressure valve and twisted hard. Superheated steam erupted in a directed blast, catching the vampire full in the face. The creature shrieked, flesh boiling away from bone as he staggered backward into a nest of hydraulic pistons that continued their relentless movement, crushing his weakened form between unyielding metal surfaces.

"Primary node compromised!" Cassie shouted over the rising mechanical protests of the calculation engine. "Secondary systems failing!"

As if in response, the chamber's lighting flickered, plunging sections into momentary darkness before emergency systems engaged. The steady rhythm of pistons faltered, becoming arrhythmic as sabotaged components sent conflicting signals through the network. Throughout the chamber, alarm klaxons began to wail, their urgent tones signaling cascading failures spreading through the Registry's surveillance network.

Alexander seized the momentary confusion to press his attack. His knife found another lieutenant's throat, silver edge parting undead flesh with terrible efficiency. The vampire collapsed, black blood spurting from the wound in defiance of natural laws as his ancient body struggled to maintain cohesion despite the fatal damage.

Anna had claimed two victims of her own, their ashes already scattered by the increasingly erratic air currents produced by failing ventilation systems. She moved to Alexander's side, blood, both hers and her enemies', staining her pale skin in stark contrast. Together they faced the last lieutenant, who backed toward the central platform, halberd raised in trembling hands as he realized his imminent defeat.

"The Dragon comes," the lieutenant hissed, something like satisfaction creeping into his voice despite his predicament. "Your deaths will be—"

Anna's blade took him mid-sentence, driving through his chest with enough force to lift him momentarily from his feet before his body dissolved around the wound, collapsing into dust that settled across control panels now flashing with urgent warnings.

"We need to finish this," Alexander said, turning toward where Cassie was planting her final sabotage devices. "How much longer?"

"Thirty seconds to complete system cascade," she replied, fingers flying across a complex array of switches and dials. "After that, the Registry network goes dark across all territories. They'll need weeks to—"

A sound cut through the chamber, silencing even the mechanical alarms that had been growing in intensity. Not a sound in the conventional sense, more a pressure against the eardrums, a physical sensation that made Alexander's teeth ache and his vision blur momentarily. The chamber's massive doors, opposite their entry point, began to move. Metal groaned against stone as gears larger than wagon wheels turned with ponderous inevitability.

"He's here," Anna whispered, her composure cracking for the first time since Alexander had known her. Fear and determination warred in her heterochromatic eyes, centuries of abuse and manipulation crystallizing into this moment of confrontation.

The doors completed their opening cycle with a sound like distant thunder. Beyond lay another chamber, this one bathed in green light that seemed to absorb rather than illuminate the space. Upon a raised dais stood a figure whose presence commanded attention with physical force—tall, aristocratic, with features that might have been sculpted by Renaissance masters if not for the inherent wrongness that no art could capture. His eyes burned crimson in the gloom, fixing first on Anna with terrible recognition, then shifting to Alexander with the cold assessment of a predator cataloging prey.

Count Dracula—the Dragon—had arrived.

The vampire lord stepped forward, each movement displaying the unnatural grace of a creature not bound by human limitations. His simple black suit seemed to absorb light, the fabric unmarked by dust or wear despite the chaos surrounding him. When he spoke, his voice carried easily across the chamber, cutting through the mechanical din like a blade through flesh.

"Daughter," he said, the single word containing centuries of ownership and expectation. "You disappoint me. Again."

Anna straightened, her fingers tightening around her bloodied blades. "Father," she replied, investing the word with equal measures of hatred and resolve.

Alexander moved to her side, rifle raised despite knowing its inadequacy against the creature before them. Cassie completed her final sabotage connection, the calculation engine's protests reaching fever pitch as systems failed in cascading sequence throughout the chamber. Emergency shutters began to descend over peripheral exits, the Registry's automated protocols attempting to contain the damage even as its brain was being systematically destroyed.

Dracula observed it all with the mild interest of one watching children's games. "You think this matters?" he asked, gesturing toward the failing machinery around them. "This is merely the first iteration. There will be others, improved by the lessons learned from your petty sabotage."

He stepped fully into the chamber, the green light seeming to follow him like an obedient pet. Behind Alexander, glass tubes shattered as pressure fluctuations exceeded their tolerances, spilling luminescent blood across control panels and floor tiles. The calculation engine was dying, its mechanical heart stuttering toward inevitable failure. However, the Dragon himself remained, the true architect of humanity's subjugation standing before them undiminished.

Alexander exchanged a glance with Anna, silent communication passing between them. Whatever happened next, they would face it together—the Last Venator and the Dragon's daughter, united against the monster who had shaped both their destinies through blood and pain. Cassie moved to join them, her tools exchanged for weapons as the final confrontation loomed.

The Dragon smiled, revealing teeth too perfect to be natural, too white against the crimson darkness of his eyes. "Shall we begin?" he asked, as if inviting them to dinner rather than their deaths.

Around them, the calculation engine gave a final, shuddering groan as Cassie's sabotage reached completion. The chamber plunged into darkness for three heartbeats before emergency lighting sputtered to life, casting everything in a bloody crimson glow. In that ghastly illumination, Dracula's smile widened, his true nature no longer concealed behind aristocratic pretense.

The End game had begun.

The Heart of Darkness

The Dragon's crimson eyes burned in the emergency lighting, their ancient depths promising torments beyond human comprehension. Alexander felt his heart hammer against his broken ribs as he raised his rifle, knowing its inadequacy even as his finger tightened on the trigger. Beside him, Anna stood with vampire grace, her blades catching the bloody light as father and daughter faced each other across the failing machinery of humanity's intended doom.

"Your weapons are meaningless," Dracula said, his voice carrying the weight of centuries. "As are your efforts here." He gestured toward the dying calculation engine, its mechanical heart still stuttering through its final spasms. "This is but a setback. I have waited centuries; I can wait decades more."

Alexander fired without warning, the rifle's report thundering through the chamber. The specialized round—one of Cassie's alchemical designs—crossed the distance in an eyeblink. Dracula didn't bother dodging. The bullet struck his chest and simply... stopped, hanging suspended an inch from his flesh before dropping to the floor with a soft clink.

"Is that all the Last Venator brings to challenge me?" Dracula asked, his lips curving into something too cruel to be called a smile.

The transformation began subtly, a lengthening of fingers into tapered claws, a shifting of bones beneath pale flesh, a deepening of the shadows around his form. Then it accelerated, his elegant suit splitting at the seams as his frame expanded. Shoulders broadened to inhuman proportions, spine elongating as his height increased by nearly a foot. The aristocratic features melted like wax near flame, reforming into something that retained a mockery of humanity while revealing the monster beneath.

"This is what your father saw before I tore out his throat," Dracula hissed at Alexander, voice dropping to a register that vibrated the chamber's metal floor. "What your mother begged me to spare her from."

Alexander tossed the useless rifle aside and drew the repeating crossbow from his back holster, his fingers automatically checking its loading mechanism despite the agony that flared through his broken ribs. Pain was temporary. Vengeance was eternal.

"Anna, flank left," he murmured, already sliding sideways to split Dracula's attention.

He pressed his back against a scorched iron pillar and unleashed a hail of silver-tipped bolts from the crossbow, each missile tracking true to its target. The bolts thudded into Dracula's obsidian breastplate, actual armor that had materialized from shadow, or perhaps his flesh had transformed into something harder than stone. Pale ichor splattered across cracked tiles where the bolts managed to penetrate, but the wounds sealed almost instantly.

Anna circled wide, her Drăculeşti rapier—an heirloom forged specifically to harm vampire nobility—held in a perfect fencing stance. Her movements blurred with preternatural speed as she darted in, the curved steel finding a gap in her father's transformed armor.

The blade sliced open Dracula's forearm with a wet, tearing sound. Bone splintered beneath with a sharp crack that echoed through the chamber. The Dragon roared, not in pain but fury, as blackish blood welled from the wound. Unlike the punctures from Alexander's bolts, this injury didn't immediately heal—the rapier's enchantments preventing the supernatural regeneration that made vampire lords so difficult to kill.

"You would use our family's own weapon against me?" Dracula snarled, his transformed face twisting with rage. "Against your father?"

"You stopped being my father centuries ago," Anna replied, dancing back from his retaliatory swipe. "When you chose dominion over decency."

Alexander continued firing, each bolt seeking vulnerable points of the joints, the neck, gaps in the shadow-armor. Most glanced off harmlessly, but enough found purchase to keep Dracula's attention divided. The vampire lord growled, a sound no human throat could produce, and thrust elongated claws through the air in a gesture Alexander initially mistook for pointless theatrics.

The error nearly cost him his life. Jagged arcs of shadow—solid despite their appearance—slammed into his plated gauntlet with bone-crunching impact. The armor crumpled like paper, and Alexander felt bones shatter in his left hand as the force sent him skidding across the floor. He crashed into a bank of failing machinery, blood mixing with oil and hydraulic fluid already pooling on the tiles.

Pain exploded through his senses, momentarily whiting out his vision. He tasted copper as blood filled his mouth from where he'd bitten through his tongue. His left hand hung useless, fingers twisted at unnatural angles.

"Alexander!" Cassie shouted from her position behind a massive gear housing. "Catch!"

She tossed something that glinted in the emergency lighting. A venator stake, its silver tip polished to mirror brightness. Alexander caught it with his functioning right hand, forcing himself upright despite the screaming protest from his ribs and shattered left hand.

Anna had engaged her father directly, rapier flashing in complex patterns that would have disemboweled any lesser opponent. Dracula matched her speed, his transformed claws parrying strikes that should have been too fast to track. Each impact produced a shower of sparks as enchanted steel met supernatural talons.

Alexander circled behind, a silver stake clutched in white-knuckled fingers. Blood dripped from his ruined left hand, leaving a trail across the floor as he sought an opening. Dracula was focused on Anna, her betrayal apparently a greater offense than Alexander's vendetta.

The moment came when Anna feinted high, then drove her rapier toward Dracula's throat. The Dragon caught the blade between transformed palms, the enchanted steel sizzling against his flesh but failing to cut through. In that moment of concentration, Alexander struck.

He hammered the silver-tipped stake into Dracula's kneecap with every ounce of strength he possessed. The impact produced a sickening pop as joints and bone gave way beneath concentrated force. Alexander struck again, driving the stake deeper as Dracula roared in genuine pain. The Dragon's leg buckled, forcing him to one knee as black ichor spurted from the wound in rhythmic pulses.

Anna wrenched her rapier free and struck again, the blade ringing against Dracula's pale wrist with a metallic clang. The vampire lord's blood splattered across her face, hissing where it touched her skin before she wiped it away with a grimace.

Around them, the dying calculation engine tore itself apart. Ruptured pipes released jets of superheated steam into the chamber. Sparks rained from overhead conduits as electrical systems failed catastrophically. The entire tower shuddered, ancient stone protesting as support structures weakened under cascading system failures.

"You cannot kill me," Dracula snarled, his voice distorted by transformation and rage. "I am eternal!"

He lashed out with his wounded arm, the limb elongating impossibly to seize Alexander by the throat. Claws dug into flesh, drawing five points of searing pain as they punctured skin and scraped against bone. Alexander felt himself lifted, feet dangling uselessly as Dracula's grip tightened with crushing force.

"I will make you watch as I reclaim my daughter," the Dragon promised, bringing Alexander's face close to his transformed visage. "Then I will keep you alive for centuries, healing you only to break you again."

Alexander couldn't speak, couldn't breathe. Darkness crept in at the edges of his vision as Dracula's claws dug deeper. With his remaining strength, he drove the silver stake upward, aiming not for Dracula's heart—too well protected—but for his throat.

The stake punched through flesh with surprising ease, silver burning vampire tissue on contact. Dracula's grip loosened reflexively, allowing Alexander to fall to the floor in a gasping heap as the Dragon clawed at the foreign object penetrating his windpipe. Black blood fountained between his fingers, spattering across the control panels of the dying calculation engine.

Anna capitalized on her father's distraction, her rapier flashing in a complex series of strikes that opened deep wounds across his chest and shoulders. Each cut hissed and smoked, the enchanted blade preventing the supernatural healing that made vampire lords so difficult to kill.

Alexander forced himself to his knees, ignoring the grinding agony of his broken ribs and shattered hand. The tower shook around them, chunks of ceiling crashing to the floor as structural supports failed. The battle had just begun, and already it threatened to bury them all beneath tons of collapsing stone and metal.

Alexander struggled to his feet, blood streaming from the puncture wounds in his neck where Dracula's claws had nearly crushed his windpipe. The calculation engine continued its death throes around them, brass gears grinding against one another with the screech of tortured metal as systems failed in cascading sequence. Dracula staggered backward, black ichor still pulsing from the stake embedded in his throat, his transformed features twisted in a rictus of pain and fury.

"The engine's failing," Cassie shouted from behind an overturned control station, her face streaked with soot and blood, "but the core system is intact! The data archives, they'll rebuild from them!"

Alexander understood immediately. Destroying the calculation engine wasn't enough. The Blood Registry's true power lay in its accumulated data—millions of blood samples, indexed and categorized, ready to fuel whatever replacement system Dracula might construct. If they didn't destroy it completely, their victory would be temporary at best.

Anna appeared at his side; her aristocratic features spattered with her father's dark blood. "The crystalline conduit cluster," she said, gesturing toward a massive array of glass tubes that pulsed with unnatural light. "It houses the central archives. Destroy that, and the Registry dies forever."

Dracula yanked the silver stake from his throat with a wet, tearing sound. Black fluid gushed from the wound before the edges began to knit together, vampire regeneration finally overcoming the silver's effects. "I will flay the skin from your bones," he snarled, his voice a ruined rasp that nonetheless carried the weight of centuries. "I will make you beg for death before I'm done."

Alexander's shattered left hand hung useless at his side, but his right found Cassie's final gift—a blood-boiling vapor grenade, its brass casing warm against his palm. The device contained alchemical compounds designed specifically to react with the preserved blood that formed the Registry's lifeblood, literally boiling it within its containment vessels.

"Cover me," he gasped to Anna, throat raw from Dracula's crushing grip.

She nodded once, stepping between him and her father with rapier raised. "Come then, Father," she taunted, her voice carrying despite the mechanical cacophony surrounding them. "Show me what the great Dragon has become—a tyrant clinging to control because he fears what free beings might become."

Dracula roared, the sound inhuman in its intensity. His transformation accelerated, humanity sloughing away like a discarded mask. Shoulders broadened to impossible width, spine elongating as his height increased by another foot. Claws extended from fingertips like obsidian daggers, dripping with venom that sizzled where it struck the floor. His face stretched into something vaguely reptilian, scaled and ancient, crimson eyes narrowing to vertical slits.

Alexander didn't wait to see the transformation complete. He lurched toward the crystalline conduit cluster, each step sending fresh waves of agony through his broken ribs. Behind him, the metal rang against claw as Anna engaged her father in a flurry of attacks designed to keep his attention fixed on her.

The conduit cluster towered over Alexander, glass tubes thick as his thigh pulsing with preserved blood—the collected essence of humanity, processed and categorized for vampire control. Each tube connected to central crystalline chambers where the blood was analyzed, its data extracted and fed into the calculation engine's neural core. Destroy this, and the Registry would lose its foundation.

Alexander slid the blood-boiling vapor grenade into a junction where multiple tubes converged. His thumb left a smear of his own blood on the activation dial as he twisted it to maximum yield. The device hummed to life, internal mechanisms whirring as they prepared to release their deadly payload.

He yanked the pin and stumbled backward, counting silently. Three seconds. Two. One.

The explosion shattered the silence with concussive force, ripping through glass and crystal with devastating efficiency. Tubes shattered in chain reaction, spraying the surrounding machinery with scalding, clotted blood that had been preserved for decades within the Registry's archives. The blood itself seemed to come alive as Cassie's compounds took effect, boiling and frothing as it spread across control panels and seeped into delicate mechanisms.

Steam valves ruptured under the sudden pressure surge, venting superheated vapor that filled the chamber with the metallic scent of blood and chemicals. The hiss of escaping steam sounded like the death rattle of some massive beast, punctuated by the crack and pop of exploding crystal as chambers designed to withstand extreme pressure finally gave way.

Alexander shielded his face with his functioning arm as glass shards and boiling blood sprayed across the chamber. His coat smoldered where droplets struck, the alchemically treated blood eating through fabric and leather with corrosive hunger.

Across the chamber, Anna had seized the opportunity his distraction provided. She launched herself at the massive calculation engines that formed the Registry's processing heart, her rapier flashing in the crimson emergency lighting. The enchanted blade sliced through hydraulic lines that spurted black-tinted blood—not human, but something older and fouler that Dracula had incorporated into his machines.

She moved with vampire speed, a blur of deadly precision as she systematically destroyed junction points and control nodes. Her blade severed copper conduits, wrenched glowing cogs from their mounts, and shattered crystalline power cells with methodical efficiency. Each strike was accompanied by the snap of breaking metal or the shriek of overtaxed gears as the calculation engine's heart suffered irreparable damage.

Alarms began to sound throughout the fortress, their urgent wailing joining the cacophony of destruction already filling the chamber. Distant screams filtered through ventilation shafts as Registry personnel fled the collapsing structure. The floor beneath them trembled as support systems failed, structural integrity compromised by cascading system failures.

Dracula howled in rage, his transformed body coiling like a serpent preparing to strike. Alexander saw the danger too late—the Dragon had abandoned his fight with Anna, recognizing that the Registry itself faced existential threat. He lunged across the chamber with supernatural speed; claws extended toward Alexander who had caused the critical damage.

"Alexander!" Anna's voice cut through the chaos.

She threw herself forward, placing her body between her father's attack and Alexander. Time seemed too slow as Alexander turned, witnessing Anna's sacrifice in horrifying clarity. Dracula's elongated talons carved a

four-inch gash across her abdomen, the blow meant to disembowel
Alexander instead tearing through his ally's flesh.

Hot blood spurted from the wound, spattering across fallen gears and
Alexander's face as Anna's cry of agony joined the mechanical wailing of the
dying Registry. She crumpled backward, and Alexander caught her collapsing
form in his arms, his shattered left hand screaming in protest as he cradled
her against his chest.

"Why?" he gasped, lowering her to the floor as Dracula recoiled in
apparent shock at having wounded his own daughter.

"Balance," Anna whispered, blood bubbling at the corners of her mouth.
Her heterochromatic eyes fixed on his, clarity fading as the wound took its
toll. "Someone had to... break the cycle."

Around them, the Blood Registry's heart gave its final death rattle.
Massive support columns buckled as the floor tilted at a sickening angle.
The neural core—the preserved brain that had coordinated the entire
network—slipped from its suspension field and shattered against unyielding
metal, decades of accumulated data lost in an instant.

Dracula staggered backward, his transformation faltering as the
Registry—the physical manifestation of his power—collapsed around him.
For the first time in their confrontation, Alexander saw something
approaching fear in the ancient vampire's eyes.

Alexander clutched Anna tighter, her blood soaking through his tattered
clothing as the fortress began to fold in upon itself. The last venator and
the Dragon's daughter, united in purpose if not in fate, witnessed the end
of Dracula's grand design as the calculation engine's destruction reached its
thunderous conclusion.

The Last Drop

Alexander cradled Anna's failing body against his chest, each labored breath sending spikes of agony through his broken ribs as he navigated the tilting floor of the collapsing tower. The calculation engine's death throes echoed through stone and metal, a symphony of destruction that masked his ragged breathing as he stumbled toward what appeared to be Dracula's inner sanctum. Black velvet banners hung in tatters from the vaulted ceiling, emblazoned with the Dragon's crest in thread that caught the flickering emergency lights like fresh blood.

Behind him, Dracula's roar of rage penetrated even the thunderous collapse of machinery. The vampire lord was recovering, his regenerative powers already knitting together the wounds Anna had inflicted. Alexander had minutes at most before the Dragon would be upon them again.

He gently laid Anna's body on the fractured marble floor, her pale skin almost translucent against the dark stone. Blood seeped from the vicious gash across her abdomen, staining her torn gown with spreading crimson. Her breathing came in shallow, wet gasps that told Alexander her lungs had been damaged in the attack.

"Stay with me," he whispered, pressing his hand against the wound in a futile attempt to stem the bleeding. His shattered left hand hung useless at his side, fingers twisted at unnatural angles that sent continuous waves of agony up his arm. Every movement threatened to drive bone fragments from his broken ribs into vital organs.

Anna's heterochromatic eyes fluttered open, recognition flickering briefly before pain clouded them again. Her lips moved, forming words he couldn't hear over the destruction surrounding them. Alexander leaned closer, feeling her breath against his ear.

"The altar," she managed, blood bubbling at the corner of her mouth. "His... weakness."

Alexander's gaze snapped to the far end of the sanctum where an obsidian altar stood, its surface-stained dark with centuries of offerings. Ancient symbols had been carved into its sides, partially obscured by the shifting shadows as emergency lighting failed throughout the tower.

A crash from the entryway announced Dracula's arrival. The vampire lord had partially reverted from his fully transformed state, now appearing as a grotesque hybrid of aristocrat and monster. His clothes hung in tatters from a frame too large and misshapen for human garments. Blackish blood still oozed from the wounds Anna's enchanted rapier had inflicted, but the flow had slowed, the edges already knitting together.

"You cannot escape," Dracula hissed, voice distorted by a mouth filled with too many teeth. "The Registry may fall, but I remain eternal."

Alexander snapped open his wrist-mounted clockwork blade, the mechanism's deployment sending fresh pain through his broken bones. The blade extended with a metallic snick, its silver-edged steel catching the failing light. He had commissioned the weapon from Cassie years ago, specifically designed to sever vampire arteries with maximum efficiency.

He launched himself at Dracula, ignoring the screaming protest from his injuries. The blade slashed toward the Dragon's exposed throat, aiming for the wound the silver stake had created earlier. Dracula moved with blinding speed, his arm rising to intercept the attack. The blade glanced harmlessly off scales that had appeared on his forearm, creating a shower of sparks but no damage.

A backhand blow sent Alexander flying across the sanctum, his body crashing into the shattered altar with bone-jarring force. Fresh blood filled his mouth as he struggled to his feet, the taste of copper overwhelming his senses. The clockwork blade had bent from the impact, its delicate mechanism jammed in half-extension.

Dracula advanced with predatory patience, savoring Alexander's desperation. "Your family's legendary weapons," he mocked, gesturing toward the bent blade. "How disappointing the Stirling arsenal has become."

Alexander's hand found a phosphorite grenade in his coat pocket, the last of Cassie's specialized weapons. He thumbed the ignition cap and lobbed it at Dracula's feet, diving behind a fallen column as the device detonated.

Emerald flames erupted in a blinding flash, enveloping the vampire lord in a supernatural fire. The phosphorite burned with unnatural hunger, designed to consume vampire flesh with voracity. For a moment, Alexander allowed himself to hope as Dracula disappeared within the green inferno.

Then came the laughter—a guttural, inhuman sound that sent ice through Alexander's veins. Dracula stepped through the flames, his skin blackened and peeling but regenerating even as the fire consumed it. The phosphorite clung to his clothing and hair, casting his features in hellish green illumination that emphasized their monstrous transformation.

"I was ancient when phosphorite was first mined from the earth," Dracula said, brushing burning fragments from his shoulders with casual disdain. "Did you think I would not have protection against such primitive weapons?"

Alexander backed away, scanning the sanctum for anything that might serve as a weapon. His gaze fell on Anna, still barely conscious on the marble floor, her blood spreading in a widening pool beneath her. She had managed to drag herself toward the wall, one pale hand extended toward a hidden alcove behind a fallen tapestry.

Without hesitation, Alexander lunged for the alcove, his fingers closing around a small vial filled with clear liquid. He recognized it immediately acetic acid, enhanced with alchemical compounds that made it particularly effective against vampire physiology. A desperate weapon, but better than nothing.

Dracula's claws slashed across his back as he rolled away, tearing through leather and flesh with equal ease. Alexander bit back a scream as fire erupted along his spine, forcing himself to focus on the vial clutched in his trembling hand. One chance, one moment of distraction to exploit.

He whirled and hurled the vial directly at Dracula's throat, where the previous wounds from the silver stake had weakened the vampire's defenses. The glass shattered on impact, splashing concentrated acid across the partially healed tissues.

Dracula's roar shook the very foundations of the already unstable tower. He clutched at his throat as the acid sizzled through undead flesh, eating away at the supernatural regeneration that had preserved him for centuries.

For the first time, genuine pain registered on the Dragon's features, his crimson eyes widening in shock and fury.

The victory was momentary. Even as Alexander watched, Dracula's flesh began to knit together around the chemical burns, slower than before but still healing. The acid had hurt him but not stopped him.

Alexander surveyed his empty holsters and spent cartridges with mounting desperation. His crossbow was gone, lost in the calculation engine chamber. The wrist-blade was bent beyond use. The grenades were spent, his knives lost or broken in previous encounters. All that remained was a silver ritual knife tucked in his boot—a ceremonial weapon, never intended for actual combat.

As Dracula recovered, snarling with renewed fury, Alexander's eyes were drawn to the floor beneath the shattered altar. A ring of charred runes had been carved into the stone, ancient symbols that predated even the Registry's formation. He recognized elements of blood magic—forbidden knowledge from venator texts his father had hidden from the Registry's purge.

With no other options remaining, Alexander knelt before the runic circle, drawing the silver ritual knife from his boot. The blade gleamed in the dying light, its edge honed for ceremonial precision rather than combat. He sliced his palm without hesitation, a clean cut that immediately welled with blood.

"Your desperation amuses me, venator," Dracula said, voice recovered enough to carry its customary arrogance. "What do you hope to accomplish with such primitive magic?"

Alexander didn't respond. Instead, he turned his cut palm downward, allowing his blood to spill over the ancient symbols. The runes had been created for a purpose—to bind, to contain, perhaps even to destroy. If his blood, carrying generations of venator heritage, could activate them, perhaps it would be enough.

The first drops struck the blackened stone, and for a heart-stopping moment, nothing happened. Then, almost imperceptibly, the runes began to glow—not with fire or light, but with a negative radiance that seemed to draw illumination inward rather than emit it. The air above the circle shimmered like heat rising from summer-baked cobblestones, distorting Alexander's view of Dracula's approaching form.

The Dragon stopped, suddenly wary, his transformed features twisting with the first hint of uncertainty Alexander had seen since their confrontation began.

The runes flared beneath Alexander's dripping blood, ancient symbols awakening with a negative light that seemed to pull the surrounding illumination into their hungry geometries. The air above the circle distorted and twisted like heat-warped glass, and a high-pitched keening filled the sanctum, emanating from nowhere and everywhere at once. Dracula reeled backward, clawed hands rising to clutch at his temples, his transformed features contorting in genuine pain as the sound penetrated defenses that had withstood centuries of attacks.

"What have you done?" The Dragon's voice cracked, its usual aristocratic control shattered by what appeared to be genuine fear. His massive frame shuddered, partial transformation reversing in patches as scales retracted and claws shortened, his body unable to maintain its battle form under the runes' assault.

Alexander recognized the effect from forbidden venator texts—blood magic that targeted vampire physiology at its most fundamental level. The runes weren't just symbols; they were conduits designed to disrupt the unnatural energies that sustained vampire existence. His Stirling blood, carrying generations of venator heritage, had activated protections built into the very foundations of the tower, perhaps by those who had originally imprisoned Dracula centuries ago.

Through pain-blurred vision, Alexander spotted Anna's ornate sword lying several feet away from where she had dropped it during their earlier struggle. The Drăculești rapier gleamed in the flickering light, its silver-inlaid hilt catching the negative radiance from the activated runes. The blade had been forged specifically to harm vampire nobility—to harm Dracula himself.

Alexander lunged for the weapon, his broken ribs screaming protest as he threw himself across the fractured marble. His fingers closed around the hilt, the metal warm against his skin as if it recognized his touch. The sword felt impossibly light in his grasp, balanced perfectly despite its ornate craftsmanship. Ancient enchantments woven into the steel hummed against his palm, resonating with the runes spread across the floor.

Dracula staggered under the runes' assault, his regenerative powers faltering as the keening grew louder. Blood—black and viscous—leaked from his eyes and ears, spattering the floor in hissing droplets that burned where they touched stone. For the first time since their confrontation began, the immortal creature looked vulnerable.

Alexander knew the moment would not last. The runes' power was already fading, their negative light flickering as the blood sacrifice that had activated them began to dry. Dracula would recover quickly once the effect dissipated, his rage multiplied by this temporary humiliation.

One chance. One strike. The culmination of a vendetta spanning generations.

Alexander gathered the last remnants of his strength, channeling pain into focus as venator training had taught him. His broken body protested every movement, but he forced himself upright, the sword rising in a two-handed grip despite his shattered left hand. Pain became irrelevant. Exhaustion became meaningless. All that mattered was this final moment of reckoning.

With a guttural cry that tore at his damaged throat, Alexander lunged forward. The sword moved as if guided by unseen hands, its arc perfect and inevitable as it swept toward Dracula's exposed neck. The Dragon attempted to raise one arm in defense, but the runes' effect had slowed his supernatural reflexes to almost human speed.

The enchanted blade met Dracula's flesh with a sound like thunder, steel parting undead tissue with supernatural efficiency. Resistance briefly tugged at Alexander's arms as the edge encountered spine, then vanished as momentum carried the stroke to completion. The blade passed through the Dragon's neck in one clean stroke, severing centuries of tyranny with cold steel and bitter vengeance.

For a suspended moment, nothing changed. Dracula's body remained upright, his face frozen in an expression of disbelief and fury. Then, with terrible slowness, his head tilted sideways and fell, tumbling to the marble floor where it landed with a wet thump that seemed impossibly mundane for such a momentous event.

Black ichor erupted from the severed neck, spraying across Alexander's chest and face. The viscous fluid hissed where it touched his skin, burning like acid as it ate through fabric and flesh alike. The sword in his hands smoked where the ichor coated its blade, ancient enchantments fighting against the corruption of Dracula's immortal essence.

Alexander staggered backward, the sword suddenly unbearably heavy in his trembling hands. His vision blurred, the sanctum tilting and spinning around him as adrenaline drained from his system, leaving only pain and bone-deep exhaustion. He watched through wavering sight as Dracula's body began to disintegrate, flesh crumbling into fine ash that drifted through the air like black snow.

The tower shuddered around them, as if the structure itself recognized its master's death. Stone groaned against metal as support beams shifted, the damage from the calculation engine's destruction spreading through connected systems. Alexander knew they had minutes at most before the entire fortress collapsed, burying the Registry's remains beneath tons of rubble.

He turned toward Anna, his movements slow and uncoordinated as his body approached its limits. She lay where he had left her, pale and still against the dark marble, the pool of blood beneath her no longer spreading. Whether that meant her bleeding had stopped or there was simply no more blood to lose, Alexander couldn't tell.

The sword dragged behind him as he stumbled to her side, its tip carving a shallow groove in the marble floor. When he reached her, his legs finally gave way, depositing him beside her with bone-jarring impact. Fresh pain exploded through his broken ribs, but he barely registered it through the numbing fog of exhaustion.

With trembling fingers, he anchored the sword haft into a crack in the rune-scarred stone, the blade standing upright like a marker or monument. It seemed important somehow that the weapon remains, a testament to what had occurred in this blood-soaked sanctum. The sword that had ended Dracula's reign should not be lost in the tower's collapse.

Around them, ash continued to drift downward, settling across dented gears and shattered vials scattered across the floor. The mechanical heart of the Registry had stopped beating, its pulsing control over humanity silenced forever. The alarms had faded to distant echoes, as if the tower itself was exhausted by the night's events.

Alexander stared at the settling ash until the last mote drifted to the floor. The Dragon was gone. The venator vendetta passed from his father to him, was finally complete. He should have felt triumph, or at least satisfaction, but found only a hollow emptiness where vengeance had lived for so long.

A soft sound drew his attention back to Anna. Her chest still rose and fell in shallow movements, each breath a defiance of the wounds that should have claimed her. Vampire physiology, perhaps, or simple stubborn will keeping her tethered to life despite devastating injury.

Alexander gathered her into his arms with careful movements, cradling her broken body against his chest as he had when they fled the calculation engine chamber. Her blood had soaked through his tattered clothing, mingling with his own and the black ichor of her father. Her skin felt cold against him, the warmth of life fading despite her continued breathing.

He rose to his feet with agonizing slowness, muscles trembling under the dual burden of Anna's weight and his own injuries. The tower's alarm bells had fallen silent now, replaced by the ominous crack and groan of failing support structures. The Registry's engines of blood had stopped, their mechanical hunger for human data finally sat still after centuries of operation.

Alexander took one final look at the sanctum where Dracula had fallen. The sword stood as their only monument, its blade catching the failing emergency light in crimson reflections. Then he turned away, carrying Anna toward whatever exit might still exist in the collapsing structure.

Victory had come at terrible cost—Victor dead, Cassie's fate unknown, Alexander himself broken almost beyond repair. But as he navigated the tilting corridors with Anna cradled against him, Alexander acknowledged a truth he had avoided for years: vengeance had never been the end, only a waypoint on a longer journey. What came after—the rebuilding, the healing, the creation of something better than what they had destroyed—that would be the true measure of their sacrifice.

The Last Venator carried the Dragon's daughter from the ruins of her father's legacy, leaving ash and silence behind as the first tentative light of dawn pierced the tower's shattered windows.

Ashes and Steam

Blood soaked through Alexander's tattered clothing as he emerged from the Registry's shadow, Anna's limp form cradled against his chest. The first rays of dawn pierced through smoke-choked skies, casting Ironbridge Boulevard in hues of copper and rust. His broken ribs screamed with each labored step, but he pressed forward, navigating the debris-strewn streets where overturned hansom cabs lay half-submerged in canal water. The Registry's fall had torn open the city's underbelly, exposing decades of vampire control to the harsh light of revolution.

Alexander knelt upon the cracked stone pavement of Slade's central plaza, gently lowering Anna against a toppled statue of her father. The irony wasn't lost on him, the Dragon's daughter, seeking refuge in the shadow of his fallen monument. He tore a strip of fabric from his already shredded coat, pressing it against the deep cut above her brow where debris from the collapsing tower had struck her.

"Stay with me," he murmured, echoing words spoken in Dracula's sanctum mere hours ago.

Brass lampposts sputtered around them, their steam-fed flames dancing erratically as pressure fluctuated through damaged pipes. The grand boulevard that had once showcased the Registry's dominance now resembled a battlefield. Steam vents had ruptured beneath the cobblestones, sending superheated vapor hissing into the morning air. Glass from shattered storefronts glittered like deadly diamonds across the plaza, reflecting the orange glow of distant fires.

Alexander's shattered left hand throbbed with each heartbeat, the bones grinding against each other when he shifted his weight. Blood matted his hair where Dracula's claws had torn his scalp. Every breath sent fresh knives of pain through his broken ribs, yet these physical torments paled against the hollow exhaustion that threatened to consume him. The vengeance that had sustained him for years had been fulfilled. Dracula was dead, the Registry destroyed. What remained was uncertain purpose and the immediate need to survive the chaos they had unleashed.

"They're hunting my kind," Anna whispered, her heterochromatic eyes fluttering open to fix on Alexander's face. Blood trickled from the corner of her mouth, her complexion ashen even for a vampire. "I can hear them. Human militias. Registry loyalists. Everyone chooses sides."

Her hand trembled as it sought his, fingers intertwining with surprising strength despite her wounds. The gesture spoke volumes—trust formed in blood and shared purpose, transcending the ancient enmity between their kinds.

Above them, the pneumatic tubes that had carried blood samples throughout the city began to sputter and fail. The transparent pipes, once filled with orderly flows of crimson fluid, now leaked their contents onto the streets below. Droplets of preserved blood spattered across cobblestones, each one representing a human life reduced to data in the Registry's vast archives. The mechanical heartbeat of vampire control faltered, then stopped entirely as pressure loss cascaded through the system.

"Look," Alexander said, nodding toward a nearby street where broken brass bracelets—the Registry's blood seals—skittered across the pavement. Citizens were tearing them off, some laughing, others weeping as they freed themselves from the physical manifestation of vampire surveillance. Yet freedom brought its own terror; many stood bewildered, having known nothing but Registry control for generations.

From the east, shouts carried across the plaza as rival human militias established barricades. Men and women clutching makeshift weapons—lengths of pipe, kitchen knives, the occasional Registry rifle seized from fallen guards—advanced in ragged formation. Their faces bore the wild exhilaration of newfound power mixed with the wariness of those who expected punishment for their rebellion.

"Kill the bloodsuckers!" a voice rang out, followed by cheers that echoed between stone buildings. "No mercy for the Registry dogs!"

In the opposite direction, surviving Registry patrols struggled to regroup. Enhanced guards moved with jerky, uncoordinated motions, their control systems compromised by the calculation engine's destruction. Pure vampires fared better, their innate abilities unaffected by the technological collapse, but their confidence had evaporated with Dracula's death. Alexander watched them retreat toward the canal district, abandoning positions they had held for decades.

"We need to move," Alexander said, scanning the plaza for immediate threats. "Neither side will welcome us."

Anna nodded, her expression a mixture of pain and something Alexander recognized as relief. Whatever came next, her father's shadow no longer loomed over her existence. She gripped Alexander's arm as he helped her to her feet, her supernatural strength diminished by injury but not extinguished.

They stood together at the threshold of a new era, vampire noble and venator united by circumstance and shared sacrifice. Around them, Slade transformed by the minute as news of Dracula's fall spread through the populace. Humans emerged from hiding places, some celebrating, others seeking revenge for centuries of oppression. Vampires fled or rallied according to their loyalties and survival instincts.

A brass loudspeaker, once used for Registry announcements, crackled to life several streets away. "Citizens of Slade," a voice proclaimed, authority straining against underlying fear, "remain in your homes. The disturbance is temporary. The Registry will—"

The message terminated in a screech of tearing metal as someone tore the speaker from its mount. Cheers erupted from nearby streets, quickly drowned by shouts of competing orders as factions began staking claims to abandoned territories.

Alexander felt Anna tense beside him as a distant explosion ripped through the eastern quarter. Orange flame bloomed against the morning sky, followed seconds later by the rumble of collapsing structures. The Registry's secondary archives, perhaps, or ammunition stores ignited by desperate loyalists determined to leave nothing for their enemies.

"This is only the beginning," Anna murmured, her words barely audible above the city's growing tumult.

Alexander tightened his grip on her hand, both of them watching as decades of suppressed chaos broke free in a single night. They had destroyed the Dragon, but in doing so, had unleashed forces neither fully understood nor controlled. The echo of destruction rolled across Slade like thunder, heralding not just the end of Dracula's reign, but the painful birth of whatever world would follow.

Alexander surveyed Cassie's hidden workshop with weary appreciation, his body still aching from wounds sustained in the Registry tower. Automata in various stages of completion lined the walls, their brass limbs frozen mid-motion like mechanical sentinels. Steam hissed through a network of copper pipes that snaked across the soot-blackened ceiling beams, providing power to an array of specialized tools and mechanisms. The forge in the corner glowed with banked coals, casting the cramped space in amber light that danced across workbenches cluttered with half-finished weapons and mechanical curiosities. It was a place of creation rather than destruction—the antithesis of Dracula's domain.

His splinted left hand throbbed dully, the pain dulled by Cassie's alchemical tinctures but still present. Three days had passed since the Registry's fall, three days of chaos in Slade's streets as the power vacuum left by Dracula's death drew opportunists from every shadow. Alexander had brought Anna to this sanctuary before returning to the streets, gathering intelligence on the rapidly shifting alliances forming across the city's districts.

A cracked pressure gauge on the wall ticked rhythmically, marking seconds that stretched into minutes as Alexander paced the confined space. He paused before a worktable where Cassie had been modifying his wrist-mounted blade, repairing the damage sustained during the final confrontation. His finger traced the silver-edged steel, remembering how it had failed against Dracula's scales but served well enough against lesser threats in the days since.

The workshop's reinforced door creaked open, then slammed shut with metallic finality. Alexander turned to see Cassie striding towards him, her red hair darkened to burgundy by canal spray, face smudged with soot and tension. She wore a leather apron over practical clothing, multiple tool belts crossing her torso like ammunition bandoliers. Her eyes found his immediately, conveying urgency before she spoke.

"Registry loyalists have seized the western district archives," she announced without preamble, shedding her outer coat to reveal arms corded with lean muscle from years of metalwork. "They're burning records, destroying evidence of vampire atrocities. Trying to rewrite history before the ink dries." She unstrapped one of her tool belts, letting it clatter onto a workbench. "Meanwhile, three human warlords have carved up the canal district between them. They're offering protection in exchange for loyalty. Trading one tyrant for many."

Alexander absorbed this with grim acknowledgment. The Registry's collapse had been necessary, but the aftermath was proving as bloody as he'd feared. "Anna?"

"Still recovering at Mariana's. The alchemist says vampire physiology is responding well to her treatments." Cassie moved to a valve, adjusting pressure with practiced efficiency. "The Drăculești name still carries weight. Some vampire houses are rallying to her, seeing her as Dracula's legitimate heir despite her role in his downfall. Others want her head on a pike."

The steam vent above the valve released a controlled burst, punctuating her assessment with mechanical emphasis. Alexander watched her movements precisely, economically, confident in her domain despite the chaos beyond its walls. Something shifted in the air between them, the professional report giving way to awareness of their solitude.

The room fell silent as the steam vent above the valve hissed in response to Cassie's practiced adjustment. He observed her movements precisely, focused, and self-assured—even amidst the chaos outside. A shift in the atmosphere caught his attention, and he glanced up from her hands to find her eyes locked onto his.

"I thought I'd lost you in that tower," she said softly in a tone he rarely heard. "When the eastern spire collapsed, I was certain..."

Alexander closed the gap between them, foregoing all caution as he pulled Cassie into the dimly lit corner by the glowing forge. Her body pressed against his, reassuring him of her presence in a world of wavering allegiances and uncertain futures. The heat from the forge was nothing compared to the newly ignited passion between them, years of unspoken tension dissolving in a single moment of certainty.

Their mouths found each other with an unexpected tenderness that quickly escalated into a fervent exchange. Overcome by desire long suppressed, Alexander gently pushed Cassie down on the workbench, eliciting a soft gasp from her as their lips met once more. She wrapped her legs around his waist with surprising strength, encouraging him to explore further.

His hands roamed over her body, traveling beneath her shirt to brush against her breasts before finding and flicking at a hardened nipple. A moan escaped her lips as they broke their kiss for a moment, allowing Alexander to trail kisses down her neck before ultimately capturing one breast with his mouth—nipping and suckling with unrestrained ardor.

Cassie's fingers deftly worked at the buttons of his shirt before clumsily yanking it off, revealing the myriad scars and fresh wounds that adorned his chest like battle trophies. She planted feverish kisses there while guiding one of Alexander's hands down between their bodies.

He felt the warmth of her core through her trousers as he followed her nonverbal instructions. A jolt of lust shot through him at the sensation, and he hastily unfastened her pants, inching them down to free her legs before pulling her closer. Their bodies pressed together, skin against skin—intimately connected.

Cassie's hands found their way to his throbbing arousal, eliciting a hoarse groan from Alexander as she stroked him teasingly before guiding it to her entrance. He hesitated for a moment until a sense of urgency surged through them both—pushing him to finally breach her wet warmth.

A guttural moan echoed through the workshop as they moved together in sync, their bodies finding pleasure in each other despite the raging storm outside. The walls seemed to vibrate with the intensity of their release as steam pipes hissed overhead, providing a mechanical symphony that only served to heighten their desire.

Amidst the carnage and uncertainty that enveloped Slade, Alexander and Cassie found solace in each other. The concrete walls of the workshop shielded them from the outside world, creating a temporary sanctuary where they could lose themselves in one another's embrace, if only for a moment. Time ceased its march forward as they clung to each other, discovering an anchor in one another amidst the chaos.

"What happens now?" she asked, her head resting in the hollow of his shoulder. "After spending your life hunting Dracula, what does the Last Venator do in a world without the Dragon?"

Alexander considered this, his fingers absently combing through her tangled hair. "I don't know," he admitted. "The Registry is broken, but the pieces remain dangerous. Someone needs to ensure no new tyrant rises from the ruins."

Cassie shifted to look at him, her expression thoughtful. "And after that? Do you ever think about..." She hesitated, uncharacteristically uncertain. "A life beyond hunting? Children, perhaps?"

The question struck Alexander with unexpected force. Children had never entered his calculations, his future extending only as far as Dracula's destruction. Now possibilities unfurled before him like blueprints on Cassie's drafting table.

"Children," he repeated, testing the word. "Raised amid gears and gunfire."

"It doesn't have to be that way." Cassie's fingers found a particularly vicious scar near his collarbone. "The world is changing. We could help shape it into something better."

Alexander closed his eyes, imagination offering glimpses of small hands working with tools instead of weapons, of knowledge passed down that created rather than destroyed. "What would they inherit, I wonder? My rage or your ingenuity?"

"Both, probably," Cassie answered, a smile in her voice. "But perhaps the rage could be channeled into something constructive. Creation can be as powerful as destruction, Alexander. You've spent your life tearing down a tyrant. Maybe now you can help build something worthy in his place."

The possibility settled between them, fragile but real, as steam continued to hiss through the workshop's arterial pipes and the distant sounds of a city in transition filtered through layers of stone and earth.

Alexander stood motionless in the vaulted chamber of the old Council Hall, dust motes dancing in shafts of afternoon light that pierced the stained-glass windows. His wounds had begun to heal, the broken ribs merely aching now rather than screaming with each breath, but exhaustion lingered in his bones like lead weights. Tattered banners hung from iron hooks along the walls, once-proud emblems of Dracula's reign now reduced to faded cloth stirring in drafts from broken windows. He traced his fingers along the edge of a splintered oak table where vampire lords had once determined human fates with casual indifference, feeling the history of oppression embedded in its polished grain.

Parched paper maps littered the table's surface, their edges curled and yellowed with age. Strategic markings in faded ink showed the expansion of Registry control across territories that had once been free human settlements. Alexander recognized his own village among them, a small dot near the eastern break now circled in red designated for "processing" decades ago. That processing had included the slaughter of his family, the beginning of his path as the Last Venator.

He moved to a shattered window, glass crunching beneath his boots. His left hand, still splinted but healing faster than any doctor had expected, clenched on the stone sill as he gazed across Slade's transformed landscape. One week had passed since Dracula's fall, seven days of bloodshed and tentative alliances as the city struggled to find new balance. From this vantage point, he could see the patchwork of control taking shape—territories marked by colored flags and makeshift barricades, the city stitched together by flickering gaslights that illuminated streets where Registry patrols no longer marched.

Smoke rose from smoldering buildings in the eastern quarter where fighting had been heaviest. The distant crack of gunfire occasionally punctuated the unusual quiet that had fallen over the city at midday, most citizens having learned to conduct their business in early morning or after dusk when the chance of being caught in crossfire diminished.

Alexander's right hand slipped into his pocket, fingers closing around a brass bracelet salvaged from the Registry's ruins. The device was deactivated now, its clockwork gears frozen and blood chamber empty, but it represented everything he had fought against—the mechanization of human control, the reduction of lives to data points in Dracula's grand design. He withdrew it, holding the bracelet to the light where its intricate machinery caught the sun's rays. Such a small thing to have caused so much suffering.

"What now?" he murmured to the empty chamber, voicing the question that had haunted him since watching Dracula crumble to ash. His life's purpose had been fulfilled, the vendetta that drove him completed with a single stroke of Anna's ancestral blade. The emptiness that followed was both liberation and burden—freedom from single-minded purpose, yet uncertainty about what should replace it.

He circled the massive table, trailing his fingers over reports bearing the Dragon's seal. Some had been charred by desperate loyalists attempting to destroy evidence before fleeing, but many remained intact—detailed accounts of human subjugation, vampire politics, and the ever-expanding reach of the Blood Registry. Each page represented lives controlled, families separated, communities destroyed in service to Dracula's vision of perfect order.

Two paths stretched before Alexander, both compelling for different reasons. He could return to what he knew best hunting the rogue vampires now fleeing into the breaks, the lawless territories between settled districts where monsters gathered and plotted. His silvered pistols would speak the language of vengeance he had mastered over decades of pursuit. The breaks needed hunters now more than ever, with Registry control shattered and ancient predators slipping their chains.

Or he could step into the murky politics emerging in Slade's power vacuum, using his reputation as the Dragon's killer to influence the formation of whatever government would replace Registry control. Humans looked to him already, a hero in their liberation narrative. He could ensure no new tyrant—human or vampire—seized the reins Dracula had dropped.

His gaze drifted to a portrait hanging askew on the far wall—Anna Drăculeşti, captured in oils during her father's reign. The artist had rendered her aristocratic features with careful attention, the heterochromatic eyes watching the viewer with calculation and intelligence. Even in paint, something of her complexity showed through, hints of the rebellion that had been building for centuries before she allied with Alexander with destroying her father.

Anna herself was gathering her own following, vampire houses that had chafed under Dracula's absolute rule now rallying to her vision of coexistence rather than dominance. Their unlikely alliance had shifted from tactical necessity to something more nuanced—not friendship, exactly, but mutual respect forged in shared struggle.

Alexander's fingers touched the healed cut on his jaw where canal water had infected a wound received in the Registry tower. Cassie's stitching had been neat, precise, like everything she created. The memory of her workshop, of bodies pressed together in rare moments of connection, pulled at him with surprising force. Another future he had never permitted himself to imagine now seemed tantalizingly possible.

His dark eyes returned to the city spread below the broken window. The venator in him noted tactical positions, identified sniper nests and patrol routes with automatic precision. Old habits. But something else stirred beneath the tactical assessment—responsibility for what came next. He had helped destroy the old order without giving sufficient thought to what would replace it.

The Blood Registry had been a monstrous system, but it had provided structure. In its absence, warlords and opportunists scrambled for control, caring little for the civilians caught between competing factions. Alexander had been so focused on Dracula that he'd given minimal consideration to the aftermath of the Dragon's fall. Now that oversight demanded attention.

He drew his silver pistol, the weapon's familiar weight offering cold comfort. The engraved barrel caught the light, Cassie's modifications visible in the elegant mechanism that allowed specialized ammunition. How many vampires had this gun dispatched to whatever hell awaited their kind? Hundreds, perhaps. Yet the Registry had fallen not through superior firepower but through alliance—human and vampire working together toward common purpose.

Perhaps that was the answer. Not hunting alone in the breaks, nor immersing himself completely in Slade's political reformation, but something between—building bridges where suspicion and hatred had ruled for centuries. The Registry's strength had been isolation, keeping humans and vampire houses divided against each other. Its weakness had been Alexander and Anna's alliance, proof that cooperation was possible even between ancient enemies.

Alexander turned from the window, resolve hardening in his shoulders. He placed the brass bracelet deliberately at the center of the oak table, a relic of oppression that would not be forgotten but need not define the future. Whatever came next would be neither wholly human nor vampire, but something new forged from the ruins of Dracula's failed vision.

He stepped toward the chamber's massive doors, decision made. The Last Venator would not disappear into the breaks to hunt monsters, nor would he become another power-hungry figure in Slade's political arena. Instead, he would stand at the intersection, ensuring that the hard-won freedom from Dracula's shadow wasn't squandered in petty power struggles or ancient vendettas.

The pistol returned to its holster as Alexander left the Council Hall behind, moving toward an uncertain future that, for the first time in decades, held possibilities beyond vengeance.

The New Dusk

The ancient tower groaned with each gust of wind, stone fragments occasionally breaking free to tumble into the abyss below. Alexander leaned against a cracked pillar, his broken ribs still protesting any sudden movement despite a week of healing. He watched Anna's slender silhouette framed against the amber twilight, her pale hand resting on the moss-covered balustrade as if testing whether it would support her weight. Beneath them, Slade stretched in fractured disarray, some streets already buzzing with reconstruction while others remained dark, abandoned to whoever claimed them in the power vacuum Dracula's death had created.

Alexander shifted weight, wincing as his splinted hand brushed against rough stone. The bandages Cassie had applied that morning were already fraying at the edges, stained with fresh blood where he'd overexerted himself. Pain was a constant companion now, almost comforting in its familiarity. It reminded him he was alive when so many others weren't.

Tattered banners snapped overhead, faded remnants of Dracula's reign still clinging to iron brackets. The Dragon's emblem was everywhere in this tower, even now, a week after his beheading. Alexander resisted the urge to tear them down. History shouldn't be erased, even painful history. Especially painful history.

"The western district has begun voluntary blood donations," Anna said without turning, her voice carrying clearly despite the wind. "Three hundred humans lined up today. Not out of fear, but choice."

Alexander studied her posture—straight-backed despite the wound across her abdomen that should have killed her. Vampire physiology or sheer stubbornness had pulled her back from death's threshold. The dark coat she wore concealed most injuries, but he noticed her favoring her left side, the slight hesitation before each movement.

"And the vampire houses?" he asked, his voice rough from disuse. He'd spent most of the day surveying barricades and checkpoints, speaking only when necessary.

Anna turned then, her heterochromatic eyes catching the dying light. The blue one seemed to absorb the sunset; the gold one reflected it back like polished brass. "Seven houses have pledged allegiance. Three remain opposed." Her lips tightened briefly. "Two others have fled to the breaks."

Steam rose from scattered chimneys below, mechanical pumps already working to restore water and heat to priority buildings. The rhythmic clanging of metal on metal echoed up from the artisan quarter where Cassie's engineer guild had established workshops. Civilization reasserting itself with rivets and gears.

"We need rules," Anna continued, brushing a strand of raven hair from her face. "Clear boundaries that both sides understand and accept."

Alexander nodded, scanning the horizon where Registry outposts still smoldered. He'd personally put two to the torch yesterday after discovering blood extraction equipment being prepared for use. Some Registry loyalists refused to accept the new reality.

"Volunteering to give blood to the city registry in exchange for the right to live here is acceptable," Anna said, her voice steady despite the wind picking up around them. "So long as vampires treat humans as equals."

Alexander arched an eyebrow. "Equals? Your father would rotate in his urn."

"My father turned vampires into parasites," she replied, a flash of ancient anger crossing her features before vanishing behind aristocratic control. "We became dependent on Registry systems rather than forming genuine bonds with our food source."

Food source. The term hung between them, a reminder that despite her progressive ideas, Anna remained vampire to her core. Alexander pushed away from the pillar, ignoring the fresh stab of pain from his ribs as he moved closer to the balustrade. Below, workers were clearing rubble from what had been the main thoroughfare, their lanterns creating pools of light in the gathering dusk.

"The human districts need rebuilding first," Anna continued. "Collapsed housing in the eastern quarter, water systems in the north. And schools for human children—real schools, not Registry indoctrination centers."

Alexander's tactical mind immediately calculated resource requirements, manpower allocations, security concerns. "You'll face opposition from your own kind. Many vampire houses profited from keeping humans ignorant."

"Those houses will adapt or perish." A simple statement delivered without heat or malice—the kind of certainty that came from centuries of existence.

The wind tugged at Alexander's coat, carrying the scents of the rebuilding city. Fresh-cut timber, molten metal, the distinctive tang of steam engines running on coal rather than blood. Underneath lay the ever-present aroma of ash and decay, reminders of what they'd destroyed to create this opportunity.

He turned his gaze to a half-restored clock tower in what had once been the financial district. Its western face had been shattered in the fighting, but workers had already replaced the massive hour hand. Time, moving forward again after Dracula's stagnant reign.

"Pretty words," Alexander said finally. "But how do we ensure these promises hold? Your kind has made pacts with humans before. They rarely survived the first food shortage."

Anna's pale fingers tightened on the stone railing, the only visible sign that his challenge had struck home. "That's why I need you, Alexander. The Last Venator. The Dragon Slayer."

The titles felt hollow now, purposes fulfilled and discarded. "I'm no politician," he said, tasting the bitterness of the word.

"No," she agreed. "You're something rarer. A man of principle who understands both worlds."

A mechanical whistle screamed from the canal district, signaling shift change at one of the reclaimed factories. Alexander closed his eyes briefly, mapping the sound to territory controlled by the former resistance. Cassie had mentioned they'd resumed manufacturing steam valves yesterday. Small victories.

"I can promise blood registry reform," Anna said, her voice dropping to ensure only he could hear, even though they were alone on the balcony.

"Voluntary donation, fair compensation, medical monitoring to prevent over-harvesting. But I need enforcement mechanisms that both sides respect."

The practical problem gave Alexander's mind something to grasp. "Joint patrols," he suggested. "Human and vampire guards working in pairs. Accountability built into the system."

Anna nodded. "And neutral judges for disputes. Perhaps those with mixed heritage."

The hum of industry rose from below as night workers took their positions, keeping the rebuilding efforts moving through darkness. Oil lamps flickered to life along major streets, their light competing with the first stars appearing overhead. In the distance, a steam tram whistle announced the resumption of limited service between central districts.

"It could work," Alexander said slowly, his strategic mind already identifying weak points and countermeasures. "If both sides see immediate benefits. Humans need security and basic services. Your kind needs willing blood donors and stability."

"Not my kind and your kind," Anna corrected gently. "Just people now. Different needs, but people."

Alexander's jaw tightened, the scar along it pulling taut. Old habits died harder than vampires. He'd spent his life seeing clear divisions—human and monster, venator and prey. Dracula's death hadn't magically erased those categories, but perhaps it had created space to question them.

"I'll need to recruit," he said finally. "Train a new generation. The old venator ways died with Victor, but something new could emerge."

Anna's expression softened, relief visible in the slight relaxation of her shoulders. "We have a foundation, then. Tomorrow we can discuss specifics."

Alexander looked once more at the clock tower, its single hand marking the passage of time in a city learning to live without its ancient tyrant. The task before them seemed impossible. Centuries of hatred and oppression couldn't be undone in weeks or months. Yet standing here, watching smoke drift over fractured rooftops while the sounds of rebuilding rose from below, he allowed himself to consider the possibility that they might actually succeed.

Alexander arrived at the plaza at first light spilled over Slade's eastern walls, turning shattered glass into glittering diamonds across the cobblestones. The night shift workers were trudging home, tools slung over their shoulders, faces streaked with soot and exhaustion. He'd slept poorly, his mind racing with plans and contingencies for the venator force Anna had inspired. His breath misted in the cool morning air as he traced the perimeter of the plaza, mentally noting defensive positions and sightlines—old habits impossible to break even in this moment of potential peace.

The fountain at the center stood as a testament to Slade's former glory and current struggle. The upper basin cracked diagonally, stone cherubs missing limbs, yet water somehow still trickling from one remaining spout. Someone had cleared the debris from its base, the first sign of restoration in this forgotten square. Alexander ran his fingers along the fountain's edge, feeling centuries of history beneath his touch. How many human children had played here before Dracula's reign? How many might return if their plans succeeded?

He withdrew a slender notebook from his coat pocket, its leather cover, newly crafted from scraps Cassie had provided. Inside, he'd spent half the night detailing governance structures, enforcement protocols, and lines of authority that might bridge the gap between vampire houses and human factions. The pages were cramped with his precise handwriting, diagrams sketched in margins, contingencies noted with asterisks. A framework built on paper that would need blood, sweat, and trust to become reality.

A shadow moved at the plaza's eastern entrance. Anna appeared silhouetted against the rising sun, her aristocratic frame wrapped in a hooded cloak that concealed most of her features. Even at this distance, Alexander noted her careful positioning in the shadowed archway. A vampire noble venturing into early morning light was unprecedented, a statement in itself to any watching eyes.

She crossed the plaza with measured steps, skirting patches of direct sunlight with practiced ease. As she drew closer, Alexander observed the subtle signs of discomfort, a tightness around her eyes, gloved hands clenched slightly, the way she angled her face away from the brightening sky. Vampire nobles could tolerate indirect daylight better than their lesser kin, but it remained unpleasant, like standing too close to a fire.

"You're early," she said by way of greeting, taking position beside the fountain where an overhanging roof fragment cast a reliable shadow.

Alexander nodded toward the sun. "Surprised to see you at all before dusk."

"Old traditions must evolve if new ones are to take root." Anna leaned against the cracked fountain spout, her heterochromatic eyes scanning the plaza with the vigilance of one accustomed to assassination attempts. "Besides, humans conduct business by day. I should adapt accordingly."

The plaza around them was gradually awakening. From the streets below came the rhythmic hammering of reconstruction, punctuated by shouted instructions and the hiss of steam vents being tested. The sharp scent of fresh mortar carried on the breeze, mingling with the surprising sweetness of early blooms pushing through cracks in the paving stones, stubborn life asserting itself amid destruction.

They shared a measured silence, both aware of the weight of what they were contemplating. Alexander paced across sun-warmed cobblestones, the notebook a solid presence in his hand as he organized his thoughts. His broken ribs complained with each step, but movement helped him think.

"A venator's purpose has always been to hunt," he said finally, voicing the conflict that had kept him awake. "To track, to kill, to protect humans from vampire predation. What you're suggesting transforms that purpose entirely."

Anna watched him pace, her stillness a counterpoint to his motion. "Not transform. Evolves. The word 'venator' simply means 'hunter' in the old tongue. Hunters enforce natural law in the wilderness. Why not the civil law in a city?"

Alexander continued his circuit of the fountain, automatically cataloging each entrance to the plaza, each potential threat vector. Three armed humans stood guard at the western approach, former resistance fighters now wearing hastily created badges of office. Near the eastern arch, a vampire in house colors observed their meeting with poorly disguised interest. Word was spreading already.

"I've mapped out jurisdictions," Alexander said, tapping the notebook. "Paired patrols—one human, one vampire—with rotating oversight to prevent corruption. Training protocols that emphasize restraint and judgment over traditional venator combat techniques."

"And recruitment?"

Alexander paused, considering the partial plans he'd sketched during the night. "Not from established vampire houses or human militias. Too much baggage, too many old hatreds. Orphans, perhaps. Outsiders. Those with nothing to lose and everything to gain from a stable city."

A flock of pigeons landed near the fountain, pecking hopefully at crumbs left by some earlier visitor. Their cooing created a gentle backdrop to the increasingly vigorous sounds of construction from surrounding streets. Scaffolding was visible on several buildings now, teams of workers hauling materials up creaking wooden structures while supervisors shouted instructions from below.

"And enforcement powers?" Anna asked, one elegant eyebrow raised.

"Limited but absolute within their domain. Authority to detain but not execute. Power to impose fines but not seize property. Rights of investigation backed by both human council and vampire houses." Alexander's words came faster now, the pieces locking together in his mind. "Transparent. Accountable. But with enough teeth that neither side dismisses them as figurehead."

Anna straightened from her position against the fountain, her movement fluid despite the injuries he knew still plagued her. She extended her hand, palm up. A gesture that carried weight beyond the simple motion. A vampire noble offering her hand to a venator, especially one who had helped kill her father, represented a fundamental shift in the natural order that had governed their world for centuries.

"Alexander Stirling," she said formally, "Will you raise this new force of Venators and bind them to enforce the laws we establish together? To hold vampire and human alike to the same standards of justice and behavior?"

Alexander looked at her outstretched hand, then at the notebook containing his night's work. A week ago, he had driven a silver-edged blade through Dracula's throat, fulfilling the vendetta that had defined his existence. Now he stood on the precipice of something far more difficult building rather than destroying.

"I will raise a new force of Venators to enforce every law you set forth," he said, his voice low and precise as he took her hand. "Ensuring vampires abide by this charter, and humans as well. Neither side will be permitted to resume old patterns of dominance or rebellion."

Her fingers were cool against his, the traditional chill of vampire flesh tempered by the morning sun that had warmed his own skin. A construction whistle pierced the air from a nearby street, workers signaling the raising of a major support beam. The timing seemed appropriate foundations being laid in more ways than one.

"The charter itself will need to be formalized," Alexander continued, releasing her hand and offering the notebook. "Written in language both sides understand, ratified by representatives from each faction."

Anna took the notebook, her gloved fingers tracing the simple cover before opening it to scan his careful notations. "You've been thorough," she observed, a hint of approval warming her typically guarded tone.

"It's just a framework. Details will need negotiation."

She closed the notebook and tucked it securely inside her cloak. "We begin with framework and add substance day by day. Like rebuilding a city, stone by stone."

Alexander's gaze swept the plaza once more, seeing beyond its current state of ruin to what might become a neutral ground where vampire and human could conduct business, perhaps even form relationships beyond the transactional blood exchange that had defined their interactions for centuries. The task seemed impossible, yet standing here in morning light with the sounds of reconstruction rising around them, he found himself believing it might actually work.

"One last thing," he said, fixing her with a steady gaze. "The first law this new force will enforce: no one, human or vampire, stands above justice. Not house nobles, not council leaders." He paused meaningfully. "Not even us."

Anna's lips curved in the barest suggestion of a smile, her heterochromatic eyes glinting with something that might have been respected. "Especially not us," she agreed. "After all, examples must be set from the top."

The sun climbed higher, forcing Anna to adjust her position to remain in shadow. Workers began arriving in the plaza, carrying tools and materials for the day's rebuilding efforts. The new day had officially begun—for Slade, for its inhabitants, and for the unlikely alliance that might yet forge a future from the ashes of Dracula's fallen empire.

Echoes of Change

Alexander stood in the shadow of the worn brick building, steam rising from vents along its weathered facade. Victor's sanctuary—no, his sanctuary now—stood as a testament to survival in a city rebuilding itself. The former venator master had hidden this place in plain sight for decades, disguised as a simple steam vehicle repair shop in the industrial district. Its windows, permanently fogged with condensation, revealed nothing of the knowledge, weapons, and history concealed within. Alexander flexed his splinted left hand, the pain less sharp than yesterday but still present, a constant reminder of what they had accomplished and what remained to be done.

The streets around him had changed in the weeks since the Registry's fall. Where Registry patrols once marched with mechanical precision, now mixed groups of humans and vampires moved cautiously, testing the boundaries of this fragile new order. A nearby factory that once produced blood extraction equipment had been repurposed to manufacture water filtration systems. Its chimneys belched white steam rather than the sickly green vapor of before, a visible sign of transformation.

Alexander approached the workshop's side entrance, withdrawing a brass key from his pocket. The lock's mechanism recognized the key's unique pattern, tumblers clicking into place with satisfying precision. Victor had been paranoid about security, installing a series of increasingly complex mechanisms between the public facade and the true sanctuary. Each one is designed to slow intruders and alert the inhabitants. Alexander had learned them all during his training, never imagining he would one day inherit this labyrinth.

The front workshop remained functional maintaining the pretense of a legitimate business served their purposes still. Half-dismantled steam carriages and mechanical components littered workbenches, genuine repair

jobs taken from locals who had no idea what lay beyond the heavy iron door
at the back. The smell of oil, heated metal, and coal smoke hung in the air,
comforting in its familiarity. Alexander ran his fingers along the edge of a
workbench, feeling the decades of nicks and burns that told the story of
Victor's cover identity.

"You stubborn old bastard," he murmured to the empty workshop,
allowing himself a rare moment of sentimentality. "You'd either approve of
what I'm doing or put a stake through my heart for it."

The reinforced door at the rear opened to his touch, recognizing another
key, seamlessly integrated into a ring he wore. The sanctuary properly
stretched before him, a vast underground space excavated beneath
neighboring buildings. Victor had expanded it gradually over decades,
adding rooms and passages as his collection and purposes grew.

Alexander had begun reorganizing the space in the two weeks since
claiming it as his base. Maps of Slade covered one wall, marked with colored
pins indicating territory control, incidents requiring intervention, and
proposed patrol routes for the new venator force. The massive wooden table
at the center—where Victor had once planned vampire hunting
expeditions—now held draft copies of laws and regulations, annotated with
Alexander's precise handwriting. The transformation from war room to
governance center was still incomplete, but progress was visible in every
corner.

He moved to the eastern section, where Victor's legendary archive of
vampire lore filled floor-to-ceiling shelves. Leather-bound volumes, scrolls in
ancient languages, and mechanical recording cylinders containing firsthand
accounts of vampire encounters—the most comprehensive collection of
knowledge on their kind ever assembled by a human. Alexander had begun
cataloging it properly, adding notes where information contradicted what
they now knew. Knowledge once used exclusively for destruction might now
serve understanding and coexistence.

"The Physiology of Vampiric Houses," Alexander read from a spine,
withdrawing the volume. Victor's handwriting filled the margins,
observations from decades of hunting. Some notes were practical" Dracula's
line resistant to standard silver compounds, requires specific alloy"—while

others reflected prejudices Alexander now questioned—"All nobles inherit blood memory, making rehabilitation impossible."

Alexander set the book on a reading stand, marking passages that might help Anna understand her own nature better. Strange to think he was now allies with a vampire noble, stranger still that he was actively seeking knowledge to help rather than harm her kind. The irony would not have been lost on Victor.

The training area beyond the archives remained mostly unchanged. Heavy canvas dummies hung from iron chains, their surfaces punctured by countless practice strikes from generations of venator weapons. The wooden floor showed decades of scuff marks from countless hours of footwork drills. Here, Victor had transformed Alexander from a grief-stricken boy into the weapon that would eventually bring down Dracula.

Alexander stood at the center of the training circle, muscle memory automatically shifting his stance to the defensive position Victor had drilled into him. His broken ribs protested the movement, but less painfully than last week. He closed his eyes, remembering Victor's gruff instructions, the punishing training regimen that had seemed cruel at the time but had kept him alive through countless encounters.

"The only good vampire is a dead vampire." Victor's favorite saying echoed in his memory. The venator master had lived and died by that creed, unable to imagine any alternative. Would he understand what Alexander was attempting now? Probably not. Victor's world had been clearly divided between human and monster, with no gray area between.

But Alexander had seen beyond that binary. Anna had shown him that vampires could choose a different path. Cassie had demonstrated that technology once used for oppression could be repurposed for good. Even Niko, the smuggler who had betrayed and then ultimately helped them, proved that people could change when presented with better options.

Alexander moved to his makeshift desk, withdrawing the notebook containing his plans for the new venator force. His quest for vengeance had consumed him for so long that its fulfillment had initially left a void. But that emptiness had quickly filled with purpose more complex and potentially more meaningful than simple revenge. Dracula's death had been necessary but ultimately destructive. Building something new from the ruins—that was the greater challenge.

He spread the schematics Anna had provided of the remaining Registry outposts across the desk. Tomorrow they would discuss which to dismantle first and how to repurpose both the materials and the personnel. Each decision they made would affect thousands of lives, vampire and human alike. The responsibility weighed heavily but also gave him a sense of direction he had lacked since watching Dracula crumble to ash.

Alexander lit the oil lamps around the sanctuary, preparing for a night of preparation. The flames cast long shadows across the training floor, illuminating weapons that would now enforce peace rather than deliver vengeance. Victor might not approve, but Alexander suspected his mentor would grudgingly acknowledge the necessity of adaptation. After all, Victor's first rule had always been survival—not just of individuals, but of humanity itself. Perhaps this new approach offered the best chance for that ultimate goal.

Alexander's head snapped up at the distinctive sound of brass tumblers turning in a pattern only two people knew. The outer door creaked open, followed by the familiar cadence of boots on the workshop floor much lighter than Victor's had been, accompanied by the gentle clink of tools in leather pouches. He set aside the registry schematics, a smile tugging at the corner of his mouth despite the exhaustion weighing on him. Cassie. She had promised to visit once her work at the eastern pumping station was complete, but he hadn't expected her until morning.

"Your security system has three vulnerabilities I could exploit with a decent spanner and some copper wire," Cassie announced as she appeared in the doorway, red hair escaping its practical knot, face smudged with the distinctive black residue of Registry machinery. She carried a covered basket that released wisps of steam, the aroma of actual cooked food cutting through the workshop's metallic scents.

Alexander rose from his chair, wincing slightly as his ribs protested. "Then I'm fortunate you've decided to exploit my company instead of my security flaws."

"For now." She set the basket on the cleared corner of his desk, brushing aside maps to make room. "You've been living on stale bread and that terrible coffee again, haven't you?"

He didn't deny it. Cassie pulled out containers of still-hot stew, fresh bread, and even a bottle of wine salvaged from some Registry official's abandoned cellar. The sight reminded Alexander he hadn't eaten since morning. His body's needs frequently forgotten when his mind focused on rebuilding plans.

"The Canal District markets reopened today," Cassie said, handing him a bowl filled with more meat than he'd seen in one place since before the Registry fell. "Real trade, not just black market. Farmers from the outskirts bringing in vegetables. Someone even had fresh eggs."

Alexander accepted the food gratefully, noting the dark circles under Cassie's eyes that matched his own. She'd been working just as relentlessly, converting Registry machinery to practical purposes that benefited the average citizen rather than vampire overlords.

"The northern aqueduct is flowing again," she continued between bites. "My apprentices figured out how to bypass the Registry filtration system that added blood preservatives to the water supply. Pure water now, though we're still checking residue levels in some neighborhoods."

They ate in comfortable silence for a few minutes, the simple pleasure of hot food and companionship, a luxury neither took for granted. Alexander studied Cassie's hands as she broke bread callused, scarred from years of mechanical work, but moving with the precise dexterity that had saved his life more times than he could count. Those same hands had rewired Registry systems, modified weapons, and touched him with surprising gentleness in rare private moments.

"Not all the news is good," she said eventually, setting down her spoon. "Registry loyalists still control the southwestern pumping station. They've barricaded themselves inside, threatened to poison the water supply if we attempt to seize it. And three vampire houses in the eastern district have rejected Anna's authority completely—they're enforcing their own blood taxation on humans in their territory."

Alexander nodded, having expected such resistance. "The old order doesn't die in a day. We knew that."

"The pumping station concerns me most." Cassie withdrew a folded schematic from one of her many pockets, spreading it across the desk between them. "This particular model integrates directly with the main water supply for a third of the city. The loyalists could make good on their threat before we could stop them."

Alexander studied technical drawing, recognizing Registry design philosophy in its unnecessarily complex mechanisms. "Can we bypass it entirely?"

"Not without leaving ten thousand people without water for weeks." She traced a series of junctures with an oil-stained fingertip. "But here and here. These are the blood integration chambers. If we could access the maintenance tunnels beneath, we might be able to neutralize the threat without direct confrontation."

This was why they worked so well together. Alexander's strategic mind complemented Cassie's technical genius. Together they could solve problems neither could manage alone. He made a mental note to discuss the pumping station with Anna at tomorrow's meeting. Perhaps vampire negotiators might succeed where human force would fail.

"What about the Registry technology itself?" Alexander asked, refilling their cups with wine that tasted better than anything had a right to in these circumstances. "Most of it was designed specifically for blood extraction and processing. How much can actually be repurposed?"

Cassie's eyes lit with enthusiasm, technical challenges always igniting her passion. "More than you'd think. The pneumatic tube system can be modified to transport messages and small goods throughout the city. The blood seal bracelets—stripped of their vials and tracking mechanisms—contain remarkable clockwork that could power personal lighting or heating devices."

She pulled out another diagram, this one her own creation. "The largest Registry machines—the calculation engines and blood processors—those need to be dismantled completely. But their components? Gears, steam valves, pressure chambers? All valuable resources that can be repurposed for everything from water purification to manufacturing."

"And jobs," Alexander added, seeing beyond the technical aspects to the social implications. "People who worked maintaining Registry equipment could be retrained to build something beneficial instead."

Cassie nodded eagerly. "Exactly. I've already identified three former Registry technicians who've volunteered to help reverse-engineer the systems they once maintained. They know these machines better than anyone and they're desperate to use that knowledge for something other than oppression."

Alexander stood, moving to the map on the wall. "We'll need to prioritize. Which facilities can be converted fastest, which will provide the most immediate benefit to surrounding neighborhoods." His finger traced the city's districts. "Anna believes stability comes from meeting basic needs first. Clean water, reliable heat, functional sewage systems."

"Starting with practical necessities builds trust," Cassie agreed, joining him at the map. "People care less about political philosophy when they're cold, hungry, or sick."

The lamplight caught the copper highlights in her hair as she leaned closer to examine the city layout. Alexander felt a familiar warmth that had nothing to do with the wine. Amid all the complexity of rebuilding a broken city, Cassie remained his constant. Brilliant, pragmatic, and unflinchingly loyal to the vision they shared.

"We're actually doing this," she said quietly, a rare note of wonder breaking through her usual practical tone. "Creating something new rather than just fighting the old."

Alexander nodded, allowing himself to acknowledge the enormity of their undertaking. Dismantling centuries of vampiric control wasn't simply about removing the Registry's physical manifestations. It meant rebuilding the foundation of society itself. The technical challenges were daunting but quantifiable. The social challenges would prove far more complex.

"One machine at a time," he said, returning to the schematics spread across his desk. "One district at a time. One day at a time."

Cassie's hand found his, warm against his scarred knuckles. "Good thing we're both too stubborn to quit, then."

The lamplight flickered across maps and diagrams as they bent over their work, planning the practical resurrection of a city emerging from centuries of darkness. Outside, Slade continued its tentative transformation, each repurposed piece of Registry technology another small victory against the legacy of the Dragon's reign.

Alexander traced his finger along the edge of Victor's old training blade, feeling the slight imperfections where countless practice strikes had nicked the once-perfect silver edge. The traditional venator arsenal surrounded him—stakes, silver-edged weapons, specialized crossbows—tools designed for a singular purpose that no longer aligned with his vision. The new venator force couldn't simply be hunters with updated orders. They needed to become something entirely different: peacekeepers who understood both worlds they were tasked with balancing.

"We need people," he said finally, turning to where Cassie sat studying the pumping station schematics. "Not just fighters. Not just technicians. People who can move between human neighborhoods and vampire territories without seeing enemies on either side."

Cassie looked up, tucking a strand of copper hair behind her ear. "A tall order. Most who survived Dracula's reign did so by picking a side and sticking to it."

"Who among our contacts might have the right qualities?" Alexander moved to the worn wooden cabinet where Victor had kept personnel files on potential recruits. Most would be useless now, the old master had sought those with hatred of vampires burning in their hearts, those easily shaped into weapons aimed at the Registry.

"There's a group of orphans in the eastern quarter," Cassie suggested, setting down her pencil. "Children who grew up in that narrow alley behind the old blood processing plant. They survived by trading information between human resistance cells and vampire houses that chafed under Dracula's control."

Alexander nodded, remembering the thin-faced youths who had sometimes carried messages for the resistance. They moved through Slade like ghosts, invisible to Registry patrols through practiced insignificance. "They know the city better than most adults. And they have no ingrained loyalty to either faction."

"Like you were," Cassie said gently, "before Victor found you again after that terrible night."

The comparison wasn't lost on Alexander. He too had been orphaned by vampire violence, his family was destroyed to make a point about human compliance. But unlike him, these children had grown up navigating the complexities of Slade rather than being shaped into a single-purpose weapon.

"There's seven I know of between fourteen and eighteen," Cassie continued. "Old enough to train, young enough to adapt to new ideas. My apprentice Tess has been feeding them and teaching basic mechanics in exchange for information about Registry movements. They trust her."

Alexander added the orphans to his mental list. Young recruits would form the foundation of the force's future, but they needed experienced guides first. "What about your apprentices themselves? Any with the right temperament?"

Cassie considered this, her fingers absently disassembling and reassembling a small pressure valve—a habit when deep in thought. "Three possibilities. Tess has good judgment and better people skills than most engineers. Marcus knows every underground passage in the city from maintaining steam tunnels. And Elyria worked Registry maintenance for years under duress. She understands their systems better than anyone except me."

All valuable skills for the new force. Alexander made notes in his ledger as Cassie spoke, already envisioning how such talents could complement traditional venator training. Technical knowledge combined with combat skills would create a force capable of addressing the complex challenges of a city transitioning from tyranny to fragile cooperation.

"We should consider Niko," Alexander said, watching Cassie's reaction carefully.

Her hands stilled on the valve, eyes narrowing. "The smuggler who betrayed you to Dracula? That Niko?"

"The same one who later helped us escape and provided the distraction that allowed us to reach the Spire," Alexander countered. "He knows every shadow dealer, informant, and black-market operator in Slade. More importantly, he understands the grey areas where vampire and human worlds overlap."

Cassie's expression remained skeptical. "He's also motivated entirely by self-interest. The moment a better offer comes along, he'll sell us out again."

"Perhaps," Alexander acknowledged, "but his self-interest now aligns with stability. Chaos is bad for business. Predictable rules enforced by a neutral party? That creates an environment where someone with Niko's talents can thrive legitimately."

He moved to the map wall, indicating the northwestern district where Niko had maintained his smuggling operation. "He survived decades under Registry control without being processed or executed. That requires intelligence, adaptability, and an understanding of power structures. All qualities we need."

Cassie set down the valve with a soft click, her practical nature weighing Alexander's arguments. "You trust him?"

"Trust is a strong word," Alexander said, a wry smile touching his lips. "Let's say I understand his motivations better now. He betrayed us when he believed Dracula was invincible and that cooperation was his only path to survival. When circumstances changed, so did his calculation."

"And you think that makes him reliable?"

Alexander considered this carefully. "It makes him predictable, which can be more valuable than blind loyalty. Besides, his knowledge of both human and vampire underworlds is unmatched. He's navigated both sides for profit for years."

Cassie rose from her seat, joining Alexander at the map. "His connections would be useful," she conceded reluctantly. "And he did risk his life during the final assault."

"He understands the consequences," Alexander said, his voice low with conviction. "He's seen firsthand what happens when power goes unchecked. That experience—even his mistakes—makes him valuable in ways someone with a spotless record couldn't be."

Alexander turned back to Victor's training floor, imagining it filled with this new generation of venators. Where Victor had taught techniques for killing vampires efficiently, Alexander would teach methods of de-escalation, negotiation, and targeted force as a last resort. Where the old master had fostered hatred as motivation, Alexander would cultivate understanding as foundation.

"The training will be different," he said, more to himself than to Cassie. "Less about hunting, more about peacekeeping. Combat skills still matter, but equally important is judgment about when not to fight."

Cassie watched him with quiet understanding, recognizing the transformation happening before her. The Last Venator was becoming something new himself—not abandoning his past, but building upon it, evolving beyond the limitations Victor had never questioned.

"You're creating something that's never existed before," she said. "Not quite venators, not quite guards, not quite diplomats. Something in between all three."

Alexander nodded, feeling the weight of the task ahead. His journey as the Last Venator wasn't ending with Dracula's death as he'd once imagined. Instead, it was evolving into something more complex and potentially more significant creating a legacy that protected rather than merely avenged.

"We start with five experienced instructors," he decided. "Your three apprentices, Niko—if he can be persuaded—and myself. Then add the orphans as trainees. A small core we can trust, expanded carefully as we prove the concept works."

Cassie nodded, practical as always. "I'll speak with my apprentices tomorrow. And I know where to find Niko—he's been running a legitimate transport service from the northeastern docks, though I suspect not everything in his cargo holds appears on the manifests."

Alexander allowed himself a moment of optimism, rare in his experience. The path forward remained treacherous, filled with potential setbacks and opposition from both human and vampire factions. But for the first time, he could envision a future beyond endless hunting—a future where venators served life rather than dealt death.

"Anna will be pleased," he said, returning to his notes. "She argued that enforcement without understanding would simply recreate the Registry's mistakes in reverse."

"Good thing the Last Venator has learned to listen, then," Cassie replied with a hint of mischief in her tone. "Even to vampires."

Alexander acknowledged the gentle teasing with a slight smile. His willingness to see beyond Victor's absolute divisions had brought them to this point—not just the defeat of a tyrant, but the possibility of building something better in his place.

The oil lamps had burned low, casting long shadows across the sanctuary as midnight came and went. Alexander's eyes burned from hours of studying schematics and drafting training protocols. He looked up to find Cassie standing by the weapons rack, her fingers tracing the outline of a modified crossbow she'd designed years ago. Something in her posture had changed subtle tension in her shoulders, a deliberateness to her movements that caught his attention. She turned to face him, and in the flickering light, he saw determination in her eyes, mixed with something softer he rarely witnessed there.

"I've been meaning to tell you something," she said, her usual direct manner tempered with uncharacteristic hesitation. "Never seemed the right moment, what with the Registry falling and the city in chaos, but..."

Alexander set down his pen, recognizing the importance of whatever had placed that unfamiliar vulnerability in Cassie's expression. He waited, giving her space to find her words.

"I'm pregnant," she said finally, her hands unconsciously moving to rest on her still-flat stomach. "About ten weeks along. I suspected before the final assault on the Spire but confirmed it three days ago."

The world seemed to stop, then restart with altered rhythms. Alexander's mind, typically quick to assess and respond, struggled to process her words. A child. His child. Their child. In the space between heartbeats, his identity transformed yet again—venator, ally to a vampire noble, architect of a new peacekeeping force, and now, father.

"Ten weeks," he said, his voice sounding distant to his own ears. That placed conception shortly before their final confrontation with Dracula, during those desperate days when survival seemed unlikely and each moment of connection had been stolen from the jaws of almost certain death.

"Say something that isn't just repeating what I've told you," Cassie prompted, a hint of her usual sharpness returning.

Alexander rose from his chair, crossing the room to stand before her. His mind raced through calculations and considerations with venator precision, then abandoned them entirely as inadequate to the moment. "Earlier, when you asked about children raised amid gears and gunfire... you already knew."

She nodded, a fleeting smile softening her features. "I was testing the waters. Seeing how you might react to the idea in theory before presenting the reality."

Alexander reached out, his scarred hand hovering uncertainly before coming to rest gently against her waist. The contrast between his battle-marked skin and the miracle developing beneath it struck him with unexpected force. "A child," he whispered, the word carrying both wonder and terror.

"In a world without Dracula," Cassie added, her eyes holding his. "That matters, Alexander. It matters tremendously."

The implications unfolded in his mind—a child born into a Slade transforming itself, neither fully under vampire domination nor caught in the chaos of constant resistance. A child who might grow up seeing cooperation where previous generations had known only oppression and rebellion. The timing felt significant, almost symbolic.

"I've never considered fatherhood," he admitted. "It seemed... incompatible with being the Last Venator." The very title had implied an ending, not a continuation.

"And yet here we are." Cassie covered his hand with hers, anchoring him to this new reality. "Neither of us has exactly had normal lives. I don't see why parenthood should be any different."

A laugh escaped him, unexpected and genuine. "I know nothing about being a father. My own died when I was barely old enough to remember him. Victor was..." He trailed off, remembering his mentor's harsh training methods, his singular focus on creating weapons against the Registry.

"Victor taught you what to fight against," Cassie said softly. "Now you get to decide what to fight for."

Alexander's gaze drifted to the maps and plans spread across his desk, the physical manifestation of the future they were trying to build. The personal and the political suddenly seemed inseparable, two aspects of the same transformation. His child would inherit the world they created from Dracula's ashes.

"I'm afraid," he confessed, the admission easier in the sanctuary's dim light. "Not of fatherhood itself, but of this world we're building. It's so fragile still. So many things could go wrong."

Cassie stepped closer, resting her forehead against his chest. "That's why this matters, Alexander. We're not just rebuilding for abstract principles or faceless future generations. We're building for our child. For a future we'll actually see."

The reality of it settled over him like a mantle heavier than his venator title had ever been, yet somehow more purposeful. Every decision he made now would shape not just Slade's future, but his child's lived experience of that future.

"We'll need safer headquarters than this," he said, practical considerations asserting themselves as his mind adapted to this new paradigm. "Better medical care than what's currently available. Schools eventually, real ones, not Registry indoctrination centers."

Cassie pulled back, eyebrow raised in amusement. "I tell you I'm pregnant and your first thoughts are infrastructure improvements?"

"Legacy of venator training," Alexander replied with a slight smile. "Identify needs, develop strategy, implement solutions."

"And here I was expecting either panic or sentimentality."

Alexander brushed a strand of red hair from her face, his expression growing serious. "There's plenty of both, believe me. But this child deserves more than just our emotions. They deserve our best efforts at creating something stable from all this chaos."

Cassie nodded, understanding perfectly as she always did. It was why they worked so well together—her practical brilliance complementing his strategic mind, both dedicated to reshaping a broken world into something better.

"What do you hope for?" he asked softly. "For the child, I mean."

Cassie considered this, her hands absently fidgeting with a gear from her pocket a self-soothing habit he'd noticed years ago. "I hope they never know what it means to wear a Registry bracelet. I hope they can walk between vampire and human districts without fear. I hope they inherit your courage and my ingenuity." She paused, a vulnerability in her voice he rarely heard. "And I hope they never have to become a weapon, as we both were in different ways."

Alexander pulled her closer, his arms encircling her with careful tenderness. The scent of machine oil and copper that always clung to her had become synonymous with home in his mind. Together they stood in

Victor's sanctuary now truly transformed into something new surrounded by the tools of the old venator's trade and the plans for a different kind of future.

"Then we have work to do," he said simply, his resolve strengthening rather than diminishing with this new responsibility. The Last Venator would not be the end of a lineage but the beginning of something new—a bridge between the world that was and the world that could be.

In the quiet sanctuary, as Slade rebuilt itself around them, Alexander allowed himself to truly believe in the future they were creating—not just as an abstract concept, but as the living reality their child would inherit. The journey that had begun with vengeance had transformed into something far more profound: the chance to build rather than destroy, to protect rather than avenge, to create a legacy defined by life rather than death.

Epilogue : The Gears OF Destiny

Alexander knelt on the dusty marble floor of the council hall, the bitter tang of heated copper filling his nostrils as his scarred fingers connected the final wires of the communication console. His healing left hand still ached when he worked too long, but the splints were gone now, replaced by only occasional stiffness. Above him, the vaulted ceiling stretched upward, its ancient stone now interlaced with fresh timber supports and gleaming steam pipes that hissed softly in the cavernous space. Eight weeks of relentless labor had transformed the shattered remnants of Dracula's inner sanctum into something new. Something that belonged to neither vampire nor human exclusively, but to the fragile alliance they were building together.

"Junction twelve is secure," he murmured, speaking to himself as much as the two apprentice engineers hovering anxiously nearby. He twisted a brass compression fitting with practiced efficiency, sealing the connection that would, in theory, allow messages to be transmitted across the city without relying on the Registry's blood-based surveillance network.

The heavy punch of hammers against metal provided a rhythmic backdrop to their work, the sound echoing off stone walls still blackened with soot from the night Dracula fell. Alexander glanced up from his work, catching sight of Anna moving among the laborers at the far end of the hall. Her raven hair was pulled back in a practical knot, her aristocratic features softened by a smudge of grime across one cheek. She paused beside a human worker, her pale hand reaching out to brush soot from a crooked support brace as she spoke quiet words Alexander couldn't hear.

Eight weeks ago, such casual contact between vampire noble and human laborer would have been unthinkable. Now it happens daily, though not without lingering tension. Alexander observed the worker's initial stiffening, followed by cautious relaxation as Anna continued speaking. Progress measured in small gestures and subtle shifts in body language.

"The primary converter still runs hot," Cassie had warned that morning before departing for the eastern pumping station. Her fingers had lingered on Alexander's as she passed him the modified pressure gauge that now sat among his tools. The memory of her touch—of the new knowledge of their child growing within her—remained a warm presence in his mind even as he focused on the technical challenges before him.

Alexander turned his attention back to the bank of communication consoles lining the wall. Each contained dozens of salvaged components from the Blood Registry bracelets that had once controlled Slade's human population. The bracelets themselves had been symbols of oppression, their clockwork mechanisms recording every movement, every interaction, every bodily function of their wearers. Now those same gears and measuring devices had been repurposed, their precision and durability serving a new function.

"Poetic justice," Anna had called it when Alexander first proposed the idea. "Using the tools of subjugation to build something that connects rather than controls."

He reached for a tarnished brass key, inserting it into the primary ignition lock of the console before him. The key once part of a Registry supervisor's control mechanism now served to prevent unauthorized access to the new communication network. Another small victory against the legacy of Dracula's reign.

Behind him, a steam valve released pressure with a sharp hiss, causing one of the younger apprentices to jump. Alexander recognized the boy as one of the orphans Cassie had mentioned, now studying engineering with the same intensity he had once applied to surviving on Slade's streets. Another transformation, another reason to ensure their fragile peace held.

"Careful with the pressure on the eastern manifold," Alexander called over his shoulder. "These fittings weren't designed for sustained high-temperature operation."

The boy nodded, making a quick adjustment to the valve with surprising dexterity. His thin face remained serious, concentrated on the task as if his life depended on it. A habit formed when existence had been far more precarious under Registry control.

Alexander returned to his own work, connecting the final circuits that would, if Cassie's calculations were correct, allow the console to transmit messages through the pneumatic tube system they'd adapted from Registry infrastructure. His fingers moved with practiced precision despite the lingering weakness in his left hand. Some wounds healed slower than others a brutal truth that applied to Slade itself as much as to his own body.

"How close?" Anna's voice came from directly behind him, startling Alexander despite his venator-trained senses. Her ability to move silently remained disconcerting, a reminder of her inhuman nature despite their alliance.

"Final connections now," he replied, sliding backward to give her space to observe his work. "If the calculations are correct, this should establish communication with the eastern district station and the northern market hub."

Anna crouched beside him, her movements fluid despite the injuries she'd sustained in the Registry tower. Like Alexander, she bore scars that had not fully healed. Including a long diagonal cut across her abdomen that had nearly killed her. Unlike him, she concealed her injuries perfectly, her aristocratic bearing revealing no hint of weakness or pain.

"The workers have done well," she said, gesturing toward the gleaming pipes and polished brass fixtures that lined the walls. "Many never imagined they would set foot in the council hall except as prisoners or blood donors."

Alexander nodded, noting how she referred to them simply as "workers" rather than "humans", a subtle but significant linguistic shift. "They take pride in reclaiming the space," he said. "Every nail they drive, every pipe they lay is an act of defiance against what this place represented."

"And what does it represent now, Alexander?" Anna asked, her heterochromatic eyes studying him with that unnerving intensity that made him feel as if she were reading more than just his expression.

He considered the question as he made the final connection inside the console. "Possibility," he said finally. "Neither vampire dominance nor human resistance. Something new between them."

A ghost of a smile touched Anna's lips, gone almost before it appeared. She rose to her feet with that characteristic grace that made even simple movements seem choreographed. "Then let us see if possibility can become reality."

Alexander closed the access panel and turned the ignition key. For a moment, nothing happened. The console remained dark, unresponsive to his efforts. A knot formed in his stomach yet another failure, another setback in their already precarious rebuilding efforts. Then, with a soft clicking that quickly built to a steady mechanical hum, amber lights flickered to life across the console's brass face. Pressure gauges twitched, their needles rising into optimal ranges as the repurposed mechanisms found their new purpose.

The workers fell silent, hammers pausing mid-strike as the amber glow spread from the primary console to those connected alongside it. Within moments, the entire bank of communications equipment glowed with warm light that reflected off polished marble floors and cast long shadows up the council hall's vaulted ceiling.

Alexander straightened, his chest tight with an emotion he rarely allowed himself to acknowledge. Not quite hope yet he had been a venator too long for that but something adjacent to it. Satisfaction, perhaps. The confirmation that destruction could lead to creation, that new purpose could emerge from the ashes of the old.

He turned to find Anna watching him, her expression unreadable to most, but after months of alliance, he had learned to recognize the subtle tells that betrayed her emotions. The slight relaxation around her eyes, the almost imperceptible easing of her typically rigid posture. She felt it too that this moment of success amid weeks of setbacks and struggles.

"It works," he said simply, the words inadequate to the significance of the moment.

The amber light pulsed once more, bathing them in a warm glow that seemed to soften the harsh edges of the rebuilt hall. In that light, vampire noble and venator stood side by side, their shadows merging on the wall behind them a visual representation of the alliance they continued to forge with each small victory.

"One system restored," Anna said, her voice carrying to the workers who had begun to gather around the glowing consoles. "Now we build the next."

Alexander nodded, already mentally calculating the resources they would need for the western district installation. But beneath the practical considerations, a deeper certainty had taken root. This moment, this small triumph of creation over destruction, was why he had chosen to stay and build rather than return to the hunt. This was the world he wanted his child to inherit: not perfect, not without struggle, but with the possibility of something better than what had come before.

Cold evening air bit at Alexander's face as he leaned against the weather-worn stone parapet, his eyes scanning the sprawling expanse of Slade that stretched beneath the watchtower. Plumes of smoke rose from chimneys and factory stacks, some still bearing the Registry's distinctive green tint while others belched the honest gray of coal-fired production. The skyline had changed in the twelve weeks since Dracula's fall some buildings reduced to rubble, others rising with surprising speed as vampire houses and human factions focused their energies on rebuilding rather than destruction. Even from this height, Alexander could distinguish the districts by their illumination: gas lamps in human quarters flickered with yellow-orange flames, while vampire territories preferred the steadier blue-white glow of alchemical lighting that mimicked moonlight.

Anna stood at his side, one pale hand adjusting the high collar of her crimson riding cloak against the persistent wind that swept across the rooftop. The color was a deliberate choice as much of a statement to both vampire houses and human factions that she would not hide her heritage nor deny her bloodline, only redirect its purpose. Her heterochromatic eyes narrowed as she studied the northern sector, where thin spirals of black smoke suggested controlled burns rather than the productive industry of the central districts.

"The ironworks district seems quiet tonight," Alexander observed, his trained eyes picking out details invisible to normal human sight. The massive forges that had once produced components for Registry extraction machines now manufactured pipes, valves, and structural support for Slade's reconstruction. Their fires should have been visible even at this distance, particularly as dusk deepened into evening.

Anna nodded, her expression revealing nothing, though Alexander had learned to read the subtle tightening around her eyes. "Too quiet. Production shouldn't have ceased yet. Not with the western district's water system still requiring pressure regulators."

The past three months had taught Alexander to trust Anna's administrative knowledge. Dracula had trained his daughter in governance despite keeping her from real power, another form of cruelty in his centuries of manipulation. That knowledge, however, reluctantly acquired, now served their joint purposes.

"Could be mechanical failure," Alexander suggested, though his instincts told him otherwise. "Or labor disputes. The northern sector foremen have been resistant to the new mixed oversight committees."

Neither of them believed this explanation. Twelve weeks of fragile cooperation had brought progress but also exposed deep fractures in Slade's social fabric. Alexander's hand unconsciously moved to touch the clockwork blade concealed beneath his coat—a habit formed through years of venator vigilance that had not diminished despite his new role.

The sound of boots scraping against stone interrupted their conversation. Alexander turned, his body automatically shifting to place himself between the approaching figure and Anna—another habit he'd been unable to break despite knowing she needed no such protection. From the narrow stairwell emerged a man in a battered leather smock, his face streaked with soot and what appeared to be dried blood on his sleeve. He carried himself with the distinctive posture of a Registry courier, though the brass insignia had been torn from his uniform, leaving only discolored patches on the leather.

The courier paused at the top step, chest heaving from the rapid climb up the watchtower's winding stairs. His eyes darted between Alexander and Anna, recognition and fear mixing in his expression. No matter how many times Alexander witnessed it, the reaction to Anna's presence never varied among former Registry employees—the instinctive terror of facing Dracula's daughter, tempered only slightly by knowledge of her role in her father's downfall.

"Speak," Anna commanded, her voice carrying the weight of centuries despite her youthful appearance.

The courier dropped to one knee, a gesture Alexander had repeatedly discouraged but that remained ingrained in those who had served the

Registry. From inside his jacket, the man withdrew a folded parchment, its edges stained dark with what Alexander immediately recognized as blood. Not the processed, preserved blood of Registry communications, but fresh human blood, hastily applied to mark the message as urgent.

"Dispatches from the northern perimeter, my lady," the courier said, his voice rough with exhaustion. "Captain Reed sends his regrets for the informal delivery, but conventional channels were compromised."

Alexander stepped forward, accepting the message as Anna remained still, her reluctance to handle blood-marked communications a boundary he had come to respect. The seal that held the parchment closed bore the impression of a stylized bat's wing—the mark of the intelligence network they had established from former Registry informants now loyal to the new order.

The courier remained kneeling, his eyes fixed on the stone floor as Alexander broke the seal. The parchment unfolded to reveal hastily scrawled notes in Reed's distinctive handwriting, the letters compressed and angular, betraying the urgency with which they had been written.

"Raids by a fledgling vampire cadre have surged around Vasilesti's northern ironworks," Alexander read aloud, his voice steady despite the implications that immediately raced through his mind. "Four dead, seventeen missing. Production halted. Evidence suggests organized resistance to joint governance. Signature confirmed—the Crimson Dawn faction."

The words landed like shards of ice in the cool evening air. Anna's jaw tightened, the only visible sign of her reaction, but Alexander felt the subtle shift in the atmosphere around them. The almost imperceptible drop in temperature that accompanied a vampire noble's anger. The courier flinched, sensing it too, though he remained kneeling with his eyes downcast.

Alexander's fingers curled around the stone railing as he swallowed the sudden rush of dread that threatened to overwhelm his carefully maintained composure. Twelve weeks of progress. Twelve weeks of rebuilding. Twelve weeks of proof that cooperation between vampire and human was possible. All threatened by a faction that had remained silent until now, striking precisely when they had begun to believe their new order might actually succeed.

"The Crimson Dawn," Anna said, the name falling from her lips like a curse. "Karayan's followers. I had thought they were scattered after my father's executed their leader."

Alexander folded the parchment carefully, his mind already calculating response options, resource allocations, defensive positions. The venator in him—never truly dormant despite his new role—assessed threat levels and tactical approaches with cold efficiency.

"Scattered but not destroyed," he replied. "And now rallying under a new banner, it seems."

The unspoken question hung between them: Was this an isolated incident or the beginning of organized resistance to everything they had worked to build? The answer would determine whether the fragile peace they had established could survive its first real test.

In the charged silence that followed, Alexander and Anna exchanged a look that contained volumes of shared purpose and understanding. No words were needed; they had faced Dracula together, had survived the Registry's collapse, had weathered the chaotic weeks that followed. This new threat, while serious, was simply another challenge to overcome.

"You'll need to inform your trainees," Anna said finally, turning her gaze back toward the northern district. "This will be their first real test."

Alexander nodded. The fledgling venator force—twelve recruits trained in both combat and negotiation—had yet to face a genuine crisis. Theory was about to become brutal practice.

Below them, the city's lamps began to flicker on in sequence as lamplighters made their evening rounds, unaware of the news that they had just arrived at the watchtower. The methodical illumination seemed suddenly poignant to Alexander, a reminder that ordinary life continued despite looming threats, that the city's heart continued beating despite the wounds inflicted upon it.

The courier finally rose, awaiting further instructions. Anna gestured toward the stairwell. "Return to Captain Reed. Tell him we depart for the northern district at dawn. Have him assemble the joint patrol units and secure the perimeter. No retaliatory actions until we arrive."

As the courier hurried away, Alexander felt the weight of their responsibility settle more heavily across his shoulders. The peace they had built remained as fragile as a clockwork mechanism precisely calibrated components working in careful harmony, vulnerable to disruption by the smallest foreign element. The Crimson Dawn faction had just thrown sand into those delicate gears.

"We knew this day would come," Anna said, reading his thoughts with unsettling accuracy. "The only question was when and where the first real challenge would emerge."

Alexander nodded, his resolve hardening as the last rays of sunlight disappeared behind Slade's western wall. The city lights spread below them like stars fallen to earth, a constellation of human and vampire existence intertwined more closely than either side had ever intended. That integration—imperfect, tense, but real—was worth defending, even against those who believed separation was the natural order.

"Then we meet it head-on," he said, turning from the parapet as the evening bells began to toll across the city, heralding the arrival of true night and whatever darkness it might bring.

About the Author

A former machine gunner in the United States Marine Corps, he first began putting words to page in a sweltering hooch at 29 Palms he was capturing fragments of thought between drills, dust storms, and the unrelenting rhythm of service life. Those early pages carried the raw honesty of a man who had seen both hardship and brotherhood up close.With steadfast encouragement from his wife and the resilience forged in uniform, Ryan transformed those rough beginnings into fully realized worlds where the stories where mythic themes collide with grounded realism, and where the extraordinary often walks hand-in-hand with the everyday. His fiction draws deeply from dreams, unanswered "what ifs," and the stark, unpolished beauty of real life.When he's not building immersive worlds on the page, Ryan lives a life as tactile and purposeful as the ones he writes. Spending time with his family, hunting and fishing in the wild places he loves, or tending to the rhythms of their micro homestead. Every moment is a reminder that stories aren't just written they're lived.